Formula Murder

A Wolf Ruger Mystery

Ross Carley

Copyright 2017

ISBN: 978-0-69284-724-4

DEDICATION

To my wife Francie,
and to my cousin Peggy

ACKNOWLEDGMENTS

Special thanks to Holly Albin and Les Roberts for their reviews, edits, and encouragement. Wolf Ruger is inspired most directly by Les' two-career LA private investigator Saxon, blended with his Cleveland PI Milan Jacovich. Sincere thanks to LeeAnna Groves, editor and publicist extraordinaire, for her expertise and cheering me on. Les, Holly, and LeeAnna have been my guides and advisors since my first Wolf Ruger novel *Dead Drive*. Finally, a tip of the hat to Andy Borme for his technical input on creating the fictional Formula Nor-Am racing class.

Chapter 1

Dust and smoke swirled in my eyes and clogged my nose. Coughing, I pushed myself to my knees off the debris-covered floor. On my left was what remained of Schumacher. I gagged on the acrid taste of the explosion and the coppery stench of blood as I looked to my right and saw Wilson's limp body.

Ringing in my ears kept me from hearing the medic squatting in front of me who seemed to be asking me if I was OK. I nodded. As I looked back toward Schumacher and called his name, I woke up, nauseous and sweating.

Damned Iraq nightmare. Fucking PTSD.

I sat on the edge of the bed with my eyes closed, waiting for the nausea to lessen. Boots rubbed against my arm, then I felt his cold nose on my hand.

He mewed, asking for breakfast. I fed him, showered, scratched his ears, then grabbed my computer bag and headed to my office.

I needed to call my buddy Tito Rodriquez, a homicide detective sergeant at the Indianapolis Metropolitan Police Department. He'd served with me in Iraq and also come back with PTSD. We provided support for each other. He was my primary support. His wife Carmen was his, but he relied on me for back-up.

It was quarter to eight when I reached him. He'd just gotten to work.

"Hey, Wolf, what's up?"

"Rough spot this morning," I replied. The words 'rough spot' were our code meaning we'd had some kind of episode triggered by PTSD.

"Nightmare?"

"Yeah, with Schumacher and Wilson. The medic was there, too." Some of my nightmares included both dead soldiers, some only one. The medic was also a part-time player. Tito had heard me describe all of the combinations. I haltingly told him about the latest version.

"Sounds like you're on the road. You OK?"

"Uh-huh. I'm headed to my office."

"You sound all right now. Call me if you need to talk."

"OK, thanks."

It was the third Thursday in September, and still godawful hot in Indianapolis. The ancient air conditioner in my office had groaned, rattled, spewed water and died a couple of weeks ago. My landlord was, of course, on vacation so it wasn't until yesterday that a replacement was installed.

My second-floor office is in Broad Ripple, a trendy area of bars and restaurants six miles north of downtown Indy. It's in a red brick building on Gilmond with Java Joe's Coffee Bar on the corner. The new air conditioner made it possible to close my windows again, stemming the aromas from the popcorn shop directly below my office.

It had only been a month since my traumatic near-death experience at the hands of a skilled murderer. The Indianapolis Star had carried a story relating how I'd shot him in self-defense. It was mostly fiction, and I had to live with it.

I was spending my first full day in three weeks in my office paying bills, answering email, and sorting through junk mail, and, since I hadn't been there for a while, changing the month on my Marilyn Monroe calendar. I was sorry to see her August photo disappear, but liked the September Marilyn just as well, possibly better. I studied it a while to decide.

The telephone brought me out of my Marilyn reverie.

"Wolf Ruger here." I always answer with both names since I run Wolf Investigations and Ruger Associates from the same office.

"Hi, Wolf. This is Nick Napoli, Hopkins-Handel Racing," said the voice on the other end. Nick spoke quickly, as if his speech couldn't keep up with his brain. His slight Italian accent belied the fact that he was born and reared in Italy. He'd hired me to write custom software for their racing team's parts inventory several months ago, and I assumed his call was in response to the marketing email I'd sent him a few days earlier.

"Morning, Nick. How's the software we developed for you working out?" Daniel Li and I wrote and installed a software application that tracked and provided the status for all racing-related items they kept in stock.

"It's working fine. That's not why I called," he replied with an edginess in his voice. "Our data telemetry system is screwed up, and

2

we need help. When you were here before, you mentioned you have experience with telemetry. Is that right?"

"Yes. What can I do?" Telemetry is the radio transmission of information about dozens of kinds, or channels, of race car performance such as speed, tire pressures, throttle position, and so on.

"We've got to have reliable telemetry at our next race. We'd like you to come out and see if you can help."

"Sure. When d'you want me there?"

I heard him take a deep breath. "I have meetings the rest of the morning. How about right after lunch?"

"Sure, no problem."

"OK, ask for our IT guy Mark White when you come in. He'll brief you on the technical problem."

I'm a big auto racing fan, and Indianapolis is regarded as the motorsports capital of the world. With its impressive list of events, topped off by the Indianapolis 500, the label isn't an exaggeration. The numerous racing teams that make their home in Indy, from Formula One teams to mom and pop weekend stock car racers, are only the tip of the corporate iceberg.

About five hundred Indiana businesses support motorsports, providing products that run the gamut from engines and brakes to communications and telemetry systems. And then there are the t-shirts, bobble-head dolls, jackets, and other memorabilia that fans gobble up at the tracks. Racing may be called motorsports, but it's really a sponsor-driven entertainment industry.

The Hopkins-Handel Racing Team, known by most racing fans as HH Racing, was founded by Gerald "Hop" Hopkins and his grandson Henry "Hal" Handel in the late 1990s. The Hopkins-Handel name had been familiar to folks in the Indianapolis area since the 1960s because of the chain of Hopkins-Handel luxury automobile dealerships that sold Mercedes-Benz, Aston Martin, and Lincoln.

Funding to establish both the dealerships and the racing team had come from Hop Hopkins who was now retired and spent most of his time in a luxury villa in Panama where he was free from taxes. Hal Handel ran the dealerships and the racing team with the same hands-on approach his grandfather had.

3

Nick Napoli, HH Racing's race engineer, had control of all engineering and technical aspects of the car. He reported directly to Hal Handel, who focused on strategy.

Indy's largest concentration of racing team facilities and support services is near the Indianapolis Motor Speedway just west of downtown. A little further away, Boone International Raceway Park is located in Boone County west of Interstate 65 and the town of Lebanon. Boone Raceway boasts a seven-tenths mile oval and a drag strip in addition to its two-and-a-half mile road course used by Formula Nor-Am. Formula Nor-Am is a regional race sequence serving as a feeder for Formula One. Boone is one of the stops on the Formula Nor-Am racing circuit.

Formula Nor-Am cars cost a fraction of their Formula One counterparts, and the racing teams usually have about fifty employees, far fewer than the four hundred employees typical for a Formula One organization. Total budgets for Nor-Am teams run around eight million dollars per year, give or take some pocket change.

From the HH Racing website, I learned that the last Nor-Am event of the current season would be held at Boone Raceway in just over a week. It would be a three-day affair, with practice on Thursday, qualifying on Friday, and the race on Saturday afternoon.

Two other racing car classes would also be competing, but the Nor-Am race, known as the Boone International Grand Prix, was the feature event. The other two classes would each have two races, one on Friday afternoon, the other Saturday morning. The opening ceremony with the introduction of the drivers and some Hollywood star singing the national anthem immediately precedes the Nor-Am Grand Prix, this event's only race carried on regional sports television networks.

HH Racing's major sponsor was Gamble Oil Company, headquartered in Houston, with a regional office just west of Indy. Other sponsors included a computerized machine tool company and a mattress manufacturer.

Their driver was a young hotshot named Scott Marks, a native of Columbus, Ohio, who was actively racing quarter midgets and karts before he was a teenager. He won national championships in each, then moved on to sprint cars and midgets, winning a rookie of the year award.

4

A year ago, at the ripe old age of nineteen, he joined the Hopkins-Handel Formula Nor-Am team, and was assigned driver's number 33, which had been used by his father on the stock car circuit. His Nor-Am car is named The Aquila, after the American eagle featured on the Gamble Oil logo.

* * *

As I drove my aging Jeep out to the meeting with Nick Napoli, a heavy haze gave the sunlight a shimmering almost milky appearance. A rainless two weeks combined with abnormally high heat had started turning leaves a brittle dry yellow, rather than the brilliant reds and oranges we see when crisp morning temperatures combine with cool rain.

HH Racing is located north of the Indianapolis Motor Speedway, in a light industrial area with other racing teams and motorsports companies. Street names in the area, like Victory Lane and Championship Drive, reflect the racing theme. They are on a street that loops around on the east side of Guion Road, appropriately called Winners Circle.

Their metal commercial-style building was set back from the road behind a well-manicured lawn featuring a flagpole surrounded by flowers. I parked in a visitor's slot, and made my way to the double glass front doors, pressing the call button. Mark opened the door and led me to the reception desk, his longish brown hair falling into his eyes as he filled out my visitor's badge.

On our way back to the glassed-in office used by the data center, we picked up cups of coffee in the break room. I marveled at the cleanliness and brightness of their facility, illuminated by numerous florescent fixtures in the ceiling. The floor was an off-white buffed to a shine in which you could see your reflection.

He motioned me to sit in a chair beside his desk as he raked the hair out of his eyes, then adjusted his round wire-rimmed glasses reminiscent of John Lennon.

Taking a sip of coffee, he sat back. "We've been having problems with our data telemetry system."

"What kind of problems?" Part of my military intelligence job in Iraq was managing telemetry data from our drone aircraft. Much of the work was classified, but the general area of handling the sensing, digitizing, and transmission of everything from weather parameters to streaming video was in my wheelhouse.

"Mainly noisy and missing data. Some kind of heavy background noise that's making it impossible to retrieve the information."

"Is this going on all the time?"

"Yes and no. We're losing data primarily in the mode where data are being transmitted continuously all the way around the track." Mark said pensively. "But once in a while we also lose it as the system dumps the data summary once a lap as the car passes the pit."

"You still have all the black box data recorded in the car, and are able to download it after a session on the track, right?" The black box was like one in an airplane.

"Yeah, but we need live data while we're on the track to monitor performance, make adjustments, and see potential safety issues like loss of tire pressure and major engine problems like loss of oil pressure. It puts us one lap behind, because we're having to analyze data from the previous lap."

"Do data losses happen at the same places on the track each time?"

"No, not always. That's one of the things that has the telemetry team pulling their hair out. And it's been getting worse. The first time, we lost data from about half of the track area. The last race we lost data about three-fourths of the time we were on the track."

"I'm glad to take a look at the system. I already have a non-disclosure agreement with HH Racing, and you can bill my consulting time at the same rate as before."

"Sounds good to me. We can really use some of your expertise." He paused, and looked at me levelly. "The telemetry and communications team is an independent bunch. That's why Nick had me talk with you first. Not sure how they'll take to some outsider looking over their shoulders. So we have to do it carefully."

"How?"

"Nick said he'll meet with them later this afternoon, and tell them we're bringing in an outside consultant that we have experience with. He'll point out that we're happy with the software you developed for us, and you can respond to us quickly. He wants to talk with you while you're here."

6

Mark briefed me on the Tau 920 telemetry system they used, and answered my questions.

"Think you can help us?" he asked.

"Yeah, it's similar to a couple of systems I've had hands-on experience with," I said. "How about seeing Nick?"

"Sure. His office is just this side of the executive conference room, on your right before you get to the lobby."

I gave him my Ruger Associates card. On an impulse, I dug out a Wolf Investigations card and handed it to him, too. "I'm also a private investigator, just in case you know anyone who could use that kind of help."

Mark looked at both cards, lingering a little longer than I expected on the Wolf Investigations one.

Nick's office door was closed, but he called out, "Come on in" as soon as I knocked. He rose to greet me and pointed at the door, indicating I should close it. I sat in a leather armchair on the other side of his desk. He wore a white HH Racing polo shirt, neatly pleated gray slacks, and a GPS watch similar to mine. I assumed he was a runner.

Nick's office wasn't opulent, but leather upholstered furniture and thick carpeting rendered it pleasant, professional, and comfortable. Framed photos taken with racing celebrities decorated the walls.

"I remember looking at your résumé. Mark sent it to me back when you wrote the inventory software. Impressive. Iraq, huh?"

I nodded.

He paused. "Thanks for what you did. My brother lost a leg over there. Above-the-knee amputation." He blinked several times and cleared his throat. "Our telemetry problem is a very serious situation. And sensitive. I'll share more about that with you when we officially bring you on board to work on it."

"OK. Mark said you wanted to check with the telemetry and communications folks."

"Yeah. I'm not about to ride roughshod over a team doing their best to solve a nasty problem. I'll tell them about your previous experience with us, that you're definitely qualified, and about your meeting with Mark. You'll hear from me by first thing tomorrow."

"Fair enough." As I got up to leave, he came around his desk and shook my hand.

By the time I was ready for lunch, it was pushing three o'clock. I walked to the Thai restaurant a couple of blocks from my office and enjoyed my usual Pad Thai and iced coffee. Thinking about the telemetry problem at HH Racing triggered memories of Iraq that I shook off as I got up from the table.

Back in my office, I booted up my computer and slogged through email detritus that accretes as surely as barnacles on a ship's hull. Given my clientless status, I hoped that HH Racing would hire me.

My mind wandered to Vanessa, the sexy Italian woman I met during my previous case. Even if I got the job, I should be free to see her on weekends.

I was fantasizing about her when my cell phone rang. It was Nick Napoli.

He got right to the point. "Wolf, I've checked with the people on the telemetry and communications team. We're going to bring you in to help us for a week or two."

I grabbed a pad of paper and pen to take notes. "What do you want me to do first, and what's the schedule?"

"First thing is to review the operations manual for the telemetry system. It'll be attached as a file to an email I'm about to send you. Don't be intimidated by its length…it's about four-hundred-fifty pages long. Skim through it today, then show up about nine tomorrow." Nick paused.

"Where do I go?"

"I'll meet you in my office so we can talk alone for a little while. Then I'll bring in the three lead people on the team: Linda Green, Ron Phillips, and Jack Berry. Ron goes by 'RF.' Those are his initials, but he's also a radio frequency, or RF, engineer. I'm forwarding your résumé to each of them now. I'll give you all a little pep talk, then you'll go into a conference room where they'll brief you on the telemetry problems."

"OK, I'll be there. Anything else?"

"Well, you might want to read their bio sketches on our website. See how they fit into the team." He paused. I sensed there was something else he wanted to say. I waited.

He cleared his throat, then said, "You may as well know that you probably won't be welcomed with open arms by RF. He's most directly responsible for the telemetry signal transmission and reception, and he may be a little threatened by you."

"I'm used to that reaction," I said. "I try to pay special attention to them, make them feel like they're in charge."

"That's good, but it brings up another dynamic. I don't want you to inadvertently stir up a hornet's nest. Linda is the lead engineer for the telemetry and communications team. RF is the oldest person in the group and has been here the longest. I don't know what grates on him more, Linda's gender or her being twenty years younger. Every so often he's in my office, griping about something related to Linda and has to be reminded of the pecking order."

"Thanks for letting me know. I assume you keep him around because he's good at what he does."

"Damn good."

After we hung up, I transferred my notes from Nick Napoli's call into a new notebook and labeled it 'HH Racing.' I keep a separate one for each Ruger Associates consulting job and each Wolf Investigations case.

Nick's email arrived while I was writing. I downloaded the manual for the telemetry system and copied it onto my thumb drive. I'd review as much as I could that afternoon, but the sheer number of pages made it clear that I'd be working at home, too. On the Hopkins-Handel website, I found biographical sketches for their key people.

Linda Green had a master's degree in electrical and computer engineering. She had been an intern for two summers at NASA, and her master's thesis was on optimizing the encoding for a NASA biomedical telemetry system for astronauts. Ron Phillips had earned a bachelor's degree in electrical engineering technology with a specialty in radio frequency antenna design. Jack Berry's diverse background featured dual bachelor's degrees in physics and computer science.

I jotted down information on each of them in my notebook; all three seemed qualified for their jobs. Then I started reviewing the owner's manual for the Tau 920, the telemetry system required for all Formula Nor-Am cars. Tau Telemetry LLC, located in Speedway near the Indy 500 track, designed and sold it.

A racecar telemetry system transfers information measured in the car on the road course to another location, usually the pit or garage area or both, via radio. Dozens of types of information, or parameters, such as individual tire pressures, engine RPM, oil pressure, temperatures at locations in the engine and tires, the gear the car is in, and so on are measured. The information is encrypted for broadcast, then decrypted by the receiver so it can be stored and analyzed in a computer.

I was about halfway through the manual at six o'clock, and decided to finish the review at home. I picked up an order of fish and chips to go from Calico Jack's Bar and Grill across the street from my office, eating a couple of chips out of the bag on the way.

Boots was at the door. His radar must have detected the food before I had the key in the lock. His nonstop mewing insisted that the fish was all his, but he had to settle for a few bits mixed into his regular cat food. I popped open a Sam Adams Light and ate while continuing the review of the manual at the kitchen table.

I discovered from the manual that I encrypted my own computer files in the same standard form as the Tau 920. I also learned the capacity of the Tau system, or how much data could be transmitted each second, and how many parameters could be transmitted.

I'd been away from telemetry systems for a few years. Adding to that was the frustrating and inexcusable length of time it takes our government to implement new developments in any military system. The Tau 920 had features I'd have given my right arm for in Iraq. The crippled government procurement system makes it unlikely that anyone in our armed forces has the new technology yet.

I was making a note to ask for a copy of the data analysis software that HH Racing used for the Tau 920, since it was probably modified from the basic software described in the manual, when my friend and lover Vanessa called.

"Hi, Wolf. I'm considering making cioppino on Saturday. We can have fresh baked Italian bread with it, and spumoni for the first dessert. Does that sound good?"

Cioppino is an Italian seafood stew originated on Fisherman's Wharf in San Francisco in the late 1800s that is cooked in a tomato broth with a variety of seasonings. Vanessa used spices from a recipe that was a closely guarded Russo family secret.

"Sounds great. I assume I'm the second dessert, right?"

"Good, and you're right. I'll see what looks good at the Italian Market on Saturday morning, then."

I told her about the consulting job I'd just taken. "I'll be at HH Racing tomorrow, looking at the telemetry system they're having problems with."

"This is a Ruger Associates job, nothing that'll get you hurt or killed, right?"

"Right," I laughed. "I don't know of any way I can get hurt analyzing their problem unless I get hit by their race car."

"That isn't funny." She had been traumatized by my being attacked by a murderer on a recent Wolf Investigations case.

"OK, sorry." To lighten the conversation I asked, "How about I bring a chilled bottle of Chardonnay?"

"Perfect. Just remember, I'm making a special effort to impress you with my cooking, so we have to eat first, screw later."

I reluctantly agreed as we hung up.

Chapter 2

After making coffee the next morning, I fed Boots, scrambled three eggs, and fried bacon. Boots rubbed my legs and mewed insufferably until I gave him two nibbles of bacon, after which he sat on the floor beside me and gave himself a bath. It was bribery and we both knew it.

The weather had continued to be dry, hot, and breezy, and swirling pieces of dry leaves lent a musty smell to the air. I blinked blowing dust out of my eyes as I got out of my Jeep at HH Racing.

Mark White signed me in. As he escorted me to Nick Napoli's office, he said quietly, "You may be in for an interesting meeting. I'm not part of it, but Nick told me to help you afterwards if you ask." He ushered me into Nick's office, then shut the door behind him as he left.

"Hi, Wolf," said Nick, standing and extending his hand from behind his desk. "Have a seat." He paused while I sat and took my notebook out. "You need to put that away for now," he said. "No notes. What I'm about to tell you is off the record. Sensitive information."

I closed my notebook.

"I'm sure you know that Gamble Oil is our main sponsor. Do you know much about them?"

"Not really," I replied. "Didn't they recently get fined by the feds for violating pollution regulations at a refinery around here?"

Nick nodded. "Yeah, around two months ago they were hit with four million bucks in fines for violations of environmental regulations, including violations of the Clean Water Act, the Clean Air Act, and improper disposal of hazardous waste."

I remembered from reading articles in the Indy Star that the refinery wasn't exactly admired by its neighbors, being infamous for a continuous downwind stench and an 'eternal flame' that produced ugly black smoke by burning off waste byproducts. But it processed fifty thousand barrels of crude oil per day and provided good-paying jobs to over three hundred taxpayers.

"It gets worse," Nick continued. "A few days after the fine was announced, they notified me that they're about to close the refinery and discontinue operations in Indianapolis. Their sponsorship of our racing team is hanging by a thread."

I thought to myself that the good news was it wouldn't stink up Indianapolis anymore. "Is it an all-or-nothing decision?"

"No. If they think they can get sufficient return on investment, they may continue as our major sponsor. They could also opt to be one of our regular sponsors at about one-tenth the cost of their current support. Or they could drop us altogether. It will be a hard-headed financial decision."

"What factors into their choice?"

"The most important factor is racing points – that is, how many points our team has accrued during the season."

"Does Formula Nor-Am use the same point structure as Formula One?"

"Yes. Are you familiar with it?"

I nodded. I couldn't recite the entire point award table, but recalled that first place was worth twenty-five points, down to tenth place getting one point.

Nick sat up, twirling a pen in his fingers. "We're battling for second in Nor-Am with one race left this season. The Laurence LeGrand first place team has over twenty points more than we have, so there's very little hope of winning overall. We're within three points of the second place Clanton-Suggs team, though, and we've beaten them all of the last three races."

"So if you can end up second in points?" I let the question hang in the air.

"Then we'll be at least twice as likely to attract a new major sponsor, or to retain Gamble Oil. They've let me know that."

"So, the fact that Gamble Oil is closing the refinery is the sensitive information you mentioned?"

"Only part of it. The other portion may or may not end up being sensitive, but treat it as such for now."

I nodded.

"It may be a coincidence, pure and simple. A couple of days after I was privately notified of the refinery closing, we first experienced telemetry problems."

"It seems improbable that the refinery closing could be related to your telemetry failures."

"I agree. Just wanted to let you know that I've speculated about it. I haven't shared it with the team we're about to meet." He paused. "So let's invite them in."

He introduced each of them to me as they filed into his office, shook my hand, and sat around the small conference table. Linda Green's brown hair was pulled back in a ponytail. Her firm handshake matched her narrow face and serious coal black eyes. Ron 'RF' Phillips' handshake was curt and barely enough to be social, and he avoided eye contact. His round head was almost bald on top, with a comb-over that wasn't worth the trouble. Jack Berry's prominent pointed chin and wavy black hair combed straight back accentuated his high forehead. Long slender fingers gave me a friendly, albeit clammy and limp, handshake.

They each wore blue jeans and a Hopkins-Handel Racing Team polo shirt. I felt out of uniform in the Cubs polo that Vanessa had given me.

Nick looked at me, then shifted his gaze to the three staff members. "First, I want to thank each of you for your hard work trying to fix our telemetry malfunction. Your team has been putting in long hours since we got back from Pocono. We have one race left this season, and I don't need to remind any of you how important it is to get this problem licked.

"I want you to include Wolf as part of your team. He isn't in charge of anything, but I want you to cooperate with him and listen to suggestions he makes. You all are accountable to me, and to Hal to find a solution before our race at Boone. Any questions?"

Three heads shook 'no.' I didn't shake mine. I had questions.

"OK, go on into the conference room and bring Wolf up to date. I'll check in occasionally. Let me know if you need anything."

As we got coffee in the break room on the way, Linda said, "We'll be in the engineering conference room. The fancy conference room next to Nick's office is mainly for entertaining sponsors and VIPs."

The meeting room was functional. A conference call phone was centered on the table, and a large HDTV that doubled as a screen for presentations was on the far wall.

Linda took charge of the meeting. "I expect you both have read Mr. Ruger's résumé, right?" She looked at RF and Jack. Jack nodded. RF looked back. She turned to me. "Anything you'd like to add before we give you our briefings?"

I nodded. "I'd like to be on a first-name basis here. Call me Wolf. The only other thing is that I don't claim to be an expert on the specific equipment setup you guys use. I skimmed through the user's manual yesterday, but it'll take me a day or two to catch up. I'll be asking some questions that may seem dumb."

RF rolled his eyes back. Linda noticed but ignored him and introduced Jack, who described the processing of the sensor array outputs that provide inputs to the telemetry system. He had a half-dozen slides illustrating where the sensors were placed, how they were hooked up, and how their signals were handled.

Jack's voice was quiet, and he looked down when he talked. Several times I had to ask him to repeat something I didn't quite hear. His intelligence was obvious, and his knowledge of sensors was both broad and deep.

Next up was RF. He started to describe what a telemetry system was using language and a slide appropriate for fifth graders. It was my turn to roll my eyes.

Linda interrupted him. "RF, did you have a chance to look at Wolf's résumé?"

RF assumed an 'aw shucks' posture and attitude. "Naw, I had a fairly busy evening. I figure he's a computer geek sorta like you. He did some inventory software for us, right? And you heard him say he's gonna ask dumb questions, so I started out really basic."

Linda picked up a copy of my résumé, then put it down. "RF, I was going to read you the part where Wolf describes his experience, but it'd be better coming straight from him." She looked at me with her eyebrows arched. "Wolf?"

Nick had been right. RF was a piece of work.

I took a deep breath. I mentioned my Purdue degree, then summarized my work in Iraq with unmanned vehicle telemetry equipment, both airborne and on the ground. I explained that I'd been involved with entire systems, including both hardware and software. As I talked, RF crossed his arms, looked at the table in front of him, and slowly sank into his chair, putting on a hangdog look.

I decided to throw him a bone. "RF, I understand from your bio on the website that you're an antenna expert." He sat up partially, but kept

15

his arms crossed. "My experience has been that antennas are often the part of communications systems that are the most critical, but least appreciated." He sat up straight and uncrossed his arms. Linda suppressed a smile.

"Yeah," he said grudgingly. "So?"

"So I'd like to hear about the antennas you use with the Tau 920. I know the telemetry frequency; it's similar to cell phones. So tell me about your antennas. I figure that the one on the car is a vertical whip, and that all of the teams use the same type. I'm most interested in what you use in the pit to receive data from the car." A whip antenna is a vertically-mounted piece of wire that is electrically insulated from its mounting.

I'd hooked him. He sat up, beginning slowly, as if hesitant to share proprietary information. "Yeah. Well, we use some pretty sophisticated equipment for receiving. I'm sure that our telemetry antennas are better than most for Formula Nor-Am." As he talked, his hands carried part of the message, and his eyebrows jumped up and down. He launched into a technical discussion of the merits and weaknesses of various types of antennas he'd evaluated, with names like Yagi and log periodic that were unintelligible to most folks.

When he paused long enough that I figured he was finished, I said, "I assume the antenna configurations are included in the recorded datasets."

"They're supposed to be," RF said.

"They are," Linda confirmed.

"OK, that's great," I said. "RF, let's you and I get together soon and look at your work area. I'm especially interested in your measurement and test equipment."

RF nodded, now reluctantly dragged into the process.

Linda cleared her throat. "I guess it's my turn. Let me give a quick overview of how we work at the track. When the car's on the course, RF monitors the overall telemetry signal quality, I listen to the voice communications, and Jack's usually been tasked by Nick to focus on two or three selected telemetry channels."

"Looking for specific things happening on certain parts of the course?"

"Yeah, that's an example," she replied. "I'm responsible for the analysis of all of the data when we're finished testing or racing and we're off the track, including the information that's transmitted continuously, what's dumped each lap at the pits, and what we download from the car afterwards back at the transporter. So I'm the first one who discovered the telemetry data dropouts."

"But I could tell we were having them by looking at the real-time data stream at the track," RF protested.

"That's true," Linda admitted, then looked at me. "We figured you'd want to look at examples of both good and problem telemetry, so I've set up a computer with telemetry processing software in a corner of the shop with files you can review."

I looked at Linda. "Can you get me some headphones? I want to listen to them, too."

RF snickered. "There's no audio. It's all digital info. Being an expert and all you should know that."

"You've never listened to the audio on digital signal telemetry?"

"Can't say as how I've ever wasted my time doing that."

"OK," Linda suggested. "Let's hook up a set of computer speakers so Wolf and anyone else can listen. I'd like to join you, Wolf."

A "me, too" from Jack elicited another roll of the eyes from RF.

We refilled our coffee cups on the way to the cubicle where Linda had the computer set up. She disappeared for a couple of minutes, returning with a pair of speakers.

"Leave the audio off for now," I said. "I'll tell you when I want to listen."

The flat-screen display made the data easily viewable. Linda and I sat in chairs. Jack and RF stood at our shoulders.

Linda ran the Tau Telemetry display software package through its paces, showing us how it displayed all thirty-two data parameters simultaneously, or any selected subset of them, down to just one kind of information at a time. We could look at the entire time period the data were collected on a single screen, or stretch out the interval so that we saw only ten seconds of information.

A miniature map of the road course was in a window at the lower right corner of the screen. As information channels scrolled by from left to right, a bright dot on the map moved around the track showing the location of the car at the time represented by the data.

It was obvious where the data dropouts occurred, no matter how many channels were being displayed. Relatively steady values for measurements such as tire pressures and temperatures suddenly looked totally random or became sequences of zeros. We looked at a couple dozen examples taken while the car was on the course, and a half-dozen received when the car dumped data going by the pit area.

I confirmed that the dropouts didn't seem to be associated with any particular track locations, then looked at each of them in turn. "So, how has your team tackled the problem? What have you looked at? What have you eliminated?"

Linda grimaced. "A short answer to all three questions is the same: hardware and software. RF and Jack have gone through the hardware with a fine-tooth comb, looking for everything from loose connections to power issues. I've looked for software bugs. For example, dropouts could occur if the software couldn't keep up with the data acquisition. But we've been using the same software all season. Why would it suddenly stop working?"

I asked questions I had entered in my notebook after reviewing the Tau 920 manual. "Have you talked with Tau Telemetry? Do they have any ideas? Are other Nor-Am teams experiencing these kinds of problems?"

RF and Linda started talking at the same time. He prevailed. "They sent a guy over. He wasn't much help; didn't seem to have any ideas we hadn't already eliminated. Said he hadn't heard of other teams having problems, and talked us into buying a spare receiver. He might have been covering his ass in addition to making a sale."

"I kind of agree with RF," Linda said. "It really isn't clear whether we're the only team with problems. That said, they send out a monthly Tau Telemetry E-newsletter and provide periodic software updates. I realize the newsletter is mainly for marketing, but we should have seen something in the newsletter or gotten a software update if there were problems." RF started to say something, but Linda held her hand up, palm out. "RF and I disagree on that."

"So you've tried the other receiver?"

RF shifted in his seat, his eyes briefly flickered discomfort. "Yeah, we've tested it here in the shop. Haven't been to the track with it yet."

Linda leveled her gaze at RF. "I'm still not sure we should have spent that kind of money on equipment we may not need, but RF convinced me it makes sense to have a backup. We already had a backup transmitter unit, the one that goes in the car. We tried it, same result."

"How come you already had a backup transmitter?" I asked. "And why not a spare receiver?"

"It's a combination of Nor-Am rules and a tight budget. Anything that's in the car or goes into the car has to be inspected at the track, so if there's a chance we'll have to replace something during the weekend, we need to have a spare because they don't do inspections real-time on demand. All inspections are done at one time."

"There's a lot higher chance something in the car might be physically damaged, right?" I asked.

"Right," she answered. "With our tight budget, we generally only buy spares for equipment or components in the car itself."

"But if it isn't in the car…?"

"The Nor-Am inspection rules don't cover electronic equipment that's used in the garage area or pits, so if we have to replace something like a receiver that doesn't have to be inspected, we can just do it." She paused, looking at me. "Ready to turn the audio on?"

"Yes, but not with this data," I answered. "You have the raw telemetry signal recorded, right?" The raw telemetry signal is what is broadcast by the car, then received via the antenna by the receiver, before it's processed into the individual channels of information that we were looking at.

"Sure. It's a huge file. We have it on DVD."

"Great. At the rate the Tau 920 can acquire data, you should get about half a gigabyte of it per hour."

She thought for a second, her eyes on the ceiling, doing a calculation in her head. "Yeah, that's about right. We get two or three hundred megabytes per practice session like the ones we've looked at on the screen, and around half a gigabyte during a race."

As she put the raw data DVD into the computer, I turned up the audio on the speakers. "OK, we're going to listen to the raw signal." I looked at RF. "If you haven't heard this before, you may learn something. What we'll hear when we have good telemetry is a sort of warbling, twittering sound."

RF crossed his arms. "So what're we gonna hear when the telemetry isn't OK?"

"I don't know."

"Thought you were the expert," he smirked. He must have taken courses in how to be irritating.

"There are lots of possibilities. If the data drop is due to the car not transmitting a signal for a little while, the warbling will stop, and a soft hissing sound due to background noise will probably replace it. If the drop is due to an interfering signal, we'll hear that instead of, maybe in addition to, the warbling."

"How does an interfering signal sound?" Linda asked.

"It may sound like someone saying 'shhh.' It's called white noise, a sort of random signal spread over a wide range of frequencies. Or we may hear another signal of some kind."

"Warbling, like our signal?" Jack asked.

"Maybe, maybe not. It could even be something completely different, such as a voice transmission. It could be due to someone else's transmission that's supposed to be on another frequency slopping over onto our frequency."

"Of course that's illegal. There are Federal Communications Commission rules," RF offered. I let him be the expert, and didn't say that interference like that happens frequently, FCC regulations notwithstanding.

"OK, I'm set," Linda said. "Let's listen to the signal at the same times as the samples we saw previously. I had those set up ahead of time before, though, and didn't know we'd be listening to the raw signal, so it'll take a few seconds for me to skip to the starting times for each example."

This time, the computer screen was blank. A specialized piece of test equipment called a spectrum analyzer was needed to view this kind of signal. I figured that RF had one, and I'd use it later, whether or not there was anything interesting on the audio.

As Linda played through the examples, we heard the predicted warbling sound of the valid telemetry signal. As each time approached when data was lost, a faint buzzing sound became louder, overwhelming the telemetry signal during the data dropout period. Even when the computer analysis software couldn't recover data, we could still hear a very faint warbling in the background.

Listening, I was vaguely aware of something tucked into the recesses of my mind, but it kept eluding me.

After the last sample had played, Linda turned toward me. "All right, so what did we hear?"

"One thing's certain," I said. "We heard the warbling of the telemetry signal, even though it was really faint, even when there was interference, so we know that the car is transmitting data continuously. Therefore, we can almost certainly rule out problems with the sensor system, and the telemetry system equipment that's in the car."

Jack let out an audible sigh. "Load off *my* mind."

"So what's the buzzing sound?" she asked.

"I'm not sure," I admitted.

RF snickered. "Not sure, or have no idea?"

I wasn't sure, and decided to give RF a chance to help. "RF, you can help me with this. I need to look at the raw signal on a spectrum analyzer. You have one, right?"

I heard him clearing his throat behind me. "Well, yeah, but it isn't working right now."

"It's eleven-thirty," Linda said. "I suggest we break for lunch. Wolf, could you stick around for a few minutes?"

"Sure." The others left the cubicle.

She looked at me with her eyebrows raised. "You got a funny look on your face while you listened to the raw telemetry signal. I don't think RF or Jack could see it, but I could. What did you hear?"

"I'm not sure. Something in the back of my mind is telling me I've heard that kind of signal before, but I can't place it."

"Is there anything I can do to help?"

"Actually, you and Mark both can. I want to look at the processed data and raw signal using my own equipment. I'd like Mark to load the Tau 920 data display software you used onto my laptop, and for you to provide me a DVD with both the multi-channel data and raw signal on it. I have a software application that I can use to listen to the raw signal like we did a little while ago."

"You have your own spectrum analyzer?"

"Not personally, but I have access to one."

"OK, Nick told me to give you anything you need as long as he's informed. If you're going to be showing it to anyone else, though, we'll need to have them sign an NDA."

"I'll be working with Daniel Li at the university. He signed an HH Racing non-disclosure agreement a few months ago when we developed the inventory software. I assume it's still valid. He'll be the only other person seeing it."

"That should be OK. I'll let Nick know."

I dropped my laptop off with Mark, then had another cup of coffee in the break area while he loaded the software and Linda prepared the DVD. I sent Daniel a text message saying I had a job for him and asking him to call me.

Linda came into the break room and handed me the DVD. "Wolf, would you like to go to lunch with us? It's kind of a Friday ritual. The telemetry and communications team and Mark go to the Pike Pub, where they have a great strip steak special. Sometimes Nick joins us; sometimes we bring something back for him."

"Steak sounds like a winner."

Mark brought my laptop in a few minutes later. "You're all set. I wrote the password on this. Memorize it and destroy it." He handed me a slip of paper.

We stopped by Nick's office on the way out. He asked us to bring a chicken taco salad back for his lunch. Linda summarized the morning's activities, including the software and data he'd OK'd their giving me.

Nick looked back and forth between Linda and me. "So, you think you're making progress?"

"I'm still getting up to speed," I explained. "I'll be working this weekend. Hope it's OK to bill you for a few hours this evening and tomorrow."

"Fine with me. The sooner we get an answer the better. Any problems with RF?"

Linda and I looked at each other as she said, "Nothing we couldn't handle. I think he's on board with Wolf's helping."

"Good," Nick said. "I want you to be in touch with me as soon as you know something, Wolf. Don't hesitate to call me this weekend." He gave me his cell number.

Pike Pub was almost full. Mark explained that the HH Racing folks were regular customers. I was impressed that our waitress, Sandy, knew all of their first names and how they wanted their steaks cooked. I ordered mine medium rare.

While we were waiting for our salads, my cell phone rang. It was Daniel.

Daniel Li, a computer engineering Ph.D. student, was my technical guru, the solver of the hardest engineering challenges for both Ruger Associates and Wolf Investigations. His wife Ying Ying, an accountant, did my bookkeeping.

"Hi, Daniel, I'm at lunch."

"Is this a bad time?"

"No, but hang on a minute. I want to go outside where I won't bother anyone." I also didn't want to be overheard.

Once outside, I said, "OK, still there?"

"Yes, still here."

"OK, good. I have a project with HH Racing, the race team we wrote that inventory software for. But not related to that. It's analyzing why they're having problems with telemetry from their race car."

"Sounds interesting. You get to go to the track? Meet the driver?"

I smiled to myself. Daniel knew how much I liked racing. "No. At least not yet. But I have some raw telemetry from a race car that I'd like to look at on the spectrum analyzer. You available in the next day or so?"

"I'm available, but the spectrum analyzer is being used by a signal processing lab course this afternoon. It'll be free tomorrow, if Saturday is OK with you."

"It'll have to do. There's also some multi-channel data I'd like you to look at. I'll meet you at the lab at ten tomorrow." Ten was first thing in the morning to Daniel, who often worked past midnight.

"OK, see you." I went back into Pike Pub.

As we waited for Sandy to bring us our checks, Linda said, "Jack and RF have asked for the rest of the day off, Wolf. I figure they've each worked over fifty hours this week and sixty hours last week. Unless you need them for something, I'll let them go home."

"I'm fine with it. I'm going to spend the afternoon at my office reading the manual for the Tau system's display software, then looking at the data a few different ways."

As I drove to my office, I briefly concentrated on the meeting with Daniel. Then my thoughts turned to my date the next evening with Vanessa.

Chapter 3

At six-thirty the next morning, I woke to Boots' paws kneading my chest. I didn't need an alarm clock anymore unless I was keeping unusual hours. Boots' hunger signals were reliable and regular.

The weather was warm and humid with clouds building in the west. The forecast called for a front to move through in the late afternoon with light showers. Gusty winds would shift to the north and the temperature would drop ten degrees.

By the time I started jogging on the Monon Trail it was in the low seventies. I went south for the first two miles so the wind would be at my back for the last half of the run. As I jogged, I considered the HH Racing telemetry problem.

I hadn't learned much more by looking at the multi-channel processed data from the telemetry system the previous afternoon. But a key issue became clear. In order to identify the interfering signal with the buzzing sound, we needed to determine the location from which it was being transmitted.

RF had been experimenting with several antenna types. Examining the dissimilarities in the signal patterns for each type might be helpful. They were probably used in differing conditions and locations, but I was looking for variations in patterns, not specific values. I'd ask RF for the files on Monday.

As I headed to campus to meet Daniel and use the spectrum analyzer, I popped in a Buddy Guy CD and cranked up the volume. His wailing blues harp provided empathy for my Saturday work day.

I wondered where I'd park. There were only ten meters in a lot with a capacity of three hundred cars, an impossible situation on weekdays. I lucked out and got one.

All but the metered spaces require a university parking permit, with patrols twenty-four seven. I had been stung before on a weekend. The meter still had twenty minutes on it, so I shucked in enough quarters for another hour and headed into Daniel's lab.

Although a late riser, he was early for our appointment, as usual. "Hi, Wolf. I have the spectrum analyzer ready."

"Great, I'd like to feed the raw data into it, and at the same time listen to the audio from my computer."

He plugged speakers into my laptop, and we started watching and listening. It only took a few examples of data dropouts to shake the cobwebs out of my brain. Recollections of telemetry I'd seen in Iraq flooded my memory.

"I've seen stuff like this before, Daniel." I felt hair rising on the back of my neck and goose bumps on my arms. My knees were so wobbly I had to sit down.

"You look like you've seen a ghost," he said soberly when he saw my face.

"In a way I have. That signal is a ghost from my electronic warfare days. It's a jamming signal. The HH Racing telemetry is being intentionally jammed by someone."

"No kidding?"

"No kidding."

A flashback to the suicide bombing in Iraq that left Shumacher and Wilson dead at my feet flickered across my vision. My breath was coming in shallow gasps, and there was perspiration on my forehead and wrists.

I was unaware of my surroundings until Daniel laid a hand on my shoulder. "You OK, Wolf?"

I took a deep breath, coming back to the present. "Yeah, thanks Daniel. Must have been something I ate."

He looked concerned, but his Asian culture prevented him from asking personal questions that could result in my "losing face." I hadn't told him about my PTSD and didn't want to. I needed to call Tito.

I stood up, still shaky, passing the back of my wrist across my forehead. "Let's record some video from the spectrum analyzer I can take with me. And make yourself a copy of the DVD. I'd like you to look at all the data channels, just to see if anything pops out at you. Remember it's proprietary, so the NDA you signed covers it."

He nodded. "Sure you're OK?"

"I'm fine," I lied. "Let's get to work."

We stored the spectrum analyzer video on separate DVDs, identical copies for each of us. Wrapping up around noon, I offered to buy him lunch, but Ying Ying had packed his meal. I thanked him, told him to send me an invoice, and left.

Walking to my Jeep, I remembered Nick's directive to call him if we found out anything. I hesitated to intrude on his weekend, but called anyway and got his voicemail. I told him we'd found something, and left my cell number.

Tito had been working day shifts recently, and was off until Monday, so I called him at home.

"How's it going?" he asked.

"Rough spot a little while ago."

"Tell me about it. I'm all ears." I heard him shut a door, and figured he was in his den where nobody else could hear.

I quickly summarized my new consulting job, explaining that I had to use a spectrum analyzer at the university because the one at HH Racing wasn't working. As I started to describe how the telemetry signals took me back to Iraq, my voice began to shake. I was reliving it again.

"Slow down. Take a deep breath. Wait a minute before you try to say any more."

After a couple of false starts, I worked my way through the episode. I was sweating and shaking, but felt better. I believed I could make it through the rest of the day.

We discussed our PTSD experiences because we inevitably revisited the trauma, and wanted that to happen together in an atmosphere where we felt safe and didn't have to worry about what other people thought. Taking a few minutes for small talk at the end of PTSD calls helped both of us to decompress.

I told him I was astounded by what I'd seen on the spectrum analyzer.

"Who'd do something like that?" he asked.

"Well, rival teams have to be high on the list. The intermittent, off and on, nature of the jamming makes me wonder if it was aimed at someone else, though."

"Call me anytime. And let me know what happens with HH racing. I'll bet you never even dreamed you'd run into jamming back here in the U.S."

"Yeah. Bad dream."

Driving back home I kept thinking that nothing made sense. I briefly pondered who had manufactured the jamming system, and how and where someone had acquired it. Ideas bounced around my head like bumper cars.

I had the refrigerator door open, deciding which leftover to reheat, half of a meatball sub, or Pad Thai, when Nick called back. Voices of chattering children made him hard to hear.

"Hi, Wolf. I'm at Mickey D's with my daughter's soccer team. Just noticed your voicemail. What's up?"

"Is she the next Mia Hamm?"

"You're behind the times. And she's a goalkeeper. Her idol is Hope Solo, but you didn't call to talk about soccer."

"No, and I'm not sure how to tell you this. First, there is probably nothing wrong with HH Racing's Tau 920 system. Second, it appears that someone's intentionally jamming your radio telemetry signal."

"What? Let me go where I can hear you better." After a pause during which the background noise dropped considerably, he said, "Say that again."

I did, adding, "Let's meet with the communications and telemetry team first thing Monday, and I'll show you all what I have. Until then, I suggest you keep this under wraps."

"Heard you right the first time. Just didn't believe it. How sure are you that we're being jammed?"

"At least ninety percent. It'll take a little time over the weekend to tie up loose ends."

"Since you're that sure there's no way I'm keeping this private. The team has worked too hard and agonized too much to make them worry needlessly another weekend. I'll call Linda, and have her get in touch with RF and Jack."

"It's your decision."

"Yes, it is." He sighed audibly. "I can't believe someone is doing this. Do you have any ideas, Wolf?"

"I have ideas, but none that make sense. You know the racing business and I don't, but I'll think about it."

It occurred to me after the call that my Ruger Associates job with HH Racing might be ending. The problem seemed to be morphing from a technical investigation into a criminal one. I needed to write a report.

I opted for the half meatball sub with a side of slightly stale potato chips, washed down with a Sam Adams Light. I counted on Vanessa's cioppino to compensate for my lousy lunch.

Most of the afternoon was spent writing and editing my report to HH Racing. An electronic warfare and radar systems handbook I'd used in the Army provided details on the type of jamming I suspected was being used. Called barrage jamming, it features the ability to cover multiple frequencies simultaneously.

Someone knew what they were doing and had the resources to do it. The sixty-four-thousand-dollar question was: Why?

I reviewed my report a couple of times. Around four o'clock, when editing started to yield diminishing returns, I decided to veg out. I rubbed Boots' stomach, which got him purring so hard he vibrated, then went out on the balcony with a Diet Pepsi and the newspaper.

Unfortunately, the pool was closed for the season, so there were no bikini babes. As luck would have it, though, two women were taking advantage of the warm weather to play tennis.

One of them was pretty and shapely, and reminded me of someone. It dawned on me that she looked like Ann Wyland, the attractive, intelligent, and recently divorced daughter of Billy Wyland, a retired electronics company executive who'd helped me with the case of the dead disk drives.

While solving the case, I met, played tennis with, fantasized about, and dated Ann. Ours was the first date she'd had since her divorce. She said she was too fragile to get into a relationship, but we'd discovered several common interests, agreed to stay in touch, and to play tennis again sometime.

The last time I saw her, I gave her a CDROM with software for a system her company, Oracle Electronics, was selling to the Navy that had been experiencing failures due to malware, or software that disrupts computers. I had to make her promise to keep the source of the CDROM confidential.

I hadn't seen her since, and hadn't heard whether the software was helpful to Oracle. Billy and I shared an interest in, and painful memories related to, backgammon. I owed him a game.

Perhaps I'd get in touch with Billy. I wondered what Vanessa would think of me calling Ann.

Instead, I decided to send Ann a personalized version of the marketing email I'd sent to previous customers seeking computer consulting jobs. Maybe we could be friends.

I finished reading the paper, stood up, and stretched. I grabbed a beer from the refrigerator, went into my office, and sent Ann the marketing email, adding a P.S. asking how she and Billy were doing and what she thought of the CD.

I'd left my smartphone on the balcony, so picked it up, and noticed that Vanessa had called. I listened to her purr, "Hi Wolf, can't wait to see you, but the cioppino is taking a little longer than I'd thought. I'd like you to wait until about seven-thirty to come over. Call me."

She answered on the first ring. "Hi, Vanessa, what's up?"

"Oh, nothing much," she said tantalizingly. "Actually, in addition to my being late making dinner, Deb's coming by this evening. We have something to show you."

I'd introduced Vanessa to Deb Lampmann right after the case involving malfunctioning computer disk drives. She and Deb had hit it off, and Vanessa had moved into a condo in the same development in Castleton.

"What's that?"

"It's a surprise. She won't stay long, promise. Seven-thirty OK?"

"Sure. I have work I can do here. I'll bring the chilled Chardonnay. See you then."

"That's good. Deb hasn't seen you since Uncle Sal was here. We'll have some wine before we kick her out," she chuckled.

We said goodbye. Something was up.

When the time came to leave, I was so preoccupied with trying to guess what Vanessa and Deb had in store that I was almost out the door before I remembered the bottle of Chardonnay. More Buddy Guy accompanied my drive, this time providing a background for my curiosity and anticipation.

* * *

I met the beautiful and sensuous Vanessa Russo Gordian a couple of months earlier. She's separated from Stan Gordian, who is out on bail awaiting trial for being an accessory after the fact in a murder.

Vanessa filed for divorce and took back her maiden name a few days after Stan was arrested. She initiated an accelerated process that takes about three months instead of the usual year. She justified it based on Stan's record, the current charges against him, and the fact that FBI agents and State Police investigators had raided their home, where computers and documents were removed. Her lawyer made a compelling case that Stan posed a risk to her that was both obvious and unacceptable.

Vanessa's family from Chicago has Italian mob ties. Her uncle, Sal Russo, like a father to her, lives in Los Angeles. His organization runs casinos in Las Vegas. Just to complicate things, her soon-to-be ex-husband Stan is part of the Armenian mob.

Following a steamy, intense sexual encounter with Vanessa, I decided that things were moving too fast and that we shouldn't see each other for a while but, during a visit to Indy a few weeks later, her Uncle Sal not only encouraged us to see each other, but also charged me with ensuring her safety.

He gave me a phone number to use to contact him if I ever came up against something I couldn't handle. That evening Vanessa and I watched fireworks and created some of our own. Since then, Vanessa and I have seen each other often.

During Uncle Sal's visit, Vanessa told him about Stan's increasingly frequent and insistent phone calls and emails trying to convince her to come back to him. Sal strongly suggested that Vanessa get a restraining order against Stan. Coming from Sal, this was equivalent to a command.

Within two weeks a restraining order that included a 'no contact' clause was issued. It applied to Stan, everyone in his family, and the employees of his company ElecRecycle. They all were required to physically stay away from her and could not contact her in any way, including electronically such as telephone, email, and social media.

Driving to Vanessa's place, I was puzzled about what Vanessa and Deb had waiting for me. I parked, grabbed the wine, climbed to her second floor condo, and rang the bell.

"Hi, Wolf, you look good enough to eat. And I mean it both ways." She ruffled my hair, wrapped her arms around my neck, and delivered a tongue-exploring kiss while she rubbed her pelvis against mine. Her hazel eyes twinkled. "I have a surprise for you. Deb helped."

I hadn't noticed what she was wearing until she pushed gently away from me, and took a step back. Saying, "Ta-da," she twirled around with her arms out from her sides, palms up.

It took a second to sink in, then hit me right between the eyes. And in the groin. She was wearing the same red peasant blouse and black flared miniskirt she had on when Uncle Sal visited and we made love in the back of her SUV after watching fireworks. I'd even glimpsed the same red satin bikini panties with white polka dots.

"Is that the surprise?" I asked teasingly.

"No, silly. Just wait."

Appearing behind Vanessa, Deb said, "Hi. Wolf. Want to give me that wine?" Her eyes twinkled as she took the Chardonnay from me and headed for the kitchen. "I'll open this and put it on ice so it stays chilled."

Vanessa took me by the hand. "OK, close your eyes and keep them closed until I tell you to open them. No peeking."

She led me down the entry hall and turned left, into her living room. The aroma of the Italian food permeated the whole living space and presaged a scrumptious dinner.

Our condos were a study in contrasts. Mine was utilitarian no-frills masculine, with serviceable but uninspiring furniture arranged haphazardly. Hers was half again as large, and could have been featured in a home decorating magazine or on HGTV.

The artwork on my walls was highlighted by framed prints from art museum gift shops, while hers featured original oils and numbered prints. Her kitchen was equipped for a top chef; mine was outfitted for someone who ate out. Her carpeting was luxuriant and off white; mine was serviceable and institutional beige.

In what I figured was her living room, she turned me around. "OK, now I want you to kiss me like you did the night of the fireworks."

I had a vivid memory of that, so I included what immediately preceded the kiss by stroking the backs of her legs, pulling her against me, lifting her skirt, and fondling her ass through her panties before fingering the ribbon bows at her hips. Then I moved my hands so one was on each side of her head, pushed her hair back, and kissed her just in front of the ear.

"Oh God, you remembered," she said huskily. "Open your eyes."

I opened them. Behind her, over the fireplace, illuminated by can lights, was a large oil painting in an ornate gilt frame of fireworks over The Navy Pier in Chicago, where Sal had taken her as a child.

"It's my housewarming gift from Uncle Sal," she cooed. "Deb helped me put it up."

"You told him what we did that night?"

"No. I wonder if he knew."

I kissed her long and deep, pressing our bodies together, her arms around my neck.

I was caressing her face, her perfume wafting over me, when from behind my back Deb cleared her throat. "I'd tell you guys to get a room, but you're already in one. Do you want me to leave?"

Vanessa pushed me away playfully. "Oh, no, Deb. You can't imagine how much I appreciate your help. Have some wine with us."

We followed Deb into the kitchen holding hands. The kitchen table was strewn with textbooks and papers, with a laptop computer sitting amidst it all. This was the main place Vanessa studied for the courses she was taking in marketing and website development. She barely used her second bedroom, which was supposed to be her office.

As Deb was filling the glasses, she said, "OK, guys, I know you're anticipating dinner and preoccupied with sex, but we have time for a toast."

She raised her glass. "To the two people whose relationship makes me jealous," adding as she looked at Vanessa, "I'll bet he's even sexier with his clothes off."

Vanessa's answer was to look at me with a wicked grin. "To Uncle Sal," she toasted.

"To fireworks," I concluded.

We clinked our glasses and sipped our wine, Vanessa still holding my hand.

We reminisced about Uncle Sal's visit over the rest of the bottle of wine, then Deb said her goodbyes, smiling at each of us. "The two of you have fun. Like you need encouragement."

Vanessa led me into her dining room, lit the two candles on the table, and pulled me to her, saying, "Kiss now. Sex later."

The cioppino was outstanding. We used the fresh-baked Italian bread to sop up leftover sauce in our bowls. For dessert, she dished out spumoni, the three-flavor Italian ice cream. She wanted the pistachio part of mine. I gave her half. She could push me only so far when it came to spumoni.

"Why don't you make coffee while I put on something more comfortable?" she asked.

What a line.

I'd finished grinding the beans and was just starting the coffee maker when she came into the kitchen wrapped in a short pink silk robe that enhanced the contrast between her fine Italian skin and lustrous auburn mane. She was holding the robe shut with one hand.

She let go of the robe. It fell open. She only wore wicked black string bikini panties. She pulled me toward her, and ground her pelvis into my bulge. Coffee would have to wait.

As she guided me into the bedroom, my cell phone on the kitchen counter rang. I checked the caller ID, prepared to let it go to voicemail, but it was from Nick Napoli.

"Hi, Nick," I said, mentally cursing his ancestors as Vanessa pulled me into the bedroom and crawled into bed.

"Sorry to bother you, Wolf. I was worried you might have turned off your cell phone."

I wished I had.

I held up my forefinger toward Vanessa, indicating I'd be just a minute. She responded by lying on her back and stroking the crotch of her panties with her forefinger.

"What's up?" I was listening to Nick but all eyes for Vanessa.

"Linda said that RF seemed quite upset when she told him about the jamming. After she talked to Jack, she called me back suggesting that we meet tomorrow morning instead of waiting until Monday. I agreed, but since then we haven't been able to reach RF. He hasn't answered voicemails, and now his land line at home seems to be off the hook."

"What do you want me to do?"

"You said you live near Broad Ripple. RF lives within five or ten minutes of you. Linda is out in Brownsburg and I live in Zionsville, so I'd really appreciate your dropping by his house."

Vanessa saw my sour look and sat up.

I muted the phone. "Trying to locate someone who works at HH Racing."

I unmuted the phone. "What's so urgent?"

33

Hearing the word 'urgent' Vanessa pulled her robe tightly around her and sat up on the edge of the bed.

"Linda has bugged me several times, asking if we've heard from RF. I'm not sure it's what *I'd* call urgent, but she's quite worried, and she has a point. We strongly prefer not to have the meeting tomorrow at eight without him, and I don't want to wait much later in the evening to postpone it. How soon could you make it?"

"I'm in the Castleton area. I can go by RF's and call you by ten or so."

"Oh, sorry. Didn't know you weren't at home, but you're still closest to him. Ten will be OK." He gave me RF's home and cell numbers.

Consulting has its downsides. This seemed like a big waste of my time, but keeping my client happy was essential.

Sex would have to wait.

I explained the situation to Vanessa and promised to be back in an hour or so. "We can pick up where we left off."

"I'll be ready," she said, illustrating her readiness with her fingers.

I followed her into the kitchen as I unsuccessfully tried to reach RF on both numbers Nick had given me.

She handed me coffee in a travel mug, then followed me to the front door. She drew me against her for a long kiss.

"Have a nice day at the office, dear." Smiling, she let her robe fall open as I shut the door.

* * *

RF had rented a small bungalow in a Butler-Tarkington working class area near 38th Street. Built in the forties, it had white siding, a screened-in front porch, and a detached garage too narrow for modern cars. A dark gray Nissan was in the driveway. Windows along the foundation indicated that it had a basement.

I parked a little way down the block facing his house and watched it for a few minutes. All the lights were off. He was probably home with the phone off the hook. He had struck me as a loner, so he wasn't likely to be out partying.

I mounted the steps, then stood on the front porch listening. Silence. I knocked, cautiously at first, then harder the next two tries, without result.

Feeling that something wasn't right, I tried the door knob. It turned. I went in. Enough light filtered through windows with open Venetian blinds to keep me from falling over furniture and guide me on a quick search of the rooms on the main floor. A yellow oak library desk in the front bedroom which seemed to serve as his office was in disarray, strewn with papers and drawers pulled out, in stark contrast with his pristine office at HH Racing.

At the back of the kitchen, past an old porcelain sink full of unwashed dishes, light shone from beneath a door on my left. At first, it appeared to be a closet, but it opened onto a steep narrow stairway into the basement. Going down the creaking wooden steps, I wished I had my revolver.

The damp concrete block wall to my right contributed to a mildewy smell. Ducking my head under the basement rafters as I continued down the stairs, I saw that the casement windows had been covered over so no light could escape. Also visible was an area floored with a checkerboard pattern of maroon and off-white vinyl tile with what at first looked like exercise equipment. Upon closer inspection, the equipment proved to be furnishings for a dungeon used by people practicing sadism and masochism, or S and M. It was the first time I'd seen one up close and personal.

Halfway back, on the left, was a large wooden structure resembling an 'X.' Partially obscured by a basement pillar, a pair of legs with stocking feet stuck out from it. A rancid odor intensified as I rounded the pillar and found RF with a studded collar around his neck attached to the center of the wooden X. In a sitting position, his head hung down and slightly to the side, his sightless eyes bulged out, and his tongue lolled out of his mouth. Jeans pulled down to his knees revealed black satiny bikini underwear.

I fought back a wave of nausea and disorientation as memories of the suicide bombing in Iraq washed over me. I took several deep breaths, and my vision cleared. I was in a cold sweat as I shuffled over to RF and felt for a pulse. Nothing. I sat on the floor with my back against the pillar.

After a minute or so, I stood and moved back to the body. A contusion on the left rear of his nearly-bald head might have been caused by a heavy blunt object, but his eyes and tongue suggested that he had strangled to death. The question was how.

As my mind cleared, I considered the possibilities. His S and M lifestyle provided several.

He could have been into the type of autoeroticism in which people restrict airflow by temporarily choking themselves to achieve very intense orgasms. His clothing arrangement indicated that he might have been masturbating and unintentionally strangled himself, which isn't as unusual as most people think.

Perhaps another individual was involved, a horrible accident occurred, and the other person fled.

He could have chosen this way to commit suicide, a not uncommon method among men who kill themselves.

Or, he could have been murdered. If the contusion on his head was recent, he could have been knocked senseless and put into the collar by his killer.

As I dialed 911, I wondered if I was in the right line of work.

My jury was out on the cause of death.

Chapter 4

I reported finding RF's body to a sergeant at the IMPD call center. Determining time and cause of death was up to them. I'd been hired to investigate a data telemetry problem, not a death that might be murder.

Then I called Tito at home.

"Hi, Wolf. Rough spot?"

"Yeah, and worse." I summarized what I'd found while I went upstairs and out to the front porch. "I've just called it in."

"You want me to come there?"

"Probably not. There'll be a patrol car here soon. I'll let you know."

"You think he was murdered?"

"Hard to tell. Could have been an accident or suicide."

"Watch your ass, mon. Just walk away from it."

"I hear you. Problem is, if he was killed, or even if it was suicide, it could be because of the jamming. I need to watch my back. Can you check out what's going on?"

"I can't call anyone tonight or tomorrow. No reason to. It'd raise red flags. I'll poke around first thing Monday morning though, and let you know what I can."

"OK, appreciate it. I hear a siren. Better go."

"Let me know if you want to talk later. Ciao."

Patrolmen Cedric Jones and Leonard Friedman worked seamlessly as a team despite disparities in appearance and culture. Jones' athletic build on a six-four African-American frame and shaved head contrasted with his partner's thin hatchet face with furtive eyes, and thick Brooklyn accent. The top of Friedman's burr haircut barely came up to Jones' chin.

After they looked over the scene, I gave them my story, and showed them my driver's license and a Ruger Associates business card.

Jones consulted his notes. "So you were sent here by someone from the company – Nick Napoli – but you don't have any company ID."

I nodded. "I'm a consultant for them."

"We'll check that out with Mr. Napoli. What's his number?"

I gave him Nick's office and cell numbers, hoping that I'd talk to him first.

"Do you have any idea how Mr. Phillips died?"

I shook my head. "I only met him once."

"Better contact homicide," Jones said to Friedman.

Friedman wrinkled his nose. "With the action on the north side and downtown tonight, they are pretty short staffed. Probably have to bring someone in." He moved a few steps away to call.

"You're in for a treat," Friedman sniggered as he walked back to us. "Homicide's sending Detective Sergeant Sam, who is not a happy camper. Apparently was attending some charity ball."

They turned their attention from me as an ambulance arrived. Jones and Friedman escorted the EMT technicians downstairs, giving me the chance to phone Nick.

I didn't pull any punches. "Nick, bad news. RF is dead."

"My God! How? What happened?"

I knew better than to give him any details. "I don't know, but with all the yellow tape around the house, the police must have preliminarily ruled it to be suspicious circumstances."

"Can't you tell me anything else?"

"No, I could get myself into deep shit. It's an active investigation now."

"I'll call Linda. It's more important than ever that we meet tomorrow. Eight o'clock. Please be there."

"OK. You'll probably be contacted by IMPD checking me out. See you tomorrow."

Then I called Tito to let him know homicide was on the way. "Some sergeant named 'Detective Sam' has been summoned away from a social event. I understand he's pissed."

Tito laughed. "Detective Sergeant Sam is Samantha Hardin; very much a 'she.' A real climber in IMPD. Plays politics. She'll make Captain before I make Lieutenant. Don't get on the wrong side of her...and for Christ's sake don't call her Sam." We hung up.

Jones came out of the house as a black Lexus sedan pulled into the driveway. A striking African-American woman with hair piled stylishly on the top of her head emerged wearing a white evening gown with a thigh-high slit. Without the hair and high heels, she would still be nearly six feet tall. The woman was all business, and all annoyed.

Opening a notebook, she strode up to Jones and stood nose to nose with him. "So, what's going on here? And who's he?" she asked, motioning at me with her thumb without turning around.

She took notes as Jones summarized. "Show me the deceased, and one of you check out his story with Mr. Napoli." She looked at me. Hard. "You come with us and walk through what you did. Don't leave anything out."

I retraced my steps and reiterated my actions. I slowed down and started to sweat as we got near the top of the basement stairway.

I must have looked a little strange, too, because she said, "OK. You don't have to go back down there. Did you touch anything? Move it around?"

I shook my head. "Oh, I checked for a pulse. Nothing else."

They didn't need me for their basement convention. Outside, I gulped in deep breaths of fresh air.

Ten minutes later the convention adjourned. A funereal parade led by RF's body on a gurney emerged from the house.

Sergeant Hardin walked up to me, flipping back through her notebook. "We checked you out with Mr. Napoli, and we have your contact information. You're free to go. You'll need to come to the North District Station and sign a statement. We'll be in touch."

I turned to leave.

"Just a second," she said, peering at me as she tapped her notebook with a pen. "Ruger…Ruger…have we met somewhere?"

I turned back. "No, I'm sure I'd remember. I don't make it to many charity balls."

Her eyes flashed sharply. She started to say something but clamped her mouth shut.

I turned and kept walking.

A few blocks from RF's house, I pulled over into a parking place and called Vanessa. "I'm on my way."

"Everything all right?" she asked.

"Not really, but I'd rather tell you in person."

"I'll wait for you to get started."

I had just hung up when the cell rang, so I figured it was Vanessa and didn't check the caller ID. "Hi, gorgeous."

There was a silence, followed by a throat clearing. "Sergeant Hardin speaking. I want to talk to you."

It was my turn to clear my throat. "Sorry. When?" I assumed she'd want to meet Monday.

"Now. North District Office. You know where that is?"

"Yes, but I have a date. What's so urgent?"

"Gorgeous can wait. I ask the questions. You answer. I'm on my way in now. Be there."

She hung up.

I stared at the phone for a few seconds. She must have connected Ruger Associates with Wolf Investigations' recent murder cases.

Bummed out, I called Vanessa again.

"Mmm…Wolf, you want me to get started before you get here?"

"I wish. I've been summoned for questioning by IMPD. I'm on my way there."

"Phooey, that sucks. Why?"

"I didn't want to tell you on the phone, but when I checked on RF, I found his body."

"Oh no, Wolf. That's terrible. You aren't involved in another murder, are you?"

"I don't think so. It was probably an accident, but the cops are labeling it 'suspicious' so they're looking into it in more detail. I'm a detail." Maybe if I wished it to be accidental death, it would be.

"God, Wolf. Be careful."

"I will. I'll call you when I can. Better not count on me for tonight."

I hadn't been honest with Vanessa. She probably knew it. If IMPD thought RF's death was accidental, yellow tape wouldn't be surrounding his house. RF was told about my discovering the jamming several hours earlier, and now was dead.

Whether suicide or homicide, I was in it up to my neck. As Aunt Edna used to say, "Life is what happens when you're making other plans."

* * *

IMPD Northwest District Headquarters is near 38th Street and Guion Road, just off I-65 with the interstate in front and a high-voltage transmission line running past the rear of the property. I parked in a lot adjacent to the one-story concrete and glass structure.

Inside, grey was the order of the day. The mayor was even wearing a grey suit in the framed photograph behind the desk sergeant who signed me in and said Sergeant Hardin was expecting me.

Expecting me and being ready to see me were not the same thing. I cooled my heels and read last year's dog-eared magazines for half an hour before being directed to her office.

Her uniform was out of sync with the hair still piled formally on her head. She peered at me without speaking, expressionless, for at least thirty seconds after I sat in the split-cushioned grey chair, then spat out, "So what the *hell* are you up to?"

It was a technique I used myself. Ask a confrontational question bordering on inappropriate just to get a reaction.

Several seconds ticked off the clock. "With respect to what?" I asked, wide-eyed.

She snorted and slammed her pen on the desk. "I know you're a private dick. Let's start with why you gave me a fake business card."

I sat back. "Because it's legitimate. I'm working for HH Racing as a computer consultant."

"Don't give me that bull crap. You were at the scene of a suspicious death."

"Murder?"

She leaned forward, blankly staring. "It's an active investigation."

"Look," I said, keeping my voice even while my blood pressure rose. "I'd have been dishonest if not unethical giving you my other card."

"You were mixed up in a shooting a month ago that the FBI was involved with, right?"

"So?" I was getting angry, and took a deep breath.

"So nobody's covering for you on *this* one. No attorney-client privileges. You will damned well tell us everything you know that's pertinent or your license is toast." She leaned over and punched a button on her phone. "Send in Corporal Gaddis."

Corporal Glen Gaddis was portly and sallow-faced, with muddy brown eyes the color of a swollen river. He read me my rights with a digital recorder running.

It was after midnight by the time my statement was transcribed and signed, and nearly one o'clock before sleep claimed my consciousness.

Sunday morning was misty and damp, but we'd only gotten a trace of badly needed rain. The cold front had passed through, and the temperature was in the upper fifties, more like autumn.

During the drive to HH Racing, I reviewed what needed to be done at the meeting. I'd explain what we'd seen on the spectrum analyzer, give them a printed copy of my report, and offer to put an electronic version on one of their computers or thumb drives. That part seemed simple enough.

Handling RF's death was going to be tricky. Keeping my ass out of a sling required saying nothing that would impede IMPD's investigation.

Not surprisingly, the outside door was locked. Nick let me in and led me into the executive conference room. Hal Handel was seated at the head of a conference table big enough to cover the infield at the Indians stadium. With his open-necked shirt, suede jacket, and feathered back sandy hair, he looked like he'd just stepped out of a commercial for used cars. Which he may have.

Mark wore cargo shorts and boat shoes with no socks. The rest of us were strictly informal, attired in jeans and t-shirts.

Hal cleared his throat. It was obviously his meeting. "We've had a grievous loss to our racing family," he intoned. "Ronald was respected and admired by us all." He paused for effect, looking up as though he had a personal channel to God.

Linda rolled her eyes, and Mark coughed. Nick, his face lined with worry, pinched the bridge of his nose with a thumb and forefinger. So much for effect.

Hal droned on, "Nick and I have discussed the way forward. He has my full support. Please give him yours. We have the Nor-Am second place trophy in the cross-hairs. I'm counting on you to bring it home." With that he rose, lumbered to the door, and turned. "Feel free to use my conference room for the rest of the day." He waved over his shoulder without looking back.

Nick took a deep breath. "Hal means well, and he really does have our team's welfare at heart. He said he'd only stay a little while, so we could work as a team without worrying about him."

"I assume you filled each of us in with the same information about RF," said Linda.

"Yes. I know that each of you had your own unique relationship with him, and will grieve in your own way. It's too early to know when, or if, a funeral will be held. If one is, we plan to shut down for a while so everyone can attend."

"Who's going to do his work?" asked Jack.

Nick shifted in his seat. "Hal and I discussed that. It's not feasible to bring someone in from the outside with only one race left in the season less than a week away. It'd take longer to get them up to speed than we have, and be a major distraction. You guys pick one of the electronics technicians to work with you. Give him or her enough training so they're useful. The rest of you will have to pick up the slack."

Linda cleared her throat. "That's OK as far as it goes. I expected something like that, and we can live with it." Nodding heads agreed. "But we need to talk about the elephant in the room." When nobody said anything, she continued, "We don't know if RF committed suicide or was murdered, but it's connected to our telemetry being jammed, right?"

They all looked at Nick. "That's one of the reasons I asked Wolf to join us."

Nick looked at me. "Hal and I would like you to continue consulting with us. Your main task is to help us do something about the jamming. Also, we want you to assist the team in getting ready for our practice session, qualifying, and race Thursday through Saturday at Boone. And provide support at the track. You have experience with the kind of equipment that RF used, so you can help Linda and Jack train the technician."

I gave him what I'd printed out. So much for it being my final report. "Sounds like a challenge. Here's what I've done so far."

Nick glanced through it, then shoved it across the table to Linda. "You'll be handling this. Wolf reports to both of us. I'm not hung up on protocol. Just keep me in the loop."

He turned to me. "Wolf, I have a purchase order for you to sign. Angie Murphy, our human resources and contracts person, emailed it to me from home. You'll be paid for ten hours a day through next Saturday, negotiable after that. We need your full attention."

43

Six hundred bucks a day was nothing to sneeze at. I signed the PO. "When do I start?"

"Now."

Linda stood up. "Let's go into the engineering conference room where we can make a list of what we need to do, and the resources required."

Jack grinned, "It's no accident that Linda and list both start with 'L.' She's known for 'em."

On the way, we detoured through the break room to make a pot of coffee. We had a long day ahead.

Linda wiped the conference room white board clean, deep in thought. She talked while she made her list. "Wolf, we need to get you an HH Racing badge and a crew pass to the track at Boone. I'll take care of those items tomorrow."

I took notes as she wrote. "I bet you have reading material for me."

"What do you mean?"

"I assume each person has a defined job, and that there's a list of tasks, guidelines, whatever, that specify what they do at a race, at qualifying, at practice sessions, maybe even getting ready for a race."

She laughed. "You were in the military. This is a racing team. For a team to actually write down what people are supposed to do is rare. It would require a different mentality. Also, it might dissuade people from doing all that's necessary. Each person's job on a race team is quite fluid."

"I'm surprised."

"So was I when I hired on here. With Nick's support, I asked Jack and RF to prepare a rough outline of what they do, just to help me understand what's going on. I'll bet you can guess what happened." She paused, looking at me.

"You got something from Jack the next day, and you never got anything useful from RF."

She nodded. "Pretty much. RF resisted giving me anything. He said his job was flexible, and that he didn't want to live and die by a notebook." Her hand went to her mouth. "Oh, God. Shouldn't have said that."

Jack cleared his throat and raised his hand like he was in a classroom, "He probably ought to see what the two of us put together."

"Good point. The material that Jack and I prepared is divided into sections, including procedures for a practice session, qualifying, and so on. There are also outlines of responsibilities when we're getting ready to travel to or from a track. It's all kinda rough, but should help you out."

"I'm sure it'll be helpful. What about RF's responsibilities?"

Linda looked at Jack. "Jack and I did our best to record what we saw him doing. I asked him to review it, and all he did was make a few corrections here and there. I know there's a lot missing, but he didn't add anything. It's going to be a real challenge out there."

I nodded. "That's probably why Nick hired me to help. I'm familiar with the various types of equipment you guys use. I still need to learn more about the Tau 920. Is the material you have in electronic or printed format?"

"Both. Mark'll load it all onto your laptop, including Jack's, mine, and what little we have for RF. Keep in mind it's highly proprietary."

"Speaking of getting ready to go to a track, what's the schedule for going to Boone?"

Linda pursed her lips, then said grimly, "Well, we usually go a day and a half before the practice session. Since we're so close to Boone, most of the team'll go out early Wednesday morning. But the communications and telemetry team isn't going to the track until that afternoon. We just can't be ready any sooner."

"I've never met a driver for a major racing team. Will Scott Marks be coming to the shop before the practice, or will he just show up at the track?"

Linda laughed. Even Jack chuckled. "Drivers don't usually show up at the factory, or shop. They can't be bothered to greet peasants like us. He has all of his required appearances in his contract, including testing days. And drivers don't like to test. They consider it a necessary evil."

"I guess I should have expected that. By the way, your mentioning 'laptop' reminded me to check on something. I assume that RF had a company laptop, and maybe a desktop computer in his cubicle, right?"

"We all have both," said Jack.

"Then I suggest that the item at the top of my list is to image those computers onto special equipment I have. If IMPD suspects foul play, they'll probably confiscate them. I'll go get everything when we finish our meeting."

Linda asked, "How do you know that?" as she added 'PC imaging' to her list.

"Let's just say I've had relevant experience recently."

"I can duplicate the hard drives in RF's computers," Mark offered.

"I'm not just copying them. I'm making a bit-by-bit replica. Deleted files and so on. A complete mirror image."

Mark nodded. "I can't do that. I know it's possible, though. I'd like to watch."

"No problem."

Linda said, "Wolf, after you image RF's drives, I want you to familiarize yourself with the gear in his test lab. There are antennas, scopes, and so on."

"Will do. Apparently the spectrum analyzer isn't working, so tomorrow I'll arrange to get it repaired and calibrated. I know a place that'll give us a loaner until ours is ready."

"Mark, Wolf needs an email account and access to our computer system. Can you take care of that?"

"Sure," replied Mark, looking at me. "You'll have email, plus access to the marketing and software areas on the system, but not the administrative or financial ones, OK?"

I nodded. "Fine."

"Anyone think of anything else for Wolf right now?" She paused. "No? All right, Wolf, why don't you go get your equipment."

"OK. I'll leave my laptop here so Mark can load the procedure outlines. Also, please load the software I'll need to support the team here and at the track. I don't want to change a single byte on either of RF's computers."

When he'd loaded the Tau 920 manual, I'd given Mark a password that would give him access to a single folder on it. The remainder of the computer was protected by another password and encrypted. I didn't trust anyone.

A light mist was still hanging around when I went out to the parking lot. It wasn't heavy enough to clean off my Jeep, which was just this side of filthy.

I called Vanessa. "Sorry about running out last night."

"So was it worth it?" she asked teasingly.

46

"Not considering what I missed. Occupational hazard." I didn't mention my session with Sergeant Sam.

"I hope there's no hazard involved. You aren't involved in a murder or anything dangerous like that, are you?"

I dodged the question. "I'm just working on their telemetry system problem. Looks like I have to put in ten-hour days through next Saturday, though. I'll be going to the track with the team Thursday through Saturday."

"Phooey. I'm all undressed and no one to fuck. Maybe I'll have to find a substitute."

"What kind of substitute?"

"I'll choose one of my options. Call me tonight if you want to find out what I picked."

She laughed as we hung up.

I assumed we were both monogamous although we hadn't discussed it. Her substitutes obviously included various ways to masturbate, but there was no reason why she couldn't screw someone else. I was ambivalent about that. We were both theoretically free to experiment sexually, but I wasn't sure how I felt about either one of us having sex with someone else.

At the moment I didn't have any options, but, while she described the guys in her university website development course as all geeks, she said there were a couple of 'hunks' in her marketing class. We probably should talk about it, even though I was afraid of what I might find out.

I let myself into my condo a little after eleven. In my office, I got my disk imaging equipment out of the safe that Max Blitzer gave me when he retired. I thought of him each time I opened it.

Also in it was my Smith and Wesson 640-1, a .357 magnum revolver with a totally enclosed action. I can carry it in my pocket without getting lint or other stuff in the action, and can fire it while it's there without worrying about it jamming when the hammer catches on something.

I was possibly in danger now. I could hear my mentor Max saying something folksy like, "Better safe than sorry," so I took the revolver out of the safe and dropped it in my pocket.

Boots was asleep on my bed. I didn't say goodbye. I put the imaging equipment in the Jeep, slid the S&W under the dash in its holder, and headed to HH Racing. The sun was peeking out now and then, but the chilly wind made that only a sham. Autumn had definitely arrived.

Linda let me in after I rang the buzzer. "I'll take you back to RF's area so you can image his computers. How long will that take?"

"Depends. Probably about a half-hour for each computer. Mark said he'd like to see what I'm doing, too."

Squeaks from the soles of her running shoes and my boat shoes on the polished floor were the only sounds in the empty shop as she led me to RF's cubicle. "Go ahead and get started, then please come see me. I'm two cubes over. I'll send Mark in after we've talked," she said, pointing.

"OK. See you later."

I glanced around his cubicle as I set up my equipment. It was plain, austere even. The guy was a neat freak. There wasn't a paperclip out of place. There were no photographs of family or anyone else. A pinup calendar from an auto parts supplier provided the only decoration. I speculated what Linda thought of it.

An antenna he probably designed himself sat on a shelf. Upside down it looked like half a dozen ten-inch bent bug legs sticking up without a body. A quick search for CDs and DVDs that might be worth copying turned up nothing.

I squeaked over to Linda's cubicle. There was no sneaking up on anyone in the shop area wearing rubber-soled shoes. I sat in a straight-backed chair pulled up to the L-shaped desk extension.

Her walls were decorated with computer program flow charts and graphs that looked like output from the Tau 920 analysis program. Two framed pictures on her desk were of an older couple, perhaps her parents, and of her with a hatchet-faced, not quite handsome man, maybe her boyfriend or brother, with San Francisco's Golden Gate Bridge in the background.

"I know we have to get ready for the events coming up next weekend," she said as I sat down, "but the telemetry jamming and RF's death give me the creeps, so let's start there. What should we be doing?"

"I need to look at the electronics lab RF used, see what test gear is there, and figure out what he was doing and how. Then I can decide what else we need. I'm fairly sure I'll want to buy a couple more antennas that can help pinpoint the direction a signal is coming from."

"Jack and I have asked Jason Lewis to assist us. He's an electronics technician and knows quite a bit about the equipment. Do you want me to call him in now?"

I reflected for a few seconds. "I hate to bother anyone on Sunday, but I'm sure he can familiarize me in an hour or so."

She nodded, picked up her phone, and began using her thumbs. "Text message," she explained. "He hates phone calls, and doesn't check his email on weekends."

Putting down the phone, she looked at me, lowering her voice. "You've only given me a technical answer to my question about what we should be doing. I'm worried about why and how RF died, and if this is a safe place to work.

"Mark showed me your other card, your private investigator one. He showed it to Nick, too. Does that have anything to do with why you were brought in to help with our telemetry problem?"

Her question took me by surprise. I sat back, crossed my arms, and shook my head. "No. At least not that I'm aware of. Nick knew about my experience with telemetry systems and called me in. I had no inkling that your Tau 920 system was being jammed."

"So you didn't offer us your services as a private investigator?"

"Absolutely not. In fact, because of a rough experience on a recent case as a PI, I've been concentrating on the computer consulting side of my work."

"You considering getting out of the investigative business?"

I shook my head slowly. "No. Maybe just taking a short break from it, and if I take a PI job, trying to make sure that it isn't potentially hazardous to my health." I smiled inwardly, thinking about getting peed on by a poodle while serving a subpoena. "At least not too hazardous."

Linda's phone beeped. "Jason's on his way in. Be here in twenty minutes or so."

"Great. I'll finish up with RF's desktop PC, and start on his laptop before Jason gets here. You can send Mark in anytime."

As I waited for the first disk image to finish, I looked around RF's work area some more. I knew that seventy percent of all suicides in the U.S. are by white males. RF didn't seem depressed or strike me as the type of person who would kill himself, but as Tito had reminded me, there's no specific type. I certainly wasn't trained to diagnose depression.

Mark came in as the first process was finishing. I showed him the equipment and explained how it worked. He watched as I set up the equipment on RF's laptop.

I had just gotten started on it when Linda brought Jason in and introduced him. With an unruly thatch of blonde hair and a serious case of acne, it was hard to believe that he was out of high school, much less that he had an associate's degree in electronics technology. His shocked look informed me that Linda had told him what was going on.

"I told him about RF, and about our telemetry being jammed," she confirmed. "He'll be helping our team 'til Boone is over. Wolf, why don't you go into the lab with Jason, and he'll orient you on the equipment. Both of you'll be studying RF's operations guidelines outline, what there is of it, with the rest of us so we can all pitch in."

"Bummer about RF," he said, pushing his hair back out of his eyes. "I'll be able to show you the lab, but some of the equipment was only used by him."

"I understand. Mark, I'll be back in a half-hour or so to finish the disk image process on RF's laptop."

I explained what I was doing as we walked to the lab. He nodded and tried to look interested. As he unlocked the door to the glassed-in electronics lab, he described the role-playing game he had been participating in on the internet when Linda called. I nodded and tried to look interested.

As we toured the lab, we asked each other questions. I recognized most of the equipment, but didn't know how it was used. So we shared our respective knowledge, filling in gaps for one another. I stopped in front of the spectrum analyzer, noting down the model and serial number.

"Why are you taking notes on that?" he asked.

"On Friday RF told me it wasn't functioning, so tomorrow I'm going to send it in for repair and calibration. We'll get a loaner while it's gone."

"Hmmm, that's funny. I'm kinda sure he was using it last week. He didn't mention it wasn't working. But then I don't use it, so I wouldn't know."

I glanced at my watch. "Time for me to make sure I got a good disk image. Is there any equipment you know of that's missing or not working?"

"No, but let me look around and think about it."

"OK, thanks." In RF's cubicle, I made sure I had good images of both disks and made a spare copy of each. I walked through the process again with Mark, answering his questions, then went back to see Linda.

I handed her the copies. "I didn't see Nick's car when I came back, so I assume he went home. Be sure you lock these up. If IMPD comes in for RF's computers, you can honestly say that not a single byte has been changed on either one since RF used them, and we'll be able to reconstruct an exact image of each one."

"Will they come for them if he killed himself?"

"I don't know, but probably not. It's possible that they'll classify his death as being 'under suspicious circumstances,' the cause of death undetermined for now. In that case, they may confiscate the computers until they make a determination."

"Did you get what you wanted from Jason?"

"Yeah, he was really helpful. The only equipment I may need is a couple of small directional antennas."

"What cost are we talking about?"

"Probably less than two hundred dollars for both antennas."

"OK, get what you need and bring me the receipts. I suggest you go home and review the operations outlines. See what you can make of RF's, and let me know what help you're going to need. You might use our outlines as a template, and develop a plan for your analysis approach."

"Makes sense to me. From a quick look, your material appears clear and easy to follow. What time do you want me here tomorrow?"

"As he was leaving, Nick told me we'll have an 'all-hands' meeting at eight-thirty. You should be there. Anything else we need to cover?"

"A couple of things. I want to talk with a technical person at Tau Telemetry. Maybe the guy who came here. I'd appreciate his contact info."

"I'll have to find it. You'll get an email from me later today. What's the other thing?"

"Where do you want me to hang out while I'm working here?"

She nodded in the direction of the lab. "I'll get you a key to the electronics lab."

"Great, thanks. I'll be here around eight-fifteen then. See you tomorrow."

I picked up my laptop from Mark, checked that I had access to the HH Racing computer system and that my email worked, then took it with the disk imaging equipment to my Jeep. I had an armful, so I went around the back of the Jeep to deposit the equipment on the passenger side front seat.

If I hadn't gone around the back, I wouldn't have noticed the clean spot on the leading edge of the Jeep's right rear fender. I put the equipment on the front seat, then carefully felt under the edge of the fender.

I discovered a small metal box, about two by three inches and an inch thick. It was magnetically attached. I popped it out and scribbled down the make and model information from the case.

It was a GPS tracking device that would broadcast my location wherever I went, an electronic tail. I quickly checked each of the other parked cars, but didn't find another one. Then I searched the Jeep for other unwanted gifts. I did an especially thorough job on the interior, looking for electronic bugs, or listening devices, but didn't find any.

I reattached the device where I'd found it. One of the tenets of the intelligence community is to be extremely careful about information disclosure. How and when can be crucial, and sometimes it's better never to divulge. I decided that for now it was better to let whoever had put it there think I didn't know about it.

Chapter 5

In the old days, well, anyway, up until a decade or so ago, if you wanted to follow, or tail, someone, it had to be done physically. You, or someone you hired, had to keep them, or the vehicle they were in, in view. Bad weather, nature's calls, and boredom could be serious obstacles.

When I started working for Max Blitzer, that was the way he did it. A reason he brought me on board, first as a consultant and then as an apprentice, was to help him learn to utilize recent technology in the private investigations business. One of the first high tech gadgets I introduced him to, after a partially successful attempt to make him computer literate, was the GPS tracking device.

Most people are familiar with GPS navigation systems installed in cars and trucks. Using signals from multiple satellites, the devices display their location, usually to an accuracy of about twenty feet.

What John Q Public doesn't know is that similar technology is being used to track vehicles and people without their knowledge. It transmits its location periodically via the cell phone system to a receiver that acts like a recorder. In other words, the tracking receiver gets and records a short message every so often.

How frequently information is reported can be programmed by the user. Since the trackers are battery powered, the more often the position is reported, the less time the transmitter lasts. Typically, a device reporting every ten minutes will broadcast for weeks, while reporting every minute reduces transmissions to a few days.

GPS tracking systems cost only a few hundred bucks plus a small monthly subscription fee. They are impervious to bad weather except extreme conditions when satellite reception is lost, never have to take a bathroom break, and don't get bored.

Max and I used such a device to trace the movements of a philandering husband. I still had it at my office. With a new battery it would probably work, but its technology was already obsolete.

As I drove out of the HH Racing parking lot, I used the hands-free feature of my smartphone to call Max at his condo in Fort Walton Beach, Florida. I hadn't told him about my consulting job or RF's death, and being electronically tailed was rattling me. I needed to talk, and he was like an uncle.

According to Max, late September through October is the best time at the ocean where he lives. It's still in the eighties during the daytime, so bikini clad women, called 'wildlife' by Max, abound, but it cools to around seventy in the evening, perfect for walking on the beach.

He answered with his usual, "Hello, Blitzer residence."

"Hi, Max. Wolf here. How's the wildlife?"

"The wildlife is colorful and plentiful, thank you very much. But I betcha didn't call about that. Whatcha been doing? I haven't heard from you for a coupla weeks."

I gave him a three-minute version of the HH Racing job, concluding with discovering the telemetry jamming, and RF's death.

Max whistled under his breath. "Wow, what did ya get yourself into? How do ya think he died?"

"Don't know. Tito is supposed to have some information for me first thing tomorrow."

"Give Tito and Carmen my regards. Anything else?"

"Yeah, well, someone just gave me a gift of a GPS tracking device mounted under a fender of my Jeep while I was parked at HH Racing."

"Oh, now we're getting to the real reason you called, right?"

"Come, on, Max," I said, "I just like to keep you up to date with my life. But you're right. Finding it shook me up a little."

"I don't blame you. It'd shake me up, too." He paused. "And you want Uncle Max to help you think through who may have done it, right?"

"Yeah, I guess so."

"Well, my experience has been that someone is usually tailed for one of two reasons, sex or money. Which one do you want to start with?"

"Let's start with money since I can't think of any reason why…" My voice trailed off.

"Hmm, I seem to remember a couple of women connected with your last case. One was Billy Wyland's daughter Ann. The other was the wife of the guy you got arrested for accessory after the fact. What's her name?"

"Vanessa."

"Yeah, Vanessa. You told me you had a date with Ann but it fizzled out. You boffing Vanessa?"

I laughed. Max would never say 'screwing,' much less 'fucking.' "Yes, Max, Vanessa and I are intimate. Her divorce should be final in a couple of months. Accelerated process."

"I'm not gonna ask you what your intentions are with her. Just remember that Marie and I have been married for over a half century, and you probably think I'm an old fuddy-duddy. But I'll tell you one thing. Her soon-to-be ex-husband would sure as heck be on my short list of people who would have you tailed."

"To tell you the truth I hadn't thought about that. I found the tracking device attached in the HH Racing parking lot. I've been trying to figure out whether someone connected with the telemetry jamming could be involved."

"So, who's your client?"

That was Max's favorite question. I was sometimes surprised by my answer. Other times, he made me think about the situation in a new way. This time was no exception.

"Nick Napoli, HH Racing's race engineer, hired me, but my client is the Hopkins-Handel Racing Team. The racing team issued the purchase order."

"But where's the money come from?" asked Max. "Remember, I lived in Indy most of my life. Racing teams get their money from sponsors."

I hadn't even considered that angle. "Gamble Oil is the major sponsor. They pay somewhere on the high side of five million a year. And their sponsorship for next year is uncertain."

"*Now* we're getting somewhere. I'm not saying that Gamble Oil is having you tracked. But I'd be willing to bet even odds that it's either someone connected with their money, or with that woman Vanessa's husband, what's-his-name Gordian. Sex and money. Trust me."

"I trust you Max, believe me. I don't know if you're right, but I'll think hard about what you said. Another thing, of course, is RF's death. There'll probably be some nasty twists and turns when we find out about that."

"If it's murder, stay the heck away from it. You've already got your hands full. This jamming business has me worried. The minute you found out about it, you should have started billing them from Wolf Investigations."

"Maybe so."

"Maybe? Horse puckey. You're into a criminal investigation now. I'd talk with them ASAP and get clear what's what."

"I will, and thanks, Max, as usual."

Even after I'd listened to the audio at HH Racing on Friday, part of me wanted to believe that the signal causing problems with their telemetry was unintended interference. What Daniel and I had seen and heard the previous morning lowered the probability of that to about zero. It took Max's wakeup call to jar me into reality.

I mulled over the electronic tail that was broadcasting my location as I drove. My experience in Iraq following land-based targets using drones had taught me a few things about GPS tracking that seeped back into my mind.

The first was that whoever is doing the tracking can often predict where you're going and get there before you do. Another was that where somebody *isn't* is often more important to know than where they *are*. Finally, GPS systems can be disabled or spoofed in a variety of ways. I didn't have the sophisticated equipment to spoof the system, to make it think it was somewhere else, but I began hatching an idea that would let me turn the tables and transform my trackers into trackees.

Max's statements had me pondering. It was conceivable that Stan Gordian was behind it, but something made me doubt that it would be about sex alone if he was involved. More likely it would also involve money.

And there was another possibility related to money: the Clanton-Suggs racing team, currently in second place by just a hair in the Nor-Am racing series. They might be gunning for Gamble Oil's sponsorship, or at least for HH Racing to lose it and be less competitive next season. I needed to dig into their organization, starting with their website, followed by a discussion with Nick.

As I pulled into the condo parking lot, I scanned the area for strange vehicles or unusual goings-on. The only activity was a pizza delivery van with its hazard lights flashing and parked in a handicapped parking slot. That is, unfortunately, not unusual.

I followed the aroma of fresh pizza up to the second floor, let myself in and put the equipment, revolver, and computer on the kitchen table. Taking a hint from what I'd seen in the parking lot and from my growling stomach, I got a pizza out of the freezer.

I told Boots I had a lot of reading to do. He let me know that he had a lot of eating to do, so I fed him. As soon as dinner was in the oven I stowed my gear and disks in the office safe.

The Colts were hosting the Denver Broncos, and the game had just started. I grabbed a Diet Pepsi, and my pizza became a TV dinner.

Early in the fourth quarter, with the Colts trailing the Broncos. I turned off the sound and followed the game intermittently as I reviewed HH Racing operations guidelines. I finished an outline for the procedure to analyze and locate the telemetry jamming for Friday's practice session at the track just as the contest was ending.

The Colts upset the Broncos. It was an especially sweet victory because the Broncos' quarterback was the ex-quarterback for the Colts. The Broncos actually beat themselves, getting numerous second-half penalties, and fumbling the ball inside their own five yard line with three minutes to go, but that didn't matter to die-hard Colts fans. I turned off the TV.

Boots was demanding attention, so I played with him using his favorite toy, a small feather at the end of a string tied to a yardstick. He went nuts over the feather as I jerked it in small steps. When I'd had enough, I stopped moving the feather, letting him 'kill' it. He rolled on his side, held it between his front paws, bit it, and kicked it with his hind legs.

I checked email. Linda had sent me the contact information for the person they were dealing with at Tau Telemetry. Following Max's advice, I prepared a report and an invoice for the work I'd done so far. I'd give them to Nick in the morning and let him know that from now on, Wolf Investigations would be HH Racing's consultant.

The website for Tau Telemetry revealed that they were founded over twenty years ago in Indianapolis, and had been providing electronics communications and telemetry systems for the auto racing industry ever since. They were acquired four years ago by a British company, Newcastle Systems. Newcastle is well known in the Formula One world for providing engines and electronics products to leading race teams, as well as high performance equipment for elite sports car manufacturers.

A recent press release touted Newcastle's diversification into small high-performance engines and telemetry systems for unmanned air vehicles. They had just signed a contract to provide unspecified electronic warfare, or EW, equipment for the U. S. Navy and Marine Corps' RQ-106 Black Eagle Unmanned Air Vehicle, or UAV. Capabilities included tracking ground targets with side-looking radar, marking targets for precision guided weapons with a laser beam, and carrying out EW missions.

On their part of the Newcastle website, Tau Telemetry was hyping its new telemetry system, the Tau 930, with more channels, higher power, etcetera, than the current model, the 920. According to their website, Tau expected the new system to be adopted by the Formula Nor-Am governing body for next year's racing season. An email address was listed to get information on it, undoubtedly a marketing type, but perhaps helpful as a conduit to an engineer or technician who could answer my questions. I fired off an email with a copy to Linda's contact, feigning interest in the 930 and asking for telephone and email information for a technical representative.

I then focused a web-based search on the Clanton-Suggs Racing Team, the Nor-Am team with the most to lose if HH Racing secured second place overall. They were headquartered near Dallas, Texas and their home track was the Super Sport Speedway near Fort Worth. Their major sponsor was Lumber Max, a supplier of lumber and building materials focused in the South and Southeast U.S.

Clanton and Suggs had merged two teams that had each been slightly better than mediocre into a competitive Nor-Am participant. Each had brought major sponsorship with them, so money hadn't been much of an issue until they started bickering over placement of promotional material, the management, the driver's contract, and just about everything else. The on-line racing publications were predicting the exit of at least one, and maybe both of the main money providers, unless they held on to their tenuous position in second place.

It was clear that they'd been present at the Pocono race where HH Racing experienced jamming of their telemetry, but that didn't mean they were directly responsible. They could easily have had a hired gun, or hired jammer. I knew from Linda that they'd be at Boone next weekend, along with all of the Nor-Am teams. I needed to find a way to poke around their operation.

Finally, on the website for the company that made the GPS tracking device attached to my Jeep, I ordered an identical model with two spare batteries. For what I had in mind, I didn't necessarily need the same system but figured someone had researched them and selected this one. Good enough. It *did* require the same battery. Another reason to order this model.

I paid the one-time registration fee and the first month of support, and specified twenty-four hour delivery with text message notification to my smartphone when it was delivered. It was late evening, so it would be delivered Tuesday. Online, I downloaded the User's Manual and located information on its setup and operation. It transmitted location as often as once a minute, and as infrequently as once an hour.

Enough work. I stood up, stretched, opened a Sam Adams Light from the refrigerator, and called Vanessa. "Hi, whatcha doing?"

"Homework, what else?" She sounded preoccupied. "We have a project due Friday. We're in teams of three, and I'm doing most of the team's work. 'Course, the other two have full time jobs."

"I've been doing homework, too, boning up on HH Racing operations procedures." I didn't tell her about being monitored electronically.

She laughed. "Interesting choice of words. Speaking of boning, you want to know what I did after you left last night?"

"Sure. Why do you think I called?"

"I figured that was why." I could visualize her hazel eyes sparkling. "I spread the blanket out on the couch and fantasized we were at the fireworks. Another couple was making out on their blanket and watching us fuck. My vibrator was a crummy substitute for you, but I came."

"That's more than I can say. Wish I'd been there."

"Me, too," she said coyly. "Want to come now?"

"Sure, but I'm wiped out. And you're doing homework. I don't think it's in the cards tonight."

"You don't have to be here. Ever have phone sex?"

My brain gears stripped. "Phone sex? Like calling a 900 number? No…"

"Like that, but I'm your 900 number. Difference is that those women just pretend to come. I'll do it for real so you can come with me. And you're in charge. You tell me what to wear, where to fantasize we're screwing, and when to put you inside me. I'll do whatever you say."

I chuckled, "That sounds like fun. How about tomorrow night? I need to figure out the details."

"Good. Selecting the scenario is half the fun. Call me ten minutes before you're ready to come so I can put on the outfit you pick and be wet and ready when you call back."

I agreed and we hung up.

I fantasized about the situation and specifics until I crawled into bed, but I had to wait for the bulge in my shorts to subside before I could go to sleep. As I dropped off into a deep slumber, I was curious whether Vanessa had *experience* with phone sex.

* * *

The next morning RF's death was reported in the Metro section of the Star. Sort of. The brief article said that a Caucasian male in his forties had been found dead in his home on the northwest side. The death had occurred under suspicious circumstances and was under investigation. Identity of the victim was being withheld pending notification of next of kin.

I gathered up my computer and paperwork, said goodbye to Boots, and headed out the door. The maples around the parking lot and tennis courts were turning shades of orange. Red leaves would start to appear in another week or so if the cool temperatures persisted.

I called Tito just before eight. His shift started at seven-thirty, and I hoped that was enough time for him to get information for me.

"Hi, Tito, so what's up with Phillips' death?"

"Hi Wolf." He lowered his voice. "I'm across the street getting coffee in City Market. Makes it a little easier to talk, but there's stuff on this one I can't tell you, mon."

"OK, so tell me what you can."

"The contusion on his head may have knocked him unconscious, but death was by strangulation. Cause unknown."

"Murder, suicide, or accident?"

"We don't know."

"What are you leaning toward?"

"I can't say. But let me suggest something if you want to learn more."

"What?"

"Talk to his ex-wife Liz."

"Is she a suspect?"

"Maybe."

"Oh for Pete's sake, Tito. What in the hell's going on?"

My answer was the dial tone.

The parking lot at Hopkins-Handel Racing was filling up. I pulled between two cars so I could go around the back of my Jeep and surreptitiously check under the edge of the fender while approaching the passenger door to get my computer. The electronic tail was still there.

The two reserved parking places were occupied. In Mr. Handel's slot was a silver Aston Martin DB9, straight out of James Bond. With over five hundred horsepower and a six-liter V12 engine, its price tag was north of two hundred grand. In the space labeled "Reserved for Gamble Oil and Refining" was a black Lincoln Town Car, with the uniformed driver listlessly buffing the left front fender while smoking a cigarette. The two cars had to have been worth more than all the rest in the lot combined.

Linda let me in immediately when I pressed the buzzer. She must have been standing by the door.

She guided me by my elbow to a corner of the lobby. "There's some big wig representing Gamble Oil in Mr. Handel's office. Nick is there and they're arguing about something. Can't tell what, but we're all walking on eggshells. I'm supposed to take you in as soon as you arrive."

"Thanks for the heads-up. Any idea why they want to see me?"

She shook her head. "It must have something to do with whatever they're arguing about."

"Great. Just the way I wanted to start Monday morning."

"Oh, and when you finish in Mr. Handel's office, see Angie Murphy for your badge. She'll take your picture and get some basic information from you: address, social, stuff like that. Shouldn't take more than fifteen minutes."

As I entered Handel's office, the conversation stopped. Handel was standing behind his desk, dressed as he had been on Saturday with the exception of a light beige linen jacket.

The other two were standing on opposite sides of the conference table that extended from Handel's desk. Nick Napoli, wearing an HH Racing polo shirt, acknowledged my presence with a handshake. He was red in the face.

The "big wig" from Gamble Oil, was a woman with black hair, pointed chin, hooked nose, and a harsh expression. She reminded me of the Wicked Witch of the West from *The Wizard of Oz*. Rail thin, and hair drawn back so severely it stretched her translucent skin, she wore a somber black midi-length skirt and black jacket over a white blouse. She oozed lawyer and reeked of a superiority complex.

My previous experiences with lawyers had generally been unpleasant. It didn't look like this would be an exception.

She was still glaring at Nick. "I'm Ellen Burkhard, representing Gamble Oil." She thrust a card in my general direction, which I took.

Hal Handel, attempting to dilute the toxic environment, crooned, "Ellen is an associate at Watterson Watson."

I nodded. Watterson Watson was the second largest law firm in Indiana, with offices in Chicago, Washington, D.C., and other cities. In addition to Gamble Oil, it counted among its clients several universities and banks. Their offices occupied the top four floors of First Hoosier Tower, a thirty-story high rise on the canal in downtown Indy that was headquarters for First Hoosier Bank and Trust.

I had attended a Christmas reception with Max in their Sky Room on the top floor overlooking the city. He'd done a job for them related to an embezzlement case. I made a mental note to ask him if he knew Ellen Burkhard.

I pulled a Wolf Investigations card out of my computer bag and offered it to her. Not even looking in my direction, she snapped, "I have your information."

Handel swept an open-palmed hand around in front of himself, indicating he was addressing us all. "Please sit down. I believe we need to tell Mr. Ruger why he's been invited to this meeting."

I was thinking the same thing. The pit of my stomach told me I'd be better off somewhere else, but I had little choice.

"They're trying to steal you away from the racing team," sputtered Nick.

"Now, now, we're all part of the same team," intoned Handel. "We're simply discussing adding a second task area to your consulting services for us."

"That will seriously impede or destroy our chances of solving our telemetry jamming problem before we go to Boone," said Nick.

Ellen Burkhard crossed her arms, still glaring at Nick. "What Mr. Napoli fails to understand is that the death of Ron Phillips is a game changer."

"How so?" I asked, reluctant to insert myself into the discussion.

"Three hundred thousand dollars, that's how."

Handel cleared his throat. "Let me explain. We carry life and long-term disability insurance on our key people. That's to compensate the team, and the investors, if we have to recruit and train a replacement. The amount is two and a half times their annual salary plus benefits, which in RF's case comes to just over three hundred thousand dollars."

"RF's been here a long time, right?" I asked.

"Over ten years," replied Handel.

I had investigated cases involving suicide. "So what's the problem? The premium will be paid regardless of whether his death was accidental, homicide, or suicide, unless your policies are unusual. There's a two-year window on suicide. If suicide occurs after two years, full payment is made."

Handel sighed. "As you know, Gamble Oil picked up major sponsorship of the team before the last season started, on the first of January. At that time, life and disability policies for our team were shifted to the insurance carrier for Gamble Oil. Each time you change insurance, the two-year window gets reset. So if RF's death was suicide, our team is out three hundred grand."

I tried to look helpful. "I read in the Star that IMPD is investigating the death as occurring under suspicious circumstances. That could mean anything."

"Exactly," interjected Burkhard. "That's why you're in here. We want you to make sure that the insurance company plays fair. If it's clearly suicide, it is what it is. But we don't know, and can't seem to find out, what the cause of death was. We want to employ your services as a private investigator."

"Why me?"

"Several reasons." She ticked them off on her fingers. "We're aware of your role in recent murder investigations. You seem to have connections at IMPD that should be useful. Your references are good. You're familiar with HH Racing, and you seem to be technically competent. We want you to keep working on the telemetry situation."

"So you're terminating my work under the HH Racing purchase order?"

"That's correct."

"I'll be paid for work to date?"

"Of course."

I shoved my report and invoice across the table to Nick. "Good, here's my final report and invoice."

Burkhard's eyebrows went sky-high. Nick started to shove it back, but I held my hand out, palm up. "Nick, I'm not quitting on you. I'm still committed as ever to solving the telemetry issue. What we're dealing with now, though, probably involves criminal activity, and you're better off having me consult as a private investigator."

Looking at Ellen Burkard, I continued, "I'm willing to look into RF's cause of death. But I hired on here to help the communications and telemetry folks, and they still must have priority."

Handel leaned forward, his hands flat on his desk. "You're working for me." Burkhard tried to interrupt but was cut off by Handel. "Mister Ruger, I want you to do both tasks. Let's say you try to split your time as evenly as feasible. Does that seem doable?"

I reflected for a few seconds. "I can split my time, but if I do that I'm afraid of doing a lousy job in both areas. If I can get help in the technical area, it might work."

Nick shook his head. "That just isn't possible. With Dick on medical leave and RF dead, we're already stretched past the breaking point."

"I wasn't suggesting someone inside. I'm recommending part-time help from someone at the university. He's familiar with HH Racing."

Nick turned to Handel and nodded. "Might work. He and Wolf developed our new inventory management software."

"And how much is *he* going to cost?" scowled Burkhard.

"No more than half of what I cost," I answered. I enjoyed watching her scowl freeze on her face.

She opened a file folder lying in front of her. "I suppose we can draw up another one of these for him," she said, clipping her words as she thrust a document across the table to me.

"What's this?" I asked.

"We want to engage you under a consulting agreement. Just routine, you understand. You sign and date it at the bottom of the last page."

Nick looked at me and rolled his eyes.

I was getting a weird feeling. "Do I get to read it first?"

Handel laughed loudly and held his hands as if he were praying, giving me the willies. "Of course, of course. It's at the same hourly rate. Take your time. It's only three pages."

It didn't take me long. "I can't sign this," I said, putting it down.

"We can make minor edits. Both parties can initial them. What's wrong, did we spell your name incorrectly?" queried Burkhard.

I ignored her question. In fact, I ignored her completely and spoke directly to Handel. "This agreement has an exclusivity clause that prohibits me from consulting to any client that is in competition in any way with either HH Racing or Gamble Oil. And the prohibition doesn't expire until two years from today."

Nick snorted. "I told you he wouldn't go for it."

So that was what the argument had been about.

"This is a perfectly reasonable and standard consulting agreement," insisted Burkhard, smirking as she tapped the document with a bony forefinger.

"It may be reasonable and standard in the world of five-hundred-dollar-an-hour lawyers, but it sure as hell isn't standard in my line of work," I snapped, looking at her. "If I signed crap like this, within a year or two I'd be prohibited from working for half of my potential clients in Indy."

"Your work will require access to Hopkins-Handel's most closely held information. They must be protected legally," snipped Burkhard.

I looked back at Handel. "I always protect my clients. If you need *this* kind of protection, you might want to review your own code of ethics."

Handel turned on his best used car salesman charm, smiling and holding his hands out to me in supplication as though he were on TV.

"This is just something we need to do. We really, really value your supporting us, Wolf. Please reconsider."

"I just reconsidered. The answer is still no." I pushed back my chair so quickly I almost knocked it over, and picked up my computer bag. On my way out the door, I looked directly at Nick. "By the way, RF's cause of death was strangulation."

There was dead silence. It took all the self-control I could muster not to slam the door behind me.

Chapter 6

I was pissed off. *Really* pissed off. My inclination was to blow out the door and say to hell with HH Racing, but I owed Linda and Jack an explanation about why I wouldn't be working with them, at least not right away. I wasn't optimistic about getting the decision reversed requiring me to sign a repressive and unreasonable consulting agreement.

I found them in the electronics lab. "Hi, I'd like to talk with you guys in private."

"Oh, hi, Wolf," replied Linda. "Sure. What happened?"

I shut the door. "I can't work here anymore."

"No way!" she exclaimed.

"Bummer," murmured Jack.

I gave them a brief summary of the meeting, then said, "I was stunned that they tried to get me to sign an agreement with a non-compete clause. You only sign something like that when you become an employee. I really don't want to leave you guys in the lurch, but I have to be able to consult with other clients."

Linda nodded. "I don't blame you. It isn't very often that Mr. Handel overrides Nick, and I think he shot himself in the foot this time." She looked at Jack. "What we're saying in here stays in here, OK?"

Jack nodded.

Looking resigned, she said, "I don't know if it'll help, but I'll talk with Nick. I've never seen him go around Mr. Handel, though. I'm not sure what else to do."

I pulled my laptop out and turned it on. "Not sure how helpful this'll be, but I have an outline of a procedure to follow at the track to analyze the jamming. I'll leave you a copy."

Jack pulled a thumb drive out of his pocket and started to insert it into one of the USB sockets. I grabbed his wrist. "Not so fast. I don't know what's on that. I don't allow anyone to access my system with one of those. Linda, please get me a CD."

Malware buried on thumb drives is a major threat to unsuspecting PC users. I transferred the file onto a CD Linda handed me after doing a security scan on it. "I could meet you outside of HH Racing and go through it with you. Answer questions, that kind of thing."

Linda and Jack looked at each other. After a few seconds she said, "I'd like that. Jack and I sometimes go to the Pan Asian Chinese buffet on Lafayette Road on Mondays. They have crab legs today. RF didn't like Chinese, so he never went, and I've never seen other HH Racing folks there."

"Chinese is fine. What time?"

"We usually leave here about eleven-thirty. Only takes five, ten minutes."

"OK, I'll show up there around eleven-forty. Another thing. Jack, you need to get the spectrum analyzer in for repair. Make sure you get a loaner. I'll do my best to find a way to get you trained to use it. For now, look at the user's guide and email me with questions."

I wrote down the name and address of the place to take it. "Ask for Jeff. He knows me."

He nodded, "OK, thanks."

I put away my computer and stood to leave. "I'd better get out of here before someone throws me out. Tell Angie not to expect me to come by for a badge."

Linda nodded grimly as I walked out.

In the parking lot, the slot that had been occupied by the Lincoln Town Car was empty. Bulldozer Burkhard had left the building. I headed out toward my office.

I still had a card to play. It had a probability of success only slightly better than drawing to an inside straight.

I called Max using the hands-free feature on my smartphone. It was still early, about seven-thirty, in Fort Walton Beach, which, despite the fact that it is straight south of Indy, is in the Central time zone and an hour earlier.

He answered in a quiet voice, "Blitzer residence."

"Hi, Max, it's Wolf. Are you OK?"

"Yeah, but Marie's still asleep. Don't wanna wake her. Just a sec while I take my coffee out on the balcony."

"Sure, take your time."

I heard his sliding glass door followed by a chair scraping on his balcony. "OK, Wolf. Seems we just talked. 'M I right?"

"Yeah. Lots going on here." I summarized what had just happened in Handel's office.

I heard him sipping coffee. "You've been a busy bee this morning. And you were right not to sign that agreement. So I bet you want me to see what I can do for you at Watterson Watson."

"I was hoping you might. The guy who invited you to their holiday party that you took me to is a partner there, right?"

"Giles Reichmann isn't just a partner, he's an equity partner. They have an ownership stake in the firm and share in its profits. Non-equity partners don't share in the wealth. Don't get me wrong, non-equity partners still pull down five, six hundred grand a year."

"Not exactly chicken feed."

"No. Another thing about Giles. He's active – read that as money – in the university and the German-American community. He and his wife endowed a chair in the law school. That takes a couple of million bucks."

"So will I run into him at the Rathskeller?"

The Rathskeller is the restaurant in the basement of the Athenaeum, the focal point for German-American activity in downtown Indy. Max and I had been frequent customers. There, he introduced me to German-American friends and clients. Tourists and natives alike visit the Athenaeum, which is on the National Register of Historic Places, to admire its stained glass windows and stepped gables.

"You might. I had lunch with him there a few times. Marie and I still get a Christmas card from him every year."

"What did you do for him?"

"I helped him nail an embezzler in a mortgage bank that was one of his clients. Geez…it's been ten or twelve years. Saved the bank millions. That case helped guarantee Giles' promotion to equity partner."

"So you'll talk with him?"

"Sure, long as he'll take my call."

"Thanks, Max."

"Let me know how it goes. And keep me up to date on what happens with your other stuff."

"Will do."

"Watch your backside. You're gettin' up into thin air."

I called the homespun expressions by Max like I'd just heard 'Maxisms.'

"Give my regards to Marie."

I still wasn't optimistic about changing the decision, but at least I'd played my card.

It was almost nine when I got to Broad Ripple. I had a couple of things I wanted to do before I met Linda and Jack for lunch.

On the way upstairs to my office, I picked up a large cup of Sumatran java from Java Joe's. The popcorn shop below me didn't open until ten, so I'd be gone before I had to mask popcorn aroma by brewing my own. I sipped the coffee while I waited for my computer to boot up.

Curiosity as to why Tito suggested I talk with RF's ex-wife got the better of me, so instead of paying bills, reading and answering email, or doing something else obviously useful, I found the address and phone number for Liz Phillips online. I called, got her voicemail, and hung up. I'd try later.

Another internet search yielded a location where the antennas needed to implement my telemetry test procedure were available. Electronic Supply Equipment Warehouse on Michigan Road was only ten minutes or so from HH Racing. I emailed the information to Linda and Jack, and confirmed I'd see them at lunch.

There are advantages and disadvantages to my having two offices, one in my condo and one in Broad Ripple. Having a commercial location facilitates meeting clients and having great choices for lunch. The office at home is a place to kick back, grab snacks from the refrigerator, and work at all hours.

A disadvantage had just revealed itself. The introductory antenna book and antenna modeling software that I wanted to loan to Linda and Jack were in my home office. I'd planned to grab them on my way to lunch, but couldn't do that and be on time.

Driving to the Chinese buffet and listening to the news on WFYI public radio, an idea occurred of a way to get technical help for Linda and Jack. I arrived on time, but they were already eating. We waved at each other, and I went to the buffet.

Luckily, the buffet was equipped with plates and there were no trays to slide along on tops of metal tubes. I still had flashbacks in buffets to the horror of the IED detonation in the cafeteria in Iraq, regardless of the different setup, but they weren't as bad as in cafeterias, which I assiduously avoided.

Carrying hot and sour soup, steamed rice, crab Rangoon, and supposedly spicy General Tso's chicken, I joined them. "Hi. The food looks great. Let's talk while we eat."

Linda put down a crab leg she was cracking. "Thanks for meeting us. We really appreciate your doing this, especially since you're not getting paid for it."

And not likely to, I thought. "So, you have any questions for me?"

"We have a few, but it's been really hard to concentrate. Everyone's thinking about RF."

I nodded. "I can understand that. Have you heard anything about a funeral or memorial service?"

She shook her head. "No. I don't know any of his family except Liz, his ex-wife. We got acquainted by talking at HH Racing social events, and several times at the track. We've become friends, and meet for coffee about once a month. I really like her, and I'm going to call her when we get back."

I decided to take a chance. "I have information that might be useful to her if she's the beneficiary of a life insurance policy on him. I'd be glad to talk with her. Things can be different depending on the cause of death and so on."

"You're not trying to sign her up as a client, are you?"

"Nope. It would be at no cost, just like I'm doing for you now. I don't see how she could possibly need my services as a private investigator, anyway." Unless she's charged with murder, I thought.

She looked at me askance like she didn't quite believe me. Luckily, Jack was busy chowing down on ribs and didn't see her look.

"OK, I'll see what I can find out about services, and let you know. And I'll mention your name to her. Also, just so you know, I talked with Nick. He agrees you got a bum deal but says his hands are tied."

"Thanks for trying, anyway. I appreciate it." I looked at Jack. "How're you doing and what questions do you have on the operations outlines, and the one for the telemetry jamming I left you?"

Jack wiped his fingers and mouth almost clean of rib sauce. "I dropped off the spectrum analyzer this morning. Jeff was really friendly. They lent us one just like ours. I'll pick up the antennas this afternoon. I'm feeling a little overwhelmed, though. I'm not sure I can do all of the stuff by myself, for one thing."

"I hear you. I got an idea on the way here. You need technical help, and there's someone who might be available. You can bring him in part time strictly on the technical side of the house, and I believe Nick'll go for it."

Linda's face brightened. "Daniel?"

"Daniel. I didn't mention his name this morning, so I don't think he'll be on anyone's radar. He'll know how to do everything in the telemetry jamming analysis procedure. That'll let you and Jason concentrate on the tasks that RF would have done."

"That's a great idea. But we'll need to justify his hiring on the basis that he'll be helping with RF's tasks. Better not to mention you, agreed?"

"Absolutely."

"All right. Please call him as soon as you can, and I'll have Angie cut him a purchase order when I get back. I'll hold off on getting it signed and getting him a track ID until I hear back, though, if that's OK."

"Fine with me. I'll send him a text message. He'll call as soon as he can, and I'll have him call you if he can help, or let you know myself if he can't."

We focused the rest of our discussion on questions that Jack had regarding tasks in RF's operations guidelines notebook. I answered most of them, and told him I'd get back to him on a couple, but that Daniel would probably know the answers. I sent Daniel a text message as we talked, saying that I had urgent work for him, and asking how much time he could free up between now and late Saturday.

When we finished discussing their questions, Linda said, "We'd better get back, and let you go."

* * *

Being unemployed, it seemed like a good idea to follow up on marketing emails from my office. On the way, I was enjoying the colorful maple trees and crisp air along Fall Creek Parkway when my cell phone rang. It was Daniel. I pulled over to admire the view.

"Hi, Wolf, what do you want me to do?"

"You're needed at HH Racing for as many hours as you can give them from now until Saturday evening."

"Well, this is kind of short notice. What's going on?"

I told him about RF's death, and explained what happened that morning. "It's sort of like I've been fired. But they can hire you as a temporary part-time technician and nobody will object."

"This is connected to the signals we examined on the spectrum analyzer on Saturday, right?"

"Yes, but unofficially. You'll be helping them figure out what the signals are and where they're coming from. But the official reason they're hiring you is to fill in for RF."

"So you won't be able to help?"

"I'll be available to answer questions and to help you flesh out the procedure to follow at the track. But I'll have to do it behind the scenes, anonymously."

"Sounds like they really need help. Sure, I'll get someone to cover my lab tomorrow afternoon and Thursday afternoon. I can supervise their labs sometime later to pay them back."

"Thanks, Daniel. You're doing me and the HH Racing team a big favor. There's a slight chance they'll hire me back, but even if they do, they'll still need your help."

I gave him Linda's contact information, and we hung up.

Daniel was always responsive to my requests, treated me with respect, and did an outstanding job. Whoever he worked for after finishing his Ph.D. was going to be lucky to have him.

Halfway up the stairs to my office my phone rang. It was Linda. "Thanks for suggesting Daniel. He just called and said he'd be here in an hour or so."

"Fantastic. He'll do great work for you."

"Only thing is, he seems pretty shy on the phone. Wouldn't quote me an hourly rate. Said to ask you."

"He's quiet, all right. I'm fairly sure he'll be happy with half as much as I was supposed to get."

"All right. That's reasonable. Thanks again."

At that pay rate, he'd be making about a third more than I could pay him. He deserved every penny.

My office computer was booting up when Max called. "Hi Max. Good news or bad news?"

"Both."

"Give me the good news first."

"Wolf Investigations has a job."

"What's the bad news?"

"You'll be reporting directly to Carol Logan, a partner at Watterson Watson."

"Equity or non-equity partner?"

"Non-equity. And therein lies a short tale I need to tell."

Max's tales were never boring. "OK."

"As you know, there's a pecking order at Watterson Watson like any other legal outfit. Your buddy Ellen Burkhard is an associate, which means she's bucking for partner. Carol Logan is the partner that oversees her work. Of course Ms. Logan is bucking for equity partner, which Giles Reichmann is."

"Interesting dynamics."

"I'm just getting started. So it appears that the head honcho at the racing team, what's his name…"

"Hal Handel."

"Yeah, Handel calls a VP at Gamble Oil suggesting that their attorney just possibly might have done something that adversely affects the racing team's competitiveness. That VP, I don't know which one it was, called Ms. Logan, who is the lead attorney on the Gamble Oil account. She, in turn, invited Ms. Burkhard into her office for a polite discussion."

"I can't see Burkhard being polite."

"Wait, it gets better. Reichmann said that after I called him, he went to Logan's office and found her in the meeting with Burkhard, who had Logan half convinced that her approach was in the best interests of the client. Reichmann persuaded both of them otherwise, and took Burkhard off the Gamble Oil account."

"Holy shit. So what am I supposed to do?"

"Carol Logan is expecting you to call, and wants to see you in her office pronto. She'll have an agreement for you to sign patterned after the one I signed with Reichmann. There's no exclusivity clause. There *is* a stringent non-disclosure clause that'll have you hanging by your thumbs over boiling oil if you violate it."

Max had a way with words. "Thanks, Max. What should I know about her before the meeting?"

74

"Glad you asked. I asked Reichmann the same question. He said that she tends to come on strong. Her way or the highway sort of thing. Pick your fights with her very carefully. Also, she can't hear you unless you're wearing a tie. I rarely saw you wear one and didn't care, but I'd wear a suit if I were you."

"OK, I'll change before I go."

"By the way, I know that you usually charge sixty bucks an hour, but the hourly rate written into your agreement with them is seventy-five."

I sucked in my breath. "What? I appreciate it. How did you manage that?"

"I didn't *manage* anything. I just told 'em. Keep in mind that Ms. Logan is making about ten times that much. Buy another suit."

"I'll consider it," I laughed. "Anything else?"

"Can't think of anything."

He gave me Carol Logan's phone number, and we said goodbye.

I headed home to change into my only suit: a gray pinstripe that I hadn't worn since somebody got married or died, I couldn't remember which. Logan's office phone was answered by a male named Barry, who I assumed was a receptionist or secretary. He gave me an appointment for three o'clock and told me to come to the twenty-ninth floor.

When I went into my bedroom, Boots was asleep on the bed, his preferred roost. I woke him up sliding open the closet doors, then endured his lecturing me and being underfoot. I tripped over him and stepped on his tail. He howled, so I rubbed his stomach, and gave him a snack. Probably did it on purpose.

I had a suit all right, but shoes were a challenge. I almost always wore boat shoes or running shoes. In the nether recesses of my closet I found a pair of loafers with tassels that were so heavily coated with dust I couldn't tell what color they were. I cleaned them off. Cordovan would have to do.

I donned a white shirt and a striped tie with the black and gold Purdue colors. I brushed off the dust that had accumulated on the shoulders of the suit jacket, and left, almost tripping over Boots. At least I didn't step on his tail again.

Chapter 7

I took Fall Creek Parkway downtown. I especially enjoy the scenery in spring and fall, with the Monon Trail running alongside between it and Fall Creek. The color of the trees was nearing peak, and joggers were enjoying the trail.

I parked in the underground garage at First Hoosier Tower and rode an elevator that moved so fast my ears popped, exiting on the twenty-ninth floor. Equity partners like Reichmann probably had their digs on the next one up, the top floor.

A receptionist buzzed me in through double glass doors, each etched with two large entwined script capital W's. Looking at her computer screen, she confirmed that I was expected, and directed me to Ms. Logan's door.

A tall narrow window provided a preview of her outer office, where I met Barry. His oval face was covered by whiskers, not exactly a beard but what you get when you don't shave for several days. Glasses with thick white frames completed his wannabe movie star look.

Her reception area was decorated by someone with feminine tastes. A vase of fresh flowers sat on an end table, and pastel oil paintings graced the walls. A framed and matted print commemorating the New York marathon a decade ago seemed a peculiar choice.

Barry ushered me into her inner sanctum, which was adorned with certificates, awards, and photographs taken with celebrities and political figures. She rose and shook hands with me across her desk. "Nice to meet you, Mr. Ruger."

Her wardrobe was Saks Fifth Avenue. A teal suit and ivory neck scarf set off her stylishly coiffed blond hair. She was ten pounds or so overweight, but carried it well on a wide-framed body that reflected athleticism in her younger days. Tastefully applied scarlet lipstick matched her nail polish.

As I returned her greeting, she noticed me scanning her walls, then looking past her through the office window at the view. She beckoned toward the window with her head. "Come on around and look."

The scene was awesome. First Hoosier Tower abutted the downtown canal which provided the panorama's foreground, with the

Indy skyline the vista behind it. People were strolling beside the canal, couples hand-in-hand, afternoon sun reflecting off high-rise windows.

Adjacent to the one-and-a-half-mile canal are attractions such as the Indiana State Museum and the Eiteljorg Museum of American Indians and Western Art. You can rent bikes and boats of various kinds, or opt to be serenaded by a gondolier in your very own gondola. One of my favorite downtown destinations, Victory Field, home of Indianapolis Indians baseball, is within easy walking distance.

I resisted the impulse to take a photo. Tacky.

She gestured me to a seat. "Call me Carol. We'll be on a first-name basis."

It was a command, not an invitation. I nodded, "OK, Carol," as we exchanged cards.

"You've caused a bit of a commotion today," she said matter-of-factly.

I nodded, and gave her space to continue.

"My number one job is to serve my clients, and Gamble Oil is a major one. The best way to do that is for you to report directly to me."

She pushed two copies of a document across her desk to me. "This is an agreement we'd like you to sign. There are no exclusivity clauses. Take your time and look it over. If it looks OK, please sign both copies."

I read it quickly. Max was right. The non-disclosure provisions were stringent, and my pay rate was seventy-five dollars an hour. I signed both copies using a non-descript ballpoint pen I fished out of my computer bag. She did the same using a replica of a vintage fountain pen that she selected from a small wooden rack of a half-dozen or so on her desk, pushing one copy over to me.

She sat back and crossed her arms. "Now, let's discuss what's going on. We have two areas, perhaps connected, that are important to us. One is Mr. Phillips' death, the other a technical issue related to something called jamming of some signal or other that sounds like science fiction to me. Tell me what you know and what you don't know."

I started to speak. She held up her hand, interrupting me. "Keep it at a non-technical level. *Really* non-technical."

I nodded, and launched into an exposition that I figured would take five minutes, but stretched out to fifteen with questions and answers. I quickly determined that her personality was Type A: alpha, assertive bordering on aggressive, and in control of all aspects of her life. During our discussion, she monitored her computer screen, occasionally typing a quick response, and made notes on her iPad that didn't appear to be relevant to our conversation. She was a master multi-tasker.

After I finished, she said, "With respect to Mr. Phillips, you called him RF I believe, our main concern is that the insurance company is pushing hard for cause of death to be ruled a suicide. We have to ensure that a thorough investigation is completed before the cause of death is finalized. You need to help us do that. And you only have a few days at best."

"I understand. I'll find what I find, though, and you may not like the outcome."

Her face flushed as she tapped the desk with a well-manicured forefinger. "I resent your implication that I would take pleasure in anything but the truth."

I sat back. "I didn't imply that. You may have inferred it."

"Fair enough," she said, taking a deep breath and sitting back. I detected the hint of a smile, but it dissolved quickly. "You said this morning in the meeting at HH Racing that the cause of death was strangulation. How do you know that?"

I took a few seconds to consider my answer. "It's part of an active police investigation. I was ordered not to discuss it."

She looked sideways at me. "Not good enough, Wolf. You need to tell me more. You are reporting to me."

"I wasn't when I obtained the information. And there may be times when I am reporting to you when I won't reveal a source."

She shifted in her seat, snapping, "You can't tell that to a judge, and you'd damn well better be prepared to do exactly that."

"I am."

"Well, if you know the cause of death, you must know whether it was murder or suicide."

I shook my head. "I wish I did. And there's a third possibility. It might have been accidental."

"You have to be kidding. How could that be?"

"I have no idea. Maybe he fell in the shower and strangled on the soap rope. Who knows?"

She grimaced. "You just made that up, right?"

"Yeah. But I know that an accident is being considered as a possible cause of death."

"So what's your plan?" she asked, taking notes.

"Poke around." Her eyebrows went up. "That's what I do. Relatives, friends, neighbors, co-workers."

"OK, but *do not* forget that you report to me on this."

"I won't." I paused. "Ready to discuss my plan for the telemetry jamming?"

"Sure. Before you tell me, though, you need to know that the VP who called me from Gamble Oil thinks that one of HH Racing's competitors is responsible."

"That's a possibility... I guess. Did this VP person think they know which competitor, or what their motive is?"

"Which one? No. Motive? To somehow lower the performance and competitiveness of HH Racing's car. Keep in mind, this VP's even less technical than I am. Also, he seems to have hatched up a theory that someone inside the racing team is involved. It's rather weird, but what with the death I thought I'd pass it along. I can honestly tell him we're working on it, right?"

"I suppose. It's not really that weird, either. What's the name of the VP?"

"Ah. Now you want *me* to reveal a source, but you don't want to reveal yours."

I stopped myself from blurting out that it wasn't the same thing, then understood that she perceived them to be analogous. After a few seconds, I realized that the information's confidentiality was protected under our attorney-client relationship and that I trusted her.

"I found the body. Homicide Detective Sergeant Samantha Hardin is in charge of the case. Please don't let that out, or contact her. My ass could be in a sling."

Her eyes widened. "Very interesting. OK, the VP is Harry Wheeler. And don't let that out, or communicate with him without my permission. It could poison our business relationship."

"Fair enough."

"So tell me about your plan to resolve the telemetry issue, and keep it simple."

"Have you heard of the six basic journalistic questions?"

"Rings a bell. Help me out."

"Journalism students are taught that every article should address who, what, when, where, why, and how.

"OK, so?"

"So we're going to use an assortment of radio equipment and antennas with fancy names to collect and then analyze information that will help us determine what, when, where, and how. From that, I hope to figure out who and why. Simple enough?"

"Simple enough," she said wryly. "Let me write that down."

"I know I'm reporting to you, but I need to work closely with the HH Racing team. You'll facilitate that?"

"Already have. You'll serve the team as an advisor, or unpaid consultant. I've asked them to issue you a VIP badge like I have for both their shop and for Boone."

We went over reporting and billing details. I had to send a report each day, and bill them each week. I'd have preferred it the other way around, but that's not the way the world works.

As I was standing up to leave, she said, "Oh. One more thing. I don't know if you're aware that another one of Watterson Watson's clients is Boone Raceway. Mr. Reichmann is their lead attorney."

In her reception area, she noticed me looking at the New York Marathon print. "That was the last marathon I ran in before I blew out my right knee. Are you a runner?"

"I'm impressed. I jog and I've run in a few 10Ks, but never even a half-marathon."

"I miss it. I work out some, but it isn't the same."

We shook hands and I waved to Barry on my way out. I made a mental note to go jogging soon. Getting on the elevator it dawned on me that Ellen Burkhard's name hadn't been mentioned.

I laid my suit jacket on the back seat, and paid an eleven-dollar ransom for fifty minutes in the underground garage. My reserved parking place in Broad Ripple only costs ten a day, and that's a twenty-four hour day. But then, I don't have the view, and I'd get reimbursed by Watterson Watson for the garage parking on my expense account.

As soon as I got out of downtown traffic, I called RF's ex-wife Liz again.

She answered on the second ring. "This is Liz."

"Hi, Ms. Phillips. My name's Wolf Ruger. I hope Linda Green mentioned me when she called."

"Oh, hello. Yes, she did. I'm quite frustrated trying to get information out of RF's insurance company. They're not even returning my calls. Do you think you can help?"

"I'm not sure, but I'll try. When and where would you like to meet?"

"I usually don't meet strange men, but Linda vouched for you. I get off work at five. How about the Open Door Coffee Shop at 56th and Illinois?"

"That's fine. Would six or six-thirty work?"

"I like to watch the news at six-thirty, but I only live five minutes away. Can you make it at five-thirty? I have short curly brown hair and wear glasses."

We settled on five forty-five.

"I have on a gray suit. I'm sure we'll find each other."

We hung up.

I turned west on 38th Street, then loosened my tie, undid the top collar button, and rolled up my sleeves a couple of turns.

I called Linda. "Hi, it's Wolf."

Before I could say anything else, she interjected. "Hi, Wolf. Great news!"

"How did you know so soon?"

"I just hung up with Angie Murphy. She said she was making you a VIP badge for here and at the track. How in the world did you manage that?"

"I'll tell you when I see you, but I'm now reporting to Watterson Watson directly. I'm headed your way. Is Daniel there yet?"

"Yes. He just got his badge and went into the electronics lab with Jason. He's so nice."

"He's very good at what he does, too. I'll be there in fifteen minutes."

"OK, I'll let you in."

"Just don't laugh at the way I'm dressed."

I hung up before she could react, called Tito, and got his voicemail. "Hey, Tito, it's Wolf. I've been fired and re-hired today. More later. Working for a different client, same matter. Meeting RF's wife. Let you know how it goes. Hope we can trade information. Ciao."

I pulled into the HH Racing lot. After locking my Jeep I checked for the GPS tracker. Still there. I grabbed my computer bag, leaving my suit jacket hanging behind the front seat.

Linda didn't laugh, but her eyes twinkled as she let me in. "You clean up pretty good."

"Lawyers," I replied. "It'd be a good idea for us to meet with Nick. He available?"

"Actually, he's waiting. He's the one who told Angie to do your badges. He came back to my cube a few minutes ago grinning like a Cheshire cat and told me to bring you in as soon as you got here."

As we entered his office, Nick shook his head and grinned. "You must know the Pope," he joked. "Nobody else I'm aware of could have caused Ellen Burkhard to have a religious experience."

I laughed. "Actually, it was more like shock therapy. She had a come-to-Jesus meeting with her boss, Carol Logan. Ms. Burkhard is now out of the picture, and I'm reporting to Ms. Logan."

He whistled softly as he motioned us to sit. "Tell us about it."

I gave them a two-minute summary, ending with, "So I send my reports and time sheets to her, and I get paid by Watterson Watson."

"You're still focusing on the two areas we discussed this morning, right?" asked Nick.

"Yes. I'll still work on the telemetry jamming with Linda and her team: Jeff, Jason, and now Daniel. Even though I report to Carol – who, by the way, is insisting that she and I be on a first-name basis – I don't foresee doing anything different."

"What're you going to do now?" asked Nick.

"Soon as we're finished here, I'm going to meet with Daniel and whoever else is available from Linda's team to review the plan for the weekend at Boone. See what needs to be done."

"That's fine, but remember Linda's in charge. It's her job to assign priorities and resources."

I nodded. "Absolutely. And even though I report to Carol, Linda will be fully informed technically, unless we get into legal areas."

Linda perked up. "What happens then?"

"I'll consult with Carol, and share what I can."

Linda looked at Nick. "I guess we'll have to live with that." Nick nodded as she turned toward me. "Don't get me wrong, it's great to have you back helping. Only wish you could focus on just the telemetry problem."

"And that gets us to the second area," I continued. "I'll strictly be going to Carol with anything I find related to the cause of RF's death."

"Can you share anything with us? Can we help?" asked Nick.

"Right now, as I told her, I'm going to poke around. Friends, family, neighbors, and, of course, people here. You can help me by letting everyone know that if I talk with them they should answer my questions. I'll do my best to keep their answers confidential."

"I'll send an email to everyone. If you run into any problems, let me know," Nick said.

"Will do. Any more questions before I talk with Daniel?"

They shook their heads.

Linda and I started into the electronics lab. "By the way," she said, "Almost forgot." She stopped and handed me a key. "To the lab door."

"Hi," said Daniel, grinning as we came in. "I heard you were working here again."

"We still need you," Linda said. "I think you've realized just how much there is to do. It's overwhelming even with this many people."

Daniel nodded.

I opened my notebook to take notes, then closed it. A different client was now paying me, so I'd have to start a new one. I got a blank pad of paper from Linda to take notes which I'd transfer later.

We reviewed the outline for gathering jamming information over the weekend, assuming it would happen again. After we'd run through it once, I said, "Daniel, I'd appreciate your observations and suggestions. How can this be improved?"

He had a cultural background that discourages criticizing his superiors, so I often have to draw things out of him. It's always worth it, and this time was no exception.

Looking at me, he said, "We need to locate the source of the jamming."

I nodded.

He pointed at the diagram of the track taped to the wall. "Your procedure requires that someone periodically move the direction the antenna is pointed and record that by hand. Then later we have to manually enter that into the electronic records."

I nodded again.

"It's easier if we use two antennas, one with one of our receivers, the other with our spectrum analyzer and spare receiver." He continued, "We'll locate one setup in the pits and the other part way around the track. Then we can determine the location of jamming automatically. With Jason and me, we have people to do it even if you can't help, Wolf."

"It's a great idea. But you didn't really mean *our* spectrum analyzer, did you? It's in for repair."

"Yes, I meant ours. They're bringing the unit we sent in for repair back to us tomorrow morning. Nothing is wrong with it. They'll pick up theirs."

Linda said pensively, "Daniel, thanks for your idea. I see why Wolf brags about you."

Daniel's response was to look at me and blush.

Since RF's death, I'd been skeptical whether the instrument we sent in for repair was malfunctioning in the first place. Maybe RF hadn't wanted us to use it.

I looked at Linda. "RF told us that the new receiver had been checked out. Where is it?"

"Yes, we ran it through its paces. It's in the electronics lab on the upper shelf in the white shipping carton with Tau Telemetry's logo on it."

I glanced at my watch. "Sounds like we have a plan. It's almost quarter after five. I have a meeting in a half-hour, so I have to leave. I may be busy until late. Daniel, please send me an email telling me what happens after I leave."

Daniel nodded. "Sure. What are you going to be doing?"

"I'll be poking around," I said as I left. I didn't mention phone sex.

Chapter 8

The Open Door Coffee Shop was located in the Butler-Tarkington neighborhood on Indy's north side. While grand homes of wealthy families line Meridian Street on the neighborhood's eastern border, and the portion along the 38th Street southern border caters to the working class, most residences belong to upper-middle-class families. It's a model of successful racial integration; about one-third of the residents are African-American. The neighborhood is named after Butler University, with its celebrity bulldog mascot, and the author Booth Tarkington, who lived there for over two decades.

At five-forty I pulled into a free parking place on Illinois Street within a half-block of the coffee shop. The rising tide of parking meters and expensive garages that has overtaken nearby Broad Ripple hasn't invaded there. Yet.

The coffee shop was on the corner, and the door opened diagonally onto both 56th and Illinois Streets. There were several tables with umbrellas outside. I scanned them unsuccessfully for a forty-something woman with short curly hair and glasses, then went inside.

Built as a corner grocery store during World War II, the Open Door had been restored to maintain the old-time charm with polished wood floors and a hammered tin ceiling from which hung globe light fixtures. A glass case featured bakery and cold sandwich items, and several varieties of coffee were available. Notices of local events including a bake sale and a 5K race covered a large bulletin board.

I didn't see anyone matching Liz's description. She must have been running late, so I got some Sumatran coffee and went back outside to sit under one of the umbrellas. Then I saw her. She'd taken her glasses off, and her hair was halfway to shoulder length.

Walking around in front of her, I asked, "Are you Liz?"

She stood, putting on her glasses. "Are you Wolf? You said you'd be wearing a suit."

"Sorry. I left the jacket in my car."

She shook my hand firmly, then smiled with her eyes as well as her mouth. "And I'd taken my reading glasses off to look for you, so you didn't recognize me, right?"

"Right."

She put them on and we both laughed.

She was probably in her mid-forties and was aging well; unless you looked closely she'd pass for forty. Her dark curly hair had a 1990s look, but her clothes were stylish. A royal blue blouse and a gold chain necklace were set off by black slacks and black pointed-toe, low-heeled shoes. She was short, barely coming up to my neck, and was shapely despite hips that were slightly too wide.

She pulled a chair next to her for me to sit in. "It'll make it easier to talk. The noise out here can be annoying, but I don't want anyone to hear us."

I wondered what she didn't want anyone to hear, but said, "OK. You'd like me to help you with something to do with a life insurance policy, right?"

She nodded. "My divorce from Ron...you knew him as RF, but I never called him that...was final about six months ago. We'd been separated for a year; he moved out. One of the terms of our divorce was that he continue to pay one-half of the mortgage on the house we were living in, the one I'm still in. The title was in both of our names, so he owned fifty percent of it. Thanks to my attorney, the judge required Ron to take out an insurance policy that would pay off his half of the remaining mortgage if he died. He also had to revise his will so that the title to the house went to me at his death."

"So you essentially get one-half of the equity in the house, plus one-half of the remaining mortgage, but now have to make the full mortgage payments?"

She nodded. "It's a blessing and a curse."

"How so?"

"His half of the equity is worth around ninety thousand dollars, and half of the remaining mortgage is around fifty thousand, which I should get from the insurance company, but now I have to come up with fifteen hundred dollars a month mortgage instead of seven hundred fifty."

"So what do you plan to do?"

"I tried and tried to get Ron to sell it, but he refused to sign the papers. I'm planning to put it on the market and move somewhere smaller."

I was making notes. "Any other beneficiaries? Children? Siblings?"

"No. After two miscarriages, I had to have my female plumbing removed, and Ron wouldn't even consider adoption. He has one brother, Leonard, we call him Len, who lives in Kalamazoo, Michigan where Ron grew up. They have been estranged for a few years."

"Mind telling me why?"

"Their father Benjamin is in a nursing home in Kalamazoo diagnosed with early onset Alzheimer's. Was diagnosed a couple of years ago. Ron pushed all of the responsibility for his care off on Len. Basically washed his hands of his father. Ron never was close to either one of them, and this was the last straw as far as Len was concerned."

"So is Len handling the arrangements for Ron?"

"I guess so. I gave the police his contact information. Nobody's gotten back with me. I expect he'll have Ron cremated after the police release the body. I have no idea what he'll do with the ashes."

She took a deep breath. "I can't get the insurance company to give me any answers. They say that until the cause of death has been determined, no action can be taken on the policy. Don't they have to pay no matter how he died?"

"Not necessarily." Her eyebrows arched as I continued. "Most life insurance policies have a suicide provision that renders the policy null and void if the policy holder commits suicide within two years of policy issuance."

"Oh." She sat back, then forward again. "Well, that's a relief, I guess. There is no way, absolutely no way, that Ron would have killed himself."

I wanted to ask her why she was so sure, but decided to take a different route to the same information. "The other two possibilities are homicide and accidental death."

She knitted her eyebrows. "To be honest with you, I don't see how it could have been either of those. He was a little rough around the edges, but I can't imagine anyone wanting to kill him."

"How about an accident?"

"Strange you should ask that. A police detective asked me the same thing. I couldn't think of anything. He had a revolver, but kept it unloaded with a trigger lock on it, and in a safe."

"Did the police share with you the cause of death?"

"No, and they clammed up when I asked them."

"He died of asphyxiation by strangulation, Liz."

It took about ten seconds to soak in, then the blood drained from her face as she put her hand to her mouth, staring into the distance. "Oh my God. Oh my God."

She looked at me, tears welling up. "In the cellar. In the dungeon. My God. He accidentally choked to death."

Revealing I'd found his body wasn't in her or my best interest. "He was into S and M?" I asked.

She fished a tissue out of her purse and blew her nose. "That's out of date. It's called B D S M." She pronounced each letter separately.

"I've heard about the S and M part, sadism and masochism. Isn't that where people get their kicks, including sexual, from receiving or inflicting pain or humiliation?"

"That's part of it, although these days, people leave out the 'and.' They just say S M."

"So what's the rest of it?"

"It includes a wide range of erotic activities that involve bondage, dominance and submissions, sadomasochism, and other things."

Looking at her, I couldn't imagine her involved in something like that. "So how did Ron get drawn into BDSM?"

Her face flushed, "I'm not sure why I'm telling you this, but it may help both of us understand what's going on. I want you to promise not to tell anyone else."

"I'll keep it confidential unless there are legal requirements. I have no interest in hurting you."

Liz looked at me steadily and lowered her voice. "I'm not sure where to start." She thought for a few seconds. "For a while, Ron and I had what I'd describe as a happy marriage, at least most of the time. But our sex life started to deteriorate a few years ago. Before that, we made love at least twice a week."

She paused to dab at her eyes, and I gave her room to continue.

"We talked about what we could do to spice it up. I suggested things like candlelit dinners and romantic movies. Ron suggested we try kinky kinds of sex. I sort of enjoyed some of the things we tried first. He'd blindfold me, and sometimes tie my hands over my head."

She looked at me, "This next part is really embarrassing to me. I caught him looking at porn on the internet. Not just people having intercourse."

"BDSM?"

88

She took off her glasses, closed her eyes and took a deep breath. "Yes. And he was, let's just say, really enjoying himself."

"What did you do?"

"I let him finish, then we had a talk. He told me about a party where there would be what's called a 'play space' in the basement. It was sort of an introductory event for people new to BDSM. I wasn't into it, but he promised all we had to do was go look, we didn't have to participate, so I agreed."

"So you were fairly naïve about it."

"That's an understatement. I tried to read up on it, look for material online, and so on. I found basic information that helped me understand what it's about."

She stopped and looked at me. "You already know about it?"

"Not much. I'm learning from you. Go on."

"Well, BDSM covers a wide range of behaviors, from cross-dressers to animal role players. Some of it sounds scary, but they supposedly emphasize the importance of safety, and stress that informed consent is essential. One way it's stated is that all activities must be safe, sane, and consensual, or SSC."

"How do they manage that?"

"The people involved sign agreements, setting limits and so on. There are two main classes of participants. Those who exert sexual dominance or control are called dominants, or doms for short. The others, who are passive, receiving, and obedient are the submissives, or subs. Ron said he was going to be a dom and wanted me to be a sub."

"Like when he tied your wrists and blindfolded you. So you went to the party."

She nodded. "They had discussions going on upstairs. You could ask questions, that sort of thing. It was almost like any other party, except instead of talking about the weather and your golf game, the discussion was focused on BDSM. Nearly everyone was wearing black latex. There was only one other couple wearing street clothes."

"Did you feel out of place?"

"A little, sure. But not that much until we went downstairs to the dungeon where all the equipment was. Benches where people got paddled and so on. You didn't have to take your clothes off if you didn't want to, and everyone had to keep at least their underwear on.

89

The other couple stripped right down. Ron wanted to, but I refused, and so he didn't either."

"How did it go?"

"Ron got turned on, and I was turned off. It went downhill from there. Ron started going to parties without me. Private parties where the subs had sex with the doms."

"This wasn't doing much for your sex life, right?"

"Yes and no. I tried to accept it as a phase he had to go through. We started having sex more often, and it was good as long as I didn't let him hit me. I found out I liked some aspects of the bondage, but nothing else."

"But he wanted more."

"He wanted a lot more. Ron thought that if we had our own dungeon, I'd be more comfortable with some of the activities. And he wanted to host sessions that included private sexual encounters."

A fire engine with its siren blaring rolled out of the fire station less than a half-block from where we were sitting outside. We waited until we could hear each other again.

She continued. "We started arguing. I finally told him that if he wanted a dungeon, he'd have to put it in some other house. I wasn't having one where I lived."

She paused, and her eyes misted over. "It was more complicated than that. I still loved him, at least most of him. I feel he loved me, too, on some level, but he increasingly acted out his dominant role at home. Even wanted me to call him 'master' when we had sex. I just couldn't go on like that."

I put down my pen. "So he rented another house and built a BDSM dungeon in the basement."

"Yes, and he still didn't give up. He must've thought that he'd convince me to come around to his way of thinking."

"He invited you over to see it."

She nodded. "I wouldn't go to his parties, but one time I went over after work and let him take me to the basement where he had his BDSM paraphernalia, including machines and accessories like paddles, blindfolds, and other stuff."

"So he had quite a few things there."

"Yes, several types of equipment. I didn't want to know what each one was for, but his pride and joy seemed to be something called a

Saint Andrew's Cross, a large wooden cross structure that looked like the letter X. It was taller than me, and a person could be restrained by the hands and feet, either facing the cross for whipping or facing out for sex. He wanted to have sex while I was restrained facing out and wearing a blindfold and the slave collar attached to the cross."

Her breath caught, and she choked back sobs. "I refused, and never went inside the house again."

"That's why you think he strangled on the collar." She nodded, unable to speak. Now wasn't the time to tell her I'd found RF.

I let her compose herself. "Do you know how to contact anyone who was into BDSM with him? I'd like to talk with them."

"No. Ron took me to the party. I know we headed toward downtown to get there, but I'm terrible at directions." She thought for a minute. "The only thing I remember is the first names of the couple hosting the party. Betty and Mike." She paused and looked me straight in the eyes. "I've shared a lot of information with you. Just who are you working for? I understood that you worked for the race team."

I handed her both of my business cards. "I'm consulting them on a technical issue as Ruger Associates. I'm looking into Ron's death for another client. I can't tell you who they are."

She looked at my cards, then at me. "Must be for the racing team's insurance company. You think he was murdered?"

"I don't know. If he didn't commit suicide, it was either an accident or murder." I didn't correct her, and I didn't add that if it was murder, she would be a prime suspect. "Just a few more questions."

She nodded.

"How well do you know Linda Green?"

She beamed. "We've become friends. She has helped me get through the divorce, and I've given her a few tips on how to deal with Ron. She's almost like a little sister to me."

"So she's been there for you since he died."

"Yes, absolutely."

"Did you know any of RF's neighbors?"

"Not really. There was a woman who was sometimes walking her dog when I took mail over to Ron's house on Sunday mornings. We'd wave, but never spoke."

"Do you know where she lives?"

91

"She came out of a house across the street. Either the one right across, or on either side, I don't remember for sure."

"What kind of a dog was it?"

"Big and black."

"Sounds like I'd better beware. Last question: What happens to his belongings, the stuff in the house?"

She pursed her lips. "I assume that Len will be in charge of disposing of it. Ron took some kitchen utensils and linens with his clothes and other stuff when he moved out, but I really don't want any of it back if it means I'd have to deal with Len."

"What about the dungeon?"

She frowned. "I guess it's a little perverse, but I'd like to be a fly on the wall when Len discovers it." She picked up her purse. "Well, I need to go. Don't want to miss the news, but I have one last question, too. How do you feel about people engaging in BDSM?"

"I'll have to think about it. I know that people don't select their sexual orientation. I met an interesting transgender person on my last case. I believe that what two consenting adults do sexually is their own business, as long as nobody gets hurt. I'm not sure what to think if they get pleasure from the pain."

"I'm sure I don't like it," she said firmly as we shook hands and parted.

I wanted to talk with the woman who'd been walking the dog. I decided on a carry-out sandwich, so crossed Illinois and walked to the Illinois Street Food Emporium across from the fire station.

It's only a five-minute drive west of my Broad Ripple office, and I go there sometimes for lunch. I picked up a turkey wrap with a side of pasta salad and a Diet Coke, and used their restroom while I waited for my order. I'd be good for a couple of hours until the coffee and soda hit me.

* * *

I parked a few spaces down from RF's house in a good place to watch the houses across the street, and ate my takeout dinner, thinking about my conversation with Liz Phillips. She seemed to have been open with me, and if what she guessed was true, RF was by himself and his death was accidental. Another possibility had raised its ugly head, though.

Her ex-husband could have been engaged with a partner in a BDSM scene that went terribly wrong. That partner could be open to charges, perhaps manslaughter.

RF hadn't seemed to me like someone who would commit suicide. He was fairly new to BDSM so probably unfamiliar with equipment like the slave collar and might have strangled unintentionally. After my meeting with Liz, that seemed the most likely. Homicide seemed less likely, but if he *had* been murdered, his ex-wife, who was disgusted by his lifestyle, had to be near the top of the list of suspects.

I was curious how much his dungeon had cost, and how he'd paid for it. It sounded like it could have been thousands of dollars.

To help me evaluate the chances that it was accidental, I wanted to talk with someone in the BDSM community who had known him. In previous cases, if I needed to talk with a representative or spokesperson of a particular business, civic, or interest group, I'd ask Max, who seemed to be networked with every conceivable organization.

This was a horse of a different color. Max was old school, and likely didn't know what LGBTQ stood for, much less BDSM. The only lead I had was the first names of the people who hosted the party RF and Liz attended.

I called Tania Bell, the transgender person I'd met briefly during my previous case. This time, I expected the male voice of her answering machine and left a message. "Tania, this is Wolf Ruger. Please call me. If you'd like, check me out with Deb Lampmann. Thanks." I left my number.

Tania had been born male, but did not accept her assigned gender role. She was undergoing feminizing hormone therapy, a common approach taken by transgender people born as men. She had found acceptance and support for her journey from a group calling themselves the Sole Sisters on the east side of Indy. Deb was a member.

I considered calling Vanessa, but decided to wait until I got back home. Instead, I mulled over the scenario I might choose for her offer of phone sex. I settled on her wearing the outfit she had on when I first met her at the Shawnee Country Club, a pink silky minidress with black lace panties. At night, off in a dark corner of the parking lot at the country club seemed like a good setting.

About seven-thirty a woman with salt-and-pepper hair styled in a bob emerged from the house across from RF's, being propelled by a black Labrador retriever. They came past me on the other side of the street.

After a few minutes I got out and started across the street, then stopped, straightened my tie, and rolled down my shirtsleeves. Might as well look official. I had my PI identification and Wolf Investigations card out as she and her dog came back.

The sun was just setting, so it was still light. She approached me warily. I could tell the dog was utterly useless as a bodyguard since it was wagging its tail so hard it almost fell over.

"Hello. My name is Wolf Ruger, and I'm investigating the death of Mr. Phillips, across the street."

She fleetingly looked at me, then her eyes scanned furtively from me to her front door, looking for an escape route.

I handed her my card and backed up a step. "I understand you were home when the police came, is that right?"

She nodded while looking at my card. I wondered if she was mute until her dog gave me a friendly greeting bark, tail still wagging.

"Elsa, be quiet, down girl."

"She's a beautiful dog," I said. "I like the name Elsa."

The woman briefly smiled, and extended her hand. "I'm Jane Hadsall. Yes, I was here. It was hard not to notice when a police car came in with its lights flashing and siren blaring."

I prompted her to keep talking. "That was Saturday evening."

"Yes, about ten."

"Had you seen or heard anything unusual earlier?"

She looked at my card again, brows knotted, again glancing at her front door. "Who did you say you work for?"

"I didn't. It's a private investigation related to insurance." Close enough.

Her face cleared. "Oh. Well. No, I didn't see anything unusual. I walked Elsa about nine. We'd gone out to dinner. It was later than she usually gets walked, and she was whining at the door when we came in. I remember that all the lights in his house were on."

"Was that unusual?"

She thought for a moment. "Yes. I'd say so. I don't remember seeing them all on like that before unless he had guests."

"Did he have guests very often?"

Just then a man stuck his head out of her front door. Slicked back dark hair complemented horn-rimmed glasses out of the fifties. He wore a checkered shirt and jeans.

Fear flickered across her face. "Sometimes. Not often. He seemed to be a private person."

The man threw the door open, lumbered up and stood unsteadily between us, reeking of beer and arching his back. "Who're you? Why're you talkin' to m'wife?"

Ms. Hadsall said, "It's all right, Del. He's an insurance investigator looking into our neighbor's death."

"Well, we din' have nuthin' ta do with it. Git the hell off m'propity."

She put her hand on his shoulder. "Now, honey."

He glanced over his shoulder, shrugging off her hand. "Don' 'now honey' me." He clenched his fists at his side and stepped forward until our chests were almost touching. His breath made my eyes water. "Git outta here."

We were standing on a public sidewalk. I didn't want to fuel the anger I felt rising in me, so I put my hands up, palms out. Backing away, I said to Ms. Hadsall, "I'll be in touch," then turned on my heel and walked to my car with Del muttering obscenities all the way.

I had intended to talk with other neighbors after I interviewed her, but I figured Del wouldn't go back into his house until I left, and I didn't feel like dealing with being attacked by a drunk. I'd continue my talk with Jane Hadsall another time.

My electronic tail was still with me.

Going out of my parking place into the narrow street, I turned on my headlights and looked both ways for traffic. I noticed someone behind me pull out a few seconds after I did, also with their lights on. I was sensitized to being followed by having the GPS tracker, so I noticed the vehicle was still on my tail as I turned north on Illinois, where it dropped back.

My condo was less than three miles from RF's house, so it didn't seem unusual that whoever it was stayed in back of me as I pulled into my parking lot. As it pulled into the entrance to the lot for the building past mine, I got a momentary glimpse of a large red pickup, maybe a Dodge Ram or a Ford 150.

I had never been followed, and dismissed what had occurred, figuring that I was just paranoid because of the electronic tail. Besides, my mind was focused on the phone sex coming up with Vanessa.

* * *

Back home, I fed Boots, then read and answered email. The detailed operations guidelines that Daniel had written from my draft were excellent. I sent a couple of comments to him, with a copy to Linda. I told them I'd be in around eight in the morning. Daniel also mentioned that the spare receiver wasn't in the box on the shelf. RF must have put it somewhere else, and they'd find it in the morning.

Ann Wyland had replied to the email I'd sent with a personal note asking how she and her dad Billy were doing:

```
Hi Wolf,
        Thanks for your note. My colleagues at
Oracle were dumbfounded when I gave them the CD
with your controller code. (Don't worry, I didn't
tell them where I got it.) The Navy systems are
installing it, and the equipment failure rates
are dropping down to what we'd expect.
        I hope you're up for another game of
tennis, and Dad said to be prepared to play
backgammon. How about later this week? Thursday
and Friday are open.
        Email or call me.
    Looking forward to seeing you,
    Ann
```

I'd half-expected an invitation back to their home, but wasn't sure what to do with it now that I had it. I still felt an attraction for Ann that went beyond platonic, even though we'd agreed to be just friends. It would be tough playing tennis with her and not wanting to get sexual, but I had to respect her statement that she was still too fragile for a relationship. With Billy there to chaperone, I'd have to keep a lid on it anyway.

I was also in a quandary on which evening I should accept. I was going to be at Boone Raceway on both days with HH Racing. We should be finished by five or five-thirty each day unless there were

96

problems we had to address, according to Linda. There was a chance of a social event on Friday, not to mention having to prepare for the race on Saturday.

Friday was an evening usually reserved for Vanessa. She had a class project due that day, and might want to celebrate in the evening. On the other hand, she might be so wiped out by the work on the project that she'd postpone until Saturday. Or celebrate with someone else.

I decided to delay replying until I'd thought about it, and was writing my daily report to Watterson Watson when Tania Bell returned my call.

"Hello, Mr. Ruger. I remember you. I didn't need to check you out with Deb."

"Thanks for calling me back, and please call me Wolf. I have a favor to ask."

"Another case?"

"Yes. This one involves someone who died, perhaps as the result of an accident in a BDSM dungeon."

"I'm not into that way of life, so I don't know how I can help," she said.

"Oh, I didn't think you were. But I hoped that with your involvement with others living non-traditional lifestyles, you might be able to refer me to someone who is. I'm especially interested in talking with a couple who hosted a party that the deceased attended."

"You think they might be responsible for his death?"

"No. Almost certainly not. I can't rule anything out, of course, but I'd like to talk with these folks to learn more about what might have happened. Their first names are Betty and Mike."

"Just a sec. Let me get something to write on."

I waited.

"OK," Tania said. "I'll ask a few people. Please plan to speak confidentially. The BDSM community is still fairly secretive. It's where we LGBT folks were a decade or more ago."

"OK. Thanks, Tania. Are you still in the Sole Sisters?"

"Yeah. I'll tell Deb we talked when I see her at the next meeting."

"Great. I just saw her Saturday."

We said goodbye.

I finished the two-section report. The first section, a copy of which I sent to Nick and Carol, focused on technical issues. The second, dealing with the cause of RF's death, went only to Carol. I provided details of my meetings with Liz Phillips and RF's across-the-street neighbors, the Hadsalls. I left out the part about being confronted by Del.

It was time to call Vanessa and set up our phone sex.

Almost all men masturbate. It was common in Iraq. Porno DVD's were freely exchanged. This was different. To have her on the other end of a phone line with both of us masturbating while engaged in the same fantasy aroused me just thinking about it.

She answered on the first ring. "Hi, Wolf. I've been getting ready. What am I going to wear, and where are we going to come?"

"Wear the same outfit you wore when we met at the country club, and let's do it in the back of your SUV in the club parking lot."

"Ooh, that's great. I'm already wet. I'll change and get in bed with my vibrator. I'll play a little."

"OK, talk to you in ten minutes."

I tried to watch TV, but all I could think about was her, so I shut Boots out of the bedroom, propped myself up with pillows, and waited for the time to go by.

When I called her we each turned out the lights, and put our phones on wireless speakers so we'd have our hands free.

"I'm wearing the pink silk dress and black panties. We're on the blanket in the back of my SUV at the club, and I'm really horny. Can anyone see us?"

"Yeah, there's a couple making out in a car next to us. They're watching."

"Umm. That turns me on."

We guided each other's fantasy.

I heard the rhythmic buzzing of her vibrator going in and out, and her bed springs creaking.

I was barely holding off ejaculating when she moaned, "Oh…*oh, I'm gonna come."*

She squealed. I grunted as I ejaculated.

Silence settled over us.

"Wow. Never came on the phone. Have to do it again," she said, breathing hard.

I laid back, panting. "That was incredible. Uh-huh, we'll definitely do it again."

"Much better than doing it alone."

I wiped myself off with a towel. "Absolutely. Good night, Vanessa."

"Mmm…good night, Wolf."

Chapter 9

Tuesday morning's Indy Star identified RF by name in a small article buried in the Metro Section, and named his place of employment. Before I left for HH Racing, I confirmed that the GPS tracking device was still in place on my Jeep. I'd be receiving my identical version that day, and had a plan to nail whoever had put it there. As soon as I was on the road at a quarter to eight, I phoned Tito. He answered on the first ring, so must have been waiting for my call.

"Hi, acho. Enjoy your talk with Phillips' ex-wife?" I could almost see him grinning. We'd started calling each other 'acho' which is short for 'muchacho,' or friend, when I'd visited him in Puerto Rico.

"It was interesting."

"His involvement with BDSM hasn't been released to the public. I couldn't give you any details."

"What else do you know that you couldn't tell me?"

"Come on. You know I can't answer that. But you might ask me a couple of specific questions and I may answer them, especially if you have information that's related."

"OK. So what was the time of death, and what about the contusion on the back of his head?"

"You have related information?"

"I believe so."

"All right, time of death was eight, plus or minus a half hour. The contusion was probably not sufficient for death, but might or might not have knocked him unconscious. Now, whatcha got, acho?"

"Still trying to rule out suicide?"

"Sure, why are you asking?"

"Because the across-the-street neighbor who walked her dog at nine said every light in the house was on. When I got there about ten, the house was dark."

"So?"

"Think, acho. If he committed suicide, how could he turn off the lights after he was dead?"

Tito was silent for a while. "Well, the only way I can think of is if they were on a timer. I'll have our guys check that out."

"Do that. I'll bet they don't find one, especially one that controls every light in the house. That'll rule out suicide, right?"

"Looks like it."

"Did you notice the clutter in his office?"

"Yeah, it looked like the usual mess a bachelor makes. Some drawers left open, stuff piled on a desk."

"RF was anal about neatness. If the place was anything but immaculate, someone was probably looking for something." I paused to let that sink in. "So you going to start a homicide investigation?"

"I don't make that decision, but, yeah, looks likely. Of course, that'll put his ex-wife right in our cross-hairs."

"She disapproved of his involvement with BDSM and was revolted by the dungeon he built, but I don't see her as the murdering type."

"Acho, you of all people should know there's no such type."

We said goodbye.

There would probably be some bickering, but it looked like Gamble Oil's insurance company would have to pay up the three hundred grand. Liz Phillips would also get her payout. Tito was right, though; if it was homicide, she'd be a prime suspect.

As far as I was concerned, that concluded the part of my work for Watterson Watson related to the cause of RF's death. I'd file my final report on that piece in the evening and would be able to focus exclusively on the telemetry issue.

I needed to let Carol Logan know sooner than that, though, so I called her office and left a voicemail summarizing what led to the conclusion that RF's death wasn't suicide. I wanted to share the information with Liz Phillips, but I should get Carol's approval to do that.

If RF was murdered, it might or might not be related to the jamming. The disordered state of RF's house made accidental strangulation less probable. Murder or accident, I needed to resolve the jamming issue and provide the information to law enforcement for follow-up related to any criminal activity.

I debated about calling Tania Bell to tell her I didn't need to talk with the couple who had hosted the BDSM party. I decided to let it ride. The information might be useful to Liz Phillips in dealing with her insurance company.

Even with a VIP badge, I needed to be buzzed in at HH Racing's front door, so I called Linda when I was five minutes away.

The shop was a beehive of activity. The high-bay doors were open to the loading dock, and a fifty-three-foot transporter with Gamble Oil and HH Racing logos was being loaded with the car and supporting equipment.

"Have you found the spare Tau receiver?" I asked Linda after she'd let me in.

"No, but it has to be around here somewhere."

Something prickled the edges of my brain that I couldn't quite grab onto. "If you don't find it this morning, let me know, OK?"

"OK, will do. I'm not too worried. RF squirreled stuff away in weird places sometimes."

She took me into Nick's office. He shut the door, his face haggard, motioning us to sit. "It's going to be a three-ring circus around here, so after this meeting I won't have much time to talk. But if you need me, I'll try to clear out a few minutes."

I nodded. "I should be able to spend most of my time working on your telemetry problem with Daniel. I can't give you details, but it appears that suicide will be ruled out by IMPD as cause of RF's death."

Linda arched her eyebrows and pulled stray hair back into her ponytail. "So was he murdered?"

"I can't say more than I just did. Maybe shouldn't have said that. The situation is still fluid, but for now, unless Carol Logan jerks my chain, I'll focus on telemetry issues."

Nick nodded, rubbing his forehead with the fingers and thumb of one hand. "That's good news for us. What's your plan for today?"

I looked at Linda. "We need to find the spare receiver so we can implement my plan." I shifted my gaze to Nick. "I want to focus on the Tau telemetry system operation, and see what I can learn, if anything, about other teams' experiences, including jamming. Nick, you've been in racing for a couple of decades. How much do people move around from team to team?"

"Quite a bit, actually. Racing has a lot of what we call rotational assets. Individuals can work several different places during their careers."

I nodded. "So do folks keep friends that they sometimes share information with?"

"As long as they're ethical and don't burn any bridges, people in the sport retain friendships, if that's what you mean." He paused, blinking and sitting back. "But your friends are now your competitors."

"Is there anyone you feel comfortable asking about their Tau 920? Whether they're having problems?"

"Maybe. Jules Hogarth is the race engineer for Laurence LeGrand. We worked together for a couple of years when we were just getting started. I don't mind talking with him; we need to catch up with each other anyway. See how his kids are doing, that kind of thing."

"Great." I hesitated, then asked, "Any contacts like him at Clanton-Suggs?"

Nick laughed. "No way, Jose. I don't know of anyone there I'd even *like* to know. You need to understand that Laurence LeGrand and Clanton-Suggs are from two different worlds. Cut from different cloth, you might say."

He paused, then continued. "Laurence LeGrand has tight ties to Formula One; it's as though they descended from there. Clanton-Suggs tries to look like a Formula One organization, but all of their original links are to stock car and midget truck racing. I don't want it repeated out of this room, but I consider them a bunch of rednecks who strut around like hillbilly peacocks."

Linda chortled, clearly agreeing. "Nick, that's awful." She looked at me. "Don't get us wrong, there are a lot of great people and class acts on the stock car circuit. Clanton-Suggs is an exception."

Nick dipped his head, concurring.

I grinned. "OK, I won't repeat it. By the way, Tau Telemetry's website is hyping a new model, the Tau 930. Says they're trying to get it approved for Formula Nor-Am for next season."

Nick snorted. "Approved isn't the right word. They're trying to ram it down our throats. Every team in Nor-Am would have to buy at least one plus spares."

"Assuming it's working right, and not getting jammed, is there a problem with the Tau 920?"

Linda shook her head. "They want to give us the ability to monitor forty-eight channels of data. The thirty-two we have now seem adequate to us."

Nick added, "And, of course, there'll be sensors that we'll have to buy. You can bet that the ones we have now won't be compatible with the new system. And Tau will be glad to provide those as well, for a hefty price."

I sat back and thought for a few seconds. "I contacted them and asked for a demo, which will probably be from a sales rep. I'll also ask for technical information that'll put me face to face with an engineer or technician, so I can learn more about their current telemetry system."

After the meeting in Nick's office, I went into the electronics lab and checked my email. I had an answer from Todd Stevens, the Tau Telemetry rep who'd visited HH Racing and been of dubious help.

He'd be delighted to give me a demo of the "fantastic" Tau 930 system anytime that morning, so I shot back an email saying I'd be there at nine, and for him to have someone available who could answer technical questions.

Then Linda and I met with Daniel. He and Jason would have the telemetry data acquisition from HH Racing's car well covered, leaving me free to concentrate on the jamming, if it occurred again. I'd be with them on the team's radio network, so could ask Daniel or Jason to do spur-of-the-moment tasks like rotate an antenna or check a specific frequency with a spectrum analyzer.

As I was getting ready to leave for Tau Telemetry, Daniel asked, "Wolf, would it be OK if I went with you? Things are under control here, and I could probably learn a lot from listening in on your demo and questions."

I looked at Linda. "I had been considering asking him, but didn't want to pull him away if he's needed here."

"Fine with me," she said. "Knowing Daniel, you'll both learn more if you go together."

* * *

Tau Telemetry was located on Main Street in Speedway, which is home to racing teams as well as more mundane establishments such as barber and beauty shops, restaurants, and tax preparers.

I expected it to be in a typical commercial building, and drove past it the first time. It was set well back from the street, and its two-story red brick and white column architecture was more usual for a bank or mortgage company.

The parking lot had room for at least thirty cars, but only about ten spaces were occupied. A blue dumpster in one corner of the lot was filled with what looked like construction waste. I parked in one of several visitor's slots, and rang the front buzzer.

It had security worthy of a military installation. After being buzzed into a small entry lobby, Daniel and I were confronted with a receptionist behind thick glass who asked to see ID and ascertained that we were not carrying firearms before issuing us visitor badges.

We signed in, were let inside a door with what looked like bulletproof glass, then into a small but plush conference room with brass-studded leather armchairs, a conference table inlaid with contrasting wood patterns, and a huge flat-screen display on the wall at one end. Todd Stevens was waiting for us, his laptop already connected to the display, ready for his sales pitch.

An African American about six-two, Todd looked like he'd just stepped out of the pages of GQ Magazine with his navy sports jacket and open-necked gray silk shirt. He struck me as a consummate salesperson who could make women melt in their shoes.

"Welcome to Tau Telemetry. We appreciate your business," he said silkily.

Like we had a choice. Their system was mandated for use by all Formula Nor-Am cars.

"Hi, I'm Wolf and this is Daniel. I'm a consultant to, and Daniel works for, HH Racing," I said as we shook hands.

Todd's countenance morphed into sorrow. "We hear you've lost a valuable member of your racing family," he said piously. "I guess you know that RF Phillips and I interacted when you acquired your Tau 920."

I nodded, keeping a straight face. He'd read the paper, too. "Yes, that's one of the reasons we're here. We'd like to hear about the new Tau 930, of course, but we're faced with the reality of having to fill in for RF at the Formula Nor-Am event this weekend. We have technical questions about the 920 system, and we need an engineering type to answer them."

"Of course, of course. I understand." Todd's face brightened. "As soon as you've heard about our great new Tau 930, I'll bring in Andy Shaffer, Chief Engineer. I'm sure he'll have all the answers."

For the next twenty minutes, we endured Todd's energetic sales pitch. Daniel took notes, nodding when appropriate. I took a few notes, nodding when Daniel nodded, but my notes were mainly related to information I needed from Andy Shaffer.

"Some of the details of the Tau 930 are still, shall we say, behind a curtain," Todd concluded, conspiratorially. Then he offered to let us in on the deep dark secrets. "If you sign non-disclosure agreements, we can let you see pretty much everything."

Daniel seemed ready to sign until I laid my hand on his arm. "Sorry, but you'll need to contact the IP, or intellectual property, people at HH Racing. We aren't authorized to sign for the team."

Even if we'd been authorized, I didn't want either of us distracted from solving the telemetry issue. I looked at Todd. "When you came over to HH Racing recently, you said that no other Nor-Am team was experiencing difficulties with the 920 system. Any change since then?"

He shook his head. "That's as much a mystery to us as it is to you."

"Well, then, it's time we talked with your engineer," I said.

"Mind if I hang around?"

"Nope. Suit yourself."

Andy Shaffer was a couple of inches shorter than Todd, but weighed nearly twice as much. Wearing a white shirt with a black and gold tie loosened at the neck, his image was closer to an NFL football tackle than an engineer. Medium-length brown hair and gray eyes set off an open and friendly face.

My right hand disappeared into his meaty paw when we shook hands. "Glad to meetcha," he said.

Noticing his tie, I asked, "Boilermaker?" I wasn't inquiring into his alcoholic drink preference, but rather whether he'd gone to Purdue University.

He nodded. "Yep. And my dad works for Gamble Oil."

It was my turn to grin. "That gives us two things in common. What was your degree?"

"Master's in computer engineering," he answered. "Yours?"

"Bachelor's in computer technology. Minor in psychology," I answered. "And Daniel is a Ph.D. student, same major as yours."

"What can I do for you two?" he asked. He pushed a stray wisp of hair out of his eyes as he settled into a chair that squeaked loudly with his weight.

"I want to discuss some general issues, then Daniel will get down in the weeds with more detailed questions. OK?"

He nodded. "Fire away."

I asked him about other teams experiencing issues with the 920 and got essentially the same reply we'd heard from Todd. I was starting to believe it was just HH Racing having problems.

Next, I asked, "How often do you update software, and does every Nor-Am team have the same version?"

"The easy answers are about twice a year, and yes. But the 920 systems used by Nor-Am were manufactured over a time span of about six months, so some of them started out with more recent software than others. As of today, though, each team is running exactly the same software version."

"Let's turn to the subject of encryption. Tell me how it's implemented in the system."

"I assume you know something about how encryption works."

I nodded. "Military intelligence. Iraq."

"Wow. OK. The encryption code is on a custom chip that is soldered onto the circuit boards, so it's hardwired into the transmitter and matching receiver."

"Is there any way to change it using software?" I asked.

"Absolutely not."

"Do you have spare chips?"

"We keep a few for each racing team, and they're in a safe. I'm the only person with the combination." He paused. "When Mr. Phillips ordered the spare receiver, I took one of the HH Racing extra chips out of the safe and personally supervised its installation. There is no way anyone else can access the encryption key, even if they have the receiver."

Gears were turning in my head, but mainly gnashing. I still didn't know what I didn't know.

I'd put my smartphone on vibrate when we went into Tau Telemetry, and it began buzzing in my pocket. Excusing myself for a minute, I went into the hall to read a text message that said that the GPS tracking system I'd ordered had just been delivered at my condo.

Back in the conference room, I listened while Andy answered a few complex questions from Daniel regarding how to set up data acquisition rates, then interjected, "Hey guys, I have to run an errand. Andy, is it OK if Daniel stays here and picks your brain? Can you give him a ride back to the shop when you're done?"

"Absolutely. In fact, we may hire Daniel if you leave him here unsupervised."

Daniel was embarrassed by the compliment, but only said, "No problem, Wolf. See you later."

"Meet you at HH Racing in an hour or so," I said as I started out the door, then stopped, looking at Andy. "Your dad doesn't know Harry Wheeler, does he?"

"Yes, but not through his work. My dad's a project engineer for Gamble's pipeline operations. Mr. Wheeler is Vice President of Refining. But they're both radio controlled, or RC, flying nuts, and belong to the Flying Tigers RC Club that flies model airplanes out of the old abandoned Speedway Airport," he replied.

"Are you into RC aircraft, too?"

"Uh-huh. It's something my dad and I still do together. Have since I was five years old. Harry's son Paul and I are about the same age, and we used to pal around at the RC club before we went to college. Paul and I both live in this area now. He dropped out of college and spent some time in the Marines with a couple of tours in Afghanistan, then came back to work with his dad at Gamble.

"We still talk at the club events, but he doesn't seem as friendly as before. He's kinda distant now." He paused. "Flying RC models is what got me interested in telemetry systems. Probably wouldn't be working here if it weren't for my dad and the Flying Tigers."

I wondered if Paul Wheeler was dealing with PTSD demons, but instead ventured, "I understand Harry Wheeler may have something to do with the company's sponsorship of Nor-Am racing."

"Yeah, he's the man. A huge race fan. He talks about it when we're at RC flying club events."

We said goodbye. I dropped off my visitor's badge with the receptionist and headed home to pick up the GPS tracking system, with the one attached to my Jeep presumably still happily transmitting. Something about the spare receiver was itching my mind, but I couldn't scratch it.

Thinking about Vanessa and our phone sex, I called her. It was mid-morning, but she didn't answer. In fact, her phone went straight to voicemail, which indicated it was turned off. That was strange. She rarely slept past seven.

I left the message, "Enjoyed last night. Call me."

Our relationship was a romantic fantasy and sexual amusement park with lots of rides and experiential variety. We called each other 'lover' but had never used the big 'L' word – love. It was at the stage, at least for me, that could be described as 'falling in love,' that initial phase of an intimate relationship that is all 'ups' and no 'downs.' I speculated what stage it was at for her.

Back home, I took the package between my storm door and my front door inside, then gave Boots a snack, scratched his ears, and told him dinner might be late. Again. Having already gone through the instruction manual, it only took me ten minutes to get the GPS tracking system operating on my kitchen table. I took it out on the balcony where it could receive satellite signals to ensure that it was working.

It took a miniature 12-volt battery similar to those used in garage door openers. My next task was to intentionally run down one of the spare batteries. I pulled a very high current out of the battery by shorting it out, connecting the positive and negative terminals with a heavy wire, for a few minutes. It was almost too hot to touch when I was finished, and very dead. After it cooled off enough to handle, I dropped it in my pocket.

I put the new GPS tracking system in a shopping bag just in case anyone was watching me, and set out for HH Racing. At a gas station along the way, I positioned the right rear of my Jeep next to the machine used to put air in tires, and dropped quarters in the slot. Kneeling down beside the tire, I removed the GPS tracking system, popped open the battery compartment, and replaced the good battery with the dead one out of my pocket. The box was easily reattached under the lip of the fender in the same place it had been, taking care not to touch the outside of the fender, so it looked the same as before.

I parked the Jeep in a slot in the HH Racing parking lot with the right side close to another car. My expected visitor would have a tight fit getting the device out of my wheel well. After Linda let me in, I checked in with Daniel, who was back from Tau Telemetry. I told them I'd be working with the Tau 920 computer modeling software outside where I could get some fresh air.

I reasoned that whoever installed the GPS tracker would come looking for it when the signal disappeared. Their most reasonable conclusion would be that the battery had died, and they'd probably bring a spare.

They must know where to find me, since I was driving toward HH Racing when they lost my signal. I was betting that they were getting paid by the hour, and each hour that went by without my location data cost them a lot more money than a two-dollar battery.

With the new GPS device in my pocket, I borrowed Jason's HH Racing cap, and sat on one of several white plastic chairs that had been put outside of the garage under a small copse of trees for use by the mechanics when they took smoking breaks. I had a view of most of the parking spaces, shouldn't attract attention, and could be in the lot in less than ten seconds.

Cumulus clouds were building in the west, and the wind was increasing out of the southwest. We could get some much needed rain later in the evening.

Since Vanessa hadn't called me back, I called her again. After several rings, it went to voicemail again. I hung up. Now I was worried and upset. The phone ringing likely meant she knew I was calling and chose not to answer. After the fantastic phone sex we'd had the previous evening, her avoiding me didn't make sense.

After about an hour, as I was running a software simulation of the Tau 920 system, an ancient black four-door Ford with a broken radio antenna circled the parking lot once, then again. It pulled into a parking place several spaces away from my Jeep, and a man got out. His white shirt had the sleeves rolled up, his face was florid, and his bald head had only a fringe around the edges. He was so fat he waddled when he walked.

I stood up and took the new GPS unit out of my pocket, cautiously moving toward the parking lot as I kept a large tree between us and speculated whether he'd fit in the space between my Jeep and the adjacent car. He looked around furtively, then disappeared behind my Jeep.

I jogged rapidly out to his car, figuring I had at least thirty seconds while he replaced the battery in the box installed on my Jeep. I quickly attached my GPS unit inside the right front wheel well on his car, and scooted back to the white chair.

I kept my head down, peering at him from under the bill of the cap. He tried to heave himself up from behind my Jeep twice before he succeeded, at which point his shirttail was hanging out and he looked thoroughly disheveled. He mopped sweat from his face as he shuffled back to his car, and pulled out of the lot. I didn't need to get his license plate, and I didn't follow him physically.

My electronic tail was on him just as sure as his was on me. Tit for tat.

Chapter 10

I went back inside HH Racing through one of the high-bay garage doors. The mechanics just looked at me and nodded. I was getting familiar enough that I didn't really need an escort as long as I was wearing my badge, and they were too busy to worry about me.

The shop area was a beehive of well-organized activity. They were going through the familiar drill of preparing for a practice and race with the precision and discipline that reminded me of a military operation.

In the engineering conference room, Linda, Jack and Jason were sitting at the table. Linda had her head in her hands, and Jack was leaning back with his arms crossed, staring at a wall.

Only Daniel noticed me. "We've looked everywhere in the building for the spare receiver."

Linda raised her head, "I've told everyone to stop looking for it. We'll just have to do our best with one receiver. We need to concentrate on getting ready for Boone."

I thought for a moment. "Did RF ever take work home with him? Could he have been testing or programming something at home that required the receiver?"

"He almost never took work home," she replied. "Once or twice, when we were getting ready for a race, he'd get behind on a task and finish it at home in the evening, but he was pretty much ready for this weekend as far as I know."

I didn't respond to that, but made a mental note to find out whether the receiver was in his house or car. If it was missing, it could be tied to RF's death, which was seeming more like murder. I needed another favor from Tito.

My stomach was rumbling for food, and my watch said it was eleven-thirty, so I asked, "What's for lunch? Where are we going?"

Linda replied, "Chez HH. Nick has sandwiches and salads brought in on the day before we leave for a practice session and race. It should be here any time."

"OK, I have a call to make. Back in a few minutes."

I went out in the shop, dialed Tito's number, and, predictably, got his voicemail. "Hi, acho. Call me when you get a chance. It's about a piece of HH Racing equipment. Ciao."

Angie Murphy was in the engineering conference room, her cart piled with white cardboard boxes containing lunches. "Pick a box and grab a drink from the fridge in the break room."

As we ate, Linda and Jack shared details about the practice, qualifying sessions, and race at Boone with Daniel and me. I could tell from the gleam in Daniel's eyes that he was excited about being at the track. My eyes probably had a similar look. I'd been a racing fan since growing up in Muncie, but this would be my first opportunity to experience it up close and personal, and Formula Nor-Am was big time.

Linda led off. "On Thursday, the practice sessions are free-for-alls. The Formula Nor-Am teams are given access to the track for a fixed period of time. At Boone, that'll be an hour in the morning and another in the afternoon. They can basically do whatever they want."

"Cars usually go out more than once, right?" I asked.

"Sure. We'll be trying various adjustments. The mechanics will be dialing in settings like suspension, and may even try different tire pressures to see what works best for track conditions."

"Tires are supplied by one manufacturer, the official tire sponsor of Nor-Am, and each team has a fixed total number of tires allocated for the entire weekend, right?" I asked.

"Yes, and that's a challenge. We get six sets of tires for all three days. We can use them any way we want, for example two sets each day."

I nodded. "And the track conditions during practice may be different than Friday's qualifying or Saturday's race."

"Sure," she replied. "And that brings us to Friday's qualifying session. It's also a fixed time period, which is an hour for Formula Nor-Am at Boone. Everyone is given access at the same time. You can run up to ten laps total, all at once or over multiple tries, and your fastest lap determines your qualifying position for the race."

"You make adjustments when the car comes in, right?"

"Almost always, but that's not the only reason to run more than once. The track may be faster at the beginning or at the end of a practice session, so it isn't unusual for a team to go out twice, even if they have everything dialed in where they want it."

There was a pause in the conversation as people ate.

I remembered the invitation to play tennis with Ann Wyland and have dinner with her and her dad Billy. "Linda, I have an invitation to dinner with friends for either Thursday or Friday night. Is one better than the other, or do I need to work both evenings, in which case I'll just turn them down?"

Linda thought for a moment. "We should be finished Thursday by five, five-thirty at the latest since it's only practice. Friday could be a different story. We may have things we need to take care of before the race. So I'd say Thursday should be fine, but I'd like to have you available Friday."

"OK, thanks." So I'd see Ann on Thursday; Vanessa would have to wait.

I went into the electronics lab, entering with the key Linda had given to me. I was accessing my personal email account when Tito called.

"Hi, acho. I'm on lunch break at City Market. What's with the HH Racing equipment?"

I summarized the situation with the missing spare receiver. "I need to find out as soon as possible whether or not it's in RF's house or car."

"We have his car impounded. There wasn't anything in it like that. You can't just go waltzing in the house and look."

"No, but you can."

"Look, acho, even if it's there, the house is a crime scene. I can't bring it out like a stray cat." I laughed. He was referring to his retrieving Boots from behind yellow tape at a murder scene.

"No need for that. We just want to know if it's there. It's important to the HH Racing operation at the track this weekend."

"What the hell do I care? Convince me that I need to make a special run past the house on my way home."

"Well, if it's there, I'll know where it is, and we'll just have to work around not having it. If it's not there, I have a feeling that someone connected to RF's murder may have it."

"Interesting. OK. Why don't we meet outside Phillips' house at five-fifteen? Oh, and bring a picture of the equipment you're looking for."

I agreed and we hung up. I printed out color copies of front and rear views of the Tau 920 receiver.

I sent an email to Ann accepting her invitation for tennis and dinner on Thursday, and asking her to please say 'hi' to Billy. I still hadn't heard from Vanessa.

After Daniel and Jack finished lunch, we worked for a couple of hours revising our system procedures to account for having only one telemetry receiver. We were still going to have two spectrum analyzers, so we could look at and listen to raw telemetry on the second one, although we couldn't decode it.

Knowing things such as the frequencies used by the other teams might be useful. We'd also be able to monitor and listen to jamming signals on all the frequencies with both spectrum analyzers. We decided to locate one analyzer with a directional antenna that would give us an indication of the direction a signal was coming from, about halfway around the two-and-a-half-mile Boone road course. We would use radio contact to coordinate our activities.

"So what else do we do now to get ready?" asked Jason.

Linda took the lead, as usual. "We should set up all of the equipment here in the shop and have a dry run tomorrow first thing. We can use the spare telemetry system, our single receiver, and whatever antennas you guys want to test."

Daniel nodded. "I like your idea, but may I make a suggestion?"

Always the polite one.

We all bobbed our heads. He continued, "Perhaps we should take it a step further. Let's test the telemetry system on a vehicle. Anybody's car will be OK. We need to determine what happens at distances similar to what we'll have at Boone."

"What about sensors?" asked Jack.

"It'd be great to test as many as possible, but I don't think we need to do that. Just hook up a couple – temperature and speed, for example – to give us some real data to broadcast and receive."

As usual, Daniel had come up with a winning idea. I worked with them for another hour, preparing for the simulation that we'd carry out the next morning.

At four-thirty I gathered up my laptop and reading material. "I have a meeting in a half-hour. Have to go."

"Racing-related?" Linda asked.

I left her question unanswered, saying, "It's something I can't talk about." Which told her, and everyone else, that it was related to RF's death.

* * *

I parked along the curb right in front of RF's house at five o'clock. I was early, but had a phone call to make that needed my undivided attention.

Vanessa answered on the third ring. "Hi, Wolf. Sorry I didn't return your calls."

She didn't offer a reason or mention our phone sex. I wanted to ask why, but instead asked, "How's your project going?"

She paused before answering. "It's fine. We're meeting at the apartment of one of the team members this evening. I probably won't get home until after midnight."

"Pretty late to be working on a project."

"We may have a few drinks after we finish."

I tried to push down my angst, unsuccessfully. "Just drinks?" I immediately regretted my question.

Another pause. "Wolf, are you asking if I'm going to have sex?"

It was my turn to pause. "I'm sorry I asked the question. Can we just forget it?"

"No, I don't think so. It's time we had a talk anyway."

"About sex?"

"About our relationship."

"Fine. OK. I'm rather happy with it, aren't you?"

"Yes, but we seem to have different expectations, and not the same perspective."

"So…what are yours?"

"I care about you, and value your friendship more than I can tell you, but we're both single. We've never discussed being monogamous, much less living together."

"But I assumed…"

116

She cut me off. "That's just what I mean about different expectations."

"OK, so you want to be free to have sex with guys besides me?"

Another pause. "Wolf, in my mind we each have *always* been free to have other relationships, including sexual."

"Well, at least now I know where I stand."

"Don't be like that. You're the most important person in my life, but I need the freedom to pursue other friendships and relationships. Sex could be involved. You have that freedom, too. That doesn't lessen my feelings for you one bit."

My mind was reeling, and I didn't want to say something else I'd regret. "I need to think about all this. We probably should talk some more."

"OK," she said. "When do you want to do that?"

"I'm working long hours until the race is over on Saturday. Maybe Sunday."

We agreed to get together then.

Our conversation jogged my memory back to the first time we met and she was trying to seduce me. She'd told me that she approached sex the same way most men did. If she saw someone she wanted to screw, she went after him. From what she'd just said, she still thought that way.

She wanted me to have the same freedom. I wondered how I'd deal with it.

We'd never agreed to a monogamous relationship. We hadn't discussed it, period. She was fresh out of a failed marriage with Stan, and was an uncaged free spirit. I couldn't realistically expect her to limit her sex partners to me. Of course, part of me wasn't realistic.

I sat, turned inward, and mulled over our conversation. Then I reviewed it again.

Oblivious to the outside world, I was startled by Tito knocking on the passenger side window. I rolled it down. He leaned on the windowsill with both forearms, sweating and shaking.

"You OK, acho?" I asked. "Rough spot?"

"Yeah," was all he could muster.

"Get in. Tell me about it."

Tito's Hum-V had been blown to smithereens by a roadside bomb while he was checking perimeter security at Al Asad Air Base in Iraq, where we were both stationed. The driver and the other passenger, a Military Police lance corporal, were killed instantly. Tito was knocked unconscious, but otherwise sustained only minor cuts and bruises. A medevac helicopter landed beside him just as he regained consciousness and discovered the lance corporal's body draped across him.

Besides suffering nightmares, Tito endured daytime PTSD episodes triggered by the unexpected sound of a helicopter. If he saw it coming in the distance, he could usually steel himself.

"I called Carmen," he said shakily, "but she didn't answer. You were less than ten minutes away, so I came straight here. I tried to call you, but my fingers wouldn't work."

"It's OK. Helicopter?"

He nodded. He'd been escorting a prisoner to Methodist Hospital when a medical helicopter unexpectedly appeared at rooftop level and landed within a hundred feet of the ER door he'd just exited.

I listened, then had him repeat it all. By then, the fear had left his eyes. He was still sweating, but his hands were steady.

As usual, we ended our session with small talk. At least he thought it was small talk.

"How are you and Vanessa?"

I winced. "We've hit what I guess you can call a bump in the relationship road."

"Want to talk about it?"

"No, not yet, but thanks for offering." I opened my computer bag and handed him pictures of the equipment. "Here's what you're looking for."

"OK, I'll look around. Probably take ten minutes max."

In seven or eight minutes, he came out and secured the front door. I could see he was empty-handed.

"No luck, acho," he said, sliding into my passenger seat and handing my photos back, which I put in my computer bag. "I see what you mean about his house. There wasn't a whole lot of stuff there. The office was messed up. That dungeon thing was weird. Never've seen one before."

"Thanks for trying. Tell Carmen hello."

"Not so fast. Why do you think the equipment not being here has something to do with his death?"

"Not sure. Maybe he knew who's responsible for the jamming. Maybe even was involved in it."

"Anything you're not telling me, acho?"

I started to say no, then remembered about my electronic tail. "One thing I haven't mentioned is that someone has a GPS tracking device on this Jeep. Been there for a couple of days. I plan to find out who it is, and if it's related to RF's murder, I'll let you know."

"How are you going to find out?"

I described what I'd done in the HH Racing parking lot.

"Watch your ass, acho. Organized crime is notorious for using electronic tails."

We said goodbye. Tito and Max had now both warned me that Vanessa's ex Stan Gordian might be involved.

The fact that the receiver was missing was a strong indication that someone else had it, someone who wanted to pirate the telemetry from HH Racing's Nor-Am car. Two organizations topped the list of suspects, Clanton-Suggs Racing and Gamble Oil.

Clanton-Suggs seemed to have the most to gain. They could guarantee their second-place position in the Nor-Am series by finishing ahead of HH Racing on Saturday, and thus likely acquire Gamble Oil sponsorship next season.

By closing its refinery in Indianapolis – a decision still unannounced – and with its corporate headquarters in Texas, somebody in Gamble Oil could be looking for a reason to justify a shift in sponsorship to Clanton-Suggs, which was also based in Texas.

Either way, the threat from someone else having the spare receiver had to be neutralized, hopefully without revealing that we knew it was missing. I thought of several approaches, then settled on one that I'd have to get approved by Nick since it would cost HH Racing serious money.

It wasn't at all clear whether RF's death was related. At least I didn't have to worry about that; I had enough on my plate.

Tito's warning about organized crime pushed finding out who was tracking my Jeep's location to the top of my list. I was about to turn on the GPS tracking tablet that was paired with the device I'd installed and download the information it had collected so far when my phone rang. It was Linda Green.

"Wolf, got a few minutes? It's about Liz."

"Sure. I have as much time as you need."

"I really appreciate this, Wolf. I just had coffee with her. The police have opened a homicide investigation into RF's death."

"I know about that."

"They interviewed Liz this afternoon downtown at IMPD. She told me that she has no idea why anyone would think she killed him, and told that to the police. She said they were very nice, but at the end told her not to leave town, and suggested that she retain legal counsel."

"Good advice."

"I agree, but she said she has absolutely no intention of wasting her money on an attorney."

"She knows that she is the prime suspect, right?"

"She doesn't accept that. She still thinks it was an accident. I asked her where she was at the time he died, and she said she was at home alone watching TV. That's not much of an alibi, is it?"

"No." I knew the contusion on the back of RF's head tended to rule out an accident, but couldn't share that with Linda. "So what do you want me to do?"

"You impressed her when you two met. With your credibility, you might have better luck than IMPD and I have had in convincing her to get an attorney. Could you please call her, maybe meet with her?"

"Sure, be glad to. Did you tell her I might call?"

"No, I wasn't sure you would."

"OK, I'll tell her I'm checking up on the progress with her insurance."

"Great, Wolf, and thanks."

Linda's call raised questions. I was supposedly working only on the telemetry issue, but things kept pointing to RF's death as being somehow connected. I wanted to find out more about Liz.

I looked across the street at Hadsall's house. There was only one car in the driveway. It was either Jane's, and I'd have a talk with her, or Del's, in which case I'd beat a quick retreat, whether or not he was drunk and belligerent.

I crossed the street and knocked at the door. Jane answered it, opening it only a few inches.

I leaned into the opening. "Is this a good time to talk?"

She nodded and slipped out of the door, looking back over her shoulder as she closed it quietly. "Let's go out on the sidewalk. I don't want Elsa to think it's time for her walk."

Once we got on the sidewalk, I asked, "You mind answering a couple more questions?"

"No, not at all, and I apologize for Del's behavior."

"It's not your apology to make, but I appreciate it. Did you ever notice a woman who came to Mr. Phillips' house on Sunday mornings?"

"Yes. A few times. Was she his wife?"

"Ex-wife. How many times did you see her?"

"Three or four times, when I walked Elsa. She always had a handful of envelopes, fliers and so on that looked like mail that she gave him."

"Did you ever see her go in the front door?"

She thought for a minute. "No, in fact she handed whatever it was she brought over in through the screen door, then turned around and left."

I heard the sound of a car, and saw Jane Hadsall's face freeze.

"Just one more question," I said. "Did you ever notice her visit at any times other than Sunday morning?"

Del's car wheeled into the driveway and he got out. He peered in our direction curiously. Recognition and anger boiled over as he loped in our direction.

"No, I never saw her at any other times. Now you'd better leave," she said urgently.

Backing away, I said to Ms. Hadsall, "He needs to be on a leash," then turned around to leave. Too slowly.

With a snarl, he leapt forward, grabbed my left shoulder with one hand, and turned me around. He might as well have telegraphed his punch from West Texas. It glanced off the side of my head as I deflected it with my forearm.

I followed through with my elbow and heard the sound of bone crunching bone as his nose broke, spewing blood. Enraged, he threw another punch which I easily dodged as I brought my knee up between his legs.

He went down on his knees whimpering, then fell over and rolled from side to side in misery, moaning while holding his groin with one hand and trying to stop the blood flow from his nose with the other.

Jane Hadsall had backed off, her lips pursed. She shook her head.

I wanted to leave, but one look at Del was all anyone needed to know that he required medical attention. Shit! I couldn't just leave him there writhing on the sidewalk.

"Del," I sighed, "I hope you're a better lover than you are a fighter." I leaned down and pulled him to his feet, then looped his left arm around my shoulder. Jane Hadsall quickly came over to help, holding up his right side, and together we helped him stagger to his front steps.

"Have him sit on the steps. I don't want him bleeding all over the carpet."

We turned him around and set him on the third step.

As she let go, she said, "Hold him up. I'll be right back."

Loathing permeated the atmosphere between us. "Don't try to talk," I said.

"Fuck you," he replied, spitting blood.

She returned quickly with gauze, cotton plugs for his nose, and washcloths and towels to clean him up. She must have had a first aid kit, preassembled and ready for regular use.

"Can you manage him?" I asked, as I got up to leave.

"I've done it before," she answered. Looking at my shirt, she said, "Wait another minute."

She came back out with stain remover in a spray can. "Hold your arms out," she commanded, then briefly sprayed each of the dozen or so blood spatters on my shirt. "They'll come out if you get them in the washer before the stain remover dries."

I nodded. As I turned to leave, I peered at Del. My anger and pity melded. "You worthless, stupid son of a bitch."

Chapter 11

Boots had to wait for dinner until I had my shirt in the washing machine. After I serviced his stomach with food and rubbing, I took aspirin for, and put ice on, my elbow. It was sore, but nothing seemed broken.

I was thankful it was my left elbow. It'd be a little stiff and tender for a day or two, but since it was only Tuesday evening, it shouldn't bother my tennis game with Ann on Thursday. Being right-handed, all I had to do with my left hand was get the ball in the air so I could serve.

I called Liz Phillips. Her phone rang several times, then went to voicemail. I left her a message to call me no matter how late.

Within half a minute she called back. "Sorry, Wolf. I didn't recognize your number. Why did you call? Did you hear that I got interviewed by the police this afternoon?"

Rather than giving a direct answer, I said, "I'm not surprised. Did they tell you not to leave town?"

"Yes, and I see no reason for that. Is that why you called?"

Again I dodged a direct answer. "How are things are going with the insurance company?"

"Not very well. Now that there is a homicide investigation, they've put everything on hold."

"Liz, do you have an attorney?"

"*No!* I didn't do anything wrong. Why should I?"

"Because you need to protect yourself. In any murder investigation, family members are automatically suspects, and ex-spouses are at the top of the list. It is absolutely essential that you get legal help right away."

There was silence on the other end of the line during which I thought I heard her sniffling. "I don't know any lawyers except the one who handled my divorce."

"They're probably not your best bet. The legal profession is compartmentalized, sort of like medicine. You wouldn't go to a heart surgeon with a back problem. You need an attorney who specializes in criminal law."

"But I am *not* a criminal."

"I didn't say you were. But that's how you need to protect yourself."

"Well…can you recommend anyone?"

I thought for a few seconds. "I don't deal with many attorneys. Only one I've worked with recently is Robert Conlan, whose office is on the east side of Indy, just off Shadeland."

"Is he good?"

"I don't have a lot of comparisons to draw from, but, yes – I'd say he's good. You might want to find someone with an office closer to you. I'm sure he could recommend someone."

"I'll think about it. Do you have his number?"

I looked it up on my smartphone and gave it to her. "Let me know if I can help further."

"I will, but I don't know if I can afford to hire a lawyer."

"Liz, you can't afford not to."

We hung up.

Having done my good deed for the day, I got a Sam Adams Light out of the refrigerator and nuked some leftover lasagna. Boots came padding into the kitchen, so I scratched his ears while eating, then went into my office, turned on my GPS tracking tablet, and started my office PC. When the tracking information had been downloaded, I settled back to see where the fat man had been since he left HH Racing.

I used the tracking tablet to look at a map of routes he had driven. A mapping application on my desktop PC provided street views that gave me information about buildings, businesses and homes, near each place he had parked.

The system was programmed to sense and relay the car's location every three minutes. I wasn't interested where he went if he stayed there less time than that, and at that rate the battery should last at least ten days. The information was received and stored at a secure internet site that I accessed with the tracking tablet.

Primarily, I wanted to know who he was and for whom he was working. That should give me information that would point me to the answer to the big question: Why? I was curious whether he'd visit the Indy Gamble Oil office or one of the racing teams. It was nearly eight o'clock, so he was likely home for the night. I'd probably learn where he lived by the location of his car now.

I started reviewing the data in the order it was sensed and stored. About ten minutes after he left HH Racing, his vehicle was stationary for almost an hour. The street view on my PC for the location he was parked indicated he was in the parking lot of a pancake house on Lafayette Road. His stomach was surely a monument to pancakes.

After a fifteen-minute lag, his location for the next half-hour was in the 300 block of Massachusetts Avenue. It's an area that features restaurants, bistros, and boutiques, including one of my favorite places to eat: The Eagle, known for its fried chicken and pulled pork. The street view of his location indicated that he was parked on the street outside a shoe store. I doubted that he was buying shoes.

Upstairs over these establishments are businesses with professional services such as medical clinics, marketing agencies, and law offices. I made a note of the range of addresses on both sides of the street within a half-block. A thirty-minute visit could have been to whomever hired him, or maybe to his own workplace.

The next stop in his itinerary lasted nearly two hours, and was in a residential neighborhood east of Haines Road just off 71st Street. The mapping software placed him about a hundred feet south of 71st Street. The street-level images were ambiguous in that he was in a driveway between two houses, and it wasn't clear which house went with the driveway. Maybe that was where he lived, and if so, maybe he worked out of his house.

At about four-thirty for forty minutes the tracker placed his car on Pendleton Pike, a few blocks outside the beltway. When I saw the location on the map, the hair went up on the back of my neck, and when the street-level imagery confirmed it, I broke out in a cold sweat.

He was parked at ElecRecycle, an electronics recycling business run by Stan Gordian, Vanessa's soon to be ex-husband. I should have listened to Max when he warned me my GPS tail might be from Gordian. Even Tito had suggested earlier that evening it might be tied to organized crime.

I had been trying to find a relationship between my being tailed electronically and the HH Racing telemetry jamming or RF's murder. A relationship that didn't exist. When I was in military intelligence, there was an Army saying that covered this situation: I'd been trying to "bash to fit and paint to match."

I was annoyed with myself for having blinders on, assuming something instead of discovering what actually existed. I was also mad as hell at Gordian.

I willed myself down off my rage and continued with the GPS tracking information. He was at the address just off 71st Street for a couple of hours. Since about an hour ago, he'd been at a business establishment that the mapping street view identified as the Golden Balls Gentlemen's Club, on Pendleton Pike. He was still there. Strip club aficionado.

I pondered what to do. First, I needed to cool down. My anger wasn't allowing me to think straight. Opening another beer helped.

Then I remembered where he'd been parked on Massachusetts Avenue. A light went on in my head. The internet listed the address of the law offices of Rudolph Kade as 333 Massachusetts Avenue, Suite 310. Kade was the shyster lawyer who had been part and parcel of the theft of intellectual property from my former clients at Stellar Electronics, and was almost certainly involved in the illegal selling of U.S. high tech information to foreign interests on the Pacific Rim.

Max had warned me about Kade as I got involved in the Stellar case. As a result of that investigation, disbarment proceedings were pending against him. But according to Max, he'd wiggled out of them previously, and it wouldn't be surprising if he dodged disbarment again.

After finishing the brew, my brain was back in gear. Why would the 'evil axis' of Gordian and Kade be tracking my movements? What if I was making incorrect assumptions again?

A possibility hit me right between the eyes. I didn't know why it hadn't occurred to me earlier. I discovered the GPS tracking system on Sunday as I was leaving HH Racing, and assumed that it was put on my Jeep there. What if it had been put on somewhere else?

I'd gone there from Vanessa's condo. What if it had been attached at her condo? What if *her* car had one, too?

A judge had put a restraining order against Stan Gordian and his associates forbidding them from contacting Vanessa via any means whatsoever, including electronic. Was an electronic tail construed as "contact?" Was Kade working for Gordian? I wasn't sure, but I needed to find out whether there was a tracking device on Vanessa's car without alerting Gordian and his goons.

I took my S&W out of the safe, put my computer and tracking system tablet in my computer bag, went down to my Jeep, and put the S&W in its holder under the dash. So that they wouldn't know I'd left home, I popped the box with the tracker off my Jeep's fender and wedged it into the fork of a tree about seven feet off the ground, next to my parking place. It was high enough that nobody would notice it even in daylight. The tree was only about ten feet from the Jeep, so was within the twenty-foot precision limit of the GPS system. They wouldn't be able to tell the Jeep had moved.

As I drove to Vanessa's condo in Castleton, lightning was beginning to flash in cumulus clouds to the west of Indy, and the wind was increasing, gusts picking up leaves and dust.

I mulled over the possibilities. What if she didn't have an electronic tail on her car, and I had the only one? Why would Gordian and Kade care about where *I* was going? What if she did have a GPS unit attached to her car? Why would they be tracking both of us? Did the restraining order have anything to do with it? If so, what? Questions with no answers.

I kept an eye out for anyone following me as I pulled into Vanessa's lot and parked several spaces away from her car. Confident that I hadn't been followed, I sat in my Jeep another few minutes before getting out.

Widely-spaced raindrops were spattering the pavement as I trotted over to her car and checked under the fenders, finding what I was looking for attached under the right rear fender, same as mine.

Now what? The questions were why, and why both of us? I was first and foremost concerned about her safety, less so about mine.

My impulse was to rip it off and throw it in the bushes. I also felt a need to tell Vanessa it was there. I beat back both urges.

As I started out of the parking lot, raindrops mixed with blowing dust temporarily rendered the Jeep's windshield wipers ineffective. I glanced out the driver's side window at her condo. All the lights were off. Maybe she was in the back bedroom where the lights didn't show outside.

Maybe she wasn't home. If not, her electronic tail was being as ineffective as mine. I repressed my inclination to call her. Better leave well enough alone. Even if she wasn't alone. Especially if she wasn't alone.

The location of the car on which I'd attached my GPS tracker was still at the strip club. I wanted more information. To get it, I needed to poke the hornet's nest, but in such a way I didn't get Vanessa or myself in more danger than we were in already.

A rough plan was taking shape in my mind as I pulled into the Golden Balls Gentlemen's Club on Pendleton Pike. They were doing a moderately good business for a Tuesday night. The parking lot was about half full. I parked in a dark corner of the lot, well away from the black Ford with the broken radio antenna.

I watched patrons come and go for about ten minutes during which the rain shower tapered off to nothing. I'd only been to a strip club like this once, during my senior year in college when a friend got married and six of us went to a place in Lafayette. I had just turned twenty-one and was already three sheets to the wind when we got there.

We paid a cover charge, a two-drink minimum, and each of us paid for a lap dance. Supposedly there was a 'no touching' policy, but it wasn't enforced unless you really groped the dancer. A dance lasted for one song – and cost twenty bucks. Allegedly, no overt sex was allowed inside the club, but after two lap dances you could pay for a third and get jerked off under a table.

I remember walking into the john and finding the groom drying the crotch of his pants with the hair dryer mounted on the wall. He hadn't needed the hand job. It also explained the hair dryer in the men's room.

I also recalled a key hanging on a hook near the scantily-clad woman who collected the cover charge. It was to a pickup truck parked out back where, for additional consideration, a patron could get a blow job.

It only took five minutes or so to ascertain that the Golden Balls' version of the pickup was a paneled van. I watched one girl with her client leave and another couple enter within a few minutes. I doubted that the activities in the van were limited to blow jobs.

I went in and paid my cover to a girl who was maybe eighteen, wearing pasties and a G-string. The clientele was mostly Caucasian and over fifty, reflecting the club's working class neighborhood. The place smelled of beer and of ammonia used in cleaning solutions. I

128

ordered a Sam Adams Light and looked around for the guy who'd put the GPS tail on my Jeep. I didn't have to look far.

There were two stages, each with a woman pole dancing while three other women worked the ringside tables. My person of interest was sitting next to one of the stages, and was being cajoled by a dancer with large breasts and tattoos on both arms. I stood back along the wall, and watched as he tucked a bill in her G-string and she straddled him for a lap dance.

I hadn't looked for a key hanging on a hook at the door, but when he tucked in more bills after the lap dance and she led him to an exit in the back, I knew where they were headed. And I had a plan.

After a few more sips of my beer, which cost me twenty dollars altogether and was worth every penny, I left the way I came in and went to my Jeep. It was unlikely he'd go back into the club after he'd shot his load in the van, at least not for very long, so his house just off 71st Street seemed the logical place to wait. The details of the conversation we were about to have were still a little vague as I parked.

Looking at the driveway indicated by the mapping software, it was clear that it belonged to the house on the left. Lights were on. A woman in what looked like a bathrobe moved by the front window, and my plan clicked into place.

I shoved the S&W into my pocket and waited. Ten minutes later the lights went off behind the front window. Five minutes after that, the black Ford rolled quietly into the driveway with its lights off. He obviously didn't want to draw attention to himself. By the time he had opened his car door, I was out of my Jeep and into the driveway, walking quickly but quietly so I didn't attract his attention.

He had just hauled himself out of his car with his shirttail hanging out and was turning to shut the door when I strode up. "I want to talk to you."

He was so startled I thought he might have peed his pants, but then transformed into a mister tough guy persona that fit him like a six-fingered glove.

"Who the fuck are you?" he demanded, speaking quietly as he started to reach back into his car.

He felt my S&W pushed into his massive belly. "Don't reach for anything. You know damn well who I am. Tell me who you are, and back it up with ID."

"I'm gonna call the cops, you son of a bitch. You're trespassing."

"Fine. Good. You do that." I turned and headed for his front door, my revolver at my side.

"You can't go in there," he protested.

I stopped, turning sideways to him. "I was just going to tell your wife where you've spent the past two hours."

"Yeah, smartass. Where's that?"

"I have a photo of you coming out of the van behind the Golden Balls." Close enough.

He sagged, sweat breaking out on his upper lip. "Oh, shit. That ain't my wife, it's my girlfriend, and she'll kill me if she finds out I went there."

"So let's see some identification. And don't make any sudden moves." I walked back to him and kept the revolver pointed in his general direction for incentive.

He dragged a wallet from his hip pocket, fumbled around in it, then thrust a photo ID at me. "I'm a private detective. See?"

His "detective" card with his photo, one of those you can get online for fifty bucks after you take an "exam" that everyone with the fifty bucks passes, identified him as Gerald Eldorp. He didn't even know that he couldn't be a detective unless he was a law enforcement officer.

"I'll make you a deal," I offered. "You give me the information I want, and I won't rat you out to your girlfriend."

"Gee, I'd like to, but I'm covered under an attorney-client privilege thing," he said smugly.

"Get off that crap. Add to my telling your girlfriend where you were my reporting you to IMPD for impersonating a licensed private detective." I took my license out and held it under his nose. "*I* am a private investigator licensed by the State of Indiana. You are nothing."

His eyes fixed on my revolver, he let out a deep breath that reminded me of a whale spouting. "So what do you want?"

"I want to know who you're working for and why. I already know part of it, and if what you tell me doesn't jibe with that, I'll be right up those steps knocking on the door, and I'll make a call to IMPD tonight."

Gears whirred in his head. There weren't many of them. "You ain't gonna tell nobody about this. Promise?"

"If I get what I want I won't tell anyone." I left out that I'd have to tell if it became part of a legal proceeding.

"OK, whaddya want to know?"

"Let's start with who you report to."

He tried to puff himself up, but he was already puffed. "Mr. Rudolph Kade, Esquire. He's a powerful lawyer, and I'll be in deep shit if he finds out we talked."

"I understand. Who else do you report to?"

"He's the only one who pays me."

"I didn't ask that. Who else do you see and give information to?"

He looked puzzled, then his face cleared. "Oh. Gotcha. When Mr. Kade tells me to, I give reports to Mr. Stan Gordian at ElecRecycle."

So far so good. "Who else?"

The last question put him into a state of confusion and fear. He began shuffling his feet around like a kid with a full bladder.

"Please. I gotta keep that confidential. I'm afraid somebody'll hurt me if I tell you."

I turned around and had started walking toward his porch when he tugged at my arm, pulling me back around the corner of the house where we'd been talking.

Sweat was glistening on his forehead. "Goddam it. You can't tell *nobody* this. Only Mr. Kade knows. Sometimes I get questions on my email reports forwarded to me by Kade from a guy in Chicago. I send answers to the guy and copy Kade."

I tried not to show my surprise. "Who? What's his name?"

"I don't know. Honest. I'm telling you God's truth. All I have is his email address." He paused, thinking. "I have it on some paper in my wallet. Don't shoot me. I'll get it out."

I memorized it and let him put the paper away.

"How do you know he's in Chicago?"

"A coupla times Mr. Kade has been talking with him when I've come inta his office, and he's asked 'im stuff like 'How's the weather in the Windy City?' and 'How about them Cubs?'"

"But you never heard a name?"

"No, honest. Just talk about Chicago. Mr. Kade said I ain't even s'posed to know he *exists*, the guy in Chicago. Mr. Gordian don't know about him, neither."

"OK," I said, my mind spinning. "Just one more question. Why? What's going on?"

"Jeez. I was afraid you'd ask me that," he said, shuffling his feet again. "Nobody tells me nothin'. I'm just doing a job."

"I can accept that. But lots of times when *I'm* doing a job, I hear things. Maybe they don't seem important at the time. What do you hear or see? Could be one end of phone calls in Kade's or Gordian's office. Maybe questions you're answering by email."

He screwed up his face, emphasizing the too-large nostrils in his bulbous nose. I gave him time. This was the main answer I'd come for.

"I don't know if it's connected, but on the phone, coupla times Mr. Gordian has talked about payments to a family. I dunno what family he's talking about. But from what I'm hearin' it seems like he, and maybe Mr. Kade too, may owe somebody big bucks, and they want payment."

I must have looked at him strangely, because he said, "Hey, I'm only tryin' to help here. Don't shoot the messenger."

I had to chuckle. "Don't worry. I won't." I turned on my heel to leave, tossing over my shoulder, "Not unless you tell anyone else about our talk."

I walked to the Jeep while he wiped sweat off his brow, tucked his shirttail in, shambled up the steps, and went into the house. When the inside light went on, I pulled away from the curb slowly with my lights off.

I'd just gotten a few more pieces to a puzzle I hadn't known existed until I connected my electronic tail to ElecRecycle and Rudy Kade, and now to some unknown person in Chicago. I didn't know who it was any more than Gerald Eldorp did, but my money was on an Armenian Mafia enforcer.

And I still didn't know *why*. OK, so Gordian and maybe Kade owed someone, maybe the Armenian mafia, lots of money. What roles could Vanessa and I possibly have in that?

I drove back home. The rain was over for the evening, leaving wet streets covered in places with wet leaves, which can be as slippery as ice. Or as Rudy Kade.

I retrieved the GPS tracking device and re-installed it where it had been. Eldorp was undoubtedly still tracking me, and I wondered what he'd think when he saw that according to the tracking system, my Jeep hadn't left the parking lot. I didn't think he'd seen what I was driving. Could have been a rental car.

As soon as I was inside, Boots ran up to greet me mewing, then backed off and circled me slowly, sniffing. I wasn't surprised. I probably smelled like a strip joint, and he'd never been in one. After I'd fed him, he plopped down in front of the refrigerator. He didn't care for my beer and ammonia odor.

Something Tito had told me about Stan Gordian was trying to surface in my consciousness, so I found the entry for that conversation in my Stellar Electronics case notebook. Another piece of the puzzle fell into place: Gordian dropped big bucks "playing the ponies," to use Tito's expression.

Gordian was charged with accessory after the fact in a murder. If he owed someone a lot of money, it made sense that they'd be disinclined to let him head off to prison for ten-to-twenty still owing it. But how was the Armenian Mob involved? They sure as hell weren't in the business of lending money to pay off bookies.

More puzzling still was what it all had to do with Vanessa and me. And what was I assuming?

One supposition I'd made was that we were somehow involved jointly, as a couple. That was still likely, but what if we were involved separately, as individuals? How might that be? With Stan Gordian it would have to include money.

Vanessa had once told me that her father recently passed away, and that she had inherited one-half of his estate, his current wife and ex-mistress the other half. But she hadn't told me how much, just that it was a burr under Stan's saddle since he didn't have a claim to a penny of it due to their prenuptial agreement.

I certainly wasn't wealthy. Did I have something besides money he was looking for? Maybe an avenue to, or something worth, money. I came up with a blank.

In my office, I turned on my computer. I had trouble clearing my head of the Gordian-Kade developments as I wrote my daily report to Carol Logan at Watterson Watson.

I included the information that HH Racing's spare receiver was still missing, and that I was assuming it was in the hands of someone who wanted to bootleg all the telemetry from their Nor-Am car. I had a plan to neutralize the receiver's loss that I'd propose to Nick Napoli in the morning. I'd submit the plan's details in the next day or two if it was approved and implemented.

I recounted what I'd learned from Jane Hadsall that led to the opening of a homicide investigation by IMPD, and reiterated what I'd said in the morning's voicemail – that I was now focused on the telemetry problem. I described the meeting at Tau Telemetry and summarized our plan for a simulation that would be a dry run of our procedure to discover answers related to the jamming problem at the track.

I concluded with a sentence that I'd be interviewing people I suspected were associated with the issue. It was vaguely worded because I wasn't sure who I'd talk with, only that I needed to poke around at both Gamble Oil and Clanton-Suggs Racing. I had the framework of a process to approach Harry Wheeler, VP of Gamble Oil, via his son Paul, who was a veteran with tours in Afghanistan. I needed to check out my idea with Linda and Nick before I sprung it on Carol.

I opened my email account and sent the report to Carol. In my inbox, buried in the spam messages including one offering me a once-in-a-lifetime investment deal in Nigeria, were one each from Ann and Daniel. Daniel had sent me the draft procedure for the simulation we were going to run the next day at HH Racing, and had asked for my review. After reading it, I replied with a few comments and thanked him for his help.

I sent an encrypted email to him saying that the shadowy organization responsible for the malware in the disk drives in the Stellar case might become a problem for us again, gave him the email address for Gerald Eldorp's Chicago contact, and asked him to find out what he could about the person or company that owned it. It was a "dot com" address, which meant it was probably assigned to a commercial entity. I told him to bill *me* for this, not HH Racing.

Ann's email confirmed our tennis match on Thursday, and dinner with Billy and her afterward. I sent the brief reply:

Ann,
Looking forward to seeing you and Billy on
Thursday.
    Wolf

Then I sent an email marked 'urgent and confidential' to Andy
Shaffer at Tau Telemetry, with a copy to Daniel, confiding that our
spare Tau 920 receiver was probably stolen. I described a number of
things I wanted him to be prepared to do as soon as I received the
approval of Nick Napoli, hopefully first thing in the morning.

Boots jumped up in my lap, and I reflected on the day's events
while I scratched his ears. My life had become significantly more
complicated. My relationship with Vanessa was no longer
monogamous, and according to her never was. She was asking for
'space.' And she was probably screwing, or intending to screw,
someone else. At the same time, I was somehow getting mired in a
situation that involved her soon-to-be ex-husband Stan, and the
crooked attorney Rudy Kade.

In my mind I could hear Max's voice sternly reminding me that my
one and only paying client at this point was HH Racing via Carol
Logan at Watterson Watson, and telling me to stay the heck away from
getting tangled up in other stuff. He'd say 'heck.'

I thought about what I knew and didn't know about the jamming.
One aspect I had briefly thought about, but had pushed down in my
mind for future consideration, was the radio transmitting equipment
that the culprits were using.

In Iraq, one of the important objectives we had when analyzing
jamming signals was to identify the specific hardware producing it,
including where it was manufactured and by whom. Each type of
equipment manufactured has unique characteristics in the jamming
signal.

Some types, such as those used on large vehicles, are complex,
relatively heavy, and hideously expensive. The jammer being used
against HH Racing was more likely a simpler system that was
relatively low cost and light weight.

In my military days, I had access to databases – many of them
classified – of electronic warfare equipment attributes. I had no way to

access that information as a civilian with no security clearance and, from the point of view of the U.S. government, no "need to know."

I needed help from someone in a company that was a government contractor that had access to the right kind of data and could provide me unclassified information. I knew that Oracle Electronics manufactured equipment that was installed in the Navy's EA-6B Growler electronic warfare aircraft.

Billy and Ann Wyland both worked at Oracle. Ann owed me a favor since I'd helped Oracle identify and fix a malware problem in a control system they sold to the Navy.

I decided to send them each an email with an attached file containing a few samples of the recorded jamming signal, and I wanted to let them know where it came from and how we'd gotten it.

```
Ann and Billy,
    I'd be grateful if you could do me a favor.
    Attached is a file with signals recorded at a
couple of road racing courses in the U.S. They
were received by a race team's telemetry
receiver. Everything was inside the tracks with
no known military activity in the area.
    I'd appreciate your passing the attachment
along to your EA-6B staff and/or other folks in
electronic warfare. I'd like to know what
equipment generated the signal. (They'll know
the signal I'm interested in as soon as they
look at it.)
    Thanks for your help, and see you both
Thursday,
    Wolf
```

I also prepared two DVDs containing all the examples of the jamming signal I had, then turned off my computer. I'd give one to each of them on Thursday evening, followed by an explanation.

As I went to sleep with Boots on his towel at the foot of the bed, I wasn't thinking about HH Racing. I was stewing over my promise to Vanessa's Uncle Sal to watch out for her.

Chapter 12

Wednesday morning I found Boots' towel and my bedcovers on the floor, and there was no sign of Boots. Probably pushed him off the bed unknowingly. I was sweaty and must have slept fretfully. I vaguely recalled dreaming about dragging something large and heavy behind my Jeep over a rutted dirt road, but, as is usual with my dreams, I couldn't remember what it was or where I was dragging it.

Boots appeared from wherever he'd been sleeping and padded along beside me as I headed to the bathroom. He mewed to let me know that all would be forgiven if I fed him.

As I gave Boots his breakfast and cleaned his box, I noticed that my elbow was a little stiff and bruised from its encounter with Del Hadsall's nose. As usual, he waited until the box was clean then immediately got in it and peed. Territory claimed.

A feature article in the sports section of that morning's Indy Star previewed the upcoming Formula Nor-Am events. The headline read 'Nor-Am at Boone This Weekend.' The sub-headline was 'Event Marred by Murder of HH Racing Crew Member.'

You could count on the press to hype anything that would sell papers. A murder wouldn't hurt the attendance at the track, either. And of course, the generosity of the Star's coverage had nothing to do with the full-page ad on the facing page paid for by Boone Raceway.

I was still shaken by the events of the previous day, when I'd found out that Stan Gordian and Rudy Kade were back in Vanessa's and my lives for unknown reasons. I had several phone calls to make: Tito, Matt Corbett at the FBI, and Max, in that order. Before I left, I called Tito and left an urgent voicemail. He'd be at work in fifteen minutes and I should hear back from him right away.

A quick check of my email revealed a short note from Ann, time-stamped at seven-fifteen, saying she'd received the file I'd sent the night before and was forwarding it as I'd requested. I was just leaving for HH Racing, my computer bag on the seat beside me and my S&W in its holder under the Jeep's dash, when Tito called.

"Hi, mon. Get fired again by that race team?"

"No, and no PTSD nastiness either, but it's still kind of bad."

"So what's up?"

"You remember our conversation about that GPS tracking system someone put on my Jeep, right?"

"Yeah, I recall saying it's the kind of thing you expect with organized crime. Tell me you found a link between the telemetry jamming and organized crime."

"I kind of wish I had. No, that electronic tail was put in place by a wanna-be private investigator with a fake PI license. Guess who he works for?"

"I give up."

"Stan Gordian and Rudy Kade."

"No shit?"

"No shit. And there's some guy in Chicago involved, maybe an Armenian mafia enforcer. I have Daniel running down info on an email address for him."

"A Chicago connection's bad news."

"I know. It gets worse. I haven't told Vanessa, but she has a GPS tail on her car, too."

"Wow, mon. Deep shit you're in. Glad you let me know. Don't know what I can do."

"Mainly just giving you a heads-up. But I'm also curious whether you've heard anything from the feds recently that might be related."

"Not a peep. You gonna call that FBI guy, what's his name?"

"Matt Corbett. Yeah, much as I hate kicking a sleeping dog, I'm going to call him. He may know something."

"Not that he'll tell you anything."

"Agreed. There's one thing you can do for me. The guy working for Gordian and Kade is named Gerald Eldorp. He showed me his mail-order, or I guess I should say internet-order, card that proclaims that he is a private detective. He and I had a confidential talk last night."

"And you want to know what we know about him."

"Right. I'm holding a couple of things over his head, including his fraudulently representing himself as a licensed PI. He could be a useful source."

"I'll be in touch. Anything interesting at HH Racing?"

"We'll be running a simulation today, and I'm starting to poke around looking for possible bad guys at Gamble Oil and Clanton-Suggs Racing."

"You aren't involved in the Phillips murder, right?"

"Right. The only reason I was looking at RF's death has gone away. Gamble Oil and HH Racing should get their three hundred grand insurance money since his death wasn't suicide."

"Good. His ex-wife Liz is at the top of our list of persons of interest."

I didn't mention that I'd convinced her to get legal help.

I was still fifteen minutes from HH Racing, so I called Special Agent Matt Corbett at the FBI's field office on Indy's northeast side. I got voicemail saying that he was out of the Indianapolis office until Monday, but could be reached by cell phone, and gave the number. I called the cell number and got another voicemail urging me to leave a detailed message. I left only my name and number.

When I arrived at HH Racing a few minutes past eight, the building was strangely quiet. Almost everyone except the communications and telemetry team was already at the track. Linda said that Nick Napoli and the rest of the team were waiting in his office for us.

As soon as we were seated at his conference table, he led off. "So, why don't you bring me up to date on the telemetry issue, and what your approach is going to be."

Linda explained the simulation we had planned for that morning, and said that by three in the afternoon, we expected to join the rest of the team at the track. Nick asked if there was anything we needed from him.

"I have a couple of things," I said, "but we don't need to take up everyone's time. I suggest that Linda and I stick around, and let Jack, Jason, and Daniel get to work setting up the simulation."

Nick nodded, and the guys went out, shutting the door behind them.

"What's up?" Nick asked.

"I have a question, a recommendation, and a request, and I'd like to let you know how I plan to operate at the track."

"Let's start with your question."

"OK. Have you heard from your friend on the Laurence LeGrand team?"

"As a matter of fact, yes. Jules Hogarth called me at home last night. We danced around a couple of subjects, telemetry being one. I approached the issue by asking him if he thought that the new model of the Tau Telemetry system they're hyping was really needed. Was he having problems with the current one?"

Linda interjected, "That was a smart move. You got the question answered without really asking it. What did he say?"

"Basically, no and no. He said that their team was going to recommend that the move to the new Tau 930 system be delayed by a year, reason being that the analysis software won't be ready in time. He didn't know of any problems with the existing system, even when I pressed the issue on the quality of data being received."

"Thanks, Nick," I replied. "I appreciate your following up on that."

"You're welcome, but I don't see how it helps."

"It narrows the possibilities. And it supports the recommendation I have."

"Which is?"

"A little background first. HH Racing's spare telemetry receiver is missing. We've searched this facility top to bottom with no luck. I convinced IMPD to search RF's house yesterday evening. It isn't there, or in his car."

"Someone steal it?" asked Nick, his eyes widening.

"That's probable. And whoever has it will be able to receive, view, and analyze all of our car's data unless we do something."

"What can we do?" asked Linda. "We can't change equipment this late before a race."

"Yes and no." I replied. "We can't change our frequency that's assigned by the Federal Communications Commission. But what I have in mind is in accordance with that, and meets the Nor-Am requirements for having equipment that's installed in the car inspected."

"Ok, let's have it," said Nick.

"First of all, we have a spare Tau 920 transmitter standing by if we need it. It's already approved for use in the car. What we do is buy another spare receiver from Tau Telemetry set up for the same frequency, but with a different encryption chip installed, and install a matching encryption chip in the spare transmitter we already have."

Linda piped up, "So that would give us two systems, the one in the car already with one encryption key, and another system, the new spare receiver and our current spare transmitter, with a different encryption key."

140

I nodded. "Where's the spare transmitter?"

"In the lab. We're planning to take it to the track with the rest of our equipment this afternoon."

"The new spare receiver's gonna cost us some money, but it looks like we need to spend it," said Nick.

"You'll also have to pay for the new encryption chips, probably several hundred bucks," I said.

"OK, let's say we do that," said Nick. "Then what?"

"Here's where you have to make a decision. I've sent an urgent message to Andy Shaffer at Tau telling him what my plan is – subject to your approval, of course. If we get our spare transmitter to them this morning, we can have the spare system with a different encryption key by tomorrow morning."

"So then we install it early tomorrow at the track?" asked Linda.

"Maybe, maybe not," I replied. "What I'd suggest is that you send the car out for the first practice session in the morning with the existing system. Before the second practice session in the afternoon, we'll have plenty of time to install the new transmitter. Then we'll use it and the new receiver for the afternoon practice."

"How long will it take to switch transmitters?" asked Nick.

Linda thought for a few seconds. "Ten minutes or so. We just need to disconnect sensors and the antenna from one transmitter and pop it out, then reverse the procedure with the spare transmitter."

"Why not just install it for both practice sessions?" asked Nick.

"To answer that, let's discuss how I'd like to operate tomorrow. I plan to be at the track with my VIP badge, but no HH Racing ID. No hat, no jacket, just street clothes like I'm wearing now. That'll let me wander around almost wherever I want to be."

"Yeah, security is fairly lax," said Linda. "We have to cater to the fans, so people with the right kinds of passes can even wander into our garage and pit areas. About all we can do is say something like 'Can I help you?' because we don't want to upset fans."

Nick smiled grimly. "We've had quite a few thefts at the track. Tools, gloves, anything that isn't tied down. Someone stole my rain suit right off a hanger at Sonoma last year. And Jules Hogarth said that they've even had tires stolen."

I was surprised at that. "I plan to poke around Clanton-Suggs tomorrow. Also a couple of other teams, just so they don't think I've singled them out. But when our car is on the track, I want to be where I can watch their communications and telemetry folks."

Linda bobbed her head. "Sure will be interesting if they are running two receiving systems."

"It'll be even more interesting to see what happens the second practice session," I ventured. "If they have our missing receiver, all of a sudden it won't be able to decode our signal."

Nick said, "This is assuming that Clanton-Suggs are the bad guys."

"Exactly," I said. "It will be important to find the location of the jamming signals, again assuming that we get jammed."

"And what happens to the jamming during our second practice?"

"Maybe it'll disappear," offered Linda.

"Or re-appear," I countered. "Another scenario is that they won't jam if they're receiving data, but will turn it on if they aren't."

Nick nodded. "I'll have Angie cut a PO for the new receiver." He paused. "Should we report this as a theft to the police?"

"I suggest we hold off officially reporting the theft until I have more information," I replied. "Let's just say IMPD is already aware it's missing under suspicious circumstances. And please include the purchase and installation of new encryption chips on the PO."

"OK," Nick replied. "Now, I seem to remember that you said you also had a request. What's that?"

This was going to be tricky. Carol Logan had forbidden me from talking with Harry Wheeler without her consent, but I needed to explore possibilities that somebody at Gamble Oil was involved with the telemetry problem.

I looked at Nick. "Do you think you might see Harry Wheeler from Gamble Oil at the track?"

Nick's eyebrows went up, his face suspicious. "Maybe, but why are you asking?"

"His son Paul is a former Marine. Pulled two tours in Afghanistan. I'd like to meet him, and figured you might mention that to his dad."

"Yeah, I guess I can do that," he said, relaxing. "How'd you know that? I didn't."

"Andy Shaffer, Chief Engineer at Tau Telemetry, told me. He and his dad fly model airplanes in the same club as Harry and Paul Wheeler. I'm also going to ask Andy to mention me to Paul if he gets the chance."

"You're just angling to get invited to HH Racing's Sky Suite at the track, or maybe Gamble Oil's," said Nick, laughing. "That's OK. I'll see what I can do. Anything else?"

Linda and I looked at each other, shaking our heads.

"I'll call Angie," said Nick, picking up the phone. "See you guys at the track."

Linda and I headed back to the electronics lab as I phoned Andy Shaffer. I got his voicemail on his office phone, so called his cell number and got lucky.

"This is Andy."

"Hi, Andy. Wolf Ruger here. How're you doing?"

"Pretty busy. I got your email. Nick approve your plan?"

"Yep, and that's mainly why I'm calling. If I send our spare transmitter over to Tau Telemetry this morning, can you put a new encryption chip in it, and pair it with a new receiver today?"

"No and yes. No, you can't take the transmitter to our Speedway facility because we're moving almost everything to Boone this morning. But yes, we can get you fixed up with a new transmitter-receiver pair on the HH Racing frequency with different encryption chips. Just bring the transmitter to Boone."

"OK, great. We're running a simulation today, so the telemetry folks won't be at the track until about three this afternoon."

"Not a problem. I figured we'd need them, so I brought a Tau 920 receiver and new encryption chips with me. We can set up the equipment and run the tests late this afternoon to make sure the transmitter and receiver are talking to each other the way they're supposed to. You can pick up your system either right before the track closes today, or first thing in the morning."

"Sounds good. I'll let Linda and Daniel know." Linda nodded, walking beside me. "And keep this quiet. Please don't let anyone know we're missing a receiver, or that we're going on the air with a different system."

"I understand. Won't say a word."

"While you're at it, please keep your eyes open for a 920 receiver that shows up where it doesn't seem to belong."

"All right." He paused. "You said you were calling mainly about the new equipment. What else can I help you with?"

"This may sound a little odd, but I'd like to meet Paul Wheeler. I've asked Nick Napoli to arrange it if he can, but if you run into him, you might mention that a fellow Middle East vet would like to meet him."

"I doubt if I'll see him. He tends to hang around the skysuites. I'm usually in the pits and garage areas and busy working, but if I do I'll mention you'd like to meet him."

"Thanks, Andy."

I felt guilty about using Paul Wheeler's veteran status to gain access to Gamble Oil, but not too guilty to do it.

I needed to find out why Harry Wheeler thought that one of HH Racing's competitors was involved in the jamming, and, further, why he thought there was an inside collaborator. That person could have been RF, or someone else. My money was still on RF's death being somehow related to his BDSM lifestyle.

When Linda and I got to the electronics lab, the others had the simulation almost ready to go. They were ready to take the equipment to the parking lot and install the transmitter in Jason's car, which would be the mobile platform.

"What route are you going to drive?" I asked Jason.

"We figured we'd drive around the street in front, Winner's Circle. It makes a loop that's about a mile long."

"I'd like to see you get a little further away. You're going to have a maximum range of over a mile at the track, so a two-mile loop would be better."

Daniel piped up, "We can go across Guion Road, but we'll have stop signs that way."

We discussed it, and settled on a route about two miles long that took Jason into a residential area for a half-mile, but we decided to locate the second receiver and antenna outside the neighborhood. Residents probably wouldn't welcome strange electronic gear set up there.

I moved away from the rest of the group, motioning for Daniel to come with me. We sat on a retaining wall at the edge of the parking lot.

"I thought you might want to talk with me alone," he ventured.

"Yeah. Did you find out anything about that email address I got from Eldorp?"

"Yes. It traces to a company in Chicago, Taravanian Real Estate."

"Great. Now I'd like a specific IP address. I'll try to get Eldorp to forward me one or more of the emails from Chicago, and if he does, I'll send them on to you." IP stands for internet protocol, and would identify the specific computer that sent the email. It is at the beginning of each email message, in an area known as the header.

Doing that would probably require another face-to-face confrontation, but it was probably a good excuse for retrieving my GPS tracking system. Continuing to tail him wasn't worth the effort, and I might be able to use the electronic tail on someone else.

As Daniel went back with the rest of the team, I called Carol Logan's number. I figured rightly that I wouldn't reach her in person since it was only nine-fifteen, so I left her a message requesting that she approve my setting up a meeting with Harry Wheeler.

My life had been complicated by learning who was responsible for the GPS tracking system on my Jeep. It got even more so by a call from FBI Special Agent Matt Corbett.

"Mr. Ruger, this is Special Agent Corbett returning your call."

I was 'Mr. Ruger' to him even though he'd saved my life. At least I wasn't just 'Ruger' like I'd been the first time he'd walked into my office what seemed like eons ago but had only been six weeks. Now that I had him on the line, I wasn't sure how to start the conversation.

"There are a couple of things that have happened that might be related to the ITAR case," I offered.

The letters I T A R, pronounced eye-tar, stand for International Traffic in Arms Regulations. They control the export and import of defense related items and services. Nothing protected by ITAR can leave the U.S. legally without special permission. A lot of high technology is covered, including advanced electronics and software, whether or not it's been designed specifically for weapons systems. Corbett and I had become acquainted on my last case, which involved ITAR violations.

"Go on." A man of few words.

"A GPS tracking system has been on my Jeep for three days or so."

"Go on." The same few words.

"It was put there by a guy working for Stan Gordian and Rudy Kade."

There was silence on the other end for so long I thought we'd lost our connection, then he said, "I'm at our satellite office in Muncie.

145

This isn't appropriate to discuss on the phone. I'll be at your office at eleven-thirty."

He hung up.

Just like that. No discussion. No asking me if I was available then. He had saved my life, but he was still an arrogant fed.

The FBI's Indianapolis Division was located in Castleton, north of the mall, on almost fifteen acres of land. One of the nine remote locations around Indiana, called satellite offices, or resident agencies, was in Muncie.

I helped get the simulation running, and we took data for several laps around the neighborhood route. With a few adjustments, everything seemed to be working well, so I left for my office about ten-thirty, telling Linda that I had an appointment with a law enforcement person. They'd be able to finish everything by early afternoon, have a late lunch, and make it to the track by three. I'd meet them there.

I wanted to prepare for my meeting with Matt Corbett. I wasn't sure *how*, but I needed to have my thoughts in order, and mentally review what had happened previously with Stan Gordian and his associates.

I picked up a coffee at Java Joe's and went upstairs to my office, steaming cup in one hand and computer bag in the other. After I unlocked and opened the door, I stepped on a manila envelope that had been shoved under it.

I read the return address with a sinking feeling. It was from attorney Bob Conlan, for whom I'd worked previously on the Stellar Electronics case, and to whom I'd referred Liz Phillips.

I put my computer bag on the desk, opened the window for some fresh air, and took a sip of coffee, delaying opening the envelope. Confirming my pit-of-the-stomach anxiety, inside was a retainer check for a thousand dollars dated two days earlier, for services related to Liz Phillips.

I resisted the urge to tear up the check, and instead called Conlan's office. The receptionist told me he wasn't available, but asked whether I'd like to leave a message. I did, saying that I had not deposited the check, and my office number. Anything more would have been obscene.

I was seething. I'd only given his name to Liz Phillips as a reference, and assumed he'd send her to someone else, and even if she hired him I had definitely *not* offered *my* services to him or to her. I already had my hands full with HH Racing and Stan Gordian.

I'd finished my coffee, and calmed down somewhat when I heard the *clump clump clump* of footsteps in the hall, followed by my office door being opened. FBI Special Agent Matthew Corbett was ten minutes early. His black suit, white shirt and designer tie were quintessential fed. The spit-shined shoes and Ray-Ban sunglasses were pure drill sergeant. His curly reddish hair and stocky build reminded me of a professional wrestler I'd seen on TV.

The first time I'd met him here in my office, I'd thought that he was trying to make me think he was one tough son of a bitch. Since we'd become better acquainted, and he'd saved my life, I'd figured out that he truly *is* one tough son of a bitch.

He stood in front of my desk, stretched himself to his full height of maybe five feet six, extended his hand, and said, "Ruger," as he took off his sunglasses.

I generally hated it when someone used only my last name, but gave him a free pass on that, this time.

I answered, "Corbett, nice to see you," as we shook hands across my desk and remained standing. "Do you have more photos to show me?" On his previous visit, he'd showed me photos of people who were involved in the ITAR investigation. One of them had been of Stan Gordian.

A smile briefly flickered across his face. "No. Nobody you haven't seen already." Still standing as if at attention, he said, "Tell me about the electronic tail you've acquired."

I summarized how I'd found it in the HH Racing parking lot, had managed to lure the person who had attached it back to the lot to replace a dead battery, and attached my own tracker to his car.

"So who's the lucky individual, and how do you know he's working for Gordian and Kade?"

"Gerald Eldorp. Calls himself a private detective. I cornered him outside his house after catching him in a compromising situation and he told me. He promised not to tell either Kade or Gordian about our conversation after I threatened to tell his girlfriend about his blow job at a night club, and to let the IMPD know he was impersonating a licensed PI."

"Interesting." He thought for a minute, twirling his sunglasses in one hand. "Looks like you've gotten yourself involved in one of our operations. Again."

I was only a little surprised, figuring that might be why he had wanted to meet in person. He had my full attention. "What do you mean? How?"

"Mr. Gordian has contacted us offering to sell information. We're obviously aware of his pending incarceration, and deduce that he needs money to pay off some kind of debt."

"Yeah, he's lost beaucoup bucks betting on the horses."

"OK, we aren't as interested in why he wants it as we are in the information itself, and how much he's asking." He paused, and looked me directly in the eyes. "You're obviously aware of the restraining order regarding contact with his wife Vanessa."

"Yeah, sure."

"What I'm about to tell you is sensitive information. You are not to reveal it to anyone, understood?"

I agreed.

"Gordian is proposing to use his wife as the intermediary. She would transport our cash payment to a meeting place and exchange it for a DVD with the detailed information on the organization involved in our investigation."

I sat down. I was beyond stunned.

He looked at me. "It is very important that you not discuss this with her. This is an FBI operation. We are negotiating with Mr. Gordian. Providing a substantial amount of cash to an informant is not routine. Your life could be in danger."

"But how can you possibly put her into such a risky situation? You know that her life *would* be in danger."

"It will be done only with her full cooperation. We will do our best to insure her safety."

"I'm not sure you can protect her against a violent criminal facing substantial prison time."

"I hear you, but he's telling us he just wants a chance to convince her to come back to him."

"Fat fucking chance." Then a light went on in my head. "So I assume you're aware of the GPS tracking system on Vanessa's car."

He nodded. "But we weren't aware of the one on *yours*. You've been spending time with her, right?"

"Yeah."

"My guess is that Mr. Eldorp outfitted your vehicle with a tracking system while it was in her condo parking lot."

"When was hers installed?"

"I'm not going to tell you that, but you finding yours on Sunday morning is consistent with the time we believe Eldorp installed hers."

"So why me?"

He paused again. "Good question. It could be as simple as Mr. Gordian wanting to keep track of how often the two of you are together."

I didn't think so, but asked, "So what do you want me to do?"

"Stay completely out of this. I hope we can count on Mr. Eldorp not informing Gordian or Kade."

"Yeah, I believe we can. In fact, it's possible he might be used as an informant himself."

"Stay away from him. Stay away from all of them. Let us handle this."

"Is this ITAR related?"

"I can't discuss the specifics of the case. But this is much bigger. It involves our Cybersecurity Division and a couple other three-letter agencies."

My incorrect assumption had been that it was same-old, same-old ITAR. "I've read about massive cyber-attacks directed at federal agencies. China and Russia have had U.S. intel fingers pointed at them."

He put on his Ray-Bans. "No comment."

"I just hope you keep me in the loop if Vanessa is involved."

"I can't promise you anything." He held out his hand. I stood and shook it. He turned to leave. "And we didn't have this conversation."

His footsteps resonated down the hallway. I watched out my office window as he got into his government-issued dark blue Ford Victoria and drove away.

Chapter 13

I sat in my office and stewed. The GPS tracking systems were now part of a federal case in which I had no official standing. And no control. And Vanessa's life could be in danger. All I could do was observe, and hope that Matt Corbett kept me informed, which he probably wouldn't.

I had a fallback position in case I needed it. I had promised Vanessa's Uncle Sal to watch out for her, which was a little hard for me if she was screwing someone else. Nevertheless, I had memorized a phone number he'd told me to call if I ever got in over my head, into a situation I couldn't handle.

It would be time to call the number if she got involved as an intermediary between Stan Gordian and the FBI. I kept that in the back of my mind; it helped me refocus on why I was being paid by HH Racing.

I checked my email, and was getting ready to go out for a quick lunch on the way to the track when I heard the *tap tap* of a woman coming down the hall. I assumed it was a customer for the accounting agency next door, since walk-in business at my office wasn't just infrequent, it was non-existent.

Max's opinion was that walk-ins were almost always trouble, and I had followed his example of not having any signage visible from the street. I didn't even have my office listed on the directory for the building that was downstairs.

If the footsteps hadn't stopped in the general location of my office, I probably wouldn't have noticed the two quiet knocks on the door. I waited. The knocks had been so hard to hear, I wondered if they were at a door down the hall. Then someone knocked again, very softly.

I took a deep breath, heaved myself out of my chair, and answered the door. Standing in the hall was a visibly distressed Liz Phillips. Her frazzled look was accentuated by dark circles under her eyes. I doubted if she'd slept much, if at all.

I must have asked, "What are you doing here?" a little more forcefully than I'd intended because she shuffled back a couple of steps, blinking at me. As she opened her mouth to answer, I blurted out, "Did Conlan sic you on me?"

She lowered her eyes, shut her mouth, slowly shook her head, then said almost inaudibly, "I came on my own."

She hardly looked like the woman I'd met with at the Open Door Coffee Shop two evenings before. Her hair was disheveled, and reading glasses were perched atop her head. She was wearing loose-fitting blue jeans and a rumpled sweatshirt.

With her eyes still lowered she asked, "Aren't you going to let me in?"

I backed up, stood to one side, then shut the door behind her. I went around my desk and sat. "Have a seat."

She dropped into one of my visitor's chairs like a bag of wet sand and raised her eyes to mine. "I was in Mr. Conlan's office when you called. I heard his secretary tell him about your message."

"So you knew he'd had a check for a retainer delivered here without my knowing?"

She dipped her head. "The calls from you and Linda really sunk in last night. I wasn't able to sleep. I called him at ten, as soon as he was in his office, and said I wanted to hire him, and wanted to meet him as soon as possible. I called in sick, and met him at eleven."

"I gave you his number. I figured you'd ask him to send you to someone else."

"I thought about that. You didn't send me elsewhere, you referred me to him. You said he's good. I didn't want to take a chance on anyone else."

"You told him I'd given you his contact information?"

"Sure. Why not? As soon as I mentioned you, he asked me what you knew about Ron's murder. I told him how you were working for HH Racing on some technical problem with their radios or something and had met Ron before his death." She paused. "Also, I put one and one together and told him you were probably involved in the police's decision that he was murdered, and didn't commit suicide."

I had figured that out after we'd talked at the coffee shop. "What made you think that?"

"Well, you said you were investigating an insurance-related issue. That's why I agreed to see you, remember?"

I sighed. "So he'd decided to involve me before you'd even met with him?"

"I'm not sure I'd call it a decision, but when he said he needed to get a private investigator involved and asked if it would it be OK to retain you, I said yes. I really thought he'd wait until after our meeting at eleven to contact you."

"Liz, I can understand that you went along with him. He can be quite assertive. But I'm up to my eyeballs in two other matters. One of them, of course, is the telemetry jamming problem for HH Racing, and the other involves a friend of mine."

"But we both believe that his death could have been tied to his BDSM activities."

"That's a good guess right now, yes. But I can't exclude other possibilities."

"Including me."

I nodded. "Right now, yes. Including you."

"So you won't help me?"

"I didn't say that. But my first priority is to take care of my existing clients. Surely you understand that."

She nodded, and started sniffling into a tissue.

"There is still a possible tie between the telemetry jamming and RF's murder, and I have to make sure my employment for Conlan isn't going to conflict with my work at HH Racing."

"How long will that take?"

"That depends on when I can reach the people I need to talk with." I was thinking mainly of Max, but maybe Carol Logan as well. "I'll try to take care of it this afternoon. We have a practice session at the track tomorrow, qualifications on Friday, and the race on Saturday. I'm afraid it might be Monday if I can't take care of it today."

"If you find out today, how soon can we meet?"

"I'll try to reach a decision this afternoon, but I can't guarantee that." I paused. She sniffled. "We can meet this evening if things work out. But I want you to remember that I have two other clients, and the situation that involves my friend could require my attention at any time."

More sniffles.

"Do you understand?" I asked softly.

She nodded, blowing her nose. "I guess I'll just have to wait for your call." She rose and walked to the door.

I started to ask where she lived, but stopped. She wasn't a client. Not yet, anyway.

She let herself out, and as her quiet footsteps faded away I punched Conlan's number into my smartphone.

This time, the receptionist put me through. "Mr. Ruger, Conlan here." At least he'd remembered that I didn't like being addressed by my last name only.

"Mr. Conlan, Liz Phillips just left my office. You have been overly presumptive in assuming that I'd agree to be involved in this case."

"Really?"

"Really. And you know it. I gave your name to her assuming you'd refer her to someone."

"Now *you're* being presumptive. She wouldn't hear of me sending her to someone else. And she agreed with my suggestion that if I took her case, you'd be the PI involved."

"Why?"

"Come on, Ruger. You knew the deceased. You have background information. Somehow – I guess it was using information you got while working for an insurance company – you convinced IMPD that Ron Phillips' death wasn't suicide." He paused. "You got my retainer. You've been working for me since prior to your conversation with Liz Phillips on Monday evening."

"Nope. No way. I was working for that other client when I interviewed her."

"So your conversation won't be protected under attorney client privilege," he snorted. "Not very smart, Ruger."

"I wasn't working for an insurance company. I was working for a law firm. It's covered. And it's confidential."

There was a long pause. "OK, let's go back to square one. I'll send you another retainer check dated today. I at least want your conversation with Liz Phillips today covered."

"I'll think about it. I need to discuss it with one or two people."

"You have to be kidding. Phillips was a BDSM weirdo. There can't be any relationship between an accident, or even manslaughter, in his...what's it called?"

"Dungeon."

"Yeah, dungeon, and technical problems with the electronics at the racing team he worked for."

153

"That remains to be seen. There are things I can't talk about with you relative to the situation at HH Racing. Let's just say that there is possible criminal activity connected with the situation I'm consulting on there."

"You'll have my retainer check hand delivered in twenty minutes. I expect to hear from you later today."

It was only mid-day on Wednesday, but I felt like I'd put in a full week.

Things were getting more complex than I could wrap my head around. I needed to talk with Max. My stomach was also telling me that it was lunchtime. Confusion won out over hunger, and I called Max.

It was still late morning in Fort Walton Beach, Florida, as Max answered, "Good morning, Wolf."

Previously, he had always answered 'Blitzer residence.'

"Good afternoon, Max. Got a new phone with caller ID, huh?"

"Yeah. We got fed up with all the sales calls. Especially Marie. So I got one of these new-fangled smartphones. I asked the salesman 'Does it make me smart?' but he didn't allow as how that was a feature of the phone. But we can tell who's calling, and don't answer unless we recognize the number."

"How's Marie?"

"Today's her birthday. You know the three little words she likes to hear most: 'Let's eat out,' so I'm taking her to AJ's over in Destin for seafood at lunch, and to Pandora's here on the island for steak at dinner."

"Tell her happy birthday."

"All right, but I know you. Your calls are counseling sessions with Uncle Max. And don't ask about the wildlife. No bikinis today. It's raining here like a cow pissing on a flat rock."

The cow Maxism made me smile.

"Things are becoming awkward. I'd like to get your opinion on a couple of things."

"You've been getting yourself in deeper and deeper recently. Don't tell me it's gotten worse."

"I'm confused about a few things, that's for sure." I summarized the situation with the GPS tracking systems on my and Vanessa's vehicles, and the meeting I'd had with Corbett. "The fact that Vanessa may be asked by the FBI to be an intermediary on some kind of payoff to Stan Gordian is sensitive information."

When I finished, Max took a few seconds before responding. "Take Corbett's advice. Stay out of it. However you feel about her, she is *not* your client."

"I promised her Uncle Sal I'd look after her."

"Don't I remember your telling me that he offered to help if you got in over your head, which you definitely are."

"Yeah."

"Then I suggest you call him. Let the Italian and Armenian mobs duke it out."

"I was considering that. Just wanted to check it out with you."

"OK. That was easy. What else ya got for me?"

I didn't think it was easy, but let Max's comment pass. "The next thing's a little stickier. Bob Conlan, the attorney I worked for on the Smithfield murder, is trying to retain me to work on the RF Phillips murder on behalf of RF's ex-wife Liz."

"And you're worried about a conflict of interest with Watterson Watson. You could be getting yourself into deep doo-doo."

"Sure, I know. But RF's murder looks to me like it might have been an accident, or maybe manslaughter, connected with his lifestyle." I gave Max a brief and sterilized version of RF's BDSM activities, referring to it as S and M. I figured that would be enough to set him off. I was right.

"The disgusting SOB! I assume his ex-wife didn't accept that crap. Probably hated it, right?"

"Right."

"Which places her at the tip-top of IMPD's list of suspects, am I right?"

"Yeah."

"And she doesn't have an alibi. Correct?"

"Uh-huh."

"I bet she's also getting a chunk of money."

I started to say 'no,' then remembered that she was getting the title to the house and one-half of the remaining mortgage, which I recalled totaled over a hundred grand. "She's getting some real estate equity."

"Don't you see a pattern here?"

155

"I suppose so. But it took lots of convincing from Linda Green at HH Racing and me to get her to even consider seeking legal advice. I referred her to Conlan, and he wants me on the case."

"Wolf, nobody's forcing you to take this case. Sounds like you think she's innocent and it's something you want to do… Good Lord knows why. From what you're saying, I don't think you need to get approval from Watterson Watson unless – and this is a big unless – you find a tie between the two cases. As soon as you do, you'd better run, not walk, to Carol Logan's office and work things out."

"OK, Max, thanks for the advice."

"You're welcome. But there's something you didn't mention."

"What's that?"

"You're getting too much on your plate. You're worried about conflicts of interest. You *should* be worrying about conflicts of *attention*. You're taking on more commitments than you can handle. Your clients are gonna suffer. Especially if this thing with Vanessa materializes."

"Are you advising me not to take on the Liz Phillips case?"

"Not necessarily. Don't you know what *I* did in a similar situation?"

"Not really. I don't think I remember that happening to you."

"You don't remember because you weren't around. When that happened to me, I found some help. I hired *you* as a consultant."

I was speechless, my brain temporarily disconnected from my tongue. It had never occurred to me that I would need help with the PI side of my business. Sure, I had Daniel there for the occasional technical job, mainly with Ruger Associates. But hiring someone, even part time, to assist with Wolf Investigations hadn't ever been on my radar.

"So what do you suggest?"

"Talk to your client about it. Conlan probably knows of resources you could use."

"Don't you know anyone?"

"I'm an old fart, and so are the folks I know in the PI business. Better for you to work through your client. If you roll snake-eyes with him, I'll try to help."

I thanked him again for his advice as we said goodbye.

So he figured that it was probably OK to work for Conlan with the proviso that Watterson Watson be informed if I found any relationship between RF's murder and the telemetry problem. Seemed fair enough.

I was left with two issues: First, what to do about the situation that might occur involving the FBI and Vanessa, and second, finding someone to help me out with Wolf Investigations if and when I got overwhelmed. The second one was tied to the first.

Concerning Vanessa, I'd prefer to wait until she'd agreed to be an intermediary for the FBI prior to calling Sal, but by then it might be too late for him to get involved. And given the way things were going between her and me, she might not tell me.

I was caught in a dilemma. I'd assured Matt Corbett that I'd stay out of it, and I'd promised Vanessa's Uncle Sal I'd seek his help if this kind of situation arose. Damned if I did, damned if I didn't. I needed to find middle ground, but I wasn't sure there was any.

* * *

Eating lunch had attained top priority, but I couldn't afford the time for a sit-down meal, so I picked up a tuna salad sandwich and chips from a deli down the block. I intended to eat in my office while catching up on email.

When I got back, a familiar-looking envelope had been pushed under my door with the revised retainer check from Conlan. I put the sandwich in the mini-fridge and made a quick trip to the bank. My favorite teller Francie was working, so I got in her line.

While she deposited the check, I again visualized her in a string bikini at the beach. I'd previously determined that she didn't wear a wedding ring, so was fair game to ask out on a date. I made a mental note that I was now free to follow up on that, given my non-monogamous status.

She flashed me a quizzical smile, asking, "Anything else I can do for you?"

I realized I'd been staring at her and stammered, "Uh, no thanks. Not today."

As I walked back to my office, my fantasizing how Ann Wyland would look in a string bikini was interrupted by a call from Carol Logan. "Hi Carol, Wolf here."

A produce truck lumbered by, belching smoke.

"Pretty noisy. Where are you?"

"I'm out on the street on my way into my office, but I can talk." At least she couldn't smell the fumes.

"All right. Good morning. Or is it afternoon? I got your voicemail requesting that I approve your meeting with Harry Wheeler. You need to convince me, but before we get into that, how are things going on the telemetry problem?"

"I'm glad you asked, since I hope the answer helps justify my meeting with Wheeler. To bring you up to date, we'll be running simulations today at HH Racing of the setup we'll use at the track starting tomorrow. Since I sent you my report last night, we've ordered a new telemetry receiver, and will put a new set of encryption chips into it and our spare transmitter."

"Whoa! Just a sec. You're too darn technical. Say that in terms I can understand."

"OK, sorry. We're going to change the way the data is coded. Someone has stolen our spare receiver, so we're going to change out the entire system so that whoever has it can't read our data anymore."

"That's better. When will you do that?"

"We should get the new system late today, first thing tomorrow latest. Then we'll put it in after our first practice session tomorrow."

"Why not right away, as soon as you get it?"

"That answer is fairly complicated, but in simple terms, I want to lull the bad guys into thinking they've got us nailed, then I want to watch what happens when we change systems and nail *them*."

"Sounds like you've thought it through. I assume that the racing team buys off on it."

"Yes. And that explanation leads into why I want to talk with Harry Wheeler. It is likely that either Clanton-Suggs Racing, another team we're trying to take second place away from, or Gamble Oil, or both, are involved in jamming our telemetry."

"Hold on. I can understand your suspecting another race team, especially one you're threatening to pass in the standings, but why Gamble Oil?"

"I don't know for sure, but there are at least a couple of possibilities. One is that someone at Gamble wants to shift their sponsorship to another team, like Clanton-Suggs." I paused. "I assume you've heard that they're closing their refinery in Indy."

"That's confidential information. How'd you find out?"

"Nick Napoli at HH Racing."

"Hal Handel must have told him." She paused. "So, why does it matter?"

"Put yourself in their shoes. With their headquarters in Texas and most of their retail operations in the southeast U.S., wouldn't it make sense for them to sponsor a team based in Texas?"

"Clanton-Suggs is headquartered there, I take it."

"Yeah. And HH Racing is only two points behind them, and has beaten them the past two races."

"So because of what Harry Wheeler told me, you want to talk with him, is that it?"

"That's pretty close. But I want to approach him indirectly via his son Paul. We're both Middle East vets, and we have enough in common that it makes sense that I'd like to talk with him."

"Let me think a minute." She thought about ten seconds. "I have a VIP pass to the Gamble Oil Sky Suite, and I might be able to get you in there while both Harry and Paul are present."

"Wouldn't that look a little strange?"

She didn't answer. I waited. "Yes, perhaps now that you mention it. A better way is to use the Boone Executive Sky Suite. As Boone's General Counsel, Giles Reichman has a VIP pass, and regularly invites major sponsors like Gamble. I'll ask him to invite Harry and Paul Wheeler. Giles will let us know when that's going to happen, and we'll show up at the same time, at Giles' invitation of course."

"That way, Giles can be the one that introduces Paul Wheeler and me."

"Yes. Just watch what you say and how you say it. I don't want you damaging Watterson Watson's relationship with Gamble Oil." Or your chances to make equity partner, I thought, my anger flaring briefly.

I didn't need a lecture. Taking a deep breath, I said between partially clenched teeth, "I'll be careful, but we both need to do our jobs."

"Fair enough."

I was unlocking my office door as we hung up. I called Conlan, got the receptionist, and left a message that I'd deposited the revised check and that there was no need for him to call.

I left a voicemail with Liz saying I'd agreed to work on her case, and could talk with her in the evening. I asked her to call back with her address and a time she could meet. I assumed it would be after the six-thirty news.

Lunch consisted of my sandwich and a Diet Pepsi out of the mini-fridge, which I ate on the way to the track. The Paul Butterfield Blues Band kept me company.

* * *

I pulled into the VIP parking area at Boone Raceway at a little before two-thirty to the strains of Butterfield's blues classic *Mellow Down Easy*. I could also have parked in the race team employee lot, but it was a little further out.

Cumulus clouds forming to the west were being pushed northeast by a gusty wind. Dust devils swirled across the lot. Last night's showers could have been just a prelude to thunderstorms this evening.

It was tornado season. Every year, a couple of dozen tornadoes touch down in Indiana. Thanks to modern warning systems that include high-definition radars, fewer people die, but in the last year six people had lost their lives.

My racing team ID was on a neck strap, so I put it on, hung my computer bag over my shoulder, and found the entrance gate marked 'Race Teams and VIPs.' There, a sweaty obese man, whose Boone Raceway Staff orange safety vest was about sixty sizes too small and whose mouth was full, crooked his forefinger at me, indicating that I needed to take the ID from around my neck and hand it to him. He held it with one greasy hand while stuffing popcorn into his mouth with the other, looked from the badge to my face several times, then asked me for an additional photo ID. I pointed out that my picture looked just like me.

"You coulda forged that," he said, sputtering partially masticated popcorn on the table in front of him where my badge was now lying. "You ain't wearin' no race team uniform, neither."

160

I almost pulled out my obviously fake Texas driver's license with a photo of a jackrabbit that I sometimes use when the person asking for a photo ID doesn't specify *whose* photo they're looking for. I wanted to blend in with the crowd, though, so showed him my driver's license, holding it up for him so he didn't have to handle it.

"Gotta look in yer bag. Cain't bring in no firearms er bombs," he snickered, thinking he'd made a funny remark.

I took the bag off my shoulder, and unzipped both compartments. I tried to hold it open for him, but he shook his head, saying, "I gotta look my own self. Gimme."

I cringed while he got grease and pieces of popcorn on my computer and its power adapter. As he started to zip up the bag, I took it from him, saying, "Let me help you with that."

He motioned me through the gate. "Have a good 'un."

I picked up a couple of copies of the program for the weekend, with the event schedules buried in pages of advertising. I grabbed napkins at a concession stand, wiped the grease off everything he'd touched, and shook the popcorn bits out of my bag.

A large awning pulled out sideways from HH Racing's transporter defined a makeshift garage area. It was the team's racing shop on wheels, with every square foot covered with sponsor advertising. Featured most prominently, of course, was Gamble Oil.

Everything needed for the weekend event was inside, from a meeting and headquarters area in the front ten feet of the trailer, to a high-tech shop in the remainder of the area to the rear.

The race car was carried in a compartment that partitioned off the upper four feet of the length of the trailer. I watched as it was unloaded by a built-in hydraulic lift. A spare frame, nose, and other major car assemblies were also transported in the upper partition.

With Linda directing operations, the communications and telemetry team was unloading equipment and setting it up for testing. We wouldn't set up all our equipment in the pit box until just before each of our practice sessions the next day, since the two other racing car classes competing also had practice sessions scheduled.

"Hi, Wolf," she said. "You're just in time to help us assemble and check out equipment."

The pit area was located on the inside of the straightaway centered on the start-finish line, as is usual at all tracks. Each team's order of

161

preference of location for the weekend was determined by the point standing in Formula Nor-Am. Laurence LeGrand thus had the first choice, and HH Racing, currently third by a hair, chose third, after Clanton-Suggs.

The locations for practice and qualifying weren't too important, since cars were entering and leaving whenever they wanted to, generally one at a time. Pit locations for the actual race were a different story.

Although a speed limit was in place for the pit area, the first and last locations were the most desirable because drivers could get into or out of them slightly faster than in the other locations. Nineteen cars were running, and Laurence LeGrand chose the first and last pit boxes, at the entry and exit. After Clanton-Suggs chose the next-to-last, HH Racing took the one next to Laurence LeGrand's at the entrance, second as the cars went through.

The main grandstand, where almost all the fans watch the race at Boone, is across from the pits and stretches nearly the entire length of the straightaway. At some road courses, you can see the entire course from upper level grandstand seats, but at Boone, the road course runs through heavily wooded areas that restrict viewing to the two turns before and first turn after the start-finish line, so some people opt to watch from other locations such as grassy mounds located near several of the seventeen turns.

Above the grandstand are the skyboxes, where major sponsors hold court with food and drink being served by long-legged hostesses in skimpy attire. Positioned directly at the start-finish line is the Boone Raceway Executive Sky Box, with the skyboxes for the official Nor-Am tire sponsor and Laurence LeGrand's sponsor, Coventry Tires, flanking it on either side. Next further out are the skyboxes for Gamble Oil and Lumber Max, major sponsors of Clanton-Suggs.

As I was hooking up cables for the Tau 920 telemetry system, I glanced up at the skyboxes, and it dawned on me that we had omitted one important parameter from our simulation. I called Jason and Daniel over.

"See how we have to look up at those sponsor skyboxes?" I asked. Daniel nodded.

I pointed at our telemetry receiving antenna. "We need to add the capability to point the antenna upward in elevation. If we get jammed from one of the skyboxes, we won't know which one exactly unless we can point at it."

Jason raised his eyebrows. "Holy shit."

Daniel slipped into thought for a few seconds. "I was able to use a regular antenna azimuth controller and motor for horizontal direction angle, but I believe I know how to add elevation." He paused. "It will cost about one or two hundred dollars, and take me a couple of hours."

"Never mind the cost. A few hundred bucks is peanuts to this operation. What do you have in mind?"

"I'll install a mount used for large security cameras. Then we can tilt and rotate the antenna at the same time."

Linda had been setting up the system for voice communications between the pits and the driver. We called her over and explained what we wanted.

"Can you get one today?"

"Yes," Daniel replied. "I saw them at the Electronic Supply Equipment Warehouse, the same place we bought the antennas."

"Go for it. I'll let Nick know," she said smiling. "That's why we have you guys out here."

The capability to point the antenna upward would prove to be crucial, but not for the reason I predicted.

Chapter 14

While Daniel was out shopping, Jack and Jason ran tests on the telemetry system using the existing antenna directional controller, and Linda checked out the voice communications system and onboard video camera.

I wandered around. I had never been inside a racing venue the day preceding the practice session. Only race teams and VIP guests were present. The Wednesday population was sparse compared to the crush of fans that would flow through the gates starting at eight the next morning.

With my VIP pass, I could roam throughout the garages and pits at will and not be approached or challenged unless I tried to venture inside a roped-off area. I could stand just outside and take pictures to my heart's content.

As expected, the Laurence LeGrand team had the classiest operation, their jumpsuits covered with advertising from Coventry Tire and other nationally-recognized sponsors. Without violating exclusion areas, I explored the garages and pits for each of the racing teams, paying special attention to the antennas used for receiving the data from the Nor-Am cars.

The Clanton-Suggs team had only one telemetry receiver set up. Of course, HH Racing's stolen receiver could be anywhere. I looked for it in the garage but came up empty.

As I walked back to the HH Racing pit area, I got a call from Tito.

"Hey, acho, you at the track?"

"Yeah. It's interesting. But you didn't call to hear about the track, right?"

"Right. You asked for info on Gerald Eldorp. You ready for this?"

"Sure. Whatcha got?"

"You said he worked for Kade, and his name rang a bell. You knew that Kade almost got disbarred for witness tampering, right?"

"Yep, Max told me that during the Stellar Electronics case. So?"

"It was Eldorp who was caught leaning on a witness. He threatened to kill them unless they changed their testimony."

"No shit. So what happened to Eldorp?"

"Two things. His Indiana PI license was revoked, and he was forbidden to possess any firearms for three years."

"So that's why he's got this fake license."

"Good guess. Was he carrying?"

I thought back to my encounter with him while he was getting out of his car, and my stopping him from reaching back for something. "My guess is yes. But it's just a hunch."

"I bet it's more than a hunch. Don't fuck around with him."

"I hear you. Thanks."

We hung up. I had been looking for a way to pry something out of Eldorp, and Tito had just handed me the lever.

Daniel came back with the new antenna controller. We installed and tested it. It would scan horizontally like the previous one, and additionally could point upward at angles of up to forty-five degrees, or halfway to vertical, sufficient to aim at the skyboxes across the track.

Midway through the testing, Liz Phillips called. "Wolf, thanks for taking my case. You don't know how relieved I am."

I didn't feel relieved. More like overloaded. "I'm at Boone Raceway right now. Are you available sometime early this evening?"

"How about after the news, at seven or so?"

"That's fine. Be prepared to answer some tough questions."

"I can't imagine you asking anything harder than you already have."

She gave me her address, and we said goodbye. My plan was to interview her, then have a conversation with Eldorp after retrieving my GPS tracking system from his car. Somewhere along the evening, I'd call Vanessa. I wasn't sure how to handle the call, but my objective was to convince her to let me know if the FBI tried to recruit her.

We finished the testing, then took apart the pieces of equipment and stowed them in the truck, leaving only the antenna and empty tables used for timing and scoring set up in the pit box. Andy Shaffer from Tau Telemetry called Linda to let us know that our new system was still being checked out, and that he'd be at the track with it at seven in the morning.

I had time for a quick stop at home to feed Boots, eat a sandwich, and pick up a new case notebook before my evening activities. I took my GPS tracking system so I could find Eldorp, and my S&W to help me convince him to assist me one more time. I removed the tracking unit attached to the inside of my Jeep's fender and put it in the same fork of the same tree I'd used before.

* * *

Liz Phillips lived in the Meridian Kessler neighborhood, an area east of Meridian Street and south of Kessler Boulevard, less than ten minutes from my office in Broad Ripple. Real estate ranges from grand estates with expansive lawns and owners with tons of money on Meridian and in the north, to middle class homes just east and south.

Its neighborhood association has been active for half a century, boasting a diversity of residents similar to its neighbors to the west, the Butler Tarkington Neighborhood, where RF had rented a house.

It was still light when I arrived. The homes on her block in the neighborhood's southeastern quadrant were small, but nice-looking. Most were seventy-five to a hundred years old, and had well-maintained yards.

In a few places, garish new edifices that stick out like sore thumbs had been erected, probably after tearing down one of the classy older structures. They sold for three-fourths of a million and up, twice the going price for the vintage homes. Luckily, there were few of them, and I hoped it stayed that way.

Liz lived in a small limestone dwelling with green and white metal awnings. It was meticulously landscaped and mowed. The small front porch with purple asters blooming on both sides contrasted with the wide porches of the adjacent bungalows.

I used the tarnished brass knocker. Liz opened the door almost immediately, still clad in a sweatshirt and jeans, her bare feet the only wardrobe change from earlier in the day. The low light in the room accentuated the circles under her eyes. The odor of fried fish revealed what she'd had for dinner.

"Come in, Wolf. Can I get you something to drink?" she asked, beckoning me into her living room, which was on the left of the entry hall. The dining room was behind it, through a broad wooden archway.

"A glass of water would be fine." I didn't really want anything to drink, but she seemed to need to make me feel welcome.

166

"Oh, I don't drink the tap water. Lots of water pipes around here are really old. Probably some lead ones. Bottled OK?"

"Sure, thanks," I nodded.

"Make yourself at home. Back in a minute," she said, vaguely waving in the direction of the couch.

The living room and dining room both had polished oak floors with throw rugs scattered around in strategic places. The furniture was eclectic and appealing. Maroon overstuffed chairs with antimacassars that were reminiscent of Aunt Edna's house where I grew up were set at a right angle to a modern off-white couch with a curved glass and chrome coffee table.

Artwork on the walls reflected the diversity of the furnishings, from framed charcoal drawings to oil paintings of Paris' Eiffel Tower and Notre Dame Cathedral. I was staring at Notre Dame remembering my argument-riddled trip to Paris with my ex-wife Susanne when Liz appeared, snapping me back to the present by handing me a bottle of water.

"Have a seat. Been to Paris?" she asked as she plopped down in one of the easy chairs.

"Yeah, once."

She didn't press me for details. "Ron promised to take me there. I had to settle for a couple of paintings I bought at an art festival."

I pondered which was worse, her unfulfilled promise or my bitter experience, as I sat on the couch and opened my notebook.

I took my pen out. "So, tell me about yourself."

"What do you want to know?"

"Let's start with where you work, your job there, and any hobbies, outside activities and so on."

"I'm a personal banker at the Glendale Branch of First Hoosier Bank and Trust, on Keystone near the Glendale Shopping Center."

"What does a personal banker do? The only interactions I have with my bank are with tellers." My mind wandered to Francie at the bank near my office wearing a bikini at the beach, and other possible kinds of interactions.

"Well, we mainly sign up people for new accounts, and sell credit card accounts to customers that the tellers have referred to us. Sometimes I refer someone to one of our money managers."

"So you outrank tellers?"

"We make more money than they do, yes. We're between the tellers and the branch manager in the office hierarchy."

"What's your salary?"

"It varies from year to year. Last year I made thirty-five thousand salary, about fifteen thousand in commissions, and a bonus of about five thousand."

"About fifty-five thousand total. What do you do when you're not working?"

"Interacting with people all day is hard for me. I've been told I'm a dyed-in-the-wool introvert. So when I come home, I shut the world out. I'm a news junkie. You probably guessed that," she laughed. "I watch local and national news in the evening, and again before I go to bed."

"What about friends, neighbors?"

"I'm involved in the neighborhood association on the architectural committee that meets quarterly. We play a role, although not always successfully, in keeping the neighborhood free of development that would erode our quality of life."

"For example?"

"We managed to block a proposal to erect a seven-story condominium and massive parking garage just a few blocks from here."

"Anything else?"

She put on her reading glasses, turned on a lamp with a Tiffany stained glass shade on the oak end table, and picked up what looked like a magazine. She riffled through the pages as she turned to me, and I could see that it was full of crossword puzzles.

"Yes, and it seems we have it in common," she said, smiling.

"What do you mean?" I asked, knitting my eyebrows.

"We both solve puzzles. Mine are crossword and Sudoku puzzles that don't really mean much. You solve puzzles involving life and death. The answers you discover change people's lives."

"I've never thought of myself in exactly those terms." I remembered something I'd learned from Max, and added, "You need to understand that I'm working for Bob Conlan."

She nodded.

I continued, "He doesn't give a damn who killed Ron."

"But *I* do, and he's supposed to be working for me!" she blurted out, leaning forward.

"His only task, and my goal, isn't to find out who killed him. It's to prove that *you* didn't do it. Establishing your innocence is the only thing we have to do."

She slumped back in her chair. Silence settled over us. Finally, she stirred herself and rubbed her eyes with thumb and forefinger. "I suppose you're right. But you yourself said that I'm the prime suspect, and I don't have anybody to confirm that I was home watching TV when he was killed."

"And that's only part of it, Liz. We also have to prove you didn't hire someone to kill him."

Her eyes widened and she gripped the arms of the chair. "What do you think I am, some kind of barbarian? How could you possibly....?" Sobbing suspended her question.

I recalled how Vanessa had cried the first time I met her in my office, and how I'd held her. This was different. Liz needed space and silence. I waited, and tried not to think about Vanessa.

When she had stopped crying, and had taken a couple of ragged deep breaths, I refocused on Liz and asked, "Did you leave home at any time that evening? Run an errand?"

"No, I was home all night."

"Did you make or receive any phone calls?"

Liz sunk into the chair, deep in thought. "I think so…I'm not positive, but I'm fairly sure I got a call about the parking garage."

"Parking garage?

"Oh. Yes. That probably didn't make sense to you. Someone's proposing to build a large parking garage on Kessler. It's on our architectural committee agenda."

"Did they call you on your home phone or your cell?"

"I only have a cell number. I got rid of my landline just after Ron and I separated. The only calls on it were sales calls, or for him, or both. It was a waste of money."

"The call still might be helpful. Your cell phone records would identify the local cell tower as having handled the call. That'd at least put you in the neighborhood." I paused to take notes. "Did you go outdoors? Would any of the neighbors have seen you?"

169

"I went out to water the flowers about dusk. I try to wait until almost sunset."

"So what time do you think you went out?"

"Around seven. Right after the six-thirty news. I don't remember seeing any of my neighbors, but then I wasn't paying any attention."

I took more notes. One of her neighbors might have seen her, perhaps from inside their house. I'd have to knock on doors.

When I looked up, Liz was looking at me intently. "So why aren't you asking me about Ron's dungeon? I thought you said that BDSM was probably involved."

"We'll get to that. Remember, my top priority is to prove your innocence." She nodded, and I continued, "Are you dating anyone?"

"I've dated a couple of guys since the divorce was final. Loretta, a friend of mine at the bank, set me up with the first one. I met the other guy downtown at a County Council meeting where they were discussing zoning for the proposed garage. We got to talking after the meeting and he asked me out."

"And?"

"I had dinner with the first one and I haven't heard from him since. I don't think he said ten words all evening. I've been out with the second one three times. He's OK, but he and I seem to be on different wavelengths."

"How so?"

"On one hand, Mike – his name's Mike Spencer – comes across as patriotic and religious. He served in the Marine Corps and has let me know he's pro-life and anti-gay. He has participated in anti-LGBT demonstrations at the State Capitol with other members of his church."

"On the other hand?"

She paused, screwing up her face. "He seems to be overly focused on peoples' sexual orientation. On our third date, when we'd agreed to share our life stories, he was a little hesitant to tell me about his former marriage and a tad too interested in Ron's BDSM pastime."

"Interested how?"

"He claimed to abhor the BDSM lifestyle, but at the same time, he kept asking questions about it."

"Voyeuristic?"

She twirled her hair around a finger. "I hadn't thought of it that way, but yeah, maybe. But also anger. He believes that anyone who's gay is condemned to hell."

"When was your most recent date?"

"A week ago Saturday." She sat up, blinking. "As a matter of fact, he asked me out for last Saturday, but I made up an excuse and put him off."

"So you'd have had an alibi if you'd been out with him, right?"

She bobbed her head pensively. "I guess so."

I decided to find out more about Mike Spencer. It was a reach to consider him a suspect in RF's murder, but his hatred of people with non-traditional lifestyles and his rigid, judgmental approach to life justified his being a person of interest.

Deep down inside, despite my earlier protestations, I wasn't only driven to prove Liz innocent. Also built into my psyche was the desire to identify the killer. I wouldn't be able to let go of the case until I, or someone else, had done both.

I realized that this altruistic motivation was melded with something else. Years spent probing into people's deepest, darkest secrets had led me to develop an inquisitiveness that went beyond my case investigations. Max called curiosity an occupational hazard for PIs.

I put down my pen. "There are a couple of possible explanations for his death that involve BDSM, either as an accident or murder. And there's also a possible Formula Nor-Am racing connection. Have you had any contact with BDSM people since you went to that party while you and Ron were still together?"

She shook her head.

"And the only time you were in Ron's house was when he invited you down to his dungeon and tried to get you to have sex, right?"

She nodded, her averted eyes tearing up.

I stood up. "I know this is hard for you. If you think of anything else, call me or Mr. Conlan. I'll let myself out."

I figured I'd gotten the information I came for. I'd check out her cell phone records, interview her neighbors, and poke around Mike Spencer's background. All that, with my plate already full with the HH Racing telemetry problem and Vanessa's possible involvement with an FBI operation involving Stan. I needed help.

* * *

Pale pulses of lightning backlighted clouds to the southwest, far enough away that the thunder was an almost imperceptible rumble. Indy's historical storm process was for storm fronts to move through from the northwest, but the pattern had been increasingly broken over the past few years, with severe weather frequently arriving from the southwest.

I flipped the Jeep's radio on to the local news, weather, and sports station while I used the GPS system to find Gerald Eldorp. He was parked in a strip mall near 75th and Shadeland. The street view provided by the mapping software put him about halfway between a liquor store and a sports bar.

If he was at the liquor store, his car would probably be on the move within a few minutes. His previous night's escapades, however, led me to bet on the sports bar.

I was about twenty minutes away from his house, and wanted to arrive before he did. My plan didn't depend on that, but it would make it easier if I could confront him as he was getting out of his car.

As I parked down the block near the same spot I'd used two nights before, the radio was describing a heavy line of thunderstorms just moving into Hendricks County west of Indy. They were due to pass through downtown Indianapolis in about half an hour. I figured it would take them another fifteen minutes to move northeast to Eldorp's house.

I checked the tracking display on the screen. His car was still at the strip mall. I took a deep breath, and pulled up Vanessa's number on my cell phone. It rang several times and I had to leave a voicemail.

"Vanessa, this is Wolf. Please call me right away. I hate to bother you, but there's something important we need to talk about." I lied about hating to bother her. I was upset and had the strong feeling that our relationship was morphing, if not eroding, but I needed to find out whether the FBI had contacted her.

She must have been monitoring her phone, because she called back within a few minutes. I heard music and laughter in the background.

"Wolf, I thought we agreed to talk on Sunday. What's so urgent?" Her voice was clipped and aloof.

No 'hello,' 'how are you doing,' or 'glad to hear from you.' I tried unsuccessfully to suppress my irritation at her brusque greeting.

"Yes. I still want to meet Sunday. But you need to know that you may be contacted by someone in law enforcement asking for your help with something involving Stan."

"And?"

"And I want you to call me if that happens. Whether or not you decide to go along with them is up to you, but it's vital that you let me know, and that you don't tell them you heard about it from me."

"Give me a break, Wolf. Aren't you being just a little melodramatic?" From the way she was slurring her words she'd had a few, or more than a few, drinks.

"No, I'm not. And it's really important that you keep me informed."

"Oh, really?" She paused. "You're just trying to keep tabs on me, and I don't like it. You can't accept that I might have sex with someone else, can you?"

"My call doesn't have anything to do with that," I said, anger simmering up in me. "I don't have anything to say about whether you screw someone else anyway, do I?"

"No, and I still think you're trying to control who I see and what I do."

"Come on, now, Vanessa."

"No, *you* come on. Or, for that matter, come with someone else."

I listened to the dial tone. The erosion of our relationship had just morphed into a landslide.

I was hurt, and angry, and frustrated. One second I thought I should have seen it coming, the next moment I reasoned that there was no way, and I went back and forth, getting nowhere except more upset.

I'd been so distracted that I hadn't noticed that Eldorp's car had left the shopping center parking lot. I figured he'd be home in less than ten minutes.

I should have waited until I had cooled down, but I didn't. Shaking and sweating, I called the number that Vanessa's Uncle Sal had made me memorize. I definitely couldn't deal with what was going on.

It rang four times, and I left a voicemail that was short and sweet. "This is Wolf. I need help. Please call."

True to his promise, he called me back within five minutes. I was still upset, and Eldorp was due in a few minutes.

"Wolf, before you say anything, I want you to know I appreciate what you have been doing for my niece."

The soothing tone of his Italian-accented voice helped me compose myself.

I took a ragged deep breath and let it out. "Thanks, Sal." I paused, not wanting to say too much or too little over the phone. "Vanessa's into a situation that involves Stan and the feds."

Before I could continue, Sal interjected, "Don't say any more. We'll be in touch soon." He hung up.

What did 'soon' mean?

I didn't have time to ponder Sal's call. Eldorp's car came down the street as the wind started to gust and the first fat raindrops splattered onto the Jeep's windshield.

My timing was important. I needed to surprise him, but not so much he didn't have time to do what I was counting on.

I jogged up to his car with my S&W revolver held out of sight in my right hand behind my leg. As he started to open his door, he glimpsed me for a second, then leaned over to his right. As he straightened up with a gun in his hand, I jerked open the car door and pressed my revolver's muzzle against his neck, making sure he heard me click off the safety.

I pushed the muzzle further into his flabby flesh than was necessary. "OK, nice and easy, hand me your piece with two fingers."

He did, muttering, "You son of a bitch. What the fuck more do you want with me?"

I eased back, reeling in my Vanessa-fueled anger. I could feel PTSD roiling just below the surface.

The rain was starting to get heavy. I pointed the S&W right between his eyes, saying "Keep your hands on the steering wheel where I can see 'em." Making sure the safety was on, I stuck his pistol in the right side of my waistband, went around the front of his car, and climbed in the passenger side door. The odors of alcohol and sweat hung thick in the car's humid interior.

I kept the weapon in my hand, but laid it in my lap. "You're going to do me another favor."

"Who the hell says so?"

I glanced at his pistol in my belt. "This does. The court prohibited you from owning, much less carrying, for three years."

174

He started to sweat and tremble. "Aw shit. How'd you find out?"

"You're a wanna-be detective. I'm a real-life PI. It's what I do."

"So what d'ya want this time?"

"It's real easy. All you have to do is forward me the emails you got from your friends in Chicago." I handed him a slip of paper with my email. "Just send them here. You probably want to get rid of the paper after you do that."

He relaxed back into his seat, looking almost relieved. It was as though he'd been expecting me to ask him to whack someone.

"Why…?"

"Just do it. Make sure you include all the stuff at the beginning of the messages, before the email text itself."

He looked at the email address, knitting his brows.

"OK. When do I have to do this?"

"As soon as you go inside. I know you have an office here. I'll expect to see them in my email when I get home."

"So what're you gonna do with my piece?"

"For now, I'm going to put it away in a safe place. Let's just say I'm carrying out the intent of the court. If you don't deliver, it'll find its way to the IMPD."

"Shit, it'll just be your word against mine. You could have gotten it six months ago. Just because my prints are on it doesn't mean jack shit."

"Maybe so, maybe not. But it'd still cause you a lot of grief. And Mr. Kade wouldn't appreciate the press that would go with it."

I let what I'd said sink in for a few seconds, then abruptly got out of his car, dropped my S&W into my front pocket, and hurried back to my Jeep in what was now a steady downpour. I stowed my S&W under the dashboard and put Eldorp's revolver into the glove compartment.

This wasn't the first time I'd used unconventional methods when on a case. I remembered being scolded by Max whenever he felt compelled to remind me of guidelines and regulations regarding correct procedures. Maybe I'd eventually let someone at IMPD know about the weapon I'd confiscated. Maybe not.

I was about to bring Sal into the picture. He was sure as hell going to call the shots from then on, but I had a hunch that the information in the email headers would provide Daniel with what he needed to nail down the sources of the messages. Those sources would likely find Sal crawling down their throats. As well as Matt Corbett.

Halfway home Tania Bell called. "Hi, Wolf. Got a minute?"

I pulled into a supermarket parking lot. "Sure. Anything I need to take notes on?"

"Yes. It's about the couple who hosted the BDSM party. Sorry it's taken a couple of days to get their information, but even with my vouching for you they wanted to check you out."

I was still uncertain how RF's BDSM activities related to his death. But I subscribe to the theory that the more I know about a victim's lifestyle, the more hints I have as to who killed them. Liz being my client made it even more relevant.

I said "Don't worry, your timing's perfect. Just a second." I found a pen and paper. "Go ahead."

"The couple you asked about are Betty and Mike Johnson. They live in the Holy Cross neighborhood just east of downtown."

"Uh-huh. I know where that is."

Tania gave me their address and phone number. "I told them the circumstances. Someone in their group had called them about the death of Mr. Phillips. I know you have to work with the police, but please try to keep your interaction with them confidential."

"I'll do my best. Thanks, Tania, I appreciate your help."

Almost home, I remembered I'd neglected to collect the GPS tracker I'd attached to Eldorp's car. In the heavy rain, the round-trip to get it would take an hour. With no immediate requirements for an electronic tail in mind, I left it where it was.

By the time I pulled into my parking lot, the rain had lightened a little and my mood had darkened a lot. Vanessa was weighing on my mind.

Chapter 15

If it hadn't been raining and I hadn't been in such a funk, I would have noticed the black Cadillac parked not far away from where I pulled in. Instead, I was startled by two dark-suited guys who opened my Jeep's front doors as soon as I shut off the ignition. It was a replay of what I'd just done to Eldorp.

"Get out and put your hands on the top of the car," commanded the one on my side of the Jeep.

He patted me down, announcing to his partner, "He's clean," and to me, "Leave your stuff in your car and get in the front seat of the Caddy."

Luckily, my S&W and Eldorp's revolver were both out of sight.

As I crawled into their car, I noticed a V-shaped antenna on top indicating it had a satellite phone. Three doors snicked shut expensively as my two escorts and I got in.

"Sorry about the frisking, Mr. Ruger. We have to be very careful."

My brain finally registered who they were. "You work for Sal Russo, right?"

The one who had patted me down said from the back seat, "Yes, we are working for Mr. Russo. We usually report to one of his colleagues here in Indianapolis."

No hands were offered, none taken.

The driver started the car and flipped on the satellite phone.

"We will call Mr. Russo, then drive around during the call so as not to be conspicuous. Our communication link will be secure."

"Encrypted?" I asked.

"Yes. Not even the feds will be able to listen to us."

The driver entered a number into the phone's keypad and pulled out of the parking lot.

On the second ring, Sal Russo answered. "Hello, Wolf. Please tell me everything that is going on. Take your time. Do not leave anything out. There is more to this than I can tell you."

"Hello, Sal. I know you said you'd be in touch soon, but I didn't expect it to be this fast."

The driver's eyebrows had gone up when I called him 'Sal.' Being on a first-name basis seemed to have significantly inflated the value of my personal stock.

I summarized everything that had happened since discovering the GPS tracking system on my Jeep, and later, on Vanessa's car. When I got to Eldorp's emails from Chicago, Sal interrupted me.

"So you know for a fact that someone, probably Armenian, in Chicago is involved?"

"It seems that way. I already have an email address in Chicago that I traced."

"Send it to me as soon as you can. Gino will give you an email address for me. And encrypt everything. Use Vanessa's maiden name as the password, upper and lowercase, no space between the first and last name."

"OK, and there's more."

"Go on."

"Eldorp is supposed to forward several complete messages from Chicago to me tonight."

"How did you manage to convince him to do that? Never mind, I don't want to know. Send them to me, too, encrypted. I'm sure you're aware that the header information may identify specific computers in the Armenian organization."

"I hope so. My IT guy is going to use that info to locate exactly where the emails originated, and ..."

Sal interrupted again. "OK, but do not do *anything* with the information, do you understand? We have our own cybersecurity people who will decide what, if any, action to take."

I paused. "Is this connected with the stuff you said you couldn't discuss with me?"

"I'm not going to answer that." But his non-answer was the answer.

"Fine, but my computer whiz is a world-class expert in cybersecurity. If you need backup here in Indy let me know."

Daniel was getting his Ph.D. in computer engineering with specialties in cybersecurity and cryptography. I doubted that he'd work for Uncle Sal's operation after he graduated; more likely he'd opt for Uncle Sam.

"Anything else?"

"Can't think of anything."

"I'm in Chicago on business for the next few days. My Indianapolis colleagues will be available as needed."

Maybe I shouldn't have been surprised. Cell phones ring anywhere. "Where are you staying?"

"At the Bella Venetian."

A Chicago boutique hotel on the lakefront where meals cost more than rooms at the Hilton, I knew of it only by reputation, not experience.

"I'll be at Boone Raceway tomorrow, Friday, and Saturday, connected with my work for HH Racing."

"Fine. I'll expect your forwarded email. Rest assured, Wolf, that the situation with Vanessa is well in hand. Do not worry yourself about it."

Sal had taken charge of the Vanessa problem, and his last statement told me to keep my nose out of it. Given my phone call with her, that shouldn't be too hard. At least that's what I told myself.

I watched the black Cadillac pull out of the parking lot. It had Illinois plates. Who knew where it was really from?

I listened to drops hitting the leaves of the maple tree I was standing under. The light rain softened the hard edge of my call with Vanessa. But only temporarily.

I took all of the stuff from the Jeep, including Eldorp's revolver and my S&W, and retrieved the GPS tracking unit that had been attached to my Jeep from the fork of the tree where I'd left it. Maybe I'd give it back to him. Maybe not.

My hands were full and I had to shift the load as I fumbled for the condo key and started to put it in the lock. The door was unlocked.

Not good.

I knew something wasn't right by what I didn't see or hear: Boots.

I quietly put everything down just inside the door, slid the S&W out of its holster, and flipped off the safety.

I'd practically telegraphed my entrance. Moving as quietly as possible, with my S&W leading the way, I explored a room at a time.

Nothing seemed out of place until I glided into my office. There was a gaping space where my desktop PC used to be. On the computer's monitor, which they'd left behind with the keyboard, was a yellow sticky note. It said, "We will contact you."

A quick survey indicated the computer was the only thing missing. A cursory inspection of the office safe with all my computer backup DVDs and CDs inside showed that it hadn't been disturbed.

A surgical strike.

After searching the remainder of the rooms and the balcony, I holstered the S&W and looked for Boots in all his hiding places. No luck.

I gathered up everything from the front hall and put it on the kitchen table, then looked for Boots again, this time with an open can of tuna, and a flashlight so I could see under and behind furniture. Finally, I made an outside search in the shrubs and bushes around the condo. Still no luck. I left the tuna near the front door.

He was definitely gone. His absence upset me as much as the PC's theft. I figured it might be a lost cause. He'd been an indoor-outdoor cat when I'd acquired him, and he could be long gone. I hoped he could survive the dangers of being on the streets.

A password was required to sign onto my stolen computer, but it could be discovered, or even bypassed, by sophisticated hackers. However, all of the files on the hard drive were encoded by a sophisticated encryption system that even NSA would have a very hard time cracking.

I booted up my laptop, which was essentially a clone of the missing desktop unit, fully capable of doing everything I needed. Just to be on the safe side, I changed the password for accessing my home wireless network, and my passwords for my personal and HH Racing email accounts. Finally, I made an image of the laptop using the equipment I kept in my safe, and put the image DVDs back in the safe with the equipment.

An insurance claim and several hours of my time reloading software would be required to get back up and operating with a new system. And about six or seven hundred bucks until the claim was paid.

I'd have to file a police report, but only because of the insurance. Whoever did it had to have been too slick to leave fingerprints.

I popped open a beer and thought about who might have been the thief, or thieves. There were several possibilities.

Someone may have thought they could learn what we knew, and didn't know, about the HH Racing telemetry jamming. Or, the robbers might have a connection with the FBI cybersecurity investigation. It was also possible that the people responsible were connected with the emails from Chicago that Sal was interested in. Finally, I couldn't overlook a previous case which had involved the FBI.

The timing of the burglary during my ride with Sal's colleagues was curious. Was Sal involved? It was remotely possible, but it was probable that my absence had provided the thieves with their opportunity. Sal was on my list, but in last place.

In any event, Matt Corbett and Sal Russo probably should be informed, but I needed to sort some things out first.

I checked the status of my office security system, and that of the building it was in, on my smartphone. An automatic notification and call to law enforcement should be sent if either was breached. Neither had been.

My mind wandered back to Boots. The condo association had an active presence on social media, so I sent a Twitter message and left a Facebook posting with his photo attached. The condo owners' association manager and the maintenance supervisor each got a personalized version.

I examined Eldorp's .38 snub-nosed Police Special. The serial number was filed off so it couldn't be traced. He'd probably bought it on the street. I stowed it and my S&W in my safe.

I made an effort to focus on tasks that needed immediate attention. In my email account, I found four messages forwarded from Eldorp that had originated in Chicago, each with complete header information.

I encrypted and forwarded them to Sal, and separately to Daniel with instructions to send me as much as he could uncover regarding the specific sources and routing for each one. I told Daniel about the burglary, and asked him if there was any way to trace the missing PC. I'd decide how to deal with Matt Corbett after I heard from Daniel.

Vanessa's acting on her declaration of independence continued to plague my psyche. I pulled my bottle of Old Fitzgerald out of the cupboard and poured myself a generous shot and tossed it off, feeling it burn all the way down into my soul.

I repeated the medicinal treatment before I felt fortified enough to write my daily report to Carol Logan. It was short and sweet, concluding with the news that our new Tau system with different encryption chips would be delivered in the morning.

It was a night for the blues. I polished off one more shot of bourbon, popped open a Sam Adams Light, leaned back my recliner, and listened to the wailing blues harp of James Cotton. About two in the morning I woke up in the chair and dragged myself to bed, shedding clothes on the way and missing Boots.

* * *

I got up at five in the morning after ragged sleep. I felt like I had cotton in my mouth and cobwebs on my brain. I needed physical exercise to clean out my system, so I put on running gear and hit the Monon Trail, keeping an eye out for Boots.

It was still dark. Although the air felt damp, the previous evening's rain had given way to a clear sky, filled at this early hour with stars. The temperature in the mid-fifties was perfect for jogging.

In order to be on time at Boone Raceway, I only went about two miles rather than my usual four. I met several other joggers, one being led by a dog, and another pushing a stroller. I speculated whether any of them were recovering from overindulging the previous night. Or if they were looking for a missing cat.

By focusing on my busy schedule for the day, I was partially successful in purging my brain of the call with Vanessa the previous evening. Front and center, of course, were the activities at the track, including the practice sessions, and installing the new Tau 920 system. Hopefully, Carol Logan would schedule a meeting for me with Harry and Paul Wheeler, if not today then tomorrow.

In clear second place was a call to Conlan to recruit assistance with Liz Phillips' case. Checking in with Sal was third on the list. He'd relieved me of duty with respect to whatever the FBI had planned for Vanessa, but I needed to let him know about the stolen computer. I was looking forward to dinner with the Wylands. Eschewing Billy's bourbon for the evening seemed wise.

It was getting light as I headed for the track after eating a quick breakfast and searching once again outside for Boots, with the same result. He had arrived as a temporary boarder and had wormed his way into my affections. I had no doubt that he thought he was doing me a favor by living with me. Hopefully, my social media posts would bring him back.

The gates opened at seven each morning of the event for the racing teams. Fans were allowed in at eight. By seven-fifteen, the HH Racing crew was assembled, coffee in hand, for the morning team meeting led by Nick Napoli, who reviewed the schedule for the day. Formula Nor-Am was the featured class, with the Boone International Grand Prix on Saturday the marquee race.

Two lower-ranking classes of racecars were also participating in the weekend event: Pro-Am 2000 and Formula Nor-Am Lights. The Pro-Am 2000 drivers were typically quite young, some only sixteen or seventeen, and this was their inauguration into major road racing. The next step up the ladder were the Nor-Am Lights, whose drivers had graduated from Pro-Am 2000 and were competing to find rides in Formula Nor-Am. A Nor-Am Light was like a Nor-Am with a smaller engine on slightly shorter chassis, but otherwise similar.

All of the events, including practicing, qualifying, and racing, happened in reverse to the pecking order. Pro-Am cars practiced first, both morning and afternoon, then the Formula Nor-Am Lights, and finally the featured class, Formula Nor-Am. Times on the track for the sessions were allocated according to status, with Pro-Am cars getting thirty minutes, and the Nor-Am Lights forty-five minutes. The Formula Nor-Ams were allocated a full hour from eleven until noon, and another from three-thirty until four-thirty.

On Friday, qualifications would be held in the same order, with the same time durations for each class as a practice session. There would be only one qualification session per class, with Pro-Am and Nor-Am Lights running in the morning, and Nor-Am on the track in the afternoon from four until five. Earlier on Friday afternoon, the Pro-Ams and Nor-Am lights would each have one of their two races, lasting forty minutes for the Pro-Ams and fifty minutes for the Lights. Starting positions on the track were based on qualifying times.

Saturday morning featured the second races for the Pro-Ams and Lights, with the same starting positions on the track and the same durations as the first one. At two in the afternoon, the official Grand Prix ceremonies got underway, with driver introductions, the National Anthem, and a parade lap by this year's Grand Marshall of the Grand Prix in the official pace car.

Unlike the other races, which were run for a fixed time length, the Grand Prix was run for a fixed number of laps, the minimum number that totaled at least two hundred miles. Since the Boone Raceway road course was 2.47 miles long, the Grand Prix was set at eighty-one laps.

The team meeting was followed by individual group get-togethers. I attended the communications and telemetry group gathering led by Linda.

We were discussing detailed assignments for the day when Andy Shaffer and Todd Stevens of Tau Telemetry rolled up in a golf cart with two boxes in the rear. Linda signed for the new Tau 920 system with changed encryption chips while Jason and I carried the boxes to the tables under the awning that served as the Boone version of the electronics lab back at HH Racing's shop.

"Hi, Andy," I said. "They don't let the Chief Engineer out without accompaniment by a sales rep?"

Todd grinned. "Well, you never know what you guys might need. And we have one of the new Tau 930 systems set up in our tent." He motioned over his shoulder toward the center of the infield. "It's in a demo car, so we can demonstrate it by driving around in here when nobody's on the track."

"Andy, you haven't run into the Wheelers, have you?" I asked. I wanted to keep my request for a meeting on his radar.

"No, but there's a good chance they'll be in later this morning. Since you guys don't practice until late morning, they'll probably show up around ten. I'll keep an eye out. Let us know if you have any questions about your new system."

"OK, thanks."

As they left, Jason and Linda were already busy setting up the new receiver and transmitter.

I pulled Daniel over to one side. "I was in a hurry to get here on time and didn't check my email this morning. You know about my PC being stolen, right?"

"Yes, I didn't send you a reply until after midnight, so I am not surprised you didn't see it."

"So, can you trace my machine?"

"Only if whoever has it puts it onto a network."

"So if they keep it disconnected from a network, we're out of luck."

"I'm afraid so. But if they connect it to a network, say to use analysis equipment on their local network to try to crack the encryption, we might be able to trace it through the media access control, or MAC, address."

A computer's MAC address is a unique identifier, like a serial number, assigned to the network communications hardware in a machine. No two MACs are the same, and, unlike the internet protocol, or IP, address, which changes with each location, the MAC never varies.

"You said 'might be able.' Please explain."

"Sure. Maltrack has software that can locate a machine if we either know what internet service provider they use, or we know what server is managing their local network. A new application they have identifies not only the IP address, but the physical street address. It's pretty cool."

"All right. Concentrate on the bad guys locally and in Chicago." I gave Daniel the PC's MAC address, which was stored with equipment serial numbers on my smartphone.

"OK. When should I start trying?"

"Please start today. Also, were you able to trace the IP addresses in the emails I sent last night?"

"Yes. You didn't open the attachment on one of the emails, did you?"

"No, to tell the truth I didn't even notice one of them had an attachment. Besides, I never ever open an attachment I'm not expecting, especially from a source I don't fully trust."

"That's a good thing. Of the four messages, that one was unique and its attachment is dangerous."

"How so?"

"Three of the four messages originated from the same computer in Chicago, and were relayed through the same email router in Chicago, then through a router here and on to Eldorp. The fourth was itself a forwarded message. On the surface, it looked like it was sent from a computer in Chicago, but had a different origin than the first three."

"Where did it originate?"

"That's what is distinctive. It was sent from a computer in Armenia and handled by a router in Belarus before going to Chicago, and then on to Mr. Eldorp."

"You said the attachment is dangerous. How?" I knew that Daniel's field of study included email network security.

He continued, "I am familiar with about forty types of attachments to emails. Some are typically used for documents, some for graphics files, and so on. Some are disruptive."

"So what kind of attachment is on this message?"

"It is a very special kind of malware that monitors every keystroke of the user of the infected computer and downloads all of them when requested by the attacking computer. It infects the computer it's in as soon as the attachment is clicked, or opened."

I nodded. "So it records not only all text entered into documents and emails, but also provides account IDs and passwords for email accounts, shopping accounts, bank accounts, and anything else keyed in, right?"

"Yes."

I suddenly realized I'd forwarded the emails to Sal, and that he might try to open the email attachment. I excused myself from Daniel, and called Sal's number. I was surprised that he answered on the second ring.

"Hello Wolf, I'm sure you are not calling me to inquire how well I slept."

"No, it's regarding the emails I forwarded last night. One of them has destructive malware in an attachment."

"What? How is it destructive?"

"If you try to open the attachment by clicking on it, the software will infect your computer, and will reveal everything you type in to whomever issued the malware, including messages, passwords, financial information, and so on."

"Thank you for the warning. I will alert my cybersecurity people."

"I'm not too worried about them. They'll probably discover the malware just as we did. It was *you* I was concerned about."

"Yes, I am a relative computer neophyte."

"Additionally, someone broke into my condo and stole my desktop PC."

"You think it might be related?"

"Maybe. I discovered the burglary right after our phone call."

"How serious is it?"

"Not very. Everything is encrypted on that machine. It would take the capabilities of NSA to break the encryption."

"Or a foreign government. Don't make light of it." He paused. "I was about to call you about another matter. You did not tell me when you asked for my assistance yesterday evening that Vanessa was not at home."

"That's because I didn't know. And how do you know?"

"She has not been in her apartment since we started looking for her yesterday evening. She is still not there, and her cell phone has been off all this time. When did you last speak with her?"

"Yesterday evening between five and six. She's been working on a project for one of her classes, and it sounded like she might have been with the project team at a party."

"Do you know why her cell phone is off?"

I decided it was time to lay it on the line. At least some of it. "She and I had, shall we say, a disagreement. She thought I was keeping tabs on her too closely, trying to control her."

"And she might have spent the night at another student's place?"

"It's quite likely."

"This student...do you know her name or number?"

"No. And Vanessa is the only female on the team."

It took a few seconds for that to sink in. Sal cleared his throat. "I see. Well. She certainly has an independent streak." The line was quiet for several seconds. "We need to locate her. You told me that someone working for Stan Gordian put an electronic tail on her car."

"Yeah, a guy named Gerald Eldorp. I'll give you his office and home addresses, and I've got an electronic tail of my own on him, so I can tell you where his car is. I'm sure you can persuade him to tell you the location of her car."

"Ordinarily I would welcome the opportunity to obtain information from Mr. Eldorp. But we do not want our activities in Indianapolis known to anyone but you."

"Not even Vanessa?"

"No, not even her."

I was beginning to get the uneasy feeling that I was being fingered for another task. "I assume that you expect *me* to get the information from him."

"That is our most logical option."

"Sal, I'm at Boone Raceway. I'm supposed to be figuring out how HH Racing's race car telemetry is being jammed and by whom, not to mention a murder case, that may be related to the telemetry jamming, where I've taken on the prime suspect as a client. You're asking me to drop everything and locate Vanessa, who has just probably spent the night with another man. And I doubt if she slept on the couch."

"We all have difficult choices to make at times."

I listened to another dial tone. Shit. Things were too damn complicated. I didn't know what to do next.

One thing was for sure, though. Sal agreeing to take control of Vanessa's situation didn't mean I wouldn't be involved, rather that he'd engage my services whenever he wanted to, expecting me to do whatever he asked.

Considering the rest of my day, it was obvious that the best time for me to confront Eldorp yet again was as soon as possible. The easiest way to contact him was by phone. I was fairly sure I could find his home number on the internet.

Trouble was, I didn't have a clue about how I was going to convince him to help me this time. It seemed like recently, whenever I needed information, I confronted him. In his mind I was probably a bad dream. He'd almost certainly hang up on me.

I pulled the tracking system for the electronic tail on his car out of my computer bag and fired it up. It was a good thing I'd left it there during the rainstorm last night. His car was in his driveway.

It was probably thirty-five to forty minutes each way between Boone and his house. My time with him could be brief, but I was going to be gone for an hour and a half, maybe more. I made some lame excuse to Linda about having to serve a subpoena, and walked out to my Jeep.

As I headed around the northern part of the beltway, I was still racking my brain for some way to get Eldorp to help me. Reflecting on the emails he had forwarded to me, I had two thoughts, almost simultaneously.

The first was that I needed to send them, especially the one with the malware attached, to Matt Corbett at the FBI. They had a huge cybersecurity operation that could probably finger the specific computer where it had originated. Also, it might be related to the negotiations they were having with Stan Gordian.

The second idea was that the malware itself provided me the crowbar I needed to pry the location information for Vanessa's car out of Eldorp. It was still early in the morning for him, and I'd probably get him out of bed. Too bad.

Satisfied that I had a plan, the rest of the way I listened to Carolyn Wonderland sing the blues. With a voice reminiscent of Janis Joplin, she represented the new generation of blues performers and was a headliner at the Canadian Blues Festival in Ottawa I'd attended. I wondered if Ann had been out to listen to blues since our date at the Slippery Noodle.

Not needing stealth, I pulled into Eldorp's driveway behind his car. I rang the doorbell. I waited and rang it again. Obviously groggy and irritated, he opened the door wearing a t-shirt and pajama bottoms.

"Not *you* again," he mumbled.

"I'm here to do you a big favor. In return, you're going to do me a small one."

"Fuck you. I don't need none of yer favors," he snarled, trying to close the door.

My foot was in the way. "I'll even do the favor for you first, before I ask for mine."

Offering him something for nothing got his attention. He came out, shutting the door quietly.

"Keep yer voice down. Ya might wake Bunny," he said, lifting each bare foot alternately off the cool porch floor. "Whatcha got?"

"Did you open the attachment that came with one of those emails you forwarded to me?" I knew the answer before I asked it. There was no way he wouldn't have.

"Maybe, maybe not. So what if I did?"

"The instant you clicked on it, your computer was infected with malware."

"Mal-ware…that's bad shit, right?"

"Right." I explained how it captured every single keystroke and sent it to someone who was spying on him.

"How do I know you ain't bullshittin' me?"

"I guess you don't. But you know I haven't lied to you before."

"So what I gotta do to fix it?"

"Take the computer to whomever installs your software. Get your computer cleaned up, get rid of the malware."

189

"Mr. Kade, too?"

I hadn't thought of that. "Yeah, that's a bonus favor I'm doing for you. You can tell him you discovered it."

"OK. So what favor d'ya want from me?"

"I want you to tell me where Vanessa Gordian's car is."

He shuffled back and forth, looking at his bare feet. "How the hell do I know?"

"You have a GPS tracking system on her car."

His head bobbed up. "How the hell?…Jeez…"

I let him stew for a few seconds. "Go inside and get the tracking tablet, and bring it out here. And don't try anything funny."

He started to object. I moved toward the door. "So you want me to wake up what's her name, Bonnie?"

He stepped in front of me. "OK. OK. I don't want to help you. I *really* don't want to help you. But I guess I hafta." As he went in, over his shoulder, he added, "It's Bunny, not Bonnie."

Less than a minute later, he came out on the porch carrying the tablet. I could see that it was on. He had a puzzled look on his face. He looked from the tablet to my car and back again.

"The tracker you provided me is stored with your weapon." Close enough.

"Aw, shit. That cost me a lot of money."

"You want it back, let's see where Vanessa Gordian's car is right now."

He knitted his eyebrows, going as deep into thought as he was capable of, as he signed on to the system with his password. A few more keystrokes, and he handed me the tablet.

The system was displaying a map with a symbol at the estimated location of Vanessa's car on the northwest side of Indy.

"I want to see the street-level view," I said, starting to hand the unit to him.

He pushed it back at me. "I don't know how to do that. What's it for?"

"You can look at the area around the vehicle's location. Here, I'll show you."

A few menu choices and clicks on the keypad later, a view showed that she was in the parking lot of a condo and townhouse development.

I panned around and identified a couple of addresses on condo buildings closest to her car's location.

"Show me again whatcha did," he pleaded.

I started over and repeated the process, pausing for him to nod that he understood at each step.

I went back out to the main menu, and handed him the tablet. "Now, you do it."

With a grimace on his face, he laboriously mimicked what I'd done. "Gotcha. OK. I think I got it."

He looked up at me, perspiration on his face, then shoved the tablet into my hands. "Shit, you might as well borrow it for now. I bought the stupid thing on my own. It's too fuckin' complicated."

"What's Rudy Kade going to think about your not having it?"

"Mr. Kade don't even know about it. Just gimme it back when you're done." He gave me the password to sign into the tablet, then turned to go in. "I gotta go take care of that mul-ware anyhow."

"That's *mal*ware." I went down the steps and got in my Jeep. I let him keep my GPS tracking unit I'd attached to his car. A free gift.

Chapter 16

I parked down the street from Eldorp's house and called Sal. He answered, "Hello, Wolf. I did not expect to hear from you so soon, if at all. I therefore assume that Mr. Eldorp was cooperative."

"You could say that." I gave him the addresses, and described the general location of Parkway Village.

"Very good. We will take over from here. My colleagues will contact you if we need anything further."

"I have Eldorp's tracking tablet, the unit that reads out Vanessa's location. Do your guys want it?"

"No. We will be using our own methods." He paused. I heard the hint of a chuckle. "I will not ask you how you got it, but I suggest you not bother yourself with tracking her. Ciao."

Vanessa's situation was Sal's problem for now, but I had the uneasy feeling I hadn't heard the last of it, especially given what I was about to do. I stopped at a Starbucks on Meridian Street near the northern beltway and forwarded the Eldorp emails to FBI Special Agent Matt Corbett with a warning to watch out for the malware attachment. It might piss him off that I wasn't staying totally out of events related to the FBI operation. I didn't care.

I also reported the theft of my computer to IMPD. They offered to send someone out to talk with me about improving the security at my residence. I declined. All I wanted was their official report number so I could file an insurance claim.

I was on the beltway, sucking down a Grande Sumatra Bold when my phone rang. I didn't recognize the number, but answered it anyway.

"It's Carol. Where are you?" Her irritation practically oozed from my phone.

"I've been serving a subpoena," I lied. "I'll be back in about fifteen, twenty minutes."

She exploded. "I am paying you damn good money for ten hours a day of your time, which does *not* include delivering subpoenas! And how the hell do you expect me to set up a meeting, at *your* request by the way, when you don't have the courtesy and common sense to let me know where you are?"

She was right, and was obviously used to dictating to anyone reporting to her, but her people skills reminded me of a World War II Patton tank: hard, hot, and rolling over everything in its path, leaving an aura of diesel fuel in its wake. I bit my tongue, grinning inwardly at the mental image of Carol's body on tank treads.

"You're right, I should have let you know," I admitted. No goddamn way I was going to apologize. "You'll get your ten hours out of me today." Close enough. "Do you have a meeting scheduled with the Wheelers?"

"Yes, at two o'clock in the Boone Executive Sky Box. We need to have a get-together before that so we're on the same page at the meeting. Let's do it in the racing team's transporter at one-thirty."

"OK, fine. Is Nick Napoli invited?"

"Yes, but he said he might be a little too busy. However, Giles Reichmann plans to join us. Be on time." She had cooled down slightly, from red hot to simmering.

"Yes, ma'am."

I wasn't sure how she'd take my calling her 'ma'am.' She grunted and hung up.

I was stretched beyond thin. So much was on my plate, some of it was falling off the edge. If there had been any doubt that I needed help, the call from Carol erased it.

A few minutes before ten I called Bob Conlan's office. I got his receptionist, and left an urgent message for him to call me from wherever he was.

Just as I was going through security at the track, Conlan called back. "Hello, Mr. Ruger. How is your investigation going regarding Liz Phillips?"

"Fine. I interviewed her yesterday evening, and have several follow-up items to pursue." I summarized my talk with Liz, including the guy she'd been dating.

"You didn't send me a report last night."

"No, it was fairly late by the time I got home. I'll send one this evening."

"What's so urgent?"

I got past the security gate without getting greasy popcorn in my computer bag. "Remember, I told you I had other work, and that some of it might require my attention. Well, that has happened."

"So what do you want from me? Sympathy?"

"No. I would appreciate your recommending someone who could help me, on Liz Phillips' case and maybe another matter to free up time for Liz."

"What kind of help are you looking for?"

"Surveillance work for sure. Interviewing potential witnesses such as Liz Philips' neighbors. Maybe running down cell phone records."

"What kind of person?"

I remembered what Max had said about law enforcement officers who were looking for moonlighting opportunities. "Maybe a cop or sheriff's deputy."

"Well, I may be able to help you. I know an IMPD officer who wants to earn some extra cash. You happen to know him, and he's a good cop."

The only officers I could think of were Tito and his colleagues in homicide. "Homicide?"

"No, missing persons. Jeff Smithfield."

I almost dropped my phone. In my previous case for Conlan, I had exonerated Smithfield in the case of his wife Sherri's murder. He was intelligent and tenacious, and I respected him.

"How do you know he's looking for work?"

Conlan chuckled. "Why don't you ask him?" He gave me Jeff's work and cell phone numbers. I still had his home number programmed into my phone.

I was getting close to the HH Racing garage area and didn't want to be overheard, so I got a coffee at a snack bar, sat at one of their tables under an umbrella, and called Jeff at work.

"Missing persons, Corporal Smithfield speaking."

"Hi, Jeff. Wolf Ruger here. Got a minute?"

"You have a missing person to report?"

I thought about Vanessa, but said, "No. This is personal business."

"Well, I'm not supposed to spend personal time on the phone, but for you I'll make an exception, at least for a couple of minutes."

"I appreciate that. I just talked with Bob Conlan, and he told me you might be looking to do a little moonlighting. Earn some extra cash. That so?"

"Yeah, and I don't believe it's you doing the asking."

"I asked Conlan why you were looking for part time work, and he said I should ask you."

Jeff snorted. "You of all people should know how much that dude charges. He's good. He's more than just good, but he costs a mint. I still owe him a couple thousand dollars."

It was my turn to laugh. "I should have known. He has a vested interest in finding you a gig."

"What do you need done?"

"Surveillance, asking some of the good citizens of Indianapolis questions. Stuff like that."

"Sure. I'm interested. Need to get off the phone for now, though. I leave work at four-thirty. Can I call you then?"

The second practice session would be over then. "That'll work. You still have my cell number?"

"Yes, and I'm seeing it on my screen. Call you later."

As I took the rest of my coffee into the HH Racing garage area, I reflected on hiring him as an assistant. Recollections of working to get him cleared of his wife's murder flooded my brain. I remembered the first time I met him, at his house, when I still thought he was probably guilty.

My reminiscence was halted by Daniel hurrying over to me. "Was your errand successful?"

"Yes, I got what I needed. I also sent the Eldorp emails to the FBI. We'll let them take charge now."

Daniel screwed up his face in disappointment. It was as close as he ever got to saying "Oh, shit," which wasn't in his vocabulary.

I leaned over to him, and said quietly into his ear, "I didn't mean for you to stop analyzing the malware. I meant we have to do it on our own."

A smile brightened his face. "Great. I'd really like to find out where it came from. I can use some software tracing tools at MalTrack. I should be able to get fairly close to the source. I'm not sure the FBI can do any better."

MalTrack was the cybersecurity company funding Daniel's Ph.D. research. An organization with over a thousand employees, they were headquartered in Silicon Valley, but their advanced research and development was done by a small elite group in Indy.

Mindful of the direction I'd gotten from Carol on giving HH Racing their due each day, I replied, "Just be sure it's not on the racing team's time. I'll pay you for your work from another project."

Daniel looked at me quizzically, but only said, "Sure. I'll be accurate with billing my hours."

Linda walked over. "We have to get our equipment ready to set up for practice. We can go in our pit box and set up at quarter to eleven."

"Who's in charge of the system with the spectrum analyzer and antenna?" I asked.

"Jason. He'll leave to set that up in a few minutes. Daniel suggested we set it up on a grassy knoll about halfway around the road course."

"Sounds fine. How do you get there?"

"By golf cart. He'll take a maintenance road, really just a two-track dirt road that gets him right behind the knoll, then carry the equipment up from there."

"He has a directional antenna, too, right?"

Daniel chimed in, "Yes, but it can't sense elevation."

"That's what we have you in the pit box for," I replied.

Linda passed out small portable radio transceivers that Max would have called walkie talkies so we could maintain radio contact with each other. Normally, they wouldn't be needed since everyone would be in or near the pit box, but with Jason nearly a mile away, and me wandering around, they were essential.

"Listen up," Linda said, getting our attention. "Over the radios I just gave you, only the five of us are on the frequency, but anyone could be listening. All of our voice communications with our driver Scott have to be in the clear so all fans can listen, though, so we've instructed him we'll be using code words 'purple' for jamming and 'rain' for when jamming stops."

Everyone nodded. I guessed that Scott was a fan of Prince. The rule that required driver voice communications to be capable of being monitored by fans was circumvented by using code words and phrases. It wasn't strictly according to the book, but all race teams did it.

"I'll be wandering around," I said. "Please let me know when we go onto the track and when we come off, and when our telemetry's being jammed, if it is. I know you'll all be busy, but tell me if you see or hear anything strange. I'll try not to bother you unless it's important."

While Linda and Daniel headed for the pit box, Jack and Jason took off with the remote system in their golf cart, and I strolled over to the Clanton-Suggs' garage area, where they were working on the car, just as everyone else. I didn't see any activity out of the ordinary in communications or telemetry.

Heading now past a canopy in the center of pit row, which housed the Tau Telemetry support staff, I waved to Andy Shaffer, who gave me a questioning look. I replied with a thumbs-up sign and continued on.

Passing the Clanton-Suggs pit box, the next to last one before the exit to the track, nothing odd caught my eye, so I made my way back to their garage area as the cars started coming out into the pits for the first practice session.

Unlike the race, when they'd all go out together in the order determined by qualifying speeds, cars would go out for practice when they were ready. A few got out within ten or twenty seconds of the start of the session; others took a few minutes to make more adjustments and wait for open spots on the track.

During both the morning and afternoon practice sessions, most cars would complete a total of twenty-five to thirty-five laps. They typically would run several laps, then come in and try different settings.

An example was the adjustment of the front and rear wings, which looked like flaps. They could be varied so that the airflow over them pushed the nose and rear end of the car down more or less. They also affected side-to-side stability.

The optimal wing settings were partially based on telemetry, but mainly by the driver's recommendations based on how the car was handling in the curves and straightaways. And everything varied with track conditions, such as the temperature of the asphalt surface.

At Boone Raceway, the highest speed achieved for a practice lap by a Nor-Am car was generally about 125 miles per hour. Cars often achieved 127 to 128 miles per hour during qualifications. Average speed for an entire race depended on how much time was spent running slowly under yellow flags due to accidents, and how much time was spent in the pits changing tires and taking on fuel, but was typically about 108 to 110 miles per hour.

About ten minutes before eleven, the cars started entering the pit boxes, and I walked back toward the garage area. I looked back across the track and up into the skyboxes, but I couldn't see inside due to the window tinting.

A couple of minutes before eleven, engines started roaring to life one by one as I wandered up to the Clanton-Suggs garage area. Only a few mechanics were there; the rest were at the pit box, standing by to make adjustments.

At precisely eleven the track announcer proclaimed, "Formula Nor-Am is on the track."

A few seconds later Linda announced via the radio, "We're headed out. Telemetry is solid."

"Let me know at each complete lap," I requested.

"Will do," she responded.

I started the timer on my jogging wristwatch. At speeds of over 120 miles per hour, each lap would take a minute and ten to twenty seconds.

A little over a minute later Linda said, "Lap one."

Almost simultaneously Daniel declared, "We're purple. I'm searching."

"Same here," said Jack.

"Let me know when you have an azimuth," I said. The azimuth was the compass reading in degrees from north that would determine the direction of the jammer.

I had a notebook with a rough map of the track and the location marked for both the Tau receiver in the pits and the spectrum analyzer out on the course. It was low tech, but would give me a good idea where the jamming was coming from. I expected it would be originating in the pits, the garage area, or the skyboxes.

Jason reported in first, and I noted his reading. As expected, their antenna was pointing in the general direction of all three candidate sources. He was almost a mile away, so it wasn't possible to tell which.

Daniel's reading from his location in the pit box should resolve the direction. From there the Clanton-Suggs pit box, their sponsor Lumber Max's skybox, and their garage area were each in a different direction. I waited.

After five or ten seconds, I called Daniel on the radio. "What do you have for an azimuth, Daniel?"

His reply was slow and deliberate. "Wolf, purple is coming from behind me. At first I thought it might be toward the skyboxes, but that direction was a false maximum signal from the back side of the antenna. I'm pointing back in the general direction of the garage area, which is also toward Jason."

"I copy you, Daniel. What's the elevation reading?"

"You may not believe this, Wolf, but the elevation is about eight to ten degrees."

"*What?*" I was incredulous.

"I know it's hard to believe, Wolf, but the elevation and direction are also varying back and forth a few degrees."

"Jason, is your azimuth reading varying?"

There was silence for five or six seconds. "Yeah. Weird. I hadn't looked at that. Figured when I had the azimuth it wouldn't move, but it's moving a few degrees back and forth, like Daniel's seeing."

Linda interjected, "Lap two. We got a good telemetry dump as Scott passed the pit box. He's coming in after two more laps for adjustments to the front wing."

Ten degree elevation was just a slight tilt upwards, only a little more than ten percent of the way to vertical, or ninety degrees. The height of the jamming antenna depended on how far away it was. A quick calculation told me that if it was as close as the garage area, it could be coming from about thirty to forty feet up. If it were coming from as far away as Jason, it would have to be around four to five hundred feet high.

The most likely scenario was that someone in the garage area was jamming with a standard telemetry antenna either I hadn't noticed or wasn't there earlier when I walked around. The problem was that the jamming source seemed to be moving around. Fixed antennas don't move, not even a little.

After another minute, Linda announced, "Lap three, another good data dump passing the pit," and Daniel said, "We're still purple. I'm getting good direction and elevation data. They are both fairly constant with slight variations."

About two minutes after that, Linda broadcast, "In the pit. Making adjustments. Back out in five minutes or so."

"Continuing purple condition?" I asked.

"Yes," replied Daniel. "I don't know why, since we're not on the track."

"Maybe whoever is doing it doesn't know we're in the pit," I ventured.

Within another minute the jamming stopped. There had been a delay in both its initiation and cessation, a pattern that repeated itself the rest of the practice session. Each time Scott went on the track it was about a minute before it started, and whenever he came into the pit a minute or so went by before it stopped.

After the practice, everyone went back to the transporter. The car was being fine-tuned for the afternoon session, while the communications and telemetry team pulled chairs into a circle under the tarp over the garage area, ate lunch, and discussed what we'd learned.

Angie Murphy, Nick's human resource person, had ordered sandwiches, pasta salad cups, chips and sodas from one of the catering trucks. A racing team's financial status was reflected in their meal arrangements.

Wealthy teams like Laurence LeGrand retained the services of a chef and portable kitchen exclusively dedicated to their culinary needs. They dined at linen-covered tables set with china and real silverware.

We shared the services of a catering truck with half a dozen other teams. The food was good, even if we had to hold our paper plates in our laps.

Those at the bottom of the revenue pecking order had to make do with hot dogs and burgers from commercial food stands frequented by the fans. They endured mediocre quality, astronomical prices, and wasted time.

Eating sandwiches, we puzzled through what we'd learned, trying to put bits of seemingly incongruous information into a cohesive picture. Nobody had an explanation for the apparent slight movement of the jammer. And we didn't really know its height, although it still seemed most reasonable to assume it was something in the garage area at a height of thirty or forty feet.

Daniel offered, "I have an idea how we can determine the altitude of the jammer, and get a better idea of where it is, assuming it stays in the same general location this afternoon. We trade locations of our two antennas."

I saw what he was getting at. "Daniel, that's great. Since you know how to run it, you go out with the antenna that can measure elevation, and Jason and Jack will use the direction-only antenna in the pit box."

Daniel nodded. "Combining the direction and elevation measurements we got this morning with what we see this afternoon will give us a good idea how high it is and where it is, including how far it is from the pit area."

"And looking at the relative strengths of the jamming signal from the two locations with both systems will give us another indication of the jammer location," I added.

Jason looked at me, "How? I don't quite get that."

Daniel explained. "If the jamming signal strength is the same from both locations, then the jammer is located midway between. If it's stronger from one location than the other, it's nearer the location with the stronger signal. We can't necessarily tell exactly how much nearer, but it'll give us a good hint."

We had a plan.

Linda chewed a potato chip thoughtfully. "I just don't understand why someone would jam us, especially since it's probably the same people who have our old receiver, and they can't receive the telemetry any better than we can."

She looked at me. "You still want us to put the new transmitter in the car before the afternoon practice, and use the new receiver?"

"Yes. I'm beginning to get an idea about their jamming method, and I believe that changing the encryption of our signal will force their hand."

"OK. We'll install the new equipment and check it out after lunch."

I looked at her. "You said that you were getting good data dumps once each lap as the car passed the pits, right?"

She nodded as she sipped her soda. "Why do you think we're getting them?"

"Probably because the car is very close to our antenna as it goes by the pit box, and is overriding the jamming. The data dumps contain everything, all the channels of telemetry, for the last lap, right?"

Another nod.

"OK. Let's assume that our stolen receiver is somewhere it can receive the data dumps as the car comes past the pits. They'll have all of our telemetry, just not in real time."

"Same as us," chimed in Jack.

"Right. So we're being deprived of our real-time telemetry that lets us read all the data while the car is on the track. We care about that, but they don't. They're satisfied to see what happened during each lap."

"So where do you think the stolen receiver is?" asked Linda.

"The most logical place is in the pits somewhere, but it could be anywhere the data dump can be received in spite of the jamming. I don't think it can be as far away as the garage area."

"The receiver could be in the grandstand," suggested Daniel.

"How about one of the skyboxes?" asked Linda.

I thought for a few seconds. "Both are possibilities. I'll check out the grandstand during the afternoon practice session."

"And the skyboxes?" asked Jason.

I had to think about that. Then I had an idea. "It would have to be one of only a couple of skyboxes. I may not be able to get into them myself, but I'll bet I know a way to find out if our stolen receiver is in one of them."

Eyebrows went up around the group. "Nope, not going to tell you how," I said with a grin. "What you don't know won't hurt you. Besides, I have to consult a lawyer."

Chapter 17

I made sure I was early for my one-thirty appointment with Carol in the meeting area at the front of the transporter. The compact eight-by-ten space was used mainly for strategy sessions prior to races, debriefings afterwards, engineering meetings, and interviews with Scott Marks, HH Racing's driver.

The décor followed Gamble Oil's corporate colors: red, white, and blue. A small couch, scarcely larger than a loveseat, was along one side wall. A wet bar with a microwave and refrigerator ran along the other. Three padded folding chairs were scattered in the middle of the carpeted floor. A Gamble Oil eagle sign illuminated with track lights adorned the front wall, while a large HDTV screen graced the back wall.

At exactly one-thirty, the door opened and Carol entered, followed by a tall, thin, balding man with a mustache, bright blue eyes and a friendly smile. Carol introduced him to me as Giles Reichmann.

As we shook hands, he put me at ease, saying, "Hi, Wolf. I remember meeting you at our holiday party. Max has sung your praises to me, and I have certainly enjoyed my associations with him over the years."

"Max has told me some of what he's done for your firm. I know he admires and respects you," I replied.

He and Carol settled onto the sofa, and I pulled over one of the chairs and sat in front of them.

Giles looked at me, his face now stern, then glanced at Carol. "You need to know two of our most important clients are involved in this meeting. We must and will protect each of them. You understand?"

I bobbed my head. The old carrot and stick.

"Carol told you about Harry Wheeler's suspicions that one of HH Racing's competitors is responsible for the problems they're having with their radios...what do you call it..."

"Telemetry," Carol chimed in. She may be non-technical, but she had learned the jargon.

"Right. Carol has briefed me on her discussions with Wheeler on the telemetry problem. Seems he also thought that someone within the racing team might be involved. And now one of the team members has died under suspicious circumstances. Any connections?" Giles asked.

"Not that I know of, but that is still an open question."

"Any new developments?"

I looked from one to the other. "Yes. We are in the process of identifying the source of the jamming. But that's only one aspect of the problem."

"Are you referring to the equipment you believe was stolen?" Carol asked.

"Yes, our Tau 920 system receiver. We're rendering it useless to whomever stole it by installing new equipment with different encryption chips."

"Translate, please," Carol said as Giles chuckled.

"The information transmitted from the car to the receiver is encrypted, or encoded, so nobody but HH Racing can read the information. We're changing the scheme used to encode the information by installing new electronic chips. The stolen receiver, with its old chip, won't be able to read our data anymore."

"So the first problem, the jamming, may not be connected with the second one, the missing and presumed stolen receiver, right?" Giles asked.

"Correct," I answered. "Based on where the jamming seems to be originating, it's likely that the receiver is in the grandstand, or, more likely, one of the skyboxes."

"And the reason you want my help is that you think someone from Gamble Oil might be involved in one or both problems, am I right?" Giles queried.

"And Harry's son, being a returning vet from the Middle East like Wolf, is an excuse for the meeting," Carol chimed in.

Giles raised his eyebrows. "Sounds plausible."

"But there's more than that," I said. "Based on what we learned this morning, I want to find out if the receiver is in either the Gamble Oil or Lumber Max Sky Box." Lumber Max was Clinton-Suggs' major sponsor.

"How on earth do you intend to do that?" Carol asked.

"As a Boone Raceway VIP, Giles has permission to go into all the skyboxes," I ventured.

Giles held up his hand, palm out. "There are two reasons I don't like that. First, I have no idea what this equipment you're looking for looks like. Second, I'd be too obvious."

I opened my computer bag and handed him the photos of the Tau equipment that Tito used when he looked for the receiver in RF's house. "Here's what we're looking for."

Giles studied the photos. "OK, that solves number one, and I have a better suggestion. Carlos Gaimano is Catering Director for the track. He regularly ducks into each skybox just to check up on things, make sure the suite occupants have everything they need, and so on. I'll have him look these over, and then visit both boxes during the practice session."

"He'll be discreet?"

Giles smiled. "Oh, yes. You can't imagine all the things he's walked in on during his fifteen years as Catering Director. He could have blackmailed employees from a number of companies renting skyboxes."

Carol glanced at her Rolex, shaking her wrist a little so we'd all notice it. "It's twenty of two. We need to head up to the Executive Box in a few minutes. Let's talk a little more about our meeting with the Wheelers."

Giles sat forward, clasping his hands in front of him on his knees. "We will take the lead in the meeting. You follow it."

"OK, how are you introducing me? As a computer consultant or a private investigator?"

"We're playing it straight up without getting specific," said Carol. "You're working for us on the telemetry problem."

"Fair enough. But I don't want to mention the stolen receiver, or the fact that we know we're being jammed. So I suggest you introduce me as a computer and communications consultant."

Carol looked quizzically at Giles.

"I don't have a problem with that," he said, "especially given what Carlos is going to do. We don't want to tip off the thief."

"So all we share with them is the fact our telemetry system is acting up big time, we're still trying to figure out why, and Tau is helping us analyze our problem."

"Works for me," said Carol as Giles nodded.

Giles had arranged for the exclusive use of the Boone Raceway's Executive Sky Box for thirty minutes, and a cleaning crew came out as he let us in with his passkey a few minutes before two. A slight aroma of ammonia was being supplanted by the scent of floral air freshener.

The suite was between opulent and decadent. Leather upholstery covered the couches, chairs, and barstools. Mirrors lightened the effect of the dark wood and thick maroon carpeting. A small kitchen next to the wet bar was set up for serious culinary activity. Large-screen closed-circuit HDTVs covered one wall. Two rows of stadium seats hugged the railing outside the glass front.

We had no sooner pulled chairs around a table at the glass front looking over the start-finish line of the track than the door opened, and a round head with rimless glasses and a mop of gray hair poked inside and looked around.

"Hello, Harry, come on in," encouraged Giles.

Harry Wheeler's short rotund body angled into the room as he swiped sweat from his brow with a white handkerchief. "Hi, Giles, Carol." He looked around, seeing me. "And this must be the Iraq veteran you want Paul to meet," he said, offering me his hand.

"Wolf Ruger. Pleased to meet you, sir."

My calling him 'sir' seemed to please all three of them.

Giles said, "I can tell that Harry needs something wet and cool. I'll be bartender."

Harry asked for a cold beer. Carol and I opted for Diet Cokes. Giles served us, then sat down with a beer. "Wouldn't want Harry drinking alone," he joked.

I looked at Harry. "Is your son on his way?"

"Oh, yes," answered Harry. "But I asked him to show up around two-ten, two-fifteen. I thought we'd discuss business first, and a personal question I have."

As we'd agreed, Giles took the lead. "OK, we might as well get right to it. You know that HH Racing has been experiencing problems with its telemetry system. You contacted us with a theory that the problems might be linked to a competitor, and, further, that someone inside the HH team might be involved."

Harry nodded. "That's correct."

Giles continued, "Initially we worked with the Tau engineers, without success. We've hired Wolf, who's a communications and computer consultant, to help us figure things out. Wolf, why don't you summarize what we've learned?"

Carol leaned forward and stared at me to remind me, as if I needed reminding, that we were only sharing part of what we knew.

I cleared my throat. "We've observed a few things. One is that the problem comes and goes. Another is that it seems to occur mainly when we're on the track. We've been troubleshooting both the hardware and the software of the telemetry system, working with Andy Shaffer at Tau."

Harry's eyes lit up. "So you know Andy. He and his dad belong to the same RC airplane club as Paul and I do."

"He mentioned that. I guess that's been a long-term father-son activity for both families."

"At least twenty years," he said, looking out the windows.

"Anyway, we haven't found any problem in the hardware. We're boring down into the software now. I hope we find something soon, with qualifications tomorrow."

Carol sat back, mollified.

Giles shifted his gaze to Harry. "Do you have any more information you can share regarding the competitor who may be involved, or the possible inside connection at HH Racing?"

Harry sat back, steepling his fingers. "I figured you'd ask that. Both the ID of the competitor and the inside person at HH Racing are rumors that have been floating around Gamble for a couple of weeks."

"Who did you first hear it from?"

"I don't remember who I initially heard it from. Maybe people talking in the break room."

He was looking Giles levelly in the eyes, and I had the feeling he was telling the truth.

"Did any fresh rumors surface when Mr. Phillips at HH Racing died?"

"Well, it doesn't take a genius to connect the dots. Whether it's valid or not is anybody's guess."

Carol had been rummaging in her purse, and had come out with a stack of business cards. "Harry, can I ask you to do me a favor?"

"Of course."

She handed Harry the stack of cards. "Please give these to anyone you think might be able to share info on where the rumors came from. I want to stress the confidential aspect of this. They can call me on my private line or send an email. I promise not to reveal the sources of anything I learn to anyone at Gamble, including you."

"Fine by me. Happy to help."

Carol had done what I'd hoped I could do. She'd reached into the Gamble Oil organization for information, not only with Harry Wheeler's approval, but with his participation.

Giles looked at his watch. "I guess that about wraps it up, business-wise. Harry, what question do you have for us?"

"It isn't for you or Carol. It's for Wolf – and it's personal. I don't want it to leave this room. Understood?"

We all nodded.

Harry looked at me uncomfortably, shifting in his seat. He took a sip of beer. I gave him time.

"In a few minutes Paul will join us. He served in the Marines in Afghanistan. He came home changed in a lot of ways, most of them negative."

I wasn't sure he was going to be able to say anymore without encouragement, but I knew where he was headed, so I offered, "And you wonder if I know anything about PTSD, is that it?"

His eyes misted over, and he had to compose himself before he went on. "That's it. Yes."

"You don't need to say any more. Yes, I know about PTSD."

"Can you and I meet privately as soon as we're finished here?"

"Sure, be glad to."

We made small talk for a few minutes. PTSD was the elephant in the room that nobody talked about.

After a few minutes the door opened. A tall gaunt man with a shaved head and blue-gray eyes swaggered into the room. He held a Miller longneck beer by three fingers on the neck. He was probably in his late twenties, but his lined sallow face added years to his apparent age.

"Hi, Paul, glad you could join us," said Harry, starting to pull a chair over to our table.

Paul's eyes darted around the room. "I'll just sit here," he said, pulling out a bar stool and perching himself on it like a predatory hawk.

Harry gestured at me. "This is Wolf Ruger, the Iraq vet I mentioned."

I got up and walked to the bar stool, my hand extended. A distant smile appeared on his face, as cold as it was correct. He shifted the beer bottle to his left hand and shook my hand nonchalantly.

"I understand you were in the Marines in Afghanistan," I said, but got no response.

"What outfit were you in? Where were you stationed?" I was still trying to start a conversation.

"I was in a Mag-Taf. We were all over the place," he responded, looking out at the track. I knew that he was talking about a Marine Air-Ground Task Force, or MAGTF.

"What unit within the Mag-Taf?"

He looked curiously at me, his eyes narrow and observant. "Fourth Radio Battalion."

I tried to keep a casual demeanor, but the hair went up on the back of my neck and my reaction must have tipped him off. A Marine Corps Radio Battalion was responsible for ground-based electronic warfare. He and I had been in the same general line of work in the military. I had a hunch he already knew that.

An uneasy silence settled over the room. Giles rose out of his chair. "I'm going to get another beer. Can I get you one, Paul?"

Paul sucked in a deep breath and expelled it impatiently as he slid off his stool. He drained his bottle and flipped it into a trash barrel, wiping his hand on his olive green t-shirt. "Nope. Gotta go."

Without another word, he went out the door with his eyes straight ahead, not seeing the concern flooding his father's face.

Carol stood and looked at Giles. "It's only two-twenty. Why don't you and I leave Harry and Wolf alone for a talk?"

"Good idea," Giles replied. "I'll make those catering arrangements we discussed." He held up the envelope with photos of the Tau equipment he would ask Carlos Gaimano to look for.

When the door had shut behind them, I turned to Harry. "Tell me about it."

He got up, went to the bar, opened another beer, and came back, still standing.

"It's bad and getting worse. Or maybe we're seeing it more clearly now. Or both."

"Can you give me examples?"

"Things that are trivial sometimes throw him into a rage. Sudden loud sounds can practically incapacitate him. But the last straw came a few weeks ago when he beat up on his girlfriend. She moved out, and he's been slapped with a restraining order."

"Has he gotten an official diagnosis of PTSD from a military doctor, like one in the Marines or at the Veterans Administration?"

"Diagnosis, yes. Help, no. He was in an armored vehicle southwest of Kandahar that was hit by an IED. All his buddies, his brothers as he thought of them, were killed. He was the sole survivor, with only minor injuries. He went before some kind of medical evaluation board, and was granted a medical discharge from the Marines, with a fifty percent disability due to PTSD."

"So he has panic attacks more than once a week, trouble following complex instructions, and impaired judgment, just to name a few things."

Harry sat down heavily in a chair at the table with me, and leaned forward. "So you really *do* know about it."

"I know about it because I have it, too."

"My God, I didn't know. I can't tell from your behavior."

"When I get riled up, there are times I go off, not as intensely as Paul, but badly enough I almost hurt my ex-wife."

"I'm sorry…"

I waved my hand in front of my face. "My disability was diagnosed at ten percent, so I have it a hell of a lot easier than Paul. Has he gone to the VA?"

"The damn doctors at the VA, when you can get in to see them, which takes about six months, always want to fill him up with meds."

"I know. It's a shitty process, and meds just dull your mind. Make you as useless as they are."

"So what do you suggest?"

I thought about Tito. "I have a support system, mainly one guy and his wife who're always there for me. I served with him in Iraq and we both came back diagnosed with PTSD. I really think that the fucking

VA ought to get rid of medication treatment for most PTSD vets, and help them build support systems."

"Could you help Paul look into that?"

"He needs to find guys who have had experiences similar to his. I don't think I'm a good candidate for helping him on a long-term basis, but I know several PTSD vets I can suggest. One group plays poker once a week. But he has to be open to considering that."

"He'd never even listen to that coming from me or his mother."

"Does he have anyone he's friends with, hangs out with? Someone he trusts?"

"No, he's a loner." He paused, then looked at me intently. "Would you be open to talking with him?"

My intuition was to say 'no,' but I considered his question for a few seconds. "Only if he's OK with it. I'd want to do it in a non-threatening environment, where the chance of his anger being triggered is minimal." I thought for a few seconds. "Is he able to work?"

"Yes…most of the time. He has a job at Gamble Oil. It's low-stress warehouse work, driving a forklift. He can wear headphones and listen to music. There are days, maybe one or two days a month, when he doesn't show up, but his boss cuts him lots of slack."

I thought while Harry sipped beer and watched the Nor-Am Lights practicing on the track. "There's a risk associated with wherever I see him. It has to be in a non-threatening environment. Have any suggestions?"

Harry sat back, rubbing the bridge of his nose with two fingers. "He's less likely to walk out on you like he just did if you meet him at his place or outdoors somewhere. Let me think about it. I'll get back to you."

I gave him my Ruger Associates card, he wrote down Paul's address and cell number, and we shook hands. I followed him out of the skybox, his body drooped in resignation.

I was paying a high price in terms of my time and emotional energy for the strategy of using Paul Wheeler to get access to Gamble Oil through his father.

* * *

Back in the garage area, I found Daniel inside the transporter working at the electronics bench. He was soldering a connector on the cable attached to the new antenna that provided elevation information.

"Hi, Wolf. I'll be using this antenna with the spectrum analyzer this afternoon, and it takes a different connector than the Tau receiver."

"I'll tag along with you. We may want to try different settings on the equipment. If so, that'll leave one of us free to aim the antenna."

He nodded, sitting up from his work. "There's room in the golf cart for you. The analyzer and antenna go in the back."

We still had a half-hour before we had to leave to set up the gear. I found Linda and Jack loading things to take to the pit box.

"Hi Linda, Jack. I'll be going out with Daniel. We'll be trying a few options with the spectrum analyzer and getting antenna direction data, so it'll take two of us, at least some of the time."

She straightened up, pushing hair out of her eyes. "What about our missing receiver? Did you really consult a lawyer about that? I saw you leaving the transporter with two people."

I laughed. "Yes, Carol Logan and Giles Reichmann, attorneys that represent Gamble Oil. I'm reporting to Carol. Mr. Reichmann has someone looking for our receiver during the practice session."

My mind drifted to Paul Wheeler, and how best to approach him. Thinking that Tito might have a suggestion, I got out of earshot of the others and called his cell phone expecting to get his voicemail, but to my surprise he answered.

"So, Wolf, why did I hear that you're working on the Phillips case from Sergeant Wilkerson instead of you?" he asked peevishly. He was not a happy camper.

"How'd that happen?"

"We wanted to call Liz Phillips in for questioning. She referred us to her attorney, Bob Conlan, and spilled the beans that you were on the case, too."

"Just trying to help you guys out. I know you're overworked." I regretted my words as soon as they were out of my mouth.

"Don't be a smartass. You get anything useful on the case, and I mean *anything*, you sure as hell better pass it on."

"OK, OK, I was just calling to let you know," I lied. Best to smooth it over.

"Better late than never," he snorted, and hung up.

I shook my head. So much for getting Tito's advice, at least for now. I'd try again later after he'd cooled down. I really wanted to find a way to help Paul Wheeler.

After loading it, Daniel and I drove the golf cart to the same grassy knoll where Jack and Jason had been set up for the morning practice session. It was about halfway around the road course, and about three-quarters of a mile as the crow flies from the grandstand and pits.

As we drove along the maintenance road, I noticed another golf cart out in front of us. It was probably two hundred yards ahead and went into and out of view as it travelled around curves on the road.

Was someone else setting up a station to receive telemetry? If so, they probably weren't using our stolen receiver since the jamming made it useless everywhere except in the area of the pits or grandstand. More likely it was another race team with enough money to afford a second receiving station.

Whoever they were, they kept going past where we pulled off, and disappeared.

We set up the spectrum analyzer we were using to receive the telemetry with the new antenna that could sense elevation as well as direction. A few minutes later, we heard Formula Nor-Am cars revving up, even though they were three-fourths of a mile away. The distance was too great to understand what the grandstand announcer was saying.

Two radio transmissions came in quick succession. "We have telemetry," said Jack, followed by, "We're on the track," from Linda. "We also see the telemetry signal," said Daniel a few seconds later.

Since this was a practice session, the cars left the pits in no particular order. The first car passed our location about fifteen seconds later. In another twenty seconds or so, HH Racing's number 33, emblazoned with Gamble Oil's eagle insignia and driven by Scott Marks, came by.

Less than fifteen seconds later, the jamming signal came on the air. "I'll handle the antenna," said Daniel, watching the signal strength vary as he changed where the antenna was pointed, both in direction and elevation.

If the jamming was coming from the garage area as we both assumed, the elevation, or tilt upward, would be minimal since the garage area was only hundreds of feet from the pits, and we were nearly four thousand feet away. As I worked at the controls of the spectrum analyzer, sharpening up the signal quality, Daniel touched my shoulder.

"Look at this, Wolf. I don't believe it." The elevation reading was hovering between ten and twelve degrees above horizontal. Combined with the eight to ten degree reading we had gotten that morning in the pit area, two things, both hard to understand, were true. First, the jammer was closer to us than to the pits, and second, that it was at an elevation of hundreds of feet.

Using my smartphone's calculator, I figured out that the jammer was about eighteen hundred feet from us or around twenty-two hundred feet from the pits, and that it was at an altitude of approximately three hundred feet. The direction information, or azimuth, from our antenna and the pit box antenna placed the source above the middle of the thick woods that filled the inside of the road course.

"Balloon?" asked Daniel, looking over my shoulder.

But my mind was back in Iraq, and I was speechless for several seconds. I was finally able to stammer, "Possibly. Not likely. Probably a hovering drone, maybe a quad-copter."

We were being jammed by a UAV, an unmanned air vehicle.

Chapter 18

After three laps, when our car went into the pits for the first time, Daniel asked, "Wolf, what are you going to do about the jamming? Shouldn't we let Linda and the others know?"

"I'm not sure what to do. I'm so surprised by the way it's being done I need to think about it. And no, I'm not going to tell anyone else on the radio. Whoever's jamming us is technically sophisticated and might be listening to our conversations."

Part of me – an angry part fueled by PTSD – wanted to charge into the woods like the cavalry. Problem was, with that approach I'd likely end up like Custer.

I needed to carefully weigh alternatives and consequences. The person or persons in the woods were emulating a military UAV jamming mission, and could be armed.

I decided to lie low for now. We hadn't said anything on the radio related to our guess that the jamming was coming from an antenna in the garage area. If they didn't know we were onto them, they would almost certainly be back tomorrow. Same place, same station.

The remainder of the afternoon practice session was a repeat performance of the morning session. Each time HH Racing's car entered the track, jamming started after about a minute, and each time it came into the pit the jamming stopped after about a minute.

We were using a different encryption code for transmitting the data, and whoever was jamming seemed not to care whether they were able to read our data. Maybe they didn't even know the encryption had been changed. The stolen receiver was almost certainly in a different location than the jammer's position in the midst of the woods. I called Giles' cell phone as we rode the golf cart back to the garage area to learn whether Carlos Gaimano had found anything noteworthy in the skyboxes.

"Hi, Wolf. I was just about to call you. Carlos is here, and has an interesting tale to tell. I'd rather you hear it from him; I'm sure I'd garble it in translation."

"You didn't tell him about the stolen receiver?"

"No, no. He was just looking, and you can rely on what he tells you going no further than him."

"OK, put him on. Turn on the speaker so I can hear both of you."
He did.

"Hello, Wolf. Carlos here. I didn't want to appear to be focusing on just the two skyboxes you mentioned, so I looked into all of them. The piece of equipment in the photo was in two of the boxes."

"*Two?* Are you sure?"

"Yes, sir. One of them was in the Coventry Tire box, Laurence LeGrand sponsors, and the other was in Lumber Max's box, one of the boxes you asked me to check."

"But none in the Gamble Oil box?"

"No sir."

"Were they being used? Were people paying attention to them?"

"Oh, yes sir, and in very different ways." In the background, I heard Giles chuckle.

"How so?"

"In the Coventry Tire Sky Box, it was sitting between two large digital screens that showed data coming from their car, and the people were looking at the Laurence LeGrand car itself by video on a third screen."

"And in the Lumber Max box?"

"Well, sir, three people were leaning over it, turning knobs and cursing," Carlos said seriously. I heard a guffaw from Giles.

I could hardly keep from laughing myself. "Thank you Carlos, you did a great job. Giles, we owe Carlos a bottle of wine."

"You're welcome, sir," said Carlos.

"I'll put the wine on your expense account," joked Giles. There was a pause. "I just took the phone off speaker. I assume that narrows your search for the receiver. Sounds like your new coding gizmo…"

"Encryption chip."

"Yes, encryption chip, had the desired effect."

"Probably. We don't have any proof that the unit in the Lumber Max box was ours, though. Could have been inept operators or some other problem."

"Now you're sounding like a defense attorney, but you're right. Can't jump to conclusions. Any news from your efforts this afternoon?"

I didn't know how to respond to that. I was almost certain that our jamming was coming from an unmanned air vehicle, or drone, but I wasn't prepared to say that until I had more evidence. It could be originating from a balloon, or from a three-hundred-foot-high antenna located in the woods. The fact that our direction and elevation measurements were varying slightly might be due to the way the signal was being affected by wind blowing the trees, or something else.

I settled for saying, "We made some significant progress that I don't want to discuss on the phone. I expect we'll get our answer tomorrow, during qualifications."

"All right. Make sure you include whatever it is you're not telling me in your report to Carol this evening."

I agreed.

As Daniel pulled the golf cart into the garage area, I cautioned him, "Don't tell anyone about our elevation readings. I'll share some of it with Nick and Linda, but not all."

He nodded. "I won't say a word."

Linda walked over as we were unloading the spectrum analyzer and antenna from the cart. "What did you guys find out? You were rather quiet on the radio."

I beckoned her away out of earshot from the others, and said, "We think the jamming is coming from the woods in the middle of the course. I need to figure out what to do about it, so keep this to yourself."

"But we were getting elevation readings of eight to ten degrees from the pits. What did you measure from your afternoon site?"

"Ten to twelve degrees." Her eyebrows shot up. "We figure the altitude of the jammer at about three hundred feet."

She pulled thoughtfully at her ponytail, looking puzzled, then asked, "Balloon?"

I didn't want to share my belief about a drone being the source, so said, "Maybe. There are other possibilities. Do you know if there is an antenna, maybe for a radio or TV station, or a cell tower, something like that, in the woods?"

"I don't think so, but I'm not sure. I'll see if I can find someone connected with Boone who can answer that."

My phone rang. I could see it was Jeff Smithfield, so pointed at the phone as I moved away. She nodded and left.

"Hi, Jeff. Off work?" My watch read four-forty.

"Yes. Do you want to talk on the phone, or meet somewhere?"

"Let's meet. I have a dinner engagement at six. I need to stop by home on the way. It's in Broad Ripple. Can you meet me there in twenty minutes?"

"Sure. Just give me the address."

About halfway there, my phone beeped, telling me I had a text message. When I stopped at a red light, I glanced at it.

`Have info and more for you, Ann`

I texted back, 'Great, see you at six, Wolf,' sending before the light turned green. I wasn't comfortable with text message shorthand. Things like 'CU@6' didn't come naturally.

She must have found information on the manufacturer of the jammer being used. I assumed 'and more' referred to additional facts such as the specific electronic warfare hardware it was used in. It turned out to be an incorrect assumption.

* * *

Jeff Smithfield was waiting for me, leaning against the wall just beyond my door, a sleeveless Pacers t-shirt draped over his barrel chest. As he straightened up to shake my hand, I glimpsed the IMPD shield tattooed on his upper right arm.

At five nine he was shorter than the average police officer, more than making up for it in bulk and athletic ability. I'd seen the workout room in his basement and knew he was an avid weightlifter.

His sandy hair in a burr haircut topped a square head that sat on a bullish neck. His nose appeared to have been broken at least once, and his swaggering demeanor told the world that he wasn't afraid of getting it broken again.

"You didn't see Boots running around, did you?" I asked as I shook his hand.

"Sherri's cat that you adopted? No. Why?"

"He's on the lam. Took off during a break-in I had last night."

He followed me into the condo and down the hall as I filled him in on the details. I motioned toward the kitchen. "Grab yourself a beer or a soda."

I carried my computer bag and S&W into the office and locked the revolver in the safe. I gathered the case notebooks for Liz Phillips and HH Racing and the notebook with entries related to the Vanessa and FBI situation, and took them to the kitchen table.

Jeff was sipping a Sam Adams Light, a notebook and pen in front of him. "Got something for me?"

"Yeah. Why don't you look these over. It'll help if you know the background on all three matters. Two are cases. One is the Phillips murder; the other is HH Racing computer consulting that now involves theft and telemetry jamming. The third is something I'm involved in that isn't really a case, since I'm not getting paid for it, but involves people you'll probably recognize. Something may come up that you can help with. I'm due for dinner at six out at Geist, so I'll jump in the shower while you read."

He nodded. "Any of them related?"

"I'm not sure. That's something you're going to help me find out."

"OK." He put the notebooks in a stack and started to review the one on top. I was back in the kitchen in fifteen minutes, dressed in a polo shirt and cargo shorts, still toweling off my hair.

He shut the third notebook and put down his pen. "I remember Stan Gordian and Rudolph Kade. They were in cahoots on the previous case, right?"

I nodded. "Also a few others, but they were key players."

"So who's this Eldorp guy that works for Kade? Looks like you've turned him into a useful source after he put the GPS tracker on your car."

"I guess so. He's a gofer for Kade, and he might come in handy." I thought to myself that his usefulness was mainly pure luck.

"You have a lot in your inbox. What do you want me to help with?"

"The telemetry jamming is quite technical. I probably need to focus there. On the murder case there is interviewing that needs to be done with RF Phillips' neighbors, Liz Phillips' neighbors, and the guy she dated, Mike Spencer, an anti-gay, pro-life ex-jarhead."

"I could do any of that. What else is there?"

I picked up the Phillips case notebook and thumbed through it. "We need to see what calls Liz Phillips got around the time RF Phillips, Ron as she called him, was murdered. She only has a cell phone, but see what you can find."

"I can look into that. Have to be careful. Anything else?"

I pointed to one of the last entries in the Phillips case notebook. "You could interview the BDSM couple to get a feel for the likelihood that RF's death was an accident."

Jeff sat back stiff-backed and held his hand up palm-out. "No thanks. I don't think I'd do very well around those folks." He paused to take a swallow of beer. "You mentioned surveillance."

"That's possible. The situation with Vanessa Russo and the FBI in the third notebook is being managed by her uncle Sal Russo. He has his own people, but I won't be surprised if he calls me for help."

"Mafia?"

"Supposedly retired."

Jeff grunted. "They only *retire* when they *expire*."

"Clever." I had him copy Liz and RF's addresses out of the notebook, along with her cell number, and Mike Spencer's information. "Start with RF's neighbors, but don't bother with the house across the street belonging to the Hadsalls." I flipped pages in the notebook, and pointed to the address. "I've already interviewed them."

"What are we looking for?"

I liked his use of the word 'we.' "Focus on what anyone saw the evening of the murder. People coming and going from Phillips' house. Find out their general impression of Phillips. Did he have any regular visitors? Was he a party animal?"

"Can do." He put down his pen and looked at me. "Who do I tell people I am?"

I gave him one of my Wolf Investigations cards. "Get some cards like this made, but with your name and cell number. You can get them at most office supply places while you wait. Bring me the bill. Tell folks you're looking into insurance-related matters. That's true as far as it goes."

"How much time do you want me to put in?"

"As much as it takes." I looked at him. "You haven't asked how much you get paid."

He fidgeted, obviously uncomfortable with the topic. "I figure you'll be fair. What do you suggest?"

I quoted an hourly rate about fifty percent more than he was making as a cop, and about two-thirds of what I was getting paid by Conlan. He agreed, and we shook on it.

"Thanks for calling me," he said. "I can use the money, and it has to be more interesting than chasing missing persons."

"You're welcome. I'm not sure about interesting. At least it'll be less boring. Wait a second, and I'll walk out with you."

I picked up my tennis racquet and bag with the DVDs and the tennis clothes I'd change into, and went downstairs to the parking lot with him. Still no sign of Boots.

* * *

It felt like the load on my shoulders had lightened. I was a little apprehensive about Jeff's inexperience doing PI-related work, but I trusted his integrity.

I punched the number of Betty and Mike Johnson, hosts of the BDSM event, into my cell phone. I didn't know what to expect.

A pleasant female voice said, "This is Betty. Who's calling, please?"

"It's Wolf Ruger. Tania Bell said you and your husband are willing to talk with me."

"It's about that poor man, Mr. Phillips, isn't it?"

"Yes. He died in his dungeon." I didn't say how, and she didn't ask.

"I don't know how we can help. He attended one of our scenes, or events, a few months ago, but we hardly knew who he was. You don't think we had anything to do with his death, do you?"

I didn't answer directly. Since I didn't know exactly how he died, I didn't feel like letting them off the hook quite yet. "I'm looking for some insight into the BDSM lifestyle, and how he was involved. I'm hoping you'll help me. I'll keep our discussion confidential."

I could hear her let out a breath. "Tania Bell vouched for you, so we're willing to talk if we keep it general. When do you want to meet?"

"I'm working all day Saturday. I could come over in the evening."

"I'm afraid that won't work. We're attending an event. How about tomorrow evening?"

"I may have an event myself tomorrow…not your kind of event, I suspect, but I can probably show up sometime between seven and eight."

She laughed. "The jargon can get in the way, that's for sure. We're here all evening. Just call when you know what time you'll be here."

I confirmed their address in the Holy Cross neighborhood and we hung up.

She had sounded perfectly normal and amiable. I didn't know what I'd expected, maybe a husky macho female dominatrix snapping at me. I realized I hadn't learned from my experience with Tania Bell to approach people with different lifestyles without preconceived notions.

The rest of the way out to the Wylands' home, or hacienda, as Billy had laughingly called it, I listened to the CD *Too Hot for the Devil* featuring the country blues mandolin of "Yank" Rachell, a revered "elder statesman" of the blues. He recorded the album at the ripe young age of eighty-seven, just before his death. He appeared regularly at the Slippery Noodle in Indy, where I had seen him perform while on leave from Iraq.

Yank's music continued to soothe the wounds in my soul.

Chapter 19

Billy Wyland's estate was on Geist Reservoir. The immense two-story limestone mansion featured a red tile roof, a four-car garage, a tennis court, and an Olympic-sized swimming pool. Sitting on two acres of pricey real estate, it was worth two or three million dollars, about average for the neighborhood.

I parked in the brick-paved circular driveway, grabbed my racquet and bag, and sprinted up the steps. Ann answered the doorbell wearing a blouse and slacks that looked like professional work clothes, and carrying black low-heeled shoes in one hand.

"Hi, Wolf," she said, smiling. "I left work a little late. Just got home."

She kissed me quickly on the lips, her icy blue eyes sparkling like the sun on water. Either she was blushing, or her face was flushed from the effort of running to the door.

"Hi, Ann. Do I change the same place as last time?"

"Yes, the guest bathroom. You know your way, right?"

"Sure."

"I'll change upstairs and meet you here, OK?"

"Yep. See you in a while."

I watched her as she ran up the stairs. Nice view, I thought, then went into the cavernous guest bathroom to change. Located there was a bookcase full of backgammon books I'd seen on my last visit. Billy Wyland and I had both played, me in Iraq and he with his now deceased wife. Painful memories for each of us.

I changed into navy tennis shorts and a blue nylon running shirt, picked up my racquet, a can of balls, and a small towel, then went back into the foyer to wait.

A few minutes later Ann appeared, as gorgeous and sexy as I'd remembered her from our previous tennis match. As she came downstairs carrying her racquet, her auburn hair in a ponytail swinging from side to side, my eyes roved over her tennis ensemble.

She came toward me, head cocked and eyebrows raised. "What are you looking at?"

"You. Is that the outfit you wore when we played before?" I asked.

Her face reddened. It was definitely a blush. "Guys usually don't remember stuff like what clothes women wear, but I think it's romantic," she replied.

"So, is it?" I asked, raising my eyebrows.

"Sort of. I was wearing a different colored top, but the tennis skirt's the same, and I believe the panties are the same color. I could tell that you were focusing below my waist last time," she said, laughing. "No wonder I beat you."

"Maybe I was. You have great legs." I paused. This conversation was not going in the direction I expected. Something was up. "When did you say your dad would be home?"

"Oh, I forgot to tell you. He won't be here for dinner."

"About what time do you expect him?"

She moved up close to me and tilted her head up, grinning, her eyes twinkling. If she'd been a cat, I'd have inspected her for canary feathers. "Well…not 'til tomorrow morning."

My knees went weak. I'd counted on Billy Wyland being there to chaperone. To keep things non-sexual. To provide dinner conversation. To drink bourbon with. Maybe play backgammon.

Instead, I was alone with a gorgeous woman who had a flirtatious look in her eyes and sex on her mind. The words 'and more' in her earlier text message took on a whole new meaning.

I stammered, "What's going on? Are you trying to seduce me?"

She laughed, then stood on her tiptoes, pressing her body against mine, and kissed me with one arm around my neck. It was a tongue exploring, fuck-me kiss.

She murmured in my ear, "We'll take things one step at a time. First tennis. Then dinner. Then, who knows what? Whatever we do after dinner will be by mutual consent."

"Mutual consent, huh?" Our pelvises were practically glued together, the bulge in my shorts pressed against her pubic mound through the thin fabric of her skirt and panties.

"Sure. Totally mutual." She rubbed her pelvis playfully against mine, then stepped away, turned and walked toward the kitchen. "I have to get dinner started before we play tennis. The last time you were here, we had lasagna and a salad. OK if we have that again?"

"Fine," I rasped, my eyes on her undulating rear, my rattled mind not focused on dinner. "You have information for me, right?"

She glanced over her shoulder. "Yes, but later. I'll put the lasagna in the oven now. We'll have forty minutes or so for tennis, then we need to come back in. I don't want it to overheat."

I wasn't worried about *it* overheating.

The last time we played tennis she had beaten me six-four. Her southpaw serves had a lethal overspin that kept the ball from bouncing very high off the court, and, as in our prior games, she had me scurrying for wicked passing shots off her backhand.

Previously it had taken me most of the set to learn that I could make her pay for aggressive net play by lobbing the ball over her head into the back of the court. This time, I started doing it earlier, which not only scored points for me, but also provided awesome rear views as she scampered back to retrieve the lobs.

I paid more attention than I should have to the white pleated tennis skirt, pink panties, and tanned legs. Never mind the ponytail. She beat me seven-five. We went in to get ready for dinner, detouring through the kitchen to take out the lasagna.

"You obviously like my tennis outfit. I'll put on another one for you," she teased, disappearing upstairs.

I cleaned up and changed back into my cargo shorts and polo shirt in the commodious first-floor bathroom, then waited at the foot of the stairs. I left the DVDs in the bag.

When she emerged, she was flushed from the effort to change in a hurry, which added to her sexy look. She wore a one-piece white silky tennis dress with a flared skirt and white high heeled sandals. I saw a flash of red panties as she descended the stairs. Her hair was brushed out and falling around her shoulders. I followed her seductively swaying body into the kitchen.

My last visit, I'd left an unopened bottle of wine with her. We had drunk lemonade that evening. She'd remembered, and the Cabernet Sauvignon was sitting on the table with a corkscrew beside it. I opened the bottle and poured two glasses.

Red wine like a Cabernet needs to breathe a few minutes before it's drunk, so we let it sit while she made the salad. She slathered French bread with garlic butter, then toasted it lightly in the broiler to serve with the lasagna.

I handed her one glass, and raised mine. "To tennis."

"To mutual consent."

"You like the Cabernet?"

"Yes, this is delicious. How about some music with dinner?"

"Great."

"OK, you pick something. My dad has a collection of big band recordings, if you're interested. It might be nice while we're eating."

"I like big bands, too. Which ones are your favorites?"

"Oh, any of them really. I often listen to Count Basie or Duke Ellington."

I selected an Ellington CD from the shelf beside the stereo in the dining room, put it into the player, and turned the volume down low.

As we sat to eat, she said, "This Ellington album's one of my favorites."

I nodded. "Mine, too." I paused. *Mood Indigo* was playing. "So what's with this mutual consent stuff? And your coming on to me after we agreed that we'd have a friendship that included tennis but not sex?"

"Whoa, just like a man. Trying to rush things. We'll get to that. For now, let's pretend we're out on a date. Tell me what you've been doing recently."

I gave her an abridged version of my consulting with HH Racing, including the telemetry jamming and my reporting to Carol Logan at Watterson Watson. I left out RF's death and my agreement to investigate it on Liz Phillips' behalf, saying only that I had another client that I couldn't discuss.

Ann furrowed her brows momentarily, then brightened. "It must be exciting being involved with the racing team. And you get to be at the track for everything, right?"

"Yeah. In fact I have to be at Boone Raceway tomorrow by eight."

"Well, I won't keep you here past midnight."

I ignored the implications of her last statement. "So, do you have the information I'm looking for on that signal?"

"Yes. It caused a bit of a stir with the electronic warfare guys at Oracle. You said it was recorded at road racing venues, right?"

"Yes."

"Mmm. They couldn't believe that. You sure there wasn't a military installation nearby?"

"I'm sure. What's more, the same signal jammed our race car telemetry at Boone today."

Her eyebrows went up as she leaned forward. "Wow. Well, the signal is from a jammer built by a company called Newcastle Systems in England. It's sold to the U.S. Navy and Marine Corps."

I felt the blood drain from my face as I sat back heavily. All I could manage to say was, "No shit."

Newcastle owned Tau Telemetry. My mind flooded with questions. Who at Tau would benefit from HH Racing's telemetry being jammed? Why only one race team?

Ann waved her hand at me. "You all right? You look like you saw a ghost."

"I'm fine. Thanks for the info. And thank the folks at Oracle." I wasn't really fine, but didn't want to get her any more involved than she already was.

"You're welcome. I will. Sure there isn't anything else you want to share with me?"

"Not right now. Just a lot of conjecture and ideas I need to run down."

"Let me know if there is, OK?"

"OK."

My agenda and priorities for the next day had just changed. For starters, I needed to get Andy Shaffer in a private conversation. His dual connection with Tau and the radio controlled flying club wasn't lost on me.

I leaned forward, wanting to change the subject. I focused on Ann, which wasn't hard to do.

"Tell me what's been happening at Oracle." She worked at Oracle Systems in Kokomo in the advanced research and development laboratory.

"First of all, as I said in my email, your CDROM with the controller software was a big hit. Several people, including my boss, asked me where it came from. I told them it came indirectly from a federal agency I was not at liberty to reveal. That shut them up."

"What are you working on now?"

"I'm working on a couple of new products, but the exciting news is that I've applied to Oracle's Ph.D. Scholar Program. If I'm accepted, the company will support me for three years while I get a Ph.D."

"Would you still get a salary?"

"Yes, I'd get full salary plus reimbursement for tuition and books."

"That's great. I remember you mentioned it the night we went to the Slippery Noodle." The date that ended with us agreeing to just be friends and play tennis.

"I was just thinking about it then. Now I've applied."

"When will you find out if you get it?"

"It should be fairly soon, within a few weeks. I've heard through the grapevine that I'll be accepted."

"Great. So what's your obligation to Oracle after you get the Ph.D.?"

"I'm committed to work for them for at least three years after that."

I wondered if that would mean her leaving the area. "Where?"

"That's a little complicated. Basically I'll be able to pick my location and then select my job from those available there, or pick exactly what I want to do and go wherever they send me."

"Are you leaning one way or the other?"

"Not strongly. I guess I'd like to stay near my dad for now, though."

After a long pause, I asked, "OK. We're on a date, and I'm curious about what you'd like to do for the rest of the evening."

"Fair enough. But I'd like to revisit our last tennis match, and our date."

"OK."

There was a long pause, filled by the haunting, mellow sax intro to *Sophisticated Lady*.

"You really took me by surprise, you know," Ann said.

"I did?"

"Coming over that first evening, then back the next for tennis, then out on a date a few days later. Most men…well, when people talk about 'most people' or 'most' anything, they're really talking about their own experience, and I've had zilch social life since my divorce…but *most* men would have taken it a bit more slowly." She smiled crookedly.

"I think I followed that. Did I come on too strong?"

"Oh, no. I was excited and flattered…and turned on. But I needed time to settle things in my mind."

"Well, you bowled me over the first time we met," I replied. "I didn't quite know how to approach you. And your asking me here

228

tonight for an evening of tennis, dinner, and…whatever… has me astonished."

"You have no idea how nervous I was inviting you. I feel like a teenager going behind my father's back. Not that it matters; he really likes you. But I don't plan to tell him about anything we do or don't do after dinner."

"So what do you want to do?"

She got up, walked over and stood beside my chair. I stood up facing her. She put her hands around my waist, pulled us together, and looked up into my eyes. "Before I answer that, you have to answer three questions."

"Fire away."

"Are you living with someone?"

"Only Boots, and he's a cat." I didn't mention that he was missing.

She laughed. "A male roommate. You told me about him. Second, are you in a monogamous relationship?"

I hesitated just a split second. Until a few days ago I thought I was, but I wasn't. Certainly not since Vanessa had told me that we'd each always been free to have sex with other people. "No. Are you looking for one?"

"I said three questions. Then I'll answer that…third, will you wear a condom when we have sex?"

"You said *when*, not *if*. And yes."

"Great. To answer your question, no, I'm not looking for anything tonight but pleasure I've been denying myself for too long, and I'd like you to give it to me."

"No strings attached?"

"No strings attached, and by mutual consent, of course."

"By mutual…" I tried to say 'consent' but she was exploring my mouth with her tongue and squeezing the bulge in my shorts with her hand. "Consent," I was finally able to articulate as she turned and led me by the hand upstairs to her bedroom. The melody of Ellington's *Satin Doll* followed us.

She lit a candle in a red glass bowl-shaped container on an end table, opened a drawer, and took out a condom packaged in gold foil. She turned out the lights and climbed onto the bed on her knees, handing me the condom.

I ran my hands over her dress, feeling her nipples and bottom through the thin fabric. She closed her eyes as I caressed her thighs. Then I moved up between her legs and she sucked in her breath sharply as I stroked the moist crotch of her panties. The dress' silky material made a soft brushing sound as I pulled it off over her head. Even with just candlelight, her red bikinis were so sheer that I could see the auburn hair on her pubic mound.

"I get to undress you," she said softly. I got up on my knees as she pulled my polo shirt off over my head. She undid my cargo shorts and pulled them down, and did the same with my black underwear, exposing my engorged shaft. She gently pushed me down on my back, and pulled them the rest of the way off. I pulled her panties down. Still on her knees, she took them the rest of the way off and I searched the wetness between her legs.

Her auburn hair fanned out behind her as she lay back on the bed, the nipples on her small perfectly formed breasts a blush of pink. I lay with her as we kissed without haste, and kissed again, our tongues and our hands exploring each other.

Our lips became more demanding, our tongues more insistent, as I fondled her nipples and clit and fingered her vagina, and she stroked my cock to rock hardness. I got up on my knees above her and took the condom out of the package.

She took the condom from me. "Let me do that."

She rolled it onto me with a playful squeeze, then laid back. "Let's screw."

She was warm and wet and imploring as she spread her legs and guided me into her, gasping, then moaning. She lifted her hands to my shoulders, her fingers spread, as I slid my hands under her, pulling her toward me. We began to move, fitfully at first, our thrusts out of sync, until we established our rhythm.

She pulled my head down next to hers, whispering into my ear, "Yes, keep going like this."

"Like this," I echoed.

Instead of pounding swiftly to orgasm, we rode gradually growing waves. Several times, she asked me to slow my thrusts into her. "I want to get right to the edge, then back off. Make it last."

She finally pushed herself too close and couldn't help herself, crying, "I'm *coming. Now!* Oh, *God!*" Her entire body clenched and twisted violently beneath me, arching her hips into my own convulsive release. Her orgasm was an earthquake, a series of jolts peaking at eight on the Richter scale, followed by aftershocks that rolled on and on. It had taken all the self-control I could muster to hold off and come with her.

"Stay. Stay inside me," she pleaded as we rolled over on our sides facing each other. I gently pushed the hair out of her eyes as she put her hands behind my ass and pulled our pelvises together. She bit her lower lip and kept shuddering.

"Ann," I whispered, kissing her forehead.

"Oh *God*, Wolf, that was incredible."

We lay side by side, me still inside her, feeling her contractions. When I slid out of her and rolled on my back, she stroked my chest, still lying on her side. We rolled over on our backs, and when I looked at her a minute later, she seemed to be asleep.

Ann had taken me totally by surprise. Tonight had been extraordinary.

I was wiped out. It wouldn't hurt to rest my eyes for a little while.

I awoke with a start, not knowing where I was for several moments. The clock on the end table said it was ten-fifteen. I realized I'd been asleep for an hour.

I kissed Ann lightly on her forehead. She murmured something inaudible but didn't open her eyes, so I got out of bed, blew out the candle, and quietly carried my clothes downstairs.

I cleaned up and dressed in the downstairs bathroom, left the DVDs on the kitchen counter with a note to call me, then turned off the downstairs lights. Making sure I had the keys to my Jeep, I let myself out, locking the door behind me.

I don't remember my drive home. I doubt that I ran any red lights or went seriously over the speed limit, but my mind was saturated with thoughts about Ann and about the information she'd provided on the hardware source of the telemetry jamming. I was on autopilot.

I thought about the tennis, the conversation, and the sex; then wondered if I was a one-night stand; then ruminated whether someone at Tau Telemetry had murdered RF, and why had my PC been stolen? Then I went back to the tennis and went around the loop a few times more.

231

I was finally able to focus on the jamming problem with frequent excursions into the incredible sex. I decided that I didn't care much whether I was a one night stand. But I hoped I wasn't.

Back at my condo, I looked around outside for Boots. Eleven at night was no time to call "Here, Boots," so I went inside.

A message from the PC crooks was waiting for me in my personal email account.

```
Ruger
It is only a matter of time until we crack
your encryption.
We will make it worth your while to expedite
our process.
Respond before midnight.
```

They pointed me to a website where I would be instructed to click a button to respond. Fat fucking chance I'd do that.

The web address, called a domain, would almost certainly disappear after midnight. Since the email had been routed via the same domain, it would become untraceable then as well.

When an internet domain name is registered and then cancelled within twenty-four hours, it's like it never existed. Hackers exploit this feature, often settling into a domain for as briefly as a few seconds before canceling it and moving on.

I sent Daniel an encrypted message from my HH Racing account pointing him to the website and asking if he could trace the IP address that owned it. He had less than an hour before it would evaporate into the ether.

He immediately replied that he was concentrating on it. I was lucky he liked to work late hours.

I focused on other tasks.

My report to Carol summarized how we determined that the origin of the jamming was at an elevation of three hundred feet, and said that I didn't want to speculate about the source just yet. I acknowledged Giles Reichmann's assistance in apparently tracking down our stolen receiver. I recommended not doing anything about it immediately since the new encryption system was making our data unreadable by anyone else.

I fired off an email to Andy Shaffer at Tau Telemetry saying it was urgent that we have a private meeting first thing in the morning. In Bob Conlan's email report, I thanked him for the referral to Jeff Smithfield. I outlined what I'd asked Jeff to do, and mentioned my planned meeting at the home of the couple with the BDSM dungeon who had hosted RF and Liz.

Just before midnight, an encrypted message came through from Daniel. The owner of the temporary website was the same organization in Chicago that he had previously linked to the Kade and Eldorp emails. Taravanian Real Estate was almost certainly a front for the Armenian mob.

Using a remote application on his Maltrack corporate computer, Daniel not only provided me the street address, but also an aerial view of the building. My stolen PC was probably there. He would monitor the company's local network for my computer's unique MAC identifier, and let me know if it was detected.

As I was going to bed, I had a momentary voyeuristic urge to use the GPS tracker I'd acquired from Gerald Eldorp to see where Vanessa's car had been all day and where it was parked for the night, but I decided to leave it in Sal's capable hands. One thing was for sure. There would be a new aspect to my discussion with Vanessa on Sunday.

Chapter 20

Friday morning, I woke up trembling and in a cold sweat. I'd had another fucking Iraq nightmare. The details were hazy, like the smoke swirling around what was left of Schumacher. Often they were like that, indistinct and disjointed, but that didn't make them any less terrifying. The horror is chaotic, and flashbacks overlap, with no clean fade-in or fade-out, no continuity.

I fought nausea as I sat up.

If I'd been religious, I might have thought that God was punishing me for the great sex I had with Ann. But I'm basically an agnostic. I don't think I have the answers. Neither does anyone else. I don't even know what I don't know.

Unlike PTSD flashbacks, which could be triggered numerous ways such as by going to a cafeteria with trays that had to be slid along metal guides, Iraq nightmares seemed to come randomly. I averaged a couple a month.

When I was able to stand, I shuffled toward the kitchen, groggily speculating where Boots was. I was halfway there before I remembered he was missing. Secondary to Tito, he had become a kind of support system for me. I needed to call Tito, which I'd do on the way to the track.

I washed down a fried egg sandwich with coffee as I watched the local weather channel. In a change from the forecast the previous evening, moderate to severe thunderstorms were now predicted for the late afternoon with a fifty-percent probability.

Qualifications for Formula Nor-Am were scheduled from four to five. If storms were on their way, the cars might all get onto the track at the beginning of the hour.

After my morning ablutions I gathered my gear, and headed to Boone, looking around quickly for Boots. I called Tito even though it was only seven-fifteen.

He answered, "Hey, Wolf, what's up?"

"Rough spot this morning," I replied.

"Nightmare?"

"Yeah, with just Schumacher. Kind of fuzzy." I briefly discussed it with him.

"You doing all right? Sounds like you're driving."

"Uh-huh. I'm headed to the track."

"You breathing OK?" One of the signs that my episode was still bothering me was ragged breathing.

"Yeah, thanks. I noticed my breath catching in the shower, but it's normal now."

"So what's happening at the track?"

I brought him up to date on the jamming situation, then added, "There has been a development you'd be interested in. I've hired part-time help. Conlan recommended a police officer who was looking for a little supplemental income."

"You gonna tell me who?"

"Sure. Jeff Smithfield."

There was a short silence. "You have to be kidding."

"No kidding."

"You know that there's lots of stuff he can't do because of his job. What are you gonna use him for?"

"Surveillance, info gathering."

"Call me if you need to talk. Watch your ass."

We hung up. I parked in the Boone lot at five of eight, the smells of coffee and frying bacon wafting out to me as I went in.

I had just gone through security when my smartphone rang. I recognized Jeff's working number.

"Sergeant Rodriguez just call you?" I asked, figuring he'd called Jeff to tell him to watch his ass, like he'd done with me.

"What? No. Why did you ask?"

"Never mind. Why'd you call? I didn't think you were supposed to make non-official calls during work hours."

"This is official."

I felt like I'd just taken strike two. "Sorry about that. What's on your official mind?"

"When I get to work, I always review the log of missing persons reports that have come in since I worked last. This morning's log says that a person named Gerald Eldorp was reported missing at five this morning by his live-in girlfriend."

"Is his girlfriend's name Bunny something?"

"Yeah, so it must be the same guy you've been tailing with your GPS tracker, right?"

"Sounds like it." I knew what came next.

"Can you turn that thing on and tell me where his car is?"

"Yeah, assuming the tracker's still attached and operating, and somewhere where satellites can see it. I'd better do it now, since I'm supposed to be working myself."

"How long will it take?"

"About five minutes. You want to stay on the line?"

"Uh-huh. I'll wait."

I got coffee at a food truck, resisting the urge to buy a cinnamon roll that seemed to be calling my name, and sat at a nearby table as I booted up the tracking system.

"OK, you still there?"

"Yes. What do you have?"

"His car is in the parking lot of the SnoreZ Inn Motel on Pendleton Pike. Looks like it's at the edge of the lot in a corner." I didn't say any more, but figured he'd shacked up with a woman from the club he frequented next door.

"OK, thanks. Sounds like this may transition to a domestic dispute," he laughed as we hung up.

I was still sipping coffee when I arrived at HH Racing's garage area. Andy Shaffer was waiting, nursing his own cup of java.

He walked up to me. "Hi Wolf. Your email and voicemail said it was urgent. What's going on?"

"Hi, Andy. Thanks for coming. Let's go into the transporter where we can have a private talk."

At that point, I suspected that someone at Tau Telemetry was responsible for the jamming since the equipment was manufactured by their parent company. I wasn't excluding anyone, including Andy Shaffer.

Andy settled his large frame in the loveseat against one wall. I pulled up a chair.

He took a sip of coffee, then balanced the cup on one knee with a meaty hand. "What's so urgent? You sounded stressed in the voicemail."

"I want to share information that is confidential. Can you keep it to yourself for now?"

"Unless it puts me in conflict with Tau Telemetry, I don't see why not."

"It involves Tau indirectly, but there's no conflict of interest that I know of." I was watching Andy closely, for any flickering of his eyes or movement of his body that would indicate he was lying. I decided to trust him. I didn't think he was involved.

"OK. What's it about?"

"We've figured out what our telemetry problem is."

Andy sat forward. "Sounds good. Can't see how that's a difficulty."

"HH Racing's telemetry's being jammed."

The incredulous look on his face indicated that either he'd been unaware of the jamming or he was eligible for an Academy Award, and Purdue geeks don't get nominated all that often.

"*What?*" He leaned forward, pushing strands of hair out of his face. "Intentional interference with the signal?"

"Exactly. And it gets worse."

"How?"

"This is where Tau is indirectly involved. Analysis of the signal has identified the hardware producing it as having been manufactured by Newcastle Systems."

Andy shook his head and sat back, blowing air out of puffed cheeks. "Wow."

I didn't say anything for a while. He looked at my face and asked, "There's more, isn't there?"

"I guess you could say that. Here at Boone, the jamming is coming from near the center of the road course at an altitude of about three hundred feet."

"You're kidding." I shook my head. "Balloon? Cell tower?" he asked, knitting his eyebrows.

"I don't think so."

He looked at me for several seconds as cogs went around in his head. Then his face cleared, and realization dropped into place. "Drone. Maybe a quad-copter."

I nodded. "Now you're on the right track. Why did you mention quad-copters?"

"The turning radius, or the amount of real estate it takes to turn, of a regular radio controlled fixed wing drone is large enough that it'd be likely to be seen by someone. A quad-copter can stay pretty much over one place."

I nodded. That fit the pattern of readings we'd taken. "Makes sense. Tell me, who do you know at Newcastle Systems?"

The question obviously took him aback. "Newcastle? The company that acquired Tau?"

"Uh-huh."

"Nobody. Until they were acquired, Tau had been privately owned for over a decade. The scuttlebutt was that the owners were shopping around for a buyer, and, in fact, had several offers. Newcastle won the bidding contest."

"Were there any reorganization changes?"

"No. We are an independent operating division, essentially autonomous. Once in a while Tau teams with Newcastle on a proposal, but that's about it, and proposal collaboration is way above my level."

"What do you know about their product line?"

Andy thought, looking at the wall behind me as he sipped his coffee and ran a hand through his hair, then looked at me. "Drones. For the U.S. military. Is that what you're getting at?"

"Close, but no brass ring. Newcastle also makes a jamming system that's used in drones. I doubt if whoever is causing our telemetry grief has access to a quarter-million-dollar military drone, much less the ability to fly it over Boone without being noticed."

"So you think they got hold of a jamming module and are using a small inexpensive drone."

"Something like that."

"What makes you believe that Newcastle hardware is involved?"

"Electronic warfare experts at Oracle Electronics analyzed the jamming signal."

Andy whistled under his breath. "So that points to someone at Tau?"

"It had crossed my mind."

"I can see why you might assume that, but I don't know of anyone at Tau besides myself who has the expertise to fly drones, and it sure isn't me."

He'd been in the Tau Telemetry tent, and out and about, during the jamming. It seemed he had a solid alibi.

"Keep an eye out for anything that might be relevant."

He nodded, we shook hands and left the transporter.

It was still early. I decided to have a look at the area in the woods where the jamming was originating. Since the HH Racing Nor-Am team appeared to be the only one with the problem, and we wouldn't be on the track until mid-afternoon, I figured that whoever was responsible wouldn't be going out until just before qualifications.

I found Linda and Daniel in conversation. Daniel was explaining how we calculated the location of the signal.

"Hi, Linda. Sorry to interrupt, but I'd like to take the golf cart out on the maintenance road and look around."

Daniel's eyes showed me he knew what I was up to. "Can I ride along?"

"I guess so, if it's all right with Linda."

Linda looked at her clipboard. "We shouldn't need it for thirty minutes or so. Long enough?"

I bobbed my head, "Sure, that'll do it."

She nodded. "OK. You can borrow the golf cart as soon as Jason finishes an errand. Be careful. I don't want either of you getting into trouble."

"I doubt if there's anyone out there this early. We'll stay in touch by radio," I responded.

Jason was back in ten minutes, and carried a five-gallon container of coffee into the garage area.

Daniel and I started around the maintenance road in the golf cart after checking that we had radio contact with Linda.

"Are we going to try to find the location on the ground below where the jamming is coming from?" asked Daniel.

"Yep. There may be a clearing in the woods there. Maybe we'll find something nearby or along the maintenance road. We'll take the longer route going there, about three-fourths of the way around to where we park. When we're done in the woods, we'll finish the last one-fourth of the loop."

After we'd gone over halfway around, I started searching for golf cart tracks leading off the road. I found what I was looking for about three hundred yards past where we'd been set up the previous day.

It was a little after nine and everything was quiet as we got out of the golf cart. The Pro-Am 2000s weren't due on the track for qualifying for another hour, followed by the Formula Nor-Am Lights.

As we started into the woods my smartphone rang. I must have been on edge, because the ringing startled me.

The caller ID indicated that it was coming from the IMPD homicide office where Tito worked. I was puzzled. Tito seldom called me during work, and almost always used his cell phone.

"Hi, Tito, it's Wolf. What's up?"

"This isn't Sergeant Rodriguez. It's Sergeant Wilkerson."

Wilkerson had been involved in the Sherri Smithfield murder and related activities. He was young and brash, in keeping with the spit and polish of his uniform. He was also a good cop.

"What can I help you with, Sergeant?"

"We were informed by Corporal Smithfield in missing persons that you provided the location of the car belonging to Gerald Eldorp, who had been reported missing early this morning. Is that true?"

I was beginning to get an uneasy feeling in the pit of my stomach. "Yes."

"Mr. Eldorp has been found deceased under suspicious circumstances, and we'd like to interview you at IMPD."

I was stunned. I felt the blood drain from my face as I shuffled back to the golf cart and leaned against a fender, waving off Daniel, who looked concerned.

"How did he die?"

"You should know better than to ask."

"OK, OK," I said, anger creeping into my voice. "When do you want me to come downtown?"

"As soon as possible."

It was an invitation I couldn't refuse. "It'll take me about an hour. I'm at Boone Raceway."

We hung up, and I slid into a seat on the golf cart. Searching the woods would have to wait.

"Daniel, we have to go back. Now. There's been a murder, and I have to go downtown to talk with IMPD."

"Somebody you know?"

"Uh-huh. Not a friend. I guess you'd call him an acquaintance."

As we started back in the golf cart, Daniel asked, "Anybody I know?"

"No. And please don't tell Linda and the others it's a murder case. It might upset them, and it isn't connected with the telemetry jamming." As we rode back in silence my thoughts were racing.

We drove up to Linda in the garage area. "That took less than fifteen minutes," she said, looking at her watch.

"Yeah. We didn't finish what we were going to do. I got a call from IMPD, and I have to go downtown."

"Why?" she asked, raising her eyebrows.

"Another case. Not related to HH Racing. But I have to go."

She arched her eyebrows and looked at Daniel, who put on his best deadpan face and remained silent.

"When will you be back?"

"I'm not sure, but it should be by noon. I'll call on my way back. I'll want to borrow the golf cart again and take a look in the woods. We should have plenty of time before Nor-Am goes out for qualifications."

As I went out to my Jeep, I noticed that the temperature and humidity had both increased significantly.

The shock of learning about Eldorp's death was with me as I headed out of the parking lot. I had to assume that murder was suspected, or Wilkerson wouldn't be insisting I come downtown.

My dealings with him disturbed me. We had put GPS electronic tails on each other. I had gotten information from him regarding the sources of malware-carrying email. Email headers he forwarded me pointed to Armenian mafia sources in Chicago, and cyber-attack sources outside the US. His email being monitored, which seemed likely, could account for my PC being stolen, and for his death.

I suddenly realized with a start that I had his revolver in my safe. It was a Saturday night special and untraceable. I was in a dilemma.

Should I reveal that I had it? A court order prohibited him from owning it, so it wouldn't be missed in the usual sense of the word. But could a ballistics test tie it to a crime?

Worrying about what to do with Eldorp's pistol led me into agonizing over whether he'd still be alive if he'd had it. I felt pain and remorse about my possible contribution to his death.

He wasn't a 'nice' person. He had tangled with the law and lost. He wasn't the sharpest pencil in the box either, but I viewed him as more of a schmuck than a hardened criminal, and as someone who was used by others like Rudy Kade and Stan Gordian. And by me.

At least he had somebody who missed him when he didn't come home at night and reported it to IMPD. That was more than I could say for myself.

His being killed was likely linked to providing me with information. That made me take his murder personally.

It was probably tied to the cybersecurity operation involving Stan Gordian that the FBI had told me to stay away from. Sticking his nose into it had cost him his life. I had the urge to contact Russo and Corbett, but decided to wait until after I knew more about Eldorp's death.

I needed to know when and where he was murdered, and how. Wilkerson wasn't likely to disclose that in my interview, but I might be able to find out from Tito if I had useful info to exchange.

I didn't know yet what I had to trade, but I called him anyway and left a voicemail. "Hi Tito, it's Wolf. I have information that you'll be interested in. Meet me for coffee at City Market at eleven. Ciao." I hoped he made it.

I parked at a meter about two blocks from the City-County Building and shelled out enough quarters to last two hours. I left everything except my smartphone in the Jeep so I wouldn't have to take it through security, and went up to Wilkerson's office. Sitting with him was Detective Sergeant Samantha Hardin. Sergeant Sam. Two on one. Just my lucky day.

Neither got up. He nodded me to a seat in front of his desk. "We meet again, Mr. Ruger."

"Another murder," Hardin said caustically.

Not a friendly greeting. I waited.

"You provided our missing persons unit with information on the location of Gerald Eldorp's car, is that right?" Wilkerson asked.

"Yes."

"How did you know him and what interactions did you have with him?"

As I started to answer, Hardin interrupted, "Don't leave anything out, and we're recording this interview as well as taking notes."

I summarized the events starting with finding the GPS tracking device on my Jeep. I told them that Eldorp had attached a tracking unit to Vanessa's car, and put one on mine only as an afterthought.

"So what did you do when you learned he was tracking Ms. Russo's vehicle?" Wilkerson asked.

I grinned, beginning to enjoy the interview. "I called the FBI."

Hardin slammed down her pen. "*What?*"

"Want me to spell that for you?"

Her eyes smoked with anger. "Don't be a smartass. Why did you call the FBI?"

"I thought they'd like to know, and I was right."

"How did you know that?"

"They told me to back off and hand the situation over to them. So I did."

"Are you telling us that we have to talk to them to get more information on Eldorp?"

"Sergeant Hardin, I wouldn't dream of telling you how to do your job, but if I were in your shoes, I'd probably contact Special Agent Matthew Corbett at the local field office."

"Do I know that name from somewhere?" Wilkerson asked.

"Maybe. He was involved in a situation related to a shooting death in an Indy Vista parking lot about six weeks ago."

"Oh, yeah. I seem to remember that IMPD covered for the FBI on that one."

I didn't answer.

She looked at her notes. "OK, let's try another direction. You can locate a vehicle with one of these electronic trackers anytime you want, right?"

"More or less."

"Could you find his vehicle right now?"

"It's a satellite-based system, so the vehicle has to be where satellites can receive its signal. If it's in a garage, probably not. If it's in an outdoor lot, yes."

By not asking how many days a GPS tracker could continuously tail a vehicle, she had given me an idea for information I'd trade to Tito.

Her eyes bored into mine. "Where were you between the hours of eight-thirty and ten last night?"

"At the home of Billy and Ann Wyland on Geist Reservoir. I can give you phone and email contact info if you want it." I'm sure she didn't understand the grin on my face as I spelled their last name.

"We'll find it if we need it." She looked up from her notes, twirling her pen with two fingers.

"Were you with 'gorgeous'?" she asked sharply.

"That's none of your business."

"*I* decide what's my business," she snapped, looking daggers at me. "And why haven't you mentioned the computer you reported stolen? Or isn't that my business?"

I felt my blood pressure taking off for the moon. "I don't know that it's related," I replied, matching her dagger for dagger.

"That's for *me* to decide," she snorted.

Wilkerson held his hand out in a peace gesture. "OK, OK. Are you licensed to carry a firearm?"

I took a deep breath. "Yes."

"Describe it."

"It's a Smith and Wesson Model 640-1, a .357 magnum."

"Do you own any small-caliber weapons?"

"No," I replied, all ears. "Did Eldorp get killed with one?" The implication, stated or not, that the killing was done with a small-caliber weapon tickled something in the back of my mind. I couldn't quite scratch it.

"You know I won't answer that." He shuffled papers. "That's all for now. We'll have your statement transcribed and printed up for you to sign on Monday."

"And I shouldn't leave town?"

Hardin replied, "You will *not* leave town."

Chapter 21

On my way downtown, I'd been too much in shock over Eldorp's murder to think clearly. Wilkerson's question about my providing his car's location to IMPD reminded me that I had GPS tracking information on his car that covered the time I attached it until after he was killed.

As I left the City-County Building, I saw a text message saying 'Meeting OK' from Tito. I had fifteen minutes to get the information I wanted to offer him, so I jogged to my car, grabbed my computer bag, and jogged back to City Market.

Covering half of a city block, City Market is directly across the street from the City-County Building. It is anchored by a restored historical brick structure with modern wings on either side.

I got coffee just inside the door to the main building. I took it upstairs, passing the wrought iron railings on the stairs, to the balcony reminiscent of the French Quarter in New Orleans. Settling on a chair with an oak seat and wire back that looked like it came from an old-time ice cream parlor, I put my computer bag on the table and fired up the GPS tracking tablet.

Wilkerson's questions as to my whereabouts the previous evening made it obvious that IMPD thought that Eldorp had died between eight-thirty and ten-thirty. I set the tracking system to display his locations after noon.

I stared at the results. He left his house about three-thirty. His car had been parked on Massachusetts Avenue near Rudy Kade's office from about four until five.

It was the location of the car from five-thirty until just after ten that took my breath away. It had been parked at ElecRecycle on Pendleton Pike, and the precision of the tracking system pinpointed the vehicle as being *inside* the high-security gates. Stan Gordian, out on bail and under indictment for accessory to murder, was the president of the company.

At a little after ten o'clock, the car moved to the parking lot of the SnoreZ Inn Motel, the location I'd reported to Jeff. My assumption had been that his body was found in the motel, but now it was obvious he'd been dead before the car was parked there.

I suddenly remembered what I'd been trying to recall when Wilkerson asked me about owning a small-caliber weapon. When Gordian had arrived home while I was staking out his house during the Stellar disk drive case, he had waved a chrome-plated .22 automatic under my nose, not exactly pointing it at me, but not pointing it away, either. It was the first time I'd seen Vanessa, who'd convinced him to put the weapon away.

When Tito walked up with his cup of coffee a few minutes later, I was ready. "Hi, acho. How's it going?"

He looked at me with his head cocked. "OK, you look pretty pleased with yourself. Your interview with Wilkerson and Hardin must have gone fairly well."

"It went fine. From their questions, I figure Eldorp was killed with a small-caliber weapon around nine or nine-thirty yesterday evening."

"What do you want from me?"

"I want to know where Eldorp's body was found and specifically how he died."

"And why should I tell you that?"

"Because I can show you where he was killed, and maybe ID his killer."

Tito looked down at the table, then slowly raised his head and sipped his coffee. "You go first."

"OK, but this has to be two-way, agree?"

He nodded.

"You know that I was tracking Eldorp's car."

Tito gave an almost imperceptible nod.

"He was reported as missing by his girlfriend. Jeff Smithfield asked me where his car was this morning, and I told him. We both assumed he was still alive, probably screwing around with someone at the motel. So I'd supposed that his body was found in the motel, but now I'm betting it wasn't."

Tito looked levelly at me. "Why're you betting it wasn't and why should I tell you?"

"Because at the estimated time of his death, Eldorp's car was in a parking lot inside of a secure chain link fence at ElecRecycle." I paused for effect. "Dead men don't drive cars, 'm I right?"

Tito leaned forward. "Show me."

I showed him the time-lapse GPS tracking of Eldrop's car from the parking place on Massachusetts Avenue to the lot at ElecRecycle to the lot at the SnoreZ Inn.

Tito pointed to the screen. "What was he doing on Mass Avenue?"

"Probably meeting with Rudy Kade."

"The lawyer?"

"Yeah. I'm curious whether Kade went out to ElecRecycle in his own car."

Tito shrugged. "Who knows?"

Then he sat back, sipped his coffee, and looked around to make sure nobody was listening to us. "Eldorp was found in the trunk of his car. He'd been handcuffed with his hands behind his back and shot twice at close range, execution style in the back of the head."

I whistled quietly through my teeth. "Holy shit. With what?"

"A .22 caliber weapon, probably a pistol, with hollow points. You don't want to know what it looked like."

He was right. I didn't. "Looks like someone killed him at ElecRecycle, then stuffed his body in the trunk of his car."

"You said you could finger the trigger man."

"I said I *might* be able to." I told him about Gordian waving a .22 pistol in my face when I staked out his house.

I continued, "If I were you, a ballistics check of his weapon would be high on my list...except for one thing."

"What's that?"

"Remember you asked if I was going to call Agent Corbett at the FBI after I found the GPS tail on my Jeep?"

Tito nodded. "Don't tell me the feds are involved with Gordian again."

"Afraid so. I had a visit from Corbett telling me to keep my nose out of whatever is going on." I didn't tell Tito about Vanessa being recruited to be the intermediary on a cash-for-information swap, or about Uncle Sal's involvement.

Tito shook his head. "We can't shit without getting their permission. Is Vanessa mixed up in this mess?"

I thought about how to answer that. "She might be."

"Look here. You'd better not be withholding information in a murder investigation."

"Damn it, Tito! I just *gave* you information. You're gonna have to talk to the FBI if you want to learn more about their operations."

He picked up his coffee. As he started to stand up, I held out my tracking tablet for the GPS electronic tail.

"You better take this. I don't want to withhold evidence." I may have sounded a little sarcastic.

He took it and strode out of City Market without saying goodbye. We were both pissed off.

I sat and stewed. Eldorp's killing had to have been linked to both the FBI operation and to Vanessa. I hoped she wasn't in danger. I still cared about her.

Corbett was telling me to stay away from the Gordian operation after letting me know that Vanessa was probably going to play a risky role. Her Uncle Sal was ostensibly protecting her and had told me to keep out of his way, but he seemed to have a hidden agenda related to the emails that came from Eldorp.

I was experiencing guilt about Eldorp's death. Lots of it. He may have been a slob and a small-time crook, but he didn't deserve what he got. I realized that I felt an obligation to find his killer. I felt like Gerald Eldorp was my client.

I had two paying clients already, Liz Phillips via Bob Conlan and HH Racing through Watterson-Watson. I would feel guilty if I took time away from them.

Guilt seemed to be the emotion-of-the-day. I shoved it aside temporarily, not easily. I thought about relationships and events related to Eldorp. I took note cards out of my computer bag that I use to diagram, doodle, and jot down ideas that are too raw, or undeveloped, to put in a case notebook.

I wrote names on some cards, thoughts on some, items on others. I shuffled them around, looking for patterns.

At the center of most of the arrangements of note cards was one name: Rudy Kade. Eldorp had worked for him, he reported to Gordian, and he'd been the original recipient of the emails forwarded to Eldorp. Sal Russo was very interested in the emails originating in Chicago that had been forwarded from Eldorp. Perhaps it wasn't a coincidence that Sal was in Chicago.

I knew Kade from the Stellar disk drive case, when Stellar's owners had hired him to find venture capital for a new product. Kade was involved in illegal activities that had culminated in murder. While only Gordian had been indicted for accessory to murder, Kade probably should have been.

I recalled a conversation about Kade with Max. He'd said something like, "There are two kinds of lawyers. One kind is constantly searching for the truth, exposing things, discovering facts, and trying to see that justice is done. The other kind is for sale to the highest bidder and engaged in covering up the truth, concealing things, trying to negate facts, and doing everything in their power to subvert justice. Rudy Kade is the second type."

Kade had to figure in Eldorp's death. The question was, how?

While it was possible that Kade was at ElecRecycle when Eldorp was killed, it wasn't likely that he pulled the trigger. Witness tampering was one thing; murder was a horse of an entirely different color.

It was plausible that Eldorp was doing an errand for Kade when he died. Or he might have gone to see Gordian freelance, something on the side.

I wanted to learn whether Kade knew Eldorp was dead. To do that, I'd have to kick a hornet's nest and quickly get the hell out of the way. Kade's office on Massachusetts Avenue was only five minutes away. I decided to pay him a visit. It would make me later than I'd planned getting back to the track, but it was important to see what his reaction was when I told him.

I found a parking place a few spaces from the door to his building, and took the elevator to the third floor where his office was. A gum-chewing receptionist with curly blond hair out of a bottle and heavy black mascara was filing her nails.

"When will Mr. Kade be in?"

She popped her gum. "Don't rightly know. He shoulda been here by now. You got an appointment?"

I shook my head and turned on my heel. I wondered for a moment if he'd suffered a fate similar to Eldorp.

I didn't have time to stake out his office, so I went back to my Jeep. I had just gotten in when I saw Kade getting out of a car a few spots down from mine. He hurried past me toward the door I'd come out of.

I recognized him from his website and the less-than-flattering pictures published in the Indy Star during Stan Gordian's indictment proceedings. Watery weasel eyes peered out of wire-rim glasses on a sallow pinched and pockmarked face. He was wearing a wrinkled black suit that hung on his scarecrow frame like a bad debt.

His car being close by gave me an idea. I took the GPS tracking unit that had been on my Jeep out of my computer bag and attached it to his car, noting the license number on his dark blue Buick. Then I hustled into the building about thirty seconds behind him.

I had Eldorp's tracking tablet, that could be used for the electronic tails on both Kade and Vanessa. I didn't intend to do anything with Vanessa's. Not that I wasn't curious.

I had no immediate plans for tracking Kade. He was a target of opportunity. I'd promised to stay away from the FBI operation, and Sal was looking after Vanessa. But I hadn't promised anyone to stay away from Kade, and I had a strong hunch he was connected to Eldorp's murder.

I caught up with him just as the elevator door was opening. "I want to talk with you."

"Make an appointment, buddy. Maybe I can work you in next month." He might as well have said 'fuck you.'

I slid in the elevator with him and punched the 'three' button as the door closed, and moved in face to face. "I have an appointment right now."

He made the mistake of trying to push me away. I grabbed his lapels with both hands and lifted him up on his toes so our noses were six inches apart. "Bad move. Try something like that again and you'll be picking your teeth off the floor."

"You son of a bitch. You have no idea who you're screwing with. I'll sue the shit out of you."

"I'm screwing with an asshole who should have been indicted for accessory to murder and disbarred."

Hatred flooded his face. "Get the hell outta here."

The elevator door opened. Still holding him up, I pushed him against the elevator's back wall.

"Let's have a reasonable discussion about what you know regarding Gerald Eldorp's murder."

"What...?" he stammered as his struggles turned to Jello. I let go of his lapels, and he left the elevator on wobbly legs. I followed him into his office.

"Kitty honey, go get me coffee."

She looked at him quizzically, then at me. I shrugged.

Kitty honey shouldered a purse half the size of a Mini Cooper and strutted out the door, popping her gum.

He closed the front door behind her, then shut and locked the door to his inner office behind us. His office was as stark as Bob Conlan's was opulent. The finish on his ancient wooden desk was dull and scratched. The windows looking out on Massachusetts Avenue were stained and streaked.

He collapsed in the squeaky wooden armchair behind his desk, and looked furtively at me. I remained standing, leaned forward on his desk, and peered directly into his eyes.

"You telling me Eldorp's dead?" he asked. Either he was a great actor, or he hadn't known. The Academy Award selection committee was still deliberating.

"That's right."

"Who are you and why do you give a damn?"

I dropped a Wolf Investigations card in front of his nose. "Insurance." Close enough. I wanted to ensure his killer was caught.

"Who you working for?"

"You're a lawyer, so you know that it's none of your damn business," I replied, implying that I was working for an attorney. "And that's the last question I'm going to answer. Now I expect you'll be answering some."

His face flushed from white to pink to red as his anger returned. "What the fuck makes you think I'm going to answer anything?"

I straightened up, absent-mindedly scratching the side of my neck with a forefinger. "Well, you don't have to, I guess. But I know about you and Gordian, and about Gordian's debt to the family, and about you and Chicago. I'm guessing the cops are going to love hearing about it."

He couldn't have looked more stunned if I'd Tasered him. He gulped and blinked repeatedly as I turned to leave his office, tossing over my shoulder, "And tell your guys in the Windy City they'll never crack the encryption on my computer."

As I breezed out the building's lobby door, Kitty honey was coming in with two cups of coffee in a holder.

I held the door for her. "Be easy on him. He's just had a bad surprise."

She nodded and popped her gum.

I got in my Jeep. I'd kicked the hornet's nest.

It would be interesting to see where Kade's car went the rest of the day. I'd check on him after my meeting that evening with the Johnsons, the BDSM couple.

I wondered whether Gordian's car had followed Eldorp's to the motel parking lot, and who had been driving each one. I assumed that both Uncle Sal and Matt Corbett knew the answers. In fact, I enjoyed pondering the number of people who probably were following Gordian everywhere. Any more and they'd need a parade permit.

But for now it was essential for me to refocus on my HH Racing client. Then, this evening I'd get information that would clarify the significance of RF Phillips' BDSM activities, hopefully pointing toward who'd killed him and why.

My smartphone chimed with a text message as I was pulling out of the parking place. I went back in.

Have your cat. Pick up at my office ASAP. Roy Dobbins

Relief, then worry, rolled over me. Dobbins didn't say whether Boots was alive.

Roy was the maintenance supervisor for the condominium association. He and two helpers were responsible for outdoor repairs, mowing, and landscaping. A faded little man with electrical tape holding his glasses together at the nose, he had always been responsive to my calls. I texted him that I'd be there in twenty minutes and kept my promise.

I knocked on the metal door that said 'Maintenance Engineering.' Roy let me into the room housing his desk. Calling it an office was a stretch. Surrounded by circuit breakers, steam lines, and shelves of paint, his windowless space seemed more like a dungeon to me.

In the middle of the floor, under an upside-down plastic laundry basket weighted down by cans of paint, was a bedraggled, frantic, howling Boots. Roy had scratches all over his arms.

"Nasty little S O B," he said ruefully.

252

"Wow. Thanks. Where was he?"

"We were repairing a garbage chute. He was down near the dumpster where it empties."

Roy loaned me an old towel that had been used as a painting drop cloth to wrap him in.

"I sure owe you," I said. "How about some Jack for your troubles?"

He nodded, smiling. I usually gave him a fifth of Jack Daniels at Christmas.

"That'd be right nice. And if there's such a thing as a cat psychiatrist, get him one. He needs help."

Boots seemed to recognize me. At least he started meowing instead of howling, but was still struggling in the towel when we got to my condo. As soon as we were inside, I rubbed his ears, told him he was home safe, and let him go. He hightailed it behind the clothes dryer.

I left him fresh food and water, figuring he'd come out when he was ready. At least I had my companion cat back. I was sure he'd tell me about his adventures.

The world seemed a better place as I got on a downtown ramp to Interstate 65 North toward Lebanon and called Linda.

"Hi, Wolf, you on your way?"

"Yeah. Had to take care of a couple of things. Any chance Daniel and I can borrow the golf cart when I get back?"

"It'll be waiting, and I'll tell Daniel. By the way, the weather looks quite iffy for the hour of Nor-Am qualifications. The current forecast is that rain could move in anytime between four and five."

"So you want to turn as fast a time as possible early in the session, right?"

"Right. And you may not have much time to find the source of the jamming."

"I'm hoping we'll identify the location when I get back."

"So then what'll you do about it this afternoon?"

"If we accurately ID the source, we'll need help from the Boone track security people. It isn't like jamming is a felony. The best we can hope for is to shut down the operation and get the person or persons responsible evicted from the track."

"Might be a good idea for me to give them a heads-up. If the jammers are associated with another racing team, HH Racing can ask the Nor-Am governing board to impose penalties."

"OK. See you soon," I said.

* * *

Daniel and I took the golf cart into the edge of the woods at the same place we'd been that morning. The wheel tracks went further into the woods.

"Daniel, you stay with our cart while I poke around. Let me know by radio if you see anyone near here, either on foot or in a cart."

"It isn't dangerous for you, is it?" he asked. He was concerned about my safety but not wanting me to 'lose face' by criticizing my decision.

"I'm sure I'll be fine. Nobody's going to be out here for another few hours. Just use your radio if you see anything."

He nodded, and I set off into the woods, following a path of flattened vegetation, which led to a small clearing that featured a small grassy knoll. The grass on the knoll had been trampled down, but there was no other sign of human intrusion. After several minutes of searching, I didn't turn up as much as a toothpick.

Satisfied that I'd found where the jamming originated, Daniel and I took the golf cart back to the HH Racing garage area. I planned to return to the woods during the Nor-Am qualification session.

A half-hour before Nor-Am qualifications, the Pro-Am 2000s and Nor-Am Lights had each completed their first of two races; each class would run again the next day before the Formula Nor-Am feature event. Linda called us together for a last-minute briefing.

"We plan to complete four or five laps early in the session, bring the car in and make adjustments, then go back out and add as many as possible before the rain, up to our maximum of ten."

"So do you plan to run at all in rain?" I asked.

"Only if we don't get any fast laps earlier. Besides, we'd have to change to rain tires, and our speed drops significantly when we run on them."

We did radio checks, and then Daniel and I drove the golf cart with the equipment back to our location about halfway around the track. By that time it wasn't a question of whether it was going to rain, it was a question of when.

254

The weather radar was showing a line of heavy precipitation about fifteen miles northwest of the track moving southeast at twenty miles an hour. At that rate, the storm front would move in around four-thirty.

There was no backup time slot for qualifications, or, for that matter, for the race. If it rained, it rained. The urgency to finish as many qualifying laps as feasible on a dry track meant that all of the cars would be on the track as soon as the session started.

Daniel and I heard the revving of the engines at three-fifty-eight. At four Linda came on the radio and announced, "Out of the pit box, moving onto the track."

A few seconds later she came on sounding breathless and excited. "Spinout in turn one. Stand by." Half a minute later, she transmitted, "It's all right. Scott drove around it. He's OK and on the track."

Timing and scoring counts the start of a lap the instant a car crosses the start-finish line. Since all the cars entered the track at the pit exit, which was beyond that line, they had all the way around the course to sort things out and position themselves for a good qualification lap. Scott seemed to be running well and had moved away from other cars as he passed us.

A few seconds later Jason announced, "Purple." We were being jammed.

Scott came in after five laps, having posted the fastest qualifying time so far. Each lap, the car successfully dumped data as it passed the pits, and as before, the jamming stopped while he was in. Nick and the tech crew were having to take valuable time to analyze the dumped performance data since the real-time telemetry wasn't available.

Linda came on the radio. "Scott's getting more downward pressure on the front wing. More control in the corners if it starts to get wet." Then ten seconds later, "On the track."

I decided it was time for me to poke around. "Daniel, when I hear that Scott's off the track, I'm going to turn off my radio for a while."

"You do not want to be disturbed while you are poking around."

"Right. I'll turn it back on and call you when I'm ready. You'll need to load the equipment, then pick me up. I'll wait for you along the road."

"Got you. Be careful, Wolf."

I had barely started walking down the maintenance road when the first scattered raindrops fell, large drops splattering in the dust. Within a minute Linda was on the radio saying, "Rain. Scott is being called in. We're done for today."

I turned off my radio and realized that our choice of code word for no jamming was unfortunate. I wasn't sure if she was relaying information on the weather, or the fact that the jamming had stopped. It didn't matter since HH Racing's car was coming off the track.

A minute later I turned into the woods following the tracks. The rain was steady and getting heavier as I slogged toward a golf cart parked back behind tall bushes.

I saw a quad-copter that had been stowed in it where it was dry. Lying on top of it was a strange wire object that looked a little like an upside-down spider, with bent legs each about a foot long poking upwards. It was probably the antenna that had been connected to the bottom of the drone so that it pointed at the ground.

I cautiously advanced, counting on the rain to cover the sounds of my approach, looking for whoever owned the equipment. I figured he or she had gone back for the other items such as the remote control. I should have realized that the rain was masking the noise made by anyone, including the person whose presence was announced by a twig snapping behind me.

Alarmed, I started to pivot, but just as I got a glimpse of a black boot and camouflage pants, someone clobbered me on the back of my head a little to the right. The trees tilted. As I tried to step to the left to straighten them up, blackness flowed through the cracks of my consciousness. I dropped to my knees, then pitched sideways into moist darkness.

Lying in the wet grass with rain pouring on me wasn't much different than being continually doused with water, and I came around in a few minutes. A bass drum playing in my head and dizziness kept me from standing for another minute.

As I stood unsteadily, brushing off wet grass and leaves, the image of the unusual antenna perched upside down on the quad-copter picked away at my memory, trying to access something that my semi-functional brain was blocking. If I gave it time, whatever it was would seep back into my awareness.

As I turned on my radio and called Daniel to pick me up, I realized who was responsible for the jamming and that I wasn't going to tell anyone else until I'd had time to think. I needed to talk with Tito. Or Jeff. Or both.

It was someone with experience flying radio controlled airplanes and with electronic warfare equipment. The leading suspect was a former Marine with PTSD.

Chapter 22

I felt the bump rising on the back of my skull just right of center, and decided to get it checked out at the first aid tent in the infield of the track. It was probable I had a mild concussion, and, if so, I figured I had to avoid going to sleep for a few hours. Two or three Ibuprofen should lessen the pounding in my head so I could function.

I was still brushing grass off myself when Daniel drove up.

"We've been off the track for almost five minutes. What happened to you?" he asked.

"I had a brief encounter with the jammer." I felt the bump on my head.

"Who was it?"

"I didn't get a good look at him," I replied. That was true, even though I knew it was Paul Wheeler.

"You need to see a doctor?"

"The first aid tent is probably a good idea."

"I'll call Linda and tell her."

"Please just tell her we're delayed. I'll fill her in when we get back."

The American Red Cross has comprehensive first aid facilities at many race tracks and race courses. Staffed by trained volunteers, including doctors and nurses, they treat a variety of ailments ranging from heat stroke to heart attacks. At Boone, an EMT vehicle was on standby to transport more serious patients to Boone Memorial Hospital.

A badge identified the woman looking at my head wound as a nurse practitioner named Cheryl Land. Short curly blond hair and penetrating blue eyes underscored her no nonsense approach to health care.

After her fingers probed the knot on my head, she examined my eyes with a small penlight, then picked up a clipboard and asked, "How'd it happen?" Her eyes roved over my grass-stained clothes.

I'd been considering what I was going to say. "I met a tree limb that didn't like me" was the best I could come up with.

She pressed her lips together and expelled air out of her nose. She wasn't buying it, but she'd obviously had stranger explanations offered for accidents at Boone. I didn't see what she wrote.

"You may have a mild concussion. Take two Ibuprofen every four hours. Get them on your way out of the tent."

"Thanks. Do I need to stay awake?"

"Used to be people were told to stay awake, but you don't have any issues with walking, and your pupils aren't dilated, so nowadays we don't suggest that. Just don't do whatever really caused that again."

As I started to reply she turned toward a limping and grimacing teenage boy coming into the tent.

Back at the HH Racing transporter, I stood under a corner of the garage area canopy out of the rain where nobody could hear us, and beckoned Linda over.

She walked up grinning. "Did you hear? We qualified second. Front row with Laurence LeGrand."

"That's great," Daniel answered.

Linda scanned me from head to toe. "What happened? You don't look too good."

"I've been better. I met the person doing the jamming, or rather, he met me."

"Who is it?"

"I didn't get a good enough look to ID him, but I have an idea."

Daniel chimed in, "He hit Wolf on the head. We've been at the first aid tent."

"You OK?" she asked, tilting her head and walking behind me.

"Nothing that Ibuprofen and time won't cure."

"Should we call track security?"

I thought for a few seconds. "Probably a good idea. Have Daniel show them where he picked me up. The jamming was coming from a clearing directly into the woods from there."

"You going to tell me who you think it was?"

"I'd rather not. I need to poke around some more. Main thing is that the jamming will probably stop, at least from that location, especially if there are a couple of security guys hanging around there tomorrow."

"You think he'll move and try again?"

"He may. But if he moves too far from where he was, he won't be able to cover the whole road course. And I aim to discourage him from trying again."

She looked at me quizzically, but I didn't elaborate. Daniel was too respectful to even think about asking.

"Go ahead and call security," I continued. "Ask them to keep the part about the jamming confidential for now; tell them it's part of a police investigation."

She nodded and moved away to call.

I looked at Daniel. "I need to make a couple of calls, too. I'll appreciate your unloading the equipment and putting it away."

"OK, Wolf. Sure you're all right?"

I nodded, and he waved, glancing anxiously back at me as he drove the golf cart to the transporter to unload it.

Nor-Am qualification was the last event of the day. People were streaming out of the track, the lucky ones with umbrellas, the semi-lucky ones with ten-buck clear plastic ponchos worth only a dollar, and the unlucky ones drenched to the skin.

I stayed under the corner of the canopy and called Jeff Smithfield.

"Hi, Wolf. I was waiting for your call."

"Had a little adventure I'll fill you in on it in a minute. Where are you?"

"I'm off work and heading home to change clothes. I'm planning to interview Mr. Phillips' neighbors and check on Mike Spencer this evening. That still OK?"

"Yes, fine. I want you to ask the neighbors specifically about any visitors they saw coming and going from his house, what they were driving, and if they carried anything in or out of the house."

"BDSM related?"

I thought for a few seconds. "Maybe, but probably not."

"Will do. What about your adventure?"

I filled him in on my encounter with Paul Wheeler, then continued, "I'm concerned about him. He has a serious case of PTSD. He's had a restraining order slapped on him by his girlfriend. I want to cut him some slack, but I'm beginning to worry that he might be somehow involved in RF's murder."

"You want to have a talk with him?"

"Yeah, with you along."

"When?"

"After I have my meeting with the Johnsons. You know, the BDSM folks. I should be finished there by eight. That'll give you time to check on Spencer and talk with RF's neighbors."

The slip of paper that Harry Wheeler had written Paul's address and cell number on indicated that he lived east of Broad Ripple. We agreed to meet at my place.

I called Tito and left a voicemail as I headed home. He was probably on the road.

A bedraggled Boots greeted me at the door, then circled around me sniffing. My rolling in the wet grass must have added some interesting outdoor scents. He let me pick him up and pet him without struggling, but he wasn't up to purring. As I was feeding him, Tito called me back.

"Hi, Tito. I believe we've figured out who's been jamming us."

"No kidding? Who?"

I recapped our location of the jamming, my initial meeting with Paul Wheeler and his father, and my encounter with him in the woods, then continued, "Jeff and I plan to visit him later this evening. I want to be careful how we deal with him, but I'd like to know whether he has a record, previous arrests and so on, other than the restraining order he's under now."

"I can check in the morning, mon."

"Any way I can get it sooner?"

"I'd need a damn good reason to ask someone to access that info tonight."

I hesitated. "This is still just a hunch, but there may be a link to RF Phillips' murder."

"Interesting, but no brass ring. I can't jump through hoops every time you have a hunch."

"Acho, there's a connection that seems to be buried in my head. I haven't grabbed it yet, but I'm sure it's there."

"Well, when you grab it, let me know. I need more than a hunch."

I didn't say anything.

"I hope your meeting with Wheeler goes OK."

I was slightly pissed at Tito, but more aggravated with myself for not being able to connect the dots. I changed into a navy pullover and jeans sans grass stains. I called Betty and Mike Johnson from my parking lot to let them know I was on the way.

* * *

The Johnsons lived in the Holy Cross neighborhood near downtown Indy, in a long narrow house on a corner across from the park. Holy Cross Catholic Church, located on the eastern edge, gives the neighborhood its name. Recently shuttered by the Catholic Church in a budget-cutting move, the church was formerly a major focus of activity.

I would have guessed that Mike's blue eyes, shock of red hair, and freckled face went with a name like O'Reilly or Flannigan. Both were wearing warm-up pants and jogging shoes, but the similarity ended there. With wavy black hair, a porcelain complexion, and a nose ring, Betty appeared as Goth as Mike did Irish.

I introduced myself and gave them each a Wolf Investigations card.

"We just got back from a walk around the neighborhood," said Mike. "Do you know much about it?"

"Only a little," I admitted. "I read about the church closing in the Indy Star."

"We've been here about a year. Lots of small investors have bought up the houses like ours and completely renovated them. There's been a renaissance happening here for the past decade."

Betty chimed in, "Mike can walk to work downtown, and I travel for my job, so it's easy to get to the airport."

At their invitation, I sat in an easy chair while Betty sat on the couch and Mike perched on one of the arms.

"What is it you'd like to know?" asked Mike, looking at my card.

I cleared my throat. "I want to ask questions that might give me insight into the death of Ron Phillips. I understand he was here with his ex-wife for an event you hosted."

"Tania Bell told us we could trust you to keep our conversation confidential," said Betty. "Just why are you interested in Mr. Phillips' death?"

"I need you to keep our conversation confidential, as well. Deal?" I asked.

They looked at each other and nodded.

"Mr. Phillips died of strangulation by a choke collar attached to the St. Andrew's cross in his dungeon."

Betty gasped, her hand going involuntarily to her neck. "My God. That wasn't in the paper, was it?"

I shook my head. "That's one reason our talk has to be confidential."

Mike pursed his lips and looked at her. "Let's show Wolf our dungeon."

As Betty led the way downstairs, I remarked, "You two don't seem different from a typical couple I'd meet in a shopping mall."

Betty turned to look at Mike and smiled.

I instantly regretted my words, and was about to say so, when Mike turned and held up a hand. "That's OK. We can see you are a little uncomfortable talking with us. We don't think of ourselves as especially unusual except for our sexual preferences."

"I guess I expected to find both of you wearing black, or something," I stammered.

Betty laughed, "Many different kinds of folks are into BDSM. There are some who practice the lifestyle 24/7, but Mike and I compartmentalize our lives a little more."

The entire downstairs was finished space. At the foot of the stairway was a modest living room area with a large screen TV. Most of the rest of the downstairs was full of BDSM gear. They led me to the other end, where there was a spacious bedroom and a full bath.

Except for the BDSM paraphernalia it could have been a very nice furnished apartment. The equipment, however, made it a big 'except.'

"Have you been in a dungeon before?" asked Mike.

"No. I probably don't need a lot of details, but an overview would be helpful."

Betty took the lead as tour guide, showing me the spanking benches, St. Andrew's Cross, a bondage chair, a sex stool with built-in dildo, and a variety of accessories, including whips, choke collars, blindfolds, and masks. The bedroom featured a king-sized bed with bondage restraints.

"You know the basics of BDSM, the fact that there are dominants and submissives, doms and subs, facts like that?"

"Yes. Liz Phillips filled me in." Based on her behavior, I looked at Betty and speculated, "I'm guessing you're a dom and Mike is a sub."

They put their arms around each other's waists and laughed.

Mike said, "You guessed right. Most people assume that the male of a couple is a dom, but not in our case, and not in many others."

"What were your impressions of Liz and Ron Phillips when they attended your event?" I asked.

They sat side by side on a spanking bench, Betty taking the lead. "Ron Phillips is the one who contacted us. He seemed as attracted to the BDSM lifestyle as anyone we've met recently, and was solidly into a dom role."

Mike interjected, "And Liz appeared as repelled as he was attracted. I didn't sense healthy interactions between the two of them."

Betty shook her head in agreement, "No. Me either. And I'm curious about him being strangled by a choke collar on a St. Andrew's Cross. No dom *I* know would allow themself to be put in a choke collar, much less attached to a cross."

"I agree," said Mike, thoughtfully. "But some people sexually arouse themselves by cutting off the oxygen to their brains. It's called autoerotic asphyxiation, and having an orgasm that way is supposedly as powerful as being on cocaine."

"Were there signs of sexual activity?" asked Betty.

"Not in the death report." Sensing their next question I added, "And it definitely wasn't suicide."

I didn't reveal the details regarding how that was determined. Almost to myself, I said, "If he wasn't into autoerotic asphyxiation, and it wasn't suicide, he must have been murdered."

They scooted closer together on the bench.

"Know anyone who'd want to do that?" I asked, looking from Betty to Mike.

"No, nobody," answered Betty, with Mike echoing, "No one."

"No one who'd been his sub and wanted revenge, or a dom who resented mistreatment of a sub, maybe theirs?"

They shook their heads again.

"We *were* uncomfortable around him, though," offered Mike. "We didn't attend an event he hosted."

"Maybe he was still searching for his niche as a dom," agreed Betty. "But he was really harsh and aggressive. He didn't seem to know how to treat subs with respect."

Mike nodded agreement. "Maybe didn't even know he was supposed to."

I figured I'd learned all I needed. I thanked them, and we said goodbye.

As I was going out the door, Betty waved. "Let us know if you'd like to attend an event."

I just waved back and nodded.

Ann would probably be troubled, perhaps even appalled, by BDSM. I wondered about Vanessa.

I called Jeff as soon as I got in my Jeep. "Hi, I'm finished with my meeting with the Johnsons. Can we meet in twenty minutes or so?"

"Yeah, sure. I'm done with my interviews of the neighbors. Couple of interesting things."

"OK, we can fill each other in at my condo."

Jeff was waiting outside my door, this time wearing a white long-sleeved shirt with rolled-up cuffs, and gray slacks. His black spit-shined shoes reflected his daytime job.

Inside, Boots, still looking a little rough around the edges, had conveniently forgotten about his escapade, and conned me out of an ear rubbing and a snack. Jeff and I sat at the kitchen table and pulled out our notebooks as I filled him in on Boots' big adventure.

I summarized my talk with Betty and Mike, then sat back. "I don't think it's likely that someone in the BDSM community killed RF. Nobody seemed to actively dislike him. They just weren't comfortable with him, and considered him a wannabe dominant who hadn't learned the ropes."

Jeff snickered, and I quickly added, "Pun not intended…so, smartass, what did you find out?"

He composed himself, and glanced at his notes. "You asked me to see if Liz Phillips had any cell calls the night Mr. Phillips was murdered.

"Before I took the trouble to call in a favor and access her cell records, I found out something that made it unnecessary. Both Mr. Phillips and his ex-wife had the same service provider."

"So?"

"So, the house where Liz lives and the one RF rented are only about a mile and a half apart. They're served by the same cell tower. She could have been either place that evening and the service provider wouldn't be able to tell which one."

"I wouldn't have thought to look at the tower locations. Smart move. A dead end, but that happens all the time. Anything on Mike Spencer?"

"Yeah, I called in a favor at the department. He's clean as a whistle. Not even any speeding tickets."

"That doesn't mean he isn't a killer."

"No, but he's active in politics."

I snickered.

"I know, I know," Jeff continued, grinning. "But he was speaking at a political rally when RF was killed. He's running for state senator."

"I guess he's another dead end. How about this evening?"

"I talked with neighbors in six houses. I'm sure that there were people home at another place, but they didn't answer the door. People in three of the homes told me about parties that he held once every month or six weeks. The black latex worn by the attendees got their attention."

"Any problems? Disturbances?"

"Not that anyone would own up to."

"Anything else?"

"Maybe. This is sort of weird, but one of his next-door neighbors, a stay-at-home mother, said she saw her neighbor, that's Mr. Phillips, walking out to a big red pickup truck with a man. Phillips was carrying something that looked kind of like an upside-down birdcage without a bottom. The man he was with put it on the front seat of the truck and drove off."

I started to say something, then closed my mouth and just sat there, staring off into space. Pieces fell into place. Dots connected.

I was startled by Jeff asking, "Is the birdcage important?"

"Wasn't a birdcage. It was an antenna."

"For what?"

"A Newcastle Systems jammer. The one that's been jamming HH Racing's telemetry."

The description of the object RF carried out of his house triggered the memory that had been hidden of a similar antenna on the shelf in his cubicle at HH Racing. I'd seen it while I was making a digital backup of his laptop and desktop computers. It was very similar, if not identical, to the antenna that I saw on the golf cart just before I got slugged by Paul Wheeler.

Jeff asked tentatively, "A link between Mr. Phillips' murder and the jamming?"

"For sure. Until now, I thought that the two might not be related. Now, I'm worried that Wheeler not only has PTSD, but might be connected to RF's death, maybe even be his killer."

"Did you get any more of a description of the pickup or the person driving?"

Jeff looked at his notes. "The woman said the pickup had four doors. She didn't remember much about the driver except that he was taller and skinnier than Mr. Phillips."

"Well, let's go see what Paul Wheeler has in his driveway." I thought for a minute. "We'll take your car; he might recognize my Jeep."

I got my computer bag with the GPS tracking tablet, and took my S&W out of my office safe.

Jeff had a silver Honda Accord with a sun roof. He flipped on the car's GPS and punched in Paul Wheeler's address. A recommended route appeared within a second.

I was jealous. "Damn, I could use something like that when I'm serving subpoenas."

He grinned. "It does come in handy."

The address was on a dead end one-block street off 65th near Allisonville Road. The streetlight at the corner was out.

The house was a small bungalow with an unkept lawn and a large red 'No Soliciting' sign affixed to the front door. The house was dark and the short gravel driveway was empty. There was no response to our knocking.

"Are we gonna wait for him?" asked Jeff.

"I guess. For a while. We didn't come equipped for a stakeout, though."

"We'd better park on 65th. This car'd stand out like a sore thumb on his block."

I agreed, and we found a place behind a black Ford about half a block down 65th.

While we waited, I pulled out my tracking tablet and turned it on. "This is my GPS electronic tailing system. You should know how to use it. Might as well start showing you the basics."

"Is that the one that was tracking you and Vanessa?"

"Yeah. Gerald Eldorp gave it to me before he was killed. It's still tracking two vehicles. One is Vanessa's car, and the other is Rudy Kade's."

"You interested in both?"

"No, not officially. Uncle Sal is covering Vanessa. Told me to lay off. But I'm interested in Kade. I think he's tied to Eldorp's murder. And while I have it on, I might as well see where Vanessa's car is."

"So show me how it works."

I showed him how to select a vehicle and display its movements for the past 24 hours. "Let's see where Kade is."

I displayed his information on the screen, then grinned.

"What's so funny?"

"I must have gotten the code for Kade's car mixed up with Vanessa's. It's indicating he's in the parking lot at Shawnee Country Club where Vanessa's a member." I started over, selecting the other vehicle in the tracking system.

"Holy shit! It's in the same parking lot. The first one was Kade's car after all. This shows Vanessa's vehicle parked about a hundred feet away, in a corner of the same lot."

The hair went up on the back of my neck. It didn't make sense, and I didn't like what I was seeing.

"What's wrong?" asked Jeff.

"I don't know what the problem is, exactly. But I suspect there's a serious one. The FBI operation involving Vanessa and Stan Gordian is under way. I'll bet that Gordian's Cadillac Escalade is there, too."

"What's Kade's role in that?"

"None. *That's* what's eating at me. He seems to have fabricated one for himself, and I doubt if any of the players officially involved even know he's in the game."

"What're you gonna do?"

"Good question…tell you what, since there's nothing happening here, take me back to my place so I can get my Jeep. You come back here and let me know when Wheeler gets home."

"You sure he'll show up?" he asked as he pulled away from the curb.

"Pretty sure."

"You going to tail Kade?"

"Probably, unless I get a better idea. Vanessa has the FBI and her uncle Sal watching her. She should be getting whatever Stan sold to the FBI from him about now. Maybe already done it."

"What do you think Kade's up to?"

"Given what's happened in similar cases, I figure that Gordian's getting at least a hundred grand in exchange for his information. One possibility is that Kade might try to relieve him of the cash."

I kept watching the location of Kade's car as Jeff drove. Just as we parked near my Jeep, it left the Shawnee Country Club heading east on Fall Creek Parkway. I checked the whereabouts of Vanessa's vehicle. She'd left the club about the same time taking the same route.

I drove toward Fall Creek Parkway, ten to twelve minutes behind each of them. Jeff went back to stake out Wheeler's house.

I doubted that Kade was following Vanessa, but I had to be prepared for that. I put his tracking information back on the tablet display. The interval between GPS location reports was three minutes, so his car's position was being updated about every mile.

Three miles up Fall Creek, Kade went east on 75th. I pulled off to the side and checked Vanessa's position. She had continued north toward her condo. I switched back to Kade's display.

I knew where he was going. As I'd expected, he was following the money.

Chapter 23

By the time I turned east on 75th, the blinking blue dot on the tracking display showed that Kade's car was directly in front of Stan Gordian's house on Royal Briarcliff Way. I didn't want to walk in on both of them, so I parked facing the street on a cul-de-sac between Gordian's house and 75th.

I don't mind kicking a hornet's nest if there's a reason and I can get away from it, but I didn't have a stake in this game. Kade wanted some or all of the hundred thousand Gordian had just collected. Or he wanted a piece of Gordian's hide for killing Eldorp. Or both.

It was a warm evening, so I opened my window and found some jazz on the radio while I was waiting. My head was down adjusting the volume, so I heard it before I saw it. A car was coming up the street. I looked up just in time to see Kade go by. The driver's side window was down, and he looked stressed. Not a sign of a congenial meeting.

With my lights off, I drove quietly down the hill past the house about fifty yards, turned around, and parked in front of his next-door neighbor. I slipped my S&W into my pocket and quietly closed the Jeep's door.

I expected to find a very pissed off Gordian. Even if Kade hadn't gotten any of the cash, there had probably been an angry confrontation.

The house was ablaze with light. Outside security lights lit up the yard, and the glow behind the living room and upstairs curtains indicated that Gordian was home. I put one hand in the pocket with my revolver and rang the doorbell with the other. No answer. Again. Nothing. Knocked. Ditto.

I listened with my ear against the door. Silence. I looked up and down the street. I didn't see anyone watching. I pulled my S&W out of the holster and flicked off the safety. Carefully, I tried the front door. It was unlocked. As I pushed it part way open, it creaked loudly. It didn't matter.

Stan Gordian's body was draped over the coffee table in front of the couch, chest down. I pushed the door open further, slipped in, and closed it behind me. Uncongealed blood, its familiar tinny copper smell assaulting me, glistened on the table's marble top and pooled on the carpet.

His right arm was dangling over the edge of the table, pointing at nothing. The left was pinned under him. His head was sideways, sightless eyes toward the large screen TV. He didn't seem interested in the ten o'clock news. He'd be part of it soon enough.

I realized I'd held my breath against the stench and exhaled. As PTSD seeped in, I felt dizzy and disoriented and confused. My eyes blurred as memories of the deaths of my buddies in Iraq flooded my consciousness. Bile rose in my throat. I willed myself not to throw up.

Taking a deep breath helped my vision start to clear. I dropped to my knees beside his hanging arm and checked for a pulse. Nada.

The main source of the blood was a bullet wound on the right side of his neck which appeared to have ruptured the carotid artery, opening a floodgate that alone would have killed him. He also had been shot in the back of the head, another fatal wound.

Under the table was the chrome-plated .22 pistol he'd threatened me with when I confronted him in his driveway during the Stellar case. It was his weapon, but this was no suicide.

Kade was probably the murderer. He was gone, but I needed to check the house before I called IMPD. If the killer was still there, not checking could be lethal.

I raised myself off the floor with one hand, holding my S&W in the other. Gordian's jacket was draped across an easy chair next to the sofa. He hadn't hung it up, so he probably hadn't been home long.

As my head cleared, I began to speculate where the hundred grand was. It wasn't an amount that he could stuff into his pockets. He probably used an attaché case or computer bag.

Holding my raised pistol, I cautiously went from room to room. I didn't find anything, and I doubted that he'd been there long enough to hide it, so the killer must have taken it. Still dizzy and nauseous, I sat on the ottoman in front of the easy chair and reviewed various scenarios that could have led to Eldorp's and Gordian's murders.

Kade could have killed both of them. Eldorp could have found out about the FBI payoff, and Kade might have silenced him to get all the money for himself. But Eldorp seemed to have been useful to Kade, and even if he was upset with Eldorp, he wouldn't have killed him.

Kade might have killed neither, stumbling upon Gordian after he was shot and fleeing the scene before he was discovered. However, the freshness of the blood suggested that Gordian had been shot very recently. I didn't see any cars but Kade's.

The most likely scenario was that Gordian had killed Eldorp, or had him killed. The GPS tracker on Eldorp's car had traced it from ElecRecycle to the SnoreZ Inn parking lot where his body was found in the trunk. Then Kade had murdered Gordian for the money, and perhaps as revenge for Eldorp.

The FBI was sure as hell not interested in what happened to Gordian after he was paid. They got the information from him and ran with it. Sal Russo, and maybe the FBI, were supposedly keeping tabs on Vanessa.

From my Jeep I called IMPD homicide and talked with a Sergeant Bartkowski. I gave the who, what, when, and where. I didn't say anything about the why or how. I asked her to contact Sergeant Rodriguez or Sergeant Wilkerson since they were aware of Gordian and his connection with a previous case. I suggested they didn't need to use lights or sirens.

I watched the movement of Kade's car on the GPS tablet as I talked. He was on a route that took him generally toward Vanessa's condo. A murderer headed her way gave me the jitters big time, especially since he was a wild card in the game that only I knew about.

I wanted to pursue him, but the IMPD cops would take a dim view of my leaving the scene of a murder. Calling the FBI was out of the question. I only had Agent Corbett's office number, and, besides, I wasn't supposed to know about their operation. I could try to re-direct Jeff to cover Kade, but I needed him where he was, watching for Paul Wheeler.

I took a deep breath and called Uncle Sal. He answered on the second ring.

"Hello Wolf. I assume you have an important situation to be calling this late."

"You could say that." I quickly filled him in on Gordian's murder.

"What is so urgent if Mr. Gordian is deceased?"

"Rudy Kade probably killed him. I'm watching Kade on my GPS tracking system and he is heading in the general direction of Vanessa's condo." I gave him information on Kade's car and license plate that

I'd noted when I installed the electronic tail, as well as his current location and direction.

"We will be watching for Mr. Kade. Anything else?"

I paused for a few seconds, then said to myself 'What the hell?'

"It's likely that Kade helped himself to a large amount of cash that had recently been paid to Gordian."

"That is most interesting," he said, and hung up.

Within ten seconds two squad cars with flashing lights came down the street. One pulled into the drive. The other parked diagonally in front of my Jeep. At least they weren't using their sirens.

As I got out of my Jeep, the officer stepped out of the car in front of it with a flashlight the size of a baseball bat which he aimed directly in my eyes, commanding, "Keep your hands where I can see 'em."

I did. "I'm the one who called this in. Wolf Ruger."

"OK, lower one hand and show me your ID. Slowly."

I did. His name tag identified him as Sergeant Delgado.

As I showed him my PI license, a voice behind him said, "I've seen him before. He's a PI." Corporal Pointer had been one of the responding officers on my previous homicide case.

Sergeant Delgado was white-haired and pudgy. He could have been somebody's grandfather. Pointer was lean, tough, and all spit and polish. The crease in his pants could have sliced the powdered sugar doughnut that Delgado had been eating.

After he checked Gordian's body, Delgado started taking my statement in the back seat of his patrol car while Pointer started stringing yellow crime scene tape.

I realized that I was here on my own. I'd come because of Eldorp's killing, and because of Kade being in the same parking lot as Vanessa. I couldn't hide behind attorney-client confidentiality. I needed to be very careful about what I said. I couldn't lie, but there were things such as the FBI operation that I considered confidential.

"OK, tell me what were you doing here, and what happened. Take your time and don't leave anything out."

I'd heard that before. Earlier that day, as a matter of fact.

I gave him the bare minimum. "I was tailing someone, and followed him here. I waited down the block, and when he left in a hurry, I decided to check out Mr. Gordian's situation." I gave them the information on Kade's car.

"Why were you following him?"

I quickly thought about that. I could say that I was doing a favor for the uncle of a friend. That was valid, but Uncle Sal would be extremely upset. I could say that I thought Kade was going to confront Gordian and take a hundred grand from him, but I wasn't even supposed to know about that.

In the end I told the truth. Most of it, anyway. Mine were sins of omission rather than commission.

"A guy named Gerald Eldorp was found murdered this morning. He worked for Kade, but he was my informant. I thought Kade might know something about Eldorp's death. I followed him here."

Accurate, as far as it went.

"How were you involved with Eldorp?"

"That information is in a statement I gave homicide Detective Sergeants Wilkerson and Hardin this morning."

Before he could ask anything else, an unmarked black Ford Victoria that had seen better days arrived just ahead of an ambulance. A plainclothes cop wearing a rumpled suit, loosened tie, and a haggard expression got out of the Vic and peered into the patrol car.

He got in the back seat on the other side of me, coffee in one hand and notebook in the other. His pinched eyes and flat nose gave him the look of a boxer who'd led with his chin. He flipped open a badge holder. His name was Thomas Tobias, Detective Lieutenant.

He looked at Delgado. "Taking his statement?"

Delgado nodded.

He looked at me and sighed. "Start again from the top."

He outranked Delgado, and they probably wanted to see if my two versions were consistent.

I was most of the way through my statement when I saw Tito's red Toyota parking beside us. He was wearing sweats, his badge in a holder hanging around his neck.

He opened the door on Delgado's side, motioned him out with his thumb, and sat in his place while I went through what had happened for a third time.

He listened, staring out the windshield, barely acknowledging my presence. From the way his dark eyes were smoldering, I knew he was angry.

He looked at Tobias. "Tom, why don't you make sure the ambulance guys have what they need. Then contact whoever is holding down the fort in forensics and give them a heads-up."

Tobias outranked him, but could tell Tito wanted to talk with me privately. He nodded and got out of the car, leaving the two of us alone in the back seat.

His eyes bored into mine. In a low, tense voice he said, "I told you to stay the fuck away from Gordian and the rest of the mobster motherfuckers. First, you get called in on the Eldorp murder, and now this. What the hell is going on?"

I told him about seeing Kade's car in the same parking lot as Vanessa's, and that he appeared to be following her home. "I started following him, then he turned off away from Vanessa and I followed him here."

"Why in hell did you care where he was going if he wasn't following Vanessa?"

I paused. "I can't tell you that."

He was about to explode. I held up my hand. "Call Matt Corbett. FBI."

Tito expelled air and sat back. "That shit again. I don't believe it. How about what happened here? What haven't you told me?"

"You'll put two and two together anyway. The gun Gordian was killed with was his. When you run ballistics on it, you'll probably find it was used to kill Eldorp."

"You'll verify that Kade's car was here when Gordian was killed, assuming time of death matches, right?"

I nodded.

"And you saw him, not just his car, leaving the scene."

"Yes."

"We have an APB out on him. State Police, too. He won't get far."

"You haven't asked me what else I haven't told you," I said smugly.

"OK, smartass. What?"

"You forgot that I told you I have a GPS electronic tail on his car."

Tito's eyes rolled up and he took a deep breath. "All right, where's his car?"

"I'll show you," I said as I took him back to my Jeep and punched a few keys on the GPS tracking tablet. I pointed at the screen. "Here. His

275

car's in an alley behind his office. Three hundred block of Mass Avenue."

"Jesus," said Tito as he reached over the front seat, grabbed the radio microphone, and called in the car's description and location.

"It's simple to use. Watch, I'll give you a quick demo." I showed him the buttons to press, then shoved the tracking tablet into his hands. "Here. Take it. If his car moves, you'll see where it goes."

I walked Tito and Tobias through the crime scene and promised to sign my statement in the homicide offices on Monday morning.

I watched Tito use the tracking tablet. Kade's car hadn't moved. "Do I need to change any of the settings on this thing?"

I shook my head. "Leave everything set like it is. I'll pick it up when I sign my statement." He didn't need to know he could also track Vanessa.

Tito and Tobias accompanied me to my Jeep.

"Must be nice, heading home to eight hours' sleep," said Tito.

"I wish. Headed to a stakeout."

"Who?"

"The guy who's been jamming the telemetry signals, Paul Wheeler."

"Ex-Marine with serious PTSD, right?"

"Yeah."

"Smithfield there?"

"Uh-huh. Figure we should both talk with him."

"Good luck. Watch your asses."

As they let me go, Tobias called out, "By the way, don't leave town."

I wondered who'd get to Kade first, IMPD or Uncle Sal. My money was on Sal.

I called Jeff as I left Gordian's house.

"What's up Wolf?" he asked.

"Gordian's dead. Kade shot him and is on the run."

"Wow. Need my help?"

"Nope. It's under control. I gave Tito my GPS unit. They're on him like stink on shit."

"How do you want to handle the situation here?"

"Stay put. I'll pick up coffee on my way to you."

I bought coffee for both of us at a 24-hour McDonalds and used their bathroom. As Max liked to say, "You don't own coffee, you just rent it." I parked my Jeep out of sight on the side street behind Jeff's car.

I handed him his coffee as I slid into his front seat. "Want me to spell you? You could run to Mickey D's and use the bathroom."

"Naw. Used the bushes in the alley. I want to hear what happened with Gordian and Kade."

As I filled him in, he sipped his coffee. "So you think Kade made off with Gordian's payoff?"

"It sure as hell wasn't anywhere I could see, and he hadn't been home long enough to hide it. If IMPD doesn't find it, we'll know for sure."

"You tell IMPD about the payoff?"

"Hell no, I'm not even supposed to know about it. If the FBI wants IMPD to know, they'll tell 'em."

"IMPD may recover it when they arrest Kade," said Jeff.

"Maybe." My money was still on Sal.

"You think Eldorp was onto the payoff, and tried to shoulder his way in?"

"I'm not sure."

"The way you've described him, he was more of a gofer than anything else, but I believe Gerald Eldorp was smarter than you give him credit for."

I nodded and sat back. "You may be right."

* * *

Midnight came and went. No sign of Paul Wheeler. The silence was broken only by sipping sounds.

I thought about Eldorp. Maybe he *was* more intelligent than I'd assumed.

He did come up with the idea to use a GPS tracking system. He always seemed a little like a buffoon, but he knew about Gordian owing money, and the Chicago connections. Seemed like he knew how to insert himself in the middle of the action. His 'aw shucks' persona could have been a put-on.

Maybe he only pretended ignorance regarding how to view someone's location on his GPS tracking tablet. And he could have been putting me on when he acted like he didn't know anything about malware.

As I thought about Eldorp, a possible analogy with RF Phillips percolated in my brain.

I broke the silence. "What you said about Eldorp makes me think about RF. What if he was smarter than he seemed? Was his 'golly gee' personality a façade?"

"I never met him, but he *was* in a job at HH Racing that required him to be technically savvy."

I nodded. "Since our first meeting, I've pondered how someone with a college degree in computer technology could be so technically ignorant about things like digital signals. And his lie about the spectrum analyzer not working should have been a red flag."

"So you think he knew about the jamming?"

"Probably. From the beginning. Or close to it. And I'll bet he knew Wheeler was doing it."

"Why did he play dumb?"

"Don't know. I can think of several reasons, but one doesn't stand out."

"What was Wheeler's role?"

I shrugged. "I hope he'll tell us."

Silence settled in again.

Jeff's dashboard clock read twelve-fifty as a large red four-door Ford 150 came down 65th from the east. It turned into Wheeler's street.

"Wait," I said. "Give him time to get inside."

Jeff nodded. A minute later, we pulled slowly onto the street, lights off.

Wheeler's pickup was in his driveway. His house was dark. We parked on the side of the street in front of the neighbor's house. I pushed my S&W under the car seat.

"Going in unarmed?" asked Jeff. "My service revolver's in the trunk."

I nodded. "He's on a hair trigger. Don't want to set him off."

"Your call."

We approached the front door. A faint blue light flickered in the front window. TV.

We stood on opposite sides of the door, backs to the wall. The knob was closer to me. I tried it. Unlocked.

I carefully pushed the door open. Nothing. At my nod, we slipped inside, one on either side of the door.

"You bastards think you're pretty fucking slick."

Paul Wheeler was sprawled on a couch against the far wall, his legs splayed out. I reached for a light switch.

"Don't," he said.

He raised a large pistol, clicked off the safety, and pointed it in our general direction. In the faint blue light it looked like a Marine-issued .45 automatic. My sidearm had been the Army version.

In a quiet monotone, he said, "This is where you pull weapons out. I kill one of you. The other one kills me."

"We're unarmed," I said, my hands out by my sides, palms forward. Jeff mirrored me.

"Well, fuck me." Paul waved the gun in my direction. "You, I've met," he said, then pointing it toward Jeff, "Who're you?"

"Smithfield. Former Spec 4, infantry, Iraq."

"That doesn't buy you shit," he muttered, laying the gun in his lap.

It may not have bought us shit, but at least we didn't have his .45 pointed in our direction. I lowered my hands and started to step toward him.

"Don't move. Either of you. Next time I point it at you, I pull the trigger."

I froze.

"Know what you're going through. Dealing with the shit myself," said Jeff, calmly.

"You can't know. And it's not the same shit!" he snapped.

"OK. Not the same. Not as bad. But we both have it."

"Why the fuck're you here? Not that I give a damn."

Answers to his question led us into dangerous, dark territory where people die.

I decided to try the noble route first. "We want to find help for you."

"Cut the bullshit. Tell me something I can believe."

I shrugged. "I have facts. Theories. Questions. You have answers."

"Skip the facts about the jamming. We both know I did that."

I nodded. "Theories, then. You could have done it because you wanted HH Racing to lose Gamble Oil sponsorship. Or, so Clanton-Suggs could pick up Gamble Oil's money."

"Close, but no kewpie doll."

"Why, then?"

He shifted on the couch, but didn't let go of the .45. "Guess again."

"RF Phillips wanted HH Racing to lose to Clanton-Suggs," I ventured.

His face briefly registered a weak smile in the blue light. "Bingo."

"Why?"

Wheeler leaned forward and picked up a long neck beer on the coffee table, took a pull, and pursed his lips. "He was offered a chunk of cash and a higher paying job with Clanton-Suggs if they beat out HH Racing."

"So he persuaded you to jam HH Racing's telemetry for a piece of the action?"

Wheeler's laugh morphed into a sneer. "No way. I didn't give a damn about his money. I started jamming for the hell of it."

"Weird hobby. Why Gamble Oil's team?"

"'Cause I wanted feedback, you know, on how I was doing, and I knew I could find out."

"Your dad?"

He nodded. "And others at Gamble."

"And when RF found out what you were up to, he offered to help you."

"Uh-huh. I was having trouble covering the track in the beginning, and could only jam for about thirty minutes before the battery ran down."

"So RF designed you a better antenna, and found a battery with larger capacity, so you could transmit longer," I guessed.

"Give the man another prize."

I thought for a while. The last puzzle piece could fall into place with the next question. Or it could be the last question I ever asked.

I tried to keep the tremor out of my voice. "So why did you kill him?"

Wheeler's eyes lost focus and his body sagged as he picked up the .45 and pointed it at the floor between us. I could tell that Jeff was on the verge of breaking for the door, so I motioned to him with my hand palm down to stay still.

Wheeler was silent for ten or fifteen seconds, head down, the flickering light from the TV reflecting off his shaved head. He teetered on the edge of deciding whether to shoot or talk. I held my breath.

"Fucking pervert," he finally muttered venomously, looking up. I exhaled.

"I went over there to pick up an antenna. We had to go through this fucking room he called his dungeon to get to his workshop."

I gave him space to continue. "Just like my depraved girlfriend. Screwed everyone in sight while I was gone. Had sex with women, too. Lesbo. When I found out, I totally blacked out. They tell me I beat her up fairly bad."

I waited for him to go on. Finally I primed the pump. "So you paid RF a visit after you got the antenna."

"Yeah, man. Fucking tried to reason with him. Told him how perverted his crap was. Chickenshit just laughed in my face."

Wheeler took a deep breath. He narrowed his eyes and looked into infinity. "I guess I completely lost it about then. I don't remember anything after that. Must've been when I hit him."

"And put him in the choke collar to strangle."

Wheeler was trembling and sweating. The gun was shaking. I didn't move.

"I don't know. I guess so."

He raised the .45 and flipped his wrist a few times, pointing it toward the door.

"Get the fuck out of here." He was blinking back tears.

Jeff and I looked at each other. Neither of us moved.

"Go on. Out."

Either he was being honest, or he wanted to get us close together so he could kill us both. Keeping it out of Wheeler's sight, I waved my left hand at the door. Jeff didn't need a second invitation. I followed close behind him.

Jeff ran behind his car in a crouch. I followed.

He was already on his cell phone calling IMPD when the shot boomed out.

I'll live with that sound for the rest of my life.

I threw up. Tears trickled from my eyes. Paul Wheeler didn't deserve to die.

Chapter 24

I sat on the curb with my head in my hands until the EMTs arrived. Paul Wheeler didn't rate a siren.

I knew the numbers by heart. Approximately three hundred fifty veterans commit suicide each year, mostly driven by PTSD. That's about one a day. Paul was on his way to being just another statistic to most people, but his suicide was deeply personal and painful to me. And to Jeff.

An estimated eight million Americans have PTSD. Included are veterans returning from the Middle East, first responders, and others who have been a victim of, or witnessed, violent crime, or been in traumatic situations such as storms or vehicle accidents where people around them died.

I heard Jeff talking with one of the guys in his PTSD poker-playing support group, and realized I needed to talk with Tito.

He answered, "Hi, Wolf. No, I don't have anything I can tell you about Gordian's death."

As I tried to talk, my breath snagged. "Not about that. Paul Wheeler just blew his brains out."

"My God, where are you?"

I was still trembling too much to stand. "Sitting on the curb in front of his house. Where are you?"

"Just got home. Fucking paperwork took me two hours. You capable of driving?"

I felt my breath catch in my throat. The thumping inside my chest felt like my heart had brass knuckles. "Not right now. Maybe in a few minutes. I'll wait 'til the EMTs leave."

"Don't push it, mon. Take your time. OK if I meet you at your condo?"

I looked at my watch. It was one-thirty. "Yeah. Thanks. I need to unload. Big-time. See you."

"How you doing?" I asked Jeff after I hung up.

"I have a couple of the guys waiting for me. You?"

I nodded. "Tito."

When the EMT van pulled out, each of us headed home where we'd have support people. If only Paul Wheeler had had someone.

Tito was waiting for me in my parking lot wearing sweats, but without his badge. "I didn't wait outside your door. Figured someone might call the police."

Boots had finally decided that Tito was OK, and rubbed against his leg as we went down the hall to the kitchen, where we sat at the table. We popped open beers, and Tito gently took me through the sequence of events that culminated in Paul Wheeler's suicide.

I was still sweaty, shaking, and upset after the first time through, so he led me through it again. And then again.

When I had finally calmed down, Tito asked with a crooked grin, "Want to hear what happened with Kade?"

"I'm all ears."

"We dispatched two patrol cars to pick him up. His car was in the alley behind his office, so one patrolman covered the front door, the other took Kade's car and the back entrance."

I could tell he was enjoying telling the story, because he was making me wait. "And?"

"The guy at Kade's car didn't find anyone in it. He was starting to walk away when he heard thumping sounds from the trunk."

"He popped the trunk open. He found Kade bound and gagged, wrists behind him, with duct tape. He'd peed his pants. When his gag was removed, he started babbling about men in black."

I smiled to myself. Uncle Sal had gotten there first.

"Find anything interesting in the car?" I asked, trying to look like it was an offhand question.

Tito narrowed his eyes. "No, nothing in their report. Should they have?"

I shrugged. "How would I know? Just curious."

"You were obviously on the stakeout. Gordian was dead. Nobody else knew where he was, right?"

I couldn't resist the urge. "Why don't you check with the FBI?"

Tito snorted, "You know damn well nobody from the FBI would do that." But I could tell that Matt Corbett would be getting a call from him.

It was almost three when Tito left. I'd had a few beers and a shot of Old Fitzgerald. I wouldn't win any prizes for efficiency, but I was functioning.

I sent an email to Nick and Linda letting them know that the telemetry problem was resolved. I said I'd explain at the track, and not to look for me before noon. The race wasn't until mid-afternoon and my job with HH Racing was finished, so there wasn't any point in showing up earlier.

I wrote a short report to Carol on the telemetry situation, and another to Bob Conlan on identifying RF's murderer. The two reports had some identical sections. I started freaking out each time I tried to write about Paul Wheeler's death, so I left it out. I told each of them I had additional details I'd share later.

It took willpower not to call Sal. I was itching to hear what happened when his 'colleagues' found Kade, and I was worried about Vanessa, but I figured Sal would let me know in his own good time.

Boots was already sound asleep when I crawled into bed around three-thirty. Thanks to the talk with Tito, I fell into a dreamless sleep.

* * *

My plan to sleep until ten was deep-sixed by my phone ringing at eight. It was Uncle Sal. "Hello, Wolf. I'm at O'Hare, on my way to Indianapolis."

I mumbled, "That's nice."

"I want to meet with you this evening. I will pick you up at your condo at nine."

I started to ask him what the subject of the meeting was, but the line went dead.

I rolled over and tried to go back to sleep. Sal's call was intriguing, to say the least. Why was he coming to Indy? You could bet it wasn't to go to the Formula Nor-Am race.

Unfortunately, Sal's call served as Boots' alarm clock. He was up and in my face, so I dragged myself out of bed, fed him, and took a mug of strong black Sumatra coffee and the Indy Star out on the balcony.

The big news on the sports page was the Colts' game against the Patriots on Sunday. On page three was a feature about the Nor-Am race. Laurence LeGrand's car earned the only photo coverage, for qualifying first.

After a plate of bacon and scrambled eggs, with bits of bacon diverted to Boots, I decided that the track was as good a place to pass the time as any, and I had an errand to run. I took Eldorp's revolver out of my safe, made sure it was wiped clean, wrapped it in a black trash bag, and took it and my computer bag to my Jeep. I stowed the black package under the seat and headed for Boone. I called Linda to let her know I was on the way and wanted to meet.

"Hi, Wolf. Wow. Great news. Your email was time-stamped after three a.m. I hope you managed to get some sleep."

"A little. I'm still waking up. I'd like to meet with you and Nick. Sometime this morning if feasible."

"Hang on a second. Nick's right here."

There was the muffled noise of background conversation.

Linda came back on the line. "Nick says we'll make time. Look us up when you get here. We'll let Daniel know, too."

As we said goodbye, she quickly whispered, "Nick's looking kind of grim. Don't know why. Just wanted to let you know."

As soon as I got to Boone, the four of us gathered in the meeting area of the HH Racing transporter. I let Nick take the lead.

"You all know who Harry Wheeler is. His son Paul died suddenly last night. Harry obviously won't be here today." Nick looked sideways at me. "He left word that Wolf is invited to watch the race from the Gamble Oil box. Said you'd understand, Wolf."

I just nodded. I couldn't say anything and keep myself together.

Nick said some things about the importance of the race, and how we all played key roles. I wasn't paying much attention. Finally, Nick asked me to give them a brief report about the jamming. I realized he'd been covering for me.

I took a ragged breath. "There definitely won't be any jamming today." I looked at Linda, "You can call off the track security."

"Was it a quad-copter?" asked Daniel.

"Yes," I replied.

"Where did the jammer come from?"

"It was a type used in the Middle East by the military."

It probably came from the same place as the .45 Paul Wheeler used to kill himself. I omitted that.

"Who was doing it, and how do you know they won't try again?" asked Linda.

286

"There are things I consider confidential. I hope they stay that way. Carol Logan at Watterson Watson will know everything. Nick will know almost everything. What gets disclosed is up to them."

"I support Wolf on this," said Nick, looking at each of them. "You can share what's been said here with other team members. Don't try to second guess anything, understood?"

Linda and Daniel nodded.

* * *

I opened a beer in the Gamble Oil Sky Box as the drivers were being introduced. The mood was so somber, I finished the beer and went back with the peons in the pits where my only job was to stay out of the way.

Everyone concentrated on doing what had to be done. Other than a polite nod once in a while, nobody paid me any attention. That was fine with me.

The race itself was an anti-climax. Scott Marks, driving the Aquila, number 33, finished a strong second to Laurence LeGrand, thus ensuring an overall season second place for the Gamble Oil sponsored team.

However, as is the case with most things in life, it wasn't that simple.

With just over a lap to go, the Clanton-Suggs Lumber Max car, running a distant third with no chance of catching Scott Marks, appeared to go out of control in the final turn. It had a spectacular crash along the home stretch in front of the grandstand. The driver walked away, unhurt and waving to the crowd, which was on its feet.

True to the nature of press coverage of auto racing, ESPN and every local station in the country covered the accident more than the results. Lumber Max got TV coverage of their logo worth millions of dollars for losing.

Nick later said the collision with the wall was intentional, and that it happened more often than race fans realized.

As the top three drivers stood on the podium receiving their trophies and accolades from the fans, Tito called.

"Hey, mon, we're watching on TV. What a crash at the end! And congratulations. You doing OK?" he asked.

"Yeah. Guess so."

"Carmen and I are making carne asada. We're putting the meat on the grill in an hour. Please join us."

I hadn't had Carmen's cooking for too long. They lived in Speedway, about a half-hour away. I welcomed the offer of food and companionship.

Sal was picking me up at nine. Spending the time until then alone or as an outsider at a victory party where people got as drunk as possible as quickly as possible wasn't appealing, so I accepted his invitation.

Eagle Creek Reservoir was only a little out of the way to my dinner engagement. I parked at one end of the bridge over the north end, and walked out where the water was deep enough. Waiting until nobody could see, I tossed the black package containing Eldorp's revolver into the water. I still suffered guilt, but at least had some closure.

* * *

When Carmen opened the door, she put a cold bottle of beer in my hand, and admonished me, "No talking business."

Her carne asada was, as usual, mouthwatering. Tito grilled flank steak, searing it slightly. Carmen served it as slices, its charred flavor enhanced with citrusy green marinade. Dessert was out-of-this-world arroz con dulce, sweet rice pudding with special rum-soaked raisins.

At eight o'clock I took a deep breath and faked a yawn. "I didn't get much sleep. Thanks for having me. I'd better call it a night."

Carmen lowered her head and looked at me over her glasses. "You have a hot date?"

I laughed, shaking my head. "No women in my evening plans."

Tito raised his eyebrows. "Seeing Vanessa tomorrow?"

"Yeah, I guess. We're supposed to have a talk."

"Good luck with that, mon."

We said our goodbyes.

* * *

I fed Boots, showered, changed to a long-sleeved blue Oxford shirt and gray slacks, and went down to the parking lot at eight-fifty. At nine sharp the same black Caddy with Illinois plates I'd ridden in earlier in the week appeared.

The same guy was driving as before. He hopped out and let me into the back seat with Sal, who was wearing a white golf shirt with a casino's logo and black dress pants.

Sal offered me his slender, well-manicured hand with a Rolex on the wrist as I settled into the leather seat. "Hello, Wolf. You've had an eventful couple of days."

He waved a hand at the driver. "Let's go, Gino." The glass partition separating us from the front raised as we pulled out onto the street.

I looked at him. "I expect we both have. Why are you here?"

The corners of this mouth briefly went up a few millimeters. For him, that was a smile. "There are a couple of things I wish to discuss with you."

I wasn't sure how to respond, so I just dipped my head.

"You probably have been curious about my interest in the emails you forwarded, including the one with malware."

I nodded. I looked outside. Darkly tinted windows made everything invisible except for bright lights.

"I will explain. As you are aware, my organization owns and operates two of the largest casinos on the strip in Las Vegas. A few weeks ago, their computer systems were compromised."

"Hacked?"

"Yes, in your terminology. They were infiltrated. Customer credit and internal financial information was stolen. We had clues regarding who was responsible, but no hard evidence."

A light went on in my brain. "The email messages I sent you…"

"Yes. We were able to identify and locate the specific source of the intrusion."

"Armenians in Chicago?"

He nodded. "There and elsewhere. We have implemented security measures to prevent future incidents. Your information on Rudy Kade's theft of Gordian's payoff money provided us an opportunity."

"So you relieved Kade of the money and sent a message."

"That is correct. We consider the cash a partial payment of a debt."

"Partial. So you're going after the rest of it."

He dipped his head. "Of course."

"Tit for tat?"

"If you are asking whether we will carry out cyber operations against them, the answer is yes."

"Why tell me?" I instantly regretted asking. I already knew.

"We wish to retain your services through your computer consulting business. Strictly legitimate."

"Nothing illegal?"

"Of course not. You will serve as an advisor."

He slid open a door in front of him, illuminating a well-stocked bar. "Wine?" he asked.

I nodded, wondering what else he wanted to discuss.

He uncorked the wine.

"From my private cellar," he said as he poured two glasses. "To our mutual endeavors." He handed me a glass and touched the rim with his.

I sipped my wine. "Excellent Cabernet. You said there was more than one reason for our meeting."

"Thank you. Yes. We will enjoy the wine first. Then we will discuss that."

The next ten minutes, we sipped and talked. I took the opportunity to tell him about tracing my stolen PC to a location in Chicago. I needed to tell Sal before I let the FBI know. I didn't want to be discovered face up in the White River with a dead canary in my mouth.

"This is the same location as before, correct?" he asked.

"Yes."

"You will, of course, provide the results of your network monitoring to us, and let us know if you detect the – what did you call it?"

"MAC identifier."

"Yes, MAC identifier of your computer."

"Of course."

As we finished our wine, I was aware we were pulling into a parking lot.

"I am delivering you to a meeting," he said, taking my glass from me, "at Vanessa's condominium."

I was stunned. I started to say something. He raised his hand. "Unfortunate things have occurred in the past few days. I am leaving you here. Go have a conversation."

Gino was already opening the door.

"I will be in touch," said Sal as Gino closed the door, got in the driver's seat and pulled away.

Holy shit. As the taillights faded down the street, I speculated what on earth I'd just gotten myself into.

Chapter 25

I looked up at Vanessa's condo and worried about what the hell was going to happen. I was too far away to walk home. I might as well find out.

She answered her door before I got my finger off the button. She must have been looking out the peephole. She was dressed in a Cubs t-shirt and a very short blue denim skirt.

Wordlessly, she motioned for me to follow her as she padded barefoot down the hall to the living room, where she sat in the easy chair, tucking her feet under her. I took the couch, remembering our last close encounter under the Navy Pier painting.

"Wolf, I don't know where to start or what to say."

"Try starting at the beginning and telling the truth."

There was silence, as she seemed to scrape her thoughts together. She looked up at me, took a deep breath, and said, "Wolf, I am so, so sorry."

I felt sorry for her, but I didn't say anything. Or move.

"The beginning. I guess that would be Tuesday morning when two FBI agents came to my door. They asked me to help them."

I nodded. Corbett didn't say he'd already recruited her when he came to my office on Wednesday. The son-of-a-bitch. No wonder she hadn't answered my calls on Tuesday.

"They told me what they wanted me to do. Then they said that I was not to say *anything* about it to you.

"They said your life would be in danger, really in danger, if you knew, and that I was to do whatever it took to keep you away."

"So you told me to go find someone else to come with," I said dully.

Tears welled up in her eyes. "That was way over the top. I should never have hurt you that way, but you were so persistent, especially your call Wednesday. I was desperate."

She sniffled and dabbed her eyes with a tissue. "I should have known you'd call Uncle Sal."

"So what's with the business of each of us being free to have sex with other people?"

She got up and walked over to me. "I don't know. I honestly don't know."

She pulled me up and put her arms around my neck. "That's something we need to work out. Stan's dead. He was a louse, but we *were* married, and in the very beginning, a long time ago, we were happy. I have a lot to deal with. I'm asking you to be patient with me."

"So did you screw the guy…" She put her forefinger on my lips.

She cocked her head and tilted it back, moving her hands down to pull our pelvises together. "Like I said, there are some things we need to discuss. But not now. Right now, I'm asking for a truce. Deal?"

The bulge in my pants and I both said, "Deal."

We kissed, tongues exploring. I pulled her skirt up to her waist so my stiff shaft could rub against her pubic mound through her panties.

"Clothes in the way," she murmured, lowering my slacks and shorts as I took off her skirt and panties. We finished undressing, our hands softly fondling each other. Then she led me to the Jacuzzi in her master bath.

With the warm bubbling water flowing past, she had me sit against the wall of the Jacuzzi with my knees up. She cupped my balls with one hand, and started stroking my cock. I closed my eyes, rising quickly, nearing ejaculation.

"I want you to come now," she murmured. "We're going out on a little adventure, and I want you to be able to last for a long, long time when we screw."

As I neared my release, she let go of my balls and played with herself with one hand while stroking me with the other. My orgasm was loud and hard as I added my hot fluid to the Jacuzzi's water.

"Better now?"

I was barely able to nod.

"Good." She kept playing with herself while I recovered. "I'll put on an outfit you'll like, and you're gonna take me out on a hot date."

We dried each other off, then she went into her bedroom to change. I dressed in the guest bedroom, then waited for her in the hallway. As she came out and I saw what she was wearing, it was clear where we were going on the 'hot date.'

She had on a pink tank top, white denim microskirt with fringe around the hem, and open-toed straw sandals with five inch heels. It was the same outfit she wore the first time we had sex on the rug in my office. I kissed her and felt the crotch of her satin panties.

"Red bikinis?"

"Um-hum," she nodded, holding my fingers against her panties with her hand for several seconds. "God, I'm horny. We're taking my car, you're driving," she said, moving away and handing me her keys.

"My office, right?" I asked as we both slid into her SUV.

"Right. Turkish rug." She grinned as she massaged my growing bulge. "Remembered, huh?"

"How could I forget?" I stroked her already moist crotch.

"Hmmm, that feels good," she said, grinning wickedly.

She reclined her seat, then slipped her hands inside her panties and played with herself as we drove. Most of the time her eyes were closed, but a couple of times she looked at me saying, "Keep watching; I like you watching me play."

I had a tough time paying attention to driving with a rock-hard cock and Vanessa masturbating. In what seemed like an eternity, we arrived at my office and pulled into the parking lot behind the building.

We walked past groups of Saturday night Broad Ripple partiers. Her sexy outfit turned heads. I imagined that every guy who came by wanted to screw her.

I let us into the building, turned off the alarm system, and followed her up the stairs and into my office. Even with the blinds shut, light filtered through from the bars and clubs.

She stood on the thick rug facing me. I slid her skirt and panties off. She peeled off her top and helped me take off my shirt.

As we kissed with our tongues probing each other, I caressed her clit and explored her steaming vagina with my fingers. She rhythmically pressed against my hand as she rubbed the bulge in my slacks, then unzipped them and slid them and my shorts down and off, and stroked my cock to a jack-hammer hard erection as we knelt on the rug.

"I think I'm hornier than I've ever been. I want to be on top, and I want to come more than once. I've never done that. You have to hold off until the second one," she said as she gently pushed me onto the rug on my back and rolled a condom onto my cock.

She straddled me face to face, then steadied my shaft as she lowered her hot wet slit around it, groaning as its full length plunged into her.

She kissed me long and hard. Then, with one hand on the rug, she put her head beside mine, her fragrant hair falling forward, as she played with herself with the other hand and we moved together.

Only a minute or so had passed when she commanded, "Fuck me harder." I was trying to delay my ejaculation, but obeyed. A little while later, she squealed as she rode my shaft to a convulsing orgasm.

"God, that was great," she whispered in my ear. It was torture to keep myself from coming. I was grateful for my earlier orgasm.

She took several deep breaths, rested her forehead against mine, then took my head in her hands and kissed me. "That was incredible. I'll stay still. Wait a little longer." That was easier said than done, but I bit my lower lip and held off.

After a few more long kisses and caresses, she shuddered and purred, "I'm still horny. Let's go again. Don't hold back this time. Fuck me hard."

I could feel her vagina contracting almost as soon as she started moving up and down on my shaft. It was like she hadn't completely stopped climaxing from the first time.

She rubbed her clit harder and faster, moaning "Oh…oh….*oh*…my *God*," then she shrieked, "Come in me *now*!" as she bucked and pounded up and down. We slammed our bodies together as I shot into her and she collapsed onto my shoulder.

"Keep fucking me," she begged. "I'm still coming." She bit her lip and played with herself with me moving inside her, trembling and having contractions which eventually tapered off in frequency and intensity. She stayed on top of me as we kissed and caressed each other.

"Aren't you sorry we didn't screw the first day we met, at the country club?" she asked impishly.

I nodded, gently touching her still-hard nipples. "But I wonder if you'd have been able to come like you just did. And was that really two orgasms or one super long one?"

"Probably not. And yes, both. It was two orgasms for sure, but I never completely stopped between them."

We rolled over on our sides and held each other, then I pulled out of her and we stood up. My legs were like rubber. She put her arms around me and kissed me gently.

We freshened up in the restrooms down the hall.

I was standing against the edge of my desk when she came back. She gave me a fuck-me kiss, then sat in a chair, sliding up her skirt and very slowly crossing her legs to show me hot pink satin bikinis like she'd worn after the first time we had sex.

"I'll buy you a drink," she suggested. "I'd like to hear what happened with the racing team."

"It's a deal. Maybe you can tell me a little about the FBI operation."

We found a quiet jazz piano bar, and sat in a back corner, nursing beers. I told her about the HH Racing telemetry problem and RF's murder.

I said that I got information on the jamming system from Ann Wyland, and that I'd gone to her place to play tennis and have dinner; then said that we planned to see each other and play a few more times at her house before it got too cold to play outside. Vanessa's eyebrows went up. She realized she wasn't the only one fooling around.

As I got to Paul Wheeler's suicide, I had trouble breathing and speaking. She laid a hand on my arm. "Don't. You can tell me some other time. Or never."

I changed the subject. "How did your project go?"

"We don't know our grade yet, but Brian, Chris and I had so much fun together we're keeping the same team for the next project that's due at the end of the semester."

Two?

I changed the subject again.

"Were you scared when you made the exchange with Stan?" I asked.

"Not really. There were enough FBI agents in the bushes to fill a baseball team lineup. It was actually rather boring."

We finished our beers and went for a walk. Arm in arm, we wandered through the crowds in Broad Ripple.

"So, Wolf, let's have that talk about where we are with each other," Vanessa ventured.

I wasn't excited about doing that, but it was as good a time as ever. "OK, where do you want to start?"

"With something we definitely agree on. That we care deeply for each other."

"That's absolutely true. What else?"

She smiled. "We agree that sex – the hot, steamy, hard-fucking kind – is the most pleasurable experience there is."

I nodded. "Definitely. And we agree that sex with each other is the most passionate either of us has had."

We were walking in public, and a couple of people turned to look at Vanessa. Whether they'd heard, or were admiring her long sexy legs, was hard to tell. I hoped it was both.

"Absolutely. Now it gets a little more complicated," she said. "I'd like to suggest that we agree that being monogamous isn't required unless we decide to live together."

We walked a few steps, still arm in arm. My opinion on that having shifted in the last few days, I replied, "I can live with that."

She looked at me, surprised. "You mean we agree that each of us has the freedom to experiment with others?"

I looked at her, grinning. "Uh-huh."

We sealed our agreement with a kiss. A mind-blowing fuck-me pelvis-grinding kiss that definitely turned heads. Even in Broad Ripple on Saturday night.

As we walked back to her car, Vanessa said, "Give me the keys. I'm driving."

"You taking me to my place?" I asked. I already knew the answer.

"No way. You're my prisoner for the night. We can pick up where we left off last Sunday morning."

Our lovemaking sessions explored new sexual territory. By the time we were finished the next morning, sheets, blankets, and pillows were scattered around the bedroom. Blindfolds and scarves were mixed in. We agreed that bondage wasn't bad, at least once in a while.

I dragged myself out on the balcony with a mug of coffee to read the paper and call Max while Vanessa put bed linens in the laundry and took a shower. The Indy Star carried a story that the FBI announced the neutralization of a major cyber-terrorist network operation. Organized crime in Chicago and Indianapolis was implicated, according to anonymous sources.

I called Max.

"Hi, Wolf," he answered. "Haven't heard from you for a long time. What's it, two, three days now? Don't know how you've managed without my advice."

I could hear the twinkle in his eyes. I filled him in on the parallel case events involving HH Racing and RF's murder, and Eldorp's and Gordian's killings.

"Sounds like you have a couple of potential new clients. Carol Logan's gonna be a great reference. I'm not so sure about Sal Russo…by the way what's with his niece, what's-her-name?"

"Vanessa. I'm at her condo now."

"On Sunday morning, even. Have a religious experience?"

I laughed. "You could call it that."

"Why don't you come visit? You keep saying you will."

"Actually, sometime in the next couple of months would be good. OK if I bring Vanessa?"

"Sure, long as you stay in another condo unit. Marie and I wouldn't want to keep you up at night."

I chuckled as I took the phone into the bedroom and asked Vanessa to say hello.

"Hi Max, Wolf has told me so much about you. You're like a father to him."

I couldn't hear what he replied, but Vanessa blushed deep red and handed the phone back to me.

"What did you say to her?"

"None of your business."

Vanessa, still blushing, tried to cover her grin with one hand as Max and I said goodbye.

She wouldn't tell me what he said.

We got airline reservations for early December to visit Max and Marie and enjoy the beach in Florida. We reserved a condo unit on the top floor of the same building as theirs, right on the water.

I'd suggested to Vanessa that we schedule the trip during the Thanksgiving holiday, when it got too cold for outdoor tennis. Her eyes sparkling, she'd insisted that we wait until early December – the end of the semester, after her final class project was due.

Tit for tat.

www.ingramcontent.com/pod-product-compliance
Lightning Source LLC
Chambersburg PA
CBHW060853250626
47159CB00008B/2717